RABINDRANATH TAGORE
AND
MAO TSE-TUNG

One was a Bengalese aristocrat, in love with the glories of the past, deeply involved with religion, devoted to the principles of nonviolence. The other is a Chinese revolutionary leader who rose through bitter and bloody struggle to become master of a quarter of the world's population.

Both are included in this volume. For both stand as poets of genius.

In this anthology, the reader will be dazzled by the variety of vision and technique to be encountered. Here is an unsurpassed tour of the great body of modern Asian literature in all its divergent tendencies, all its rich complexity, all its meaningful portents for the future.

ABOUT THE EDITOR: *Dorothy Blair Shimer received her A.B. in English at Skidmore College, her A.M. at Middlebury College, and went on to study at Columbia University, Syracuse University, Oxford University, and the University of Hawaii. With her noted educator husband, William A. Shimer, she has worked and traveled widely throughout Asia, as well as editing and publishing the international quarterly* Brotherhood. *Currently Mrs. Shimer is Lecturer in World Literature at the University of Hawaii.*

Other MENTOR Books
of Special Interest

The Mentor Book of
MODERN
ASIAN LITERATURE
From the Khyber Pass to Fuji

edited by Dorothy Blair Shimer

With an introduction, critical
commentary, and biographical notes

A MENTOR BOOK

Published by The New American Library, New York
and Toronto
The New English Library Limited, London

PERMISSIONS NOTICES

TO BILL AND MOTHER

without whose faith, encouragement, and sacrifice this work would not have been possible.

Acknowledgments

It would be impossible to acknowledge all those who have contributed to the realization of this volume—from undergraduate instructors at Skidmore College, who sparked love of literature; to scholars at Middlebury College's Bread Loaf School of English and Oxford University, whose demands at the graduate level provided "the refiner's fire"; to innumerable associations with men and women of all classes and occupations during three years of life and work in more than a dozen countries "from the Khyber Pass to Fuji" and beyond; and, perhaps above all, to college and university students in Hawaii who have responded with special enthusiasm to the literatures of those "Eastern" countries that lie to Hawaii's west.

Special thanks are due Dr. K. C. Leebrick, then President of Mauna Olu College on the Island of Maui, Hawaii, who gave constant encouragement in practical terms of schedule adjustments and working space during five years of research and writing. Helping to reach authors and translators for copyright permissions and sometimes advising on final selection of works (though not to be charged with the final results) were such friends as Tomas C. Benitez, Ambassador-at-Large, Republic of the Philippines; Dr. Jal C. Daruvala, Professor of English, Wilson College, Bombay; Horace G. Underwood, Librarian, Yonsei University, and E. Otto DeCamp, Christian Broadcasting System, Seoul, Korea; Jim Wanigatunga, Colombo, Ceylon; U Thein Han, Librarian, University of Rangoon, Burma; Professors Marjorie Sinclair and Yukuo Uyehara, University of Hawaii; Milton Rosenthal, UNESCO, Paris; and the Rev. William W. Simpson, Council of Christians and Jews, London.

Editorial advice and critical judgment came especially from Professor John C. Yohannan, City College of the University of New York; William A. Pullin, Dorothy S. Arnof, W. L. Parker, John M. Pickering, Phillip Flayderman, Tom McCormack, and Ellen Asher.

Invaluable research and reading facilities were afforded by general and specialized collections at the International House, Tokyo; East Asian Library, Columbia University; Bodelian Library, Oxford University; East-West Center, Graduate, and Sinclair Libraries, University of Hawaii.

CONTENTS

INTRODUCTION   17

POETRY   23

The Poetry of India, Pakistan, and Nepal   25

  India   25

    Henry Louis Vivian Derozio—
      "The Harp of India"   31
      "To India—My Native Land"   31
    Bankim Chandra Chatterjee—
      "Mother, I Bow to Thee"   32
    Rabindranath Tagore—Songs from *Gitānjali*   33
    Vir Singh—"I Made My Mind a Beggar's Bowl"   40
    Maithili Sharan Gupta—
      "Now, Those Days Are Gone for Good"   41
    Umashankar Joshi—"The Washerman"   41
    Agyeya (Sachchidananda Vatsyayan)—
      "Borrow in the Morning, Lend at Night"   42
    Mohan Singh—"Evening"   44
    Bachchan (Harivansh Rai)—"My Garden Plant"   44
    G. S. Sivarudrappa—"Krishna"   45

  Pakistan   46

    Muhammad Iqbal—*Ghazals*   49
                "Ruba'iyat"   52
                "Jehad"   52
                "Two Planets"   53
    N. M. Rashed—"Near the Balcony"   53
             "Sheba in Ruin"   54
    Taufiq Rafat—"Poem 4"   55
    Abdul Ghani Hazari—
      "At the Death of a Friend's Son"   55

  Nepal

    Balakrishna Sama—"The Song"   58

The Poetry of Southeast Asia   60

Thailand   60

   H.R.H. Prince Phanuphan Yukhon—
     "The White Lotus"   61
   Chayasi Sunthonphiphit—"Till Heart's End"   61

Indonesia   62

   J. E. Tatengkeng—"Traveler First Class"   65
                 "On the Shore: Twilight"   66
   Amir Hamzah—"Because of You"   66
   Chairil Anwar—"At the Mosque"   67
       "My Love's on a Faraway Island"   68
       "My Love Far in the Islands"   68
   Sitor Situmorang—"Swimming Pool"   69
   Asrul Sani—"Remember Father, Remember
     Father"   69
   Toto Sudarto Bachtiar—"Djakarta in the
     Evening"   71
   W. S. Rendra—"Little Sister Narti"   72

Philippines   73

   José Rizal—"My Last Farewell"   75
   Rafael Zulueta da Costa—"Like the Molave"   77
   Bienvenido N. Santos—"The March of Death"   79
   Nick Joaquin—"Six P.M."   81

The Poetry of China and Korea   82

China   82

   Hu Shih—"Dream and Poetry"   90
        "Old Dream"   90
   Wen Yi-tuo—"Forget Her"   91
       "Dead Water"   92
       "I Wanted To Come Home"   92
   Feng Chih—Sonnets XV and XVI   93
       "Han Po Chops Wood"   94
       "I Sing of Anshan Steel"   96
       "For Tu Fu"   97
   Pien Chih-lin—"A Monk"   97
       "The First Lamp"   98
       "To the Young Pioneers of the
         Northwest"   98
   Ai Ch'ing—"Snow Falls on China"   99
   Tien Ch'ien—"Freedom Is Walking toward Us"   101
       "Children's Festival"   101
   Mao Tse-tung—"The Long March"   102
       "The Snow"   102

    "Sixteen-Syllable Stanza"   103
    "On the Liu-p'an Mountain"   103
    "After Swimming across the
        Yangtze River"   104

Korea   104

  Sijo poems, anonymous   107
  Manhae (Han Yong-un)—"I Do Not Know"   108
  Kim Sowŏl (Kim Chŏng Sik)—"Wild Flowers
    of the Mountains"   109
  Sim Hun—"When That Day Comes"   109
  Yu Ch'i-hwan—"Flowers"   110
  Sŏ Chŏng-ju—"Self-Portrait"   110
  Yi Sang-hwa—"Does Spring Come to Stolen
    Fields?"   111
  Pak Tu-jin—"River of Solitude"   112
  Pak Mok-wol—"The Wild-Peach Blossom"   113
           "On a Certain Day"   114
  Cho Chi-hun—"Ancient Temple"   114
The Poetry of Japan   115

  Tanka by Ryōkan   122
    Ōkuma Kotomichi   123
    Tachibana Akemi   123
  Haiku by Kobayashi Issa   124
    Mizuhara Shūōshi   124
    Nakamura Kusatao   124
    Katō Shūson   125
  Yosano Akiko—"A Mouse"   125
  Kitahara Hakushū—"Secret Song of the Heretics"   126
  Hagiwara Sakutarō—"Night Train"   127
           "Harmful Animals"   127
           "The New Road of Koide"   127
  Nakahara Chūya—"The Hour of Death"   128
  Nakano Shigeharu—"Song"   128
  Kitagawa Fuyuhiko—"Early Spring"   129
  Tanikawa Shuntarō—Two sonnets   130
  Takamura Kōtarō—"My Poetry"   131

DRAMA   133

The Drama of India   136
  Rabindranath Tagore—*Sacrifice*   138

The Drama of Japan   160
  Kikuchi Kan—*The Madman on the Roof*   163

The Drama of China   172
  Lao Sheh (Shu Sheh-yu)—*Dragon Beard Ditch*   176

THE ESSAY AND OTHER EXPOSITORY PROSE 197

Essays of India and Ceylon 199
  Swami Vivekānanda—"Modern India" 202
  Santha Rama Rau—"On Learning To Be an
    Indian" 206
  J. Vijayatunga—"Village Goes to Town" 214

Essays of China 219
  Hu Shih—"A Chinese Literature of National
    Speech" 221
  Mao Tse-tung—"Literature for the Masses" 223

Essays of Japan 229
  Motoori Norinaga—"The True Tradition of the
    Sun Goddess" 231
  Hirata Atsutane—"The Land of the Gods" 235
  Lafcadio Hearn—"Mosquitoes" 236
  Hino Ashihei—"Earth and Soldiers" 239

THE NOVEL 247

  A Novel of the Philippines 249
    Noli me Tangere, José Rizal 251
  A Novel of India 275
    Godan, Premchand (Dhanpat Rai) 276
  A Novel of Japan 295
    The Temple of the Golden Pavilion,
      Mishima Yukio (Kimitake Hiraoka) 297

THE SHORT STORY 321

  Short Stories of India 323
    Dhumektu (Gaurishanker Goverdhanram
      Joshi)—"The Letter" 324
    Khwaja Ahmad Abbas—"The Sword of Shiva" 331
    Khushwant Singh—"Riot" 341

  Short Stories of Southeast Asia 345

  Burma

    Zawgyi (U Thein Han)—"His Spouse" 346

  Thailand

    Pratoomratha Zeng—"My Thai Cat" 352

  Philippines

    Amador Daguio—"Wedding Dance" 358
    N. V. M. Gonzalez—"A Warm Hand" 365

  Short Stories of China & Korea 375

China

Lu Hsun (Chou Shu-jen)—"A Little Incident" 377
Mao Tun (Shen Yen-ping)—"Spring Silkworms" 379

Korea

Yu-Wol Chong-Nyon—"The Nonrevolutionaries" 394
Choe Chong-Hi—"Chom-nye" 399

Short Stories of Japan 407
Ogawa Mimei—"The Handstand" 409
Shiga Naoya—"The Patron Saint" 423
Akutagawa Ryûnosuke—"The Spider's Thread" 432

BIBLIOGRAPHY 437

INTRODUCTION

> . . . poetry is something more
> philosophic and of graver im-
> port than history, since its state-
> ments are of the nature rather
> of universals, whereas those of
> history are singulars.
>
> ARISTOTLE

Aristotle's statement of the case for poetry might well be applied to literature in general, in all its forms. The literary product—poetry, drama, imaginative prose—has the advantage over historical record of being at once a first-hand reflection of history on the spot and an interpretation of the timely and specific in terms that make them universal.

So Shakespeare's *Richard II* is not only a slice of the life of fifteenth-century England; it is also a reflection of the mores of the England for whose audiences it was written. But, beyond these, it is a penetrating study of character under stress and of motives and ambitions that are basic to human beings no matter what their time or culture. So the com-pendious *Shah Namah,* or *Book of Kings,* is of living in-terest to today's readers, East and West, not because of its dubious historicity—or even, perhaps, because of the broad sweep of Persian culture and accomplishment it presents—but because Firdausi's poetic genius has embued Bizhan, Sohrab, Rustem, and the other great heroes with those quali-ties that make them have life and meaning for us today.

Paradoxically, it is by way of the "universals" of literature, then, that we can most readily and most palatably become educated in the "singulars" that may be of immediate prac-tical concern. Through the universal appeal of Savitri's devo-tion and courage, we understand present-day Indian woman-hood better. The universally human qualities of Shakespeare's characters, as they reveal themselves in French dialogue on the Paris stage, help to make even contemporary England more understandable to the Gallic mind.

Sociologist Vera Micheles Dean emphasized just this point in a UNESCO Orient-Occident report in 1963:

> Above all, we must use literature and the arts in our teaching —and I speak as one trained in the social sciences. I believe that a

17

few novels, or plays, or poems ... are far more important for the
student than any number of books on politics, economics, or
anthropology. For it is in literature and the arts that are reflected
the emotions, the hopes and fears, the aspirations of human beings, and basically what we must train our students to do is to
understand human beings.

The literature of lasting worth provides a bridge of understanding not only to the past but to our neighbors of
today. Relationships can be established and connections to
living concerns made through literature, which Thornton
Wilder has so aptly called "the notation of the heart." And
if we are to become really acquainted with our Asian neighbors as they live and think *today,* we must not confine our
literary acquaintance to the early classics but must become
more contemporaneous in our reading. There are several
excellent anthologies that will carry the reader to the sixteenth
century A.D., but few include works that come down to our
own time. There is an excitingly expanding library of non-
Western literature moving to Western shelves, but the available material is scattered, still largely ignored in the classroom,
or directed toward the specialist. Some sort of catalyst seems
desirable. This volume would perform such a service.

Whenever we deal with works that originated in languages
other than our own, we are faced with the so-called translation problem. How can we expect to get an adequate
counterpart in English of a writing that may include so
many elements that cannot possibly be reproduced in another
language? We cannot, of course, get a fully precise ren-
dition, especially of poetry, in another tongue. Should we
allow ourselves to founder on this reef, however? Western
culture is firmly established on that of Greece, which came
through Arabic Africa into Europe largely by the Latin, not
the Greek, tongue. Today we are inclined to accept the
works of Aeschylus, Plato, Sappho, *et al.,* almost as though
they originated in English, or in any of the languages of
Europe to which we may lay claim. We have not rejected
Greek literature and culture because it must come to us
"secondhand." It is time now that we enriched Western
thought with the wealth of Asia, even though we as in-
dividuals cannot hope to master the many languages and
dialects in which that wealth has been stored.

Let us tackle this criticism now, and then relegate it to
the back of our minds. There it will remain as a discomforting

awareness of the obvious fact that we can never fully appreciate all the nuances and beauties of a translated literature, but it will not be an insuperable barrier to exciting and informative exploration. Also, we should be aware that being born to a language and its literature is not always the first requirement for the good translator. The Chinese scholar-statesman Hu Shih, for instance, agreed with Chi-chen Wang, professor of Chinese at Columbia University, in his belief that the best translator of Chinese verse is Gerald Bullitt, an English poet who knew no Chinese but collaborated with Chinese scholars. Wang contends that the important thing is to be able to translate into good readable English.

It must be recognized, of course, that the approach by way of translation is admittedly "second-best." As has already been said, it certainly offers special problems in regard to poetry. Here we always come closest to *traduttore, traditore*. It is obvious that in the poetic tradition of China, in which the visual element of calligraphy and the aural subtlety of tone levels are added to other more usual ingredients of verse, translation will rarely give more than an approximation. And yet Achilles Fang concludes a rather caustic article on "The Difficulty of Translation" by saying, "I see no reason why we should desist from translating Chinese texts." The reader—and surely the student—should, however, be forewarned concerning difficulties and adjustments as he approaches his reading.

Another consideration in regard to literature in translation that should be recognized is that such reading cannot be considered in the strictly literary terms in which the reader or student often approaches his native products. If translation alters or even eliminates certain elements, this must necessarily affect critical judgment. It seems to me it must be agreed, then, that the considerations that may come first in our critical appraisal of literature in our native tongue may not come first as we read literatures in translation, especially those from such different milieu as the cultures of Asia. The well-turned phrase, the effective metaphor, may be transmuted as it enters another language. But the author's revelation of character, his power to reflect human emotions and needs, his ability to make culture and way of life live and have meaning—these, it seems to me, are the elements that come to the forefront as we judge writings from other lands.

The authors and selections included here have been judged competent by their homegrown critics. Further, they reflect the life of the people from whom they emanate. Where several works by the same author are judged equal as literature—as in the dance dramas of Rabindranath Tagore, for instance—those selected for inclusion here offer the "foreign" reader more value by way of cultural insights.

Another factor should be considered in the selection of writings of the modern period: the evidences of interaction between East and West. More and more Western forms have replaced earlier indigenous ones. But it is stimulating and often exciting to see the ways in which these newer forms contain age-old habits of thought or the ways in which they have been influenced by the native forms. A modern short story of Thailand, for instance, may be the vehicle for revelation of persistent animistic superstitions. Or a Japanese play, written in the Western manner, may in its production be so influenced by the traditions of *Nō* and *Kabuki* that, as authority Earle Ernst says, "a play that would require no more than two and a half hours playing time in the American theater cannot be performed in less than four hours in Japan."

In this volume "modern" has been interpreted to mean that period from the beginning of the nineteenth century to the present. By 1800 indigenous forms show increasing evidences of outside influences, especially the impact of the West. After a century of colonialism in India and Southeast Asia, Western powers—especially England—had exerted considerable cultural influence. In China the long span of the Ch'ing or Manchu Dynasty (1644–1912) endured through several traumatic experiences with the West, ranging from the coming of the Jesuit missionaries at the very beginning of the rule, through the Opium War of 1839–42 and the Boxer Rebellion of 1900, to the beginning of the Republic in 1911. Early in the eighteenth century Japan began to relax its edict against foreign learning and lower the barriers that had blocked influences from the West for almost a century. The establishment of diplomatic relations with the United States in 1856 was followed by the Meiji Restoration twelve years later. By this time the floodgates were down and Japan was inundated by foreign pressures in all areas of her life.

Recent years have witnessed unusual interest in the publication of improved translations of contemporary works of Asia, as well as of updated versions of classic Asian masterpieces. We have both the urgent incentive and the increased facilities for escape from provincialism by acquainting ourselves with the literature of humanity, wherever and whenever great artistry appears.

POETRY

Poetry, it is generally agreed, was the earliest literary expression in virtually all cultures. Its mnemonic qualities mark it as having been originally oral, devised to be recited, chanted, and perpetuated by word of mouth from generation to generation. Being looked upon as extra-ordinary expression, it was probably the first to become fixed, also, in the written heritage. When writing was difficult and rare, only the choicest expression would have been recorded. Certainly, it is verse that right down to contemporary times has been the most highly regarded literature in all the cultures of Asia. It is natural, then, to open an anthology of Asian literature with selections of poetry.

Also, to begin our readings in Asian literature with poetry brings us to grips with fundamental elements in literature and at the same time gives us an appreciation of the striving toward beauty and awareness that is elemental in mankind. Literature, especially poetry, is the recorded evidence of such striving toward higher values. As such, it is as essential to us as are the things we are apt to refer to as the "necessities of life." As anthropologist John Greenway puts it:

> Poetry is far older than prose; thousands of years before man burned clay into culinary ware, the Paleolithic people of Ariège painted a ritual dance on the walls of a cave, a dance that was certainly accompanied by singing. And poetry is far more important than pottery; many peoples get along well without kitchenware, but none is without some form of literature.

Peoples of distinctive cultures may differ sharply in certain specifics of poetic expression—for example, the Chinese who delight in rhyme, and the Japanese who reject rhyme entirely, because of their language structure. When we go beyond Western verse, we must often abandon the accent on which the meter is based (as in Japanese).

It is exciting, however, to note certain ingredients that are common and basic. Elizabeth Drew maintains that the "chiefest thing" about poetry is its rhythm. Certainly, a rhythm of some sort is one of the primary elements in verse, but the rhythms of the Orient may not be caught readily by the Occidental ear or may not be reproducible in another language. But the poet's assumption that his reader or listener will be ready to think in metaphor—this remains basic. And it is through simile and metaphor that we get our most intimate insights into other ways of life. If it is to be successful, however, thinking in metaphor other than our own requires that we virtually slough off our own mental skin and assume another. Here is one of the challenging and rewarding aspects of experiencing the poetry of another's culture.

In addition to metaphor and rhythm, parallelism and repetition—carry-overs from primitive verse—are devices still prevalent in much of the poetry of Asia.

The Poetry of India, Pakistan, and Nepal

INDIA

We can approach the literatures of India with the comforting realization that even the native must resort to translation if he is to become acquainted with the writing of any area of his country other than his own. In fact, since English continues to be the chief binding force throughout the subcontinent, it is likely that the educated Indian knows literature in English as well as, or perhaps even better than, in any Indian dialect other than his own. In the case of the Bengali poet Rabindranath Tagore, we may even read works translated into English by the poet himself. A fellow-countryman goes so far as to say that the English versions sometimes surpass the Bengali.

It is also interesting to note that in the case of the writings of Tagore, and of certain other major literary figures of India, translations into other Indian languages and dialects often went by way of English. This means that the English-language reader may often come at an Indian writing more directly than would the native reader.

However, we must also recognize the peculiar difficulties facing us as we attempt to come to any understanding of a literature that might be considered Indian. Although Hindi and English are the "official" languages of present-day India, thirteen others also have official recognition. In addition to these there are 120 tongues recognized as "minor languages," plus some 500 dialects. Even the fourteen major native languages are so different that a Tamil-speaking husband and his Urdu-speaking wife, for instance, would find it necessary to resort to English for home use.

Nevertheless, there are certain observations that may safely be made. Of prime significance, as is generally true throughout Asia, poetry is a "first love." Probably because down to the most recent times India's heritage has been dependent upon an oral tradition, poetry with its mnemonic qualities has gone beyond the refinements of literature as such and has also served the practical uses of religion, philosophy, politics, law, economics, history, geography, and science.

But it is as a pleasurable art form that it has its chief *raison d'être* today. Poetry recitals are common occurrences, especially in small towns and villages where illiteracy is still prevalent. These simple, almost spontaneous, gatherings help to preserve the ancient religious hymns and also encourage new creative expression. Often the verses are sung or chanted to musical accompaniment, thus helping to keep modern poetry close to its earliest roots.

There are other evidences, too, of the elemental forms. Anyone who has heard the songs sung today in the marketplaces of India and in the fairs and carnivals will recognize the age-old appeal of the repeated word and tone, which provide the strong warp of memory on which the web of ancient poetry and song is perpetuated in full color and design.

Eunice Tietjens notes that from its earliest beginnings to the present, Indian poetry has been essentially lyrical in nature, marked by a peculiarly Indian blend of subjectivity and detachment.

These are some of the features that, I believe, we may find pertain largely to the poetic expression of India as a whole, irrespective of the specific language media. Another is the theory of *rasa* against which poetry, drama, and to a certain extent prose works, are measured. Although the idea of *rasa* was first set down in the *Natyasastra* by Bharata as one of his critical guides for the judgment of Sanskrit poetry and drama, the concept has largely permeated all Indian poetic and dramatic expression.

In his *History of Sanskrit Poetics*, Amiya Kumar Dev says that *rasa* has generally been accepted as the main element in poetry, and he goes on to define it thus:

Rasa is viewed as a pleasant sentiment belonging to the reader whose dominant emotions, derived from experience or inherited instincts, are evoked by the reading of poems into an ideal and impersonalized form of joy; an appreciation or enjoyment, consisting of a pleasant mental condition. . . . The sentiment thus evoked is essentially universal in character, and the aesthetic pleasure resulting from it is not individual . . . but generic and disinterested, being such as would be common to all trained readers.

He summarizes by terming *rasa* a "sentiment" that becomes "dominant" as a poem is experienced. The term has been translated into English as "emotion" or "literary flavor" or "relish."

Ananda K. Coomaraswamy believes that all great writers "are agreed that the one essential element in poetry is what they term *Rasa*, or Flavor . . . which is the equivalent of Beauty or Aesthetic Emotion." We sense *rasa*, then, to be the subtle essence in a work of art that arouses pleasurable response and brings us into rapport with the creative imagination of the artist. It is essentially quiet, gentle, and pervasive. The theory has gathered about it a whole literature of analysis, but in broadly generalized terms it is what Dev and Coomaraswamy have distilled here. It would be helpful if the Western reader could come to have a feeling for the subtleties of the term and incorporate it untranslated into his own critical thinking as he becomes acquainted with Indian poetry and drama.

The poems selected for inclusion here are representative of English expression, as well as of several of the major language traditions—Bengali, Punjabi, Gujarati, and Kannada. They range in time from the early nineteenth century to the present. Although obviously influenced by Western form and thought, they reveal Indian life and culture.

Henry Louis Vivian Derozio (1809–1831) was the son of a Portuguese-Indian father and an English mother. A present-day Indian critic (K. R. Srinivassa Iyengar), however, finds him "wholly Indian in spirit." Although he was part English, was educated in the finest English tradition in Calcutta, and wrote most of his poetry in English, Derozio's poems are strongly nationalistic. He is regarded as India's earliest poet of national aspiration, and it was probably because of his unorthodox political views that he was forced to resign from the headmastership of Hindu College in Calcutta, a post he had assumed at the age of nineteen.

Derozio's early love lyrics had brought him acclaim when he was only seventeen; at twenty-two he was dead of cholera. Yet the harvest of those five short years significantly influenced later Bengali poets and found a permanent place in contemporary Indian literature.

The English-language poems "The Harp of India" and "To India—My Native Land" are written in the finest tradition of the sonnet, yet they cry against the British colonialism that had made India's heritage like a "ruined monument" and had brought the nation "groveling in the lowly dust."

Bankim Chandra Chatterjee (1838–1894), as both poet and novelist, also lent his pen to the cause of India's pride and worth. Inspired by the historical novels of Sir Walter Scott, he drew upon India's past for fictional material.

In Bankim Chandra's day, English had come to be regarded as the only worthy literary medium. By using his native Bengali with the dignity and polish of Sanskrit, he at the same time restored his mother tongue to its earlier esteem and opened his writings to the non-English-speaking masses. From the Bengali his novels and poetry were translated into several other regional languages, as well as into Sanskrit.

The poem "Mother, I Bow to Thee" (*"Bande Mātaram"*) first appeared in Bankim Chandra's famous novel of national aspiration, *Anandamath* (*The Abbey of Bliss*). The "Mother" he apparently thought of as both Bengal and the goddess-mother Durga, or Kali. Later, the poem was taken as a rallying cry for the nationalist movement with the "Mother" representing India herself.

Rabindranath Tagore (1861–1941), Asia's first Nobel Prize poet, lived a life so productive of notable achievement that it is difficult to hold introductory comment to allowable limits—as it is difficult to determine which of his works must be omitted from this collection of modern Indian poetry.

Rabindranath was the brightest star in a family galaxy that had added luster to Bengal's magnificent cultural history. Early in life Rabindranath's father, Debendranath, turned his back on the business world, which had made his father a man of considerable wealth. Instead, he turned to an investigation of religion. Debendranath's studies and meditations were to lead to a nonaggressive movement to rid Hinduism of idolatry and Indian society of abuses made in the name of religion. His *Autobiography* reveals the spirit of a saint, the mind of a scholar, and the proficiency of a skillful writer.

The fourteenth child in a family of fifteen, Rabindranath felt the stimulation not only of his saintly father and sensitive mother but also of brothers and sisters whose artistic

interests surrounded his youth. Music, poetry, drama, philosophy, were everyday factors in his formative years.

He tried his talents in a variety of media, but his earliest
and most enduring love was poetry. His first volume of poems
appeared when he was only twenty and established him as
a poet of genius. When his English version of *Gitānjali* (*Song
Offerings*) was published in 1912, it brought him the Nobel
Prize for Literature and thrust him into the international
literary world.

He later traveled widely to England, America, Russia,
and Japan, meeting and influencing poets wherever he went.
Especially interesting are the evidences of the impression he
left on the poets of Japan.

The metaphor of his beloved homeland cannot be divorced
from Rabindranath's poetic expression, no matter how universal his themes may be. Also, religious faith is fundamental
in all his poetry, even the love lyrics.

Vir Singh (1872–   ), as his name indicates, is a Sikh.
He writes in Punjabi, the language of the Punjab, an area
now divided between north India and West Pakistan. A prolific writer, Vir Singh has turned his pen to fiction, bi-
ography, and religious commentary, as well as to verse.

Vir Singh was the first Punjabi poet to experiment successfully with blank verse. His later poetry introduced another
innovation, a short meter not traditional to Punjabi, which
he often used in the rubaiyat form.

The brief poem included here, "I Made My Mind a
Beggar's Bowl," is replete with peculiarly Indian metaphor
and idiom. It also reveals an interesting insight into Vir
Singh's religious philosophy. Though he himself was a translator of, and astute commentator on, the sacred Sikh texts,
here we find him advocating a direct perception into the
mind of God rather than by way of sacred learning.

Maithili Sharan Gupta (1886–1964) published forty volumes of Hindi poetry during sixty years of writing. His
work combines new themes with traditional verse forms,
thus providing a link with later poetry, which would feel
free to use new forms for its expression of new ideas. His
writings, therefore, should be esteemed for their influential
importance, as well as for their intrinsic worth.

In his single poem included here, "Now, Those Days Are
Gone for Good," we perhaps see a reflection of the innately
traditional poet questioning the wisdom or the value of his
experimentation in the modern idiom.

Umashankar Joshi (1911–   ) takes us into another of

India's major language heritages—Gujarati, of the Bombay area. Although he wrote short stories and one-act plays early in his career, he is esteemed chiefly for his poetry. Mansukhlal Jhaveri commends him for his "superb use" of the *Natya Rupak* form, which he defines as dealing with "a single dramatic situation, significant and pregnant with the mystery of life . . . in the form of a dialogue in verse."

"The Washerman," which was translated into English by Umashankar Joshi himself, is a good example of this form.

Sachchidananda Vatsyayan (1911–   ), who writes in Hindi under the pen name Agyeya, is another of India's talented versatile writers. In addition to a half-dozen volumes of verse, Agyeya has published three novels and several collections of short stories and essays and has edited anthologies of contemporary Hindi poetry and other creative writing. In his young manhood he served with Britain's India forces in Burma during World War II and later shared with other patriots the "horror" of imprisonment for the cause of India's independence.

Mohan Singh (1905–   ), another poet and editor of the Punjab, is called by the noted novelist Khushwant Singh one of the "best of the younger poets." The only indication now of his brief espousal of communist doctrine is in the recurring theme urging action on behalf of the poor and oppressed.

"Evening," the poem quoted here, sustains a delicate metaphor with the "spontaneous beauty" that Khushwant Singh believes may help to make him "one of the greatest poets in the language."

Harivansh Rai (1907–   ), educated in the great cultural traditions of Varanasi (Benares) and Allahabad, publishes both verse and short fiction under the name Bachchan. His doctorate at Cambridge University followed special study of the poetry of William Butler Yeats.

By combining traditional poetic forms with the idiom of contemporary Hindi, Bachchan has helped to break down the earlier idea that poetry had to employ a special poetic language.

G. S. Sivarudrappa (1926–   ) is the youngest of the poets included here and the only one writing in the Kannada language. Geographically Kannada is closest to Gujarati, since it is the official language of the Karnataka State, which was formed in recent times from portions of what had been included in the states of Bombay, Mysore, and Hyderabad.

According to critic V. K. Gokak, Sivarudrappa employed

"new diction and imagery" in an old poetic tradition which he terms "unending." Affected by the technics of modern poets of the West, Sivarudrappa developed new meters and forms. Nevertheless, as we see from his poem here, he has not abandoned the old gods, places, and metaphors.

HENRY LOUIS VIVIAN DEROZIO

THE HARP OF INDIA

Why hang'st thou lonely on yon withered bough?
　　Unstrung, forever, must thou there remain?
Thy music once was sweet—who hears it now?
　　Why doth the breeze sigh over thee in vain?—
　　Silence hath bound thee with her fatal chain;
Neglected, mute and desolate art thou
　　Like ruined monument on desert plain—
O! many a hand more worthy far than mine
　　Once thy harmonious chords to sweetness gave,
And many a wreath for them did Fame entwine
　　Of flowers still blooming on the minstrel's grave;
Those hands are cold—but if thy notes divine
　　May be by mortal wakened once again,
　　Harp of my country, let me strike the strain!

TO INDIA—MY NATIVE LAND

My country! in thy day of glory past
A beauteous halo circled round thy brow,
And worshiped as a deity thou wast.
Where is that glory, where that reverence now?
Thy eagle pinion is chained down at last,
And groveling in the lowly dust art thou:
Thy minstrel hath no wreath to weave for thee
Save the sad story of thy misery!
Well—let me dive into the depths of time,
And bring from out the ages that have rolled
A few small fragments of those wrecks sublime,
Which human eye may never more behold;
And let the guerdon of my labor be
My fallen country! one kind wish from thee!

translated by Francis Bradley Bradley-Birt

BANKIM CHANDRA CHATTERJEE

MOTHER, I BOW TO THEE

Mother, I bow to thee!
Rich with thy hurrying streams,
Bright with thy orchard gleams,
Cool with thy winds of delight,
Dark fields waving, Mother of might,
Mother free.
Glory of moonlight dreams
Over thy branches and lordly streams,
Clad in thy blossoming trees,
Mother, giver of ease,
Laughing low and sweet!
Mother, I kiss thy feet,
Speaker sweet and low!
Mother, to thee I bow.
Who hath said thou art weak in thy lands,
When the swords flash out in twice seventy million hands
And seventy million voices roar[1]
Thy dreadful name from shore to shore?
With many strengths who are mighty and stored,
To thee I call, Mother and Lord!
Thou who savest, arise and save!
To her I cry who ever her foemen drave
Back from plain and sea
And shook herself free.
Thou art wisdom, thou art law,
Thou our heart, our soul, our breath,
Thou the love divine, the awe
In our hearts that conquers death.
Thine the strength that nerves the arm,
Thine the beauty, thine the charm.
Every image made divine
In our temples is but thine.
Thou art Durga,[2] Lady and Queen,
With her hands that strike and her swords of sheen,
Thou art Lakshmi [3] lotus-throned,

[1] When used as a national anthem, this figure was changed to 300 million.

[2] The goddess-mother, much worshiped in Bengal.

[3] The goddess of wealth.

And the Muse a hundred-toned.
Pure and Perfect without peer,
Mother, lend thine ear.
Rich with thy hurrying streams,
Bright with thy orchard gleams,
Dark of hue, O candid-fair
In thy soul, with jeweled hair
And thy glorious smile divine,
Loveliest of all earthly lands,
Showering wealth from well-stored hands!
Mother, mother mine!
Mother, sweet, I bow to thee
Mother great and free!

translated by Aurobindo Ghose

RABINDRANATH TAGORE

SONGS FROM GITĀNJALI

3

All fruitless is the cry,
All vain this burning fire of desire.
The sun goes down to his rest.
There is gloom in the forest and glamour in the sky.
With downcast look and lingering steps
The evening star comes in the wake of departing day
And the breath of the twilight is deep with the fullness of a
    farewell feeling.

I clasp both thine hands in mine,
And keep thine eyes prisoner with my hungry eyes;
Seeking and crying, Where art thou,
Where, O, where!
Where is the immortal flame hidden in the depth of thee!

As in the solitary star of the dark evening sky
The light of heaven, with its immense mystery, is quivering,
In thine eyes, in the depth of their darkness
There shines a soul-beam tremulous with a wide mystery.

Speechless I gaze upon it.
And I plunge with all my heart

Into the deep of a fathomless longing:
I lose myself.

translated by the author

6

I have ever loved thee in a hundred forms and times,
Age after age, in birth following birth.
The chain of songs that my fond heart did weave
Thou graciously didst take around thy neck,
Age after age, in birth following birth.

When I listen to the tales of the primitive past,
The love-pangs of the far distant times,
The meetings and partings of the ancient ages,
I see thy form gathering light
Through the dark dimness of Eternity
And appearing as a star ever fixed in the memory of the All.

We two have come floating by the twin currents of love
That well up from the inmost heart of the Beginningless.
We two have played in the lives of myriad lovers
In tearful solitude of sorrow,
In tremulous shyness of sweet union,
In old old love ever renewing its life.

The on-rolling flood of the love eternal
Hath at last found its perfect final course.
All the joys and sorrows and longings of heart,
All the memories of the moments of ecstasy,
All the love-lyrics of poets of all climes and times
Have come from the everywhere
And gathered in one single love at thy feet.

translated by the author

16

O Man Divine, sanctify our efforts
with the light of thy sacred touch.
Dwell in our hearts,
hold before us the image of thy greatness.
Forgive our transgression,
teach us to forgive.

Guide us into serene fortitude
through all joys and sorrows,
inspire us with love

overcoming pride of self,
and let our devotion for thee
banish all enmity.

translated by the author

20

My heart, like a peacock on a rainy day,
spreads its plumes tinged with rapturous colors of thoughts,
and in its ecstasy seeks some vision in the sky,—
with a longing for one whom it does not know.
My heart dances.

The clouds rumble from sky to sky—
the shower sweeps horizons,
the doves shiver in silence in their nests,
the frogs croak in the flooded fields,—
and the clouds rumble.

O, who is she on the king's tower
that has loosened the braid on her dark hair,
has drawn over her breasts the blue veil?
She wildly starts and runs in the sudden flashes of lightning
and lets the dark hair dance on her bosom.

Ah, my heart dances like a peacock,
the rain patters on the new leaves of summer,
the tremor of the crickets' chirp troubles the shade of the
    tree,
the river overflows its bank washing the village meadows.
My heart dances.

translated by the author

30

The battle is over. After strife and struggles the treasure is
    gathered and stored.
Come now, woman, with your golden jar of beauty. Wash
    away all dust and dirt, fill up all cracks and flaws, make
    the heap shapely and sound.
Come, beautiful woman, with the golden jar on your head.

The play is over. I have come to the village and have set up
    my hearthstone.
Now come, woman, carrying your vessel of sacred water;
    with tranquil smile and devout love, make my home pure.
Come, noble woman, with your vessel of sacred water.

The morning is over. The sun is fiercely burning. The wandering stranger is seeking shelter.

Come, woman, with your full pitcher of sweetness. Open your door and with a garland of welcome ask him in.

Come, blissful woman, with your full pitcher of sweetness.

The day is over. The time has come to take leave.

Come, O woman, with your vessel full of tears. Let your sad eyes shed tender glow on the farewell path and the touch of thy trembling hand make the parting hour full.

Come, sad woman, with your vessel of tears.

The night is dark; the house is desolate and the bed empty, only the lamp for the last rites is burning.

Come, woman, bring your brimming jar of remembrance. Open the door of the secret chamber with your unbraided streaming hair and spotless white robe, replenish the lamp of worship.

Come, suffering woman, bring your brimming jar of remembrance.

translated by the author

35

Where the mind is without fear and the head is held high;
    Where knowledge is free;
    Where the world has not been broken up into fragments
        by narrow domestic walls;
    Where words come out from the depth of truth;
    Where tireless striving stretches its arms towards perfection;
    Where the clear stream of reason has not lost its way
        into the dreary desert sand of dead habit;
    Where the mind is led forward by thee into ever-widening thought and action—
    Into that heaven of freedom, my Father, let my country awake.

translated by the author

39

The flood, at last, has come upon
your dry river-bed.
Cry for the boatman,
cut the cordage,
launch the boat.

Take your oars, my comrades,
your debt has grown heavy,
for you have spent idle days at the landing,
hesitating to buy and sell.
Pull up the anchor,
set the sails,
let happen what may.

translated by the author

51

Thou art the ruler of the minds of all people,
Thou Dispenser of India's destiny.
Thy name rouses the hearts
of the Punjab, Sind, Gujrat and Maratha,
of Dravid, Orissa and Bengal.
It echoes in the hills of the Vindhyas and Himalayas,
mingles in the music of Jumna and Ganges,
and is chanted by the waves of the Indian Sea.
They pray for thy blessing and sing thy praise,
Thou Dispenser of India's destiny,
Victory, Victory, Victory to thee.

Day and night, thy voice goes out from land to land,
calling Hindus, Buddhists, Sikhs and Jains round thy throne
and Parsees, Mussalmans and Christians.
Offerings are brought to thy shrine by the East and the West
to be woven in a garland of love.
Thou bringest the hearts of all peoples into the harmony of
   one life,
Thou Dispenser of India's destiny,
Victory, Victory, Victory to thee.

Eternal Charioteer, thou drivest man's history
along the road rugged with rises and falls of Nations.
Amidst all tribulations and terror
thy trumpet sounds to hearten those that despair and droop,
and guide all people in their paths of peril and pilgrimage.
Thou Dispenser of India's destiny,
Victory, Victory, Victory to thee.

When the long dreary night was dense with gloom
and the country lay still in a stupor,
thy Mother's arms held her,
thy wakeful eyes bent upon her face,
till she was rescued from the dark evil dreams

that oppressed her spirit,
Thou Dispenser of India's destiny.
Victory, Victory, Victory to thee.

The night dawns, the sun rises in the East,
the birds sing, the morning breeze brings a stir of new life.
Touched by golden rays of thy love
India wakes up and bends her head at thy feet.
Thou King of all Kings,
Thou Dispenser of India's destiny,
Victory, Victory, Victory to thee.

translated by the author

This lyric has been adopted as the national anthem of independent India. The first stanza refers to major states, mountains, and the sacred Jumna and Ganges rivers; the second, to India's several religious sects. The reference to the "Eternal Charioteer" in the third stanza takes the mind at once to the great epic of religious devotion, the *Bhagavad Gita,* in which the god Krishna is incarnated as a charioteer for the hero Arjuna to show him the course he must follow in performing life's duty in reverence to God.

86

Let the links of my shackles snap at every step of thy dance,
O Lord of Dancing,
and let my heart wake in the freedom of the eternal voice.
Let it feel the touch of that foot that ever sets swinging the
    lotus-seat of the muse,
and with its perfume maddens the air through ages.
Rebellious atoms are subdued into forms at thy dance-time,
the suns and planets,—anklets of light,—twirl round thy mov-
    ing feet,
and, age after age, Things struggle to wake from dark slum-
    ber, through pain of life, into consciousness,
and the ocean of thy bliss breaks out in tumults of suffering
    and joy.
Before I leave, tinge my heart in secret with thine own colour,
the colour of the young smile, of tears shaded with ancient
    sadness.
Let it tinge my thoughts, my deeds, the flame of my evening
    lamp,
the waking moment of my midnight.
Before I leave, rouse my heart with the swing of thy dancing
    feet,
the swing that wakens stars in the deep of night,

frees the stream from the rocky cave,
gives voice to clouds in thunder and rain,—
the swing by which the balance in the center of existence is
    swayed in endless cycles of movement.

translated by the author

Shiva, the god of music and dance, is also the early god of destruction. A favorite representation in art and sculpture, Shiva is
depicted as having four arms and as dancing in a circle of fire, his
movements representing the rhythm of the universe and the eternal
cycle of life and death.

129

> Your creation's path you have covered
> with a varied net of wiles,
> Thou Guileful One.
> False belief's snare you have
> laid with skillful hands
> in simple lives.
> With this deceit have you left a mark
> on Greatness;
> for him kept no secret night.
> The path that is shown to him
> by your star
> is the path of his own heart
> ever lucid,
> which his simple faith
> makes eternally shine.
> Crooked outside yet it is straight within,
> in this is his pride.
> Futile he is called by men.
> Truth he wins
> in his inner heart washed
> with his own light.
> Nothing can deceive him,
> the last reward he carries
> to his treasure-house.
> He who has easefully borne your wile
> gets from your hands
> the unwasting right to peace.

translated by the author

130

In front lies the ocean of peace.
Launch the boat, Helmsman.
You will be the comrade ever,
Take, O take him in your lap.
In the path of the Infinite
will shine the *Dhruva-tārā*.[1]
Giver of freedom, your forgiveness, your mercy
will be wealth inexhaustible
in the eternal journey.
May the mortal bonds perish,
May the vast universe take him in its arms,
And may he know in his fearless heart
The Great Unknown.

translated by the author

Although written two years before the poet's death, this poem was first heard when it was sung at his funeral (following his request) and was then published posthumously.

VIR SINGH

I MADE MY MIND A BEGGAR'S BOWL

I made my mind a beggar's bowl.
I begged the bread of learning door to door;
With crumbs that fell from houses of learning
Did I cram it.
It was heavy,
I was proud,
I was a Pandit.[2]
I strove to walk in the clouds,
But even on the earth I stumbled.
One day I went to my Guru [3]
And placed the bowl before him as an offering.
"Dirt," he said, "dirt."
And turned it upside down.

---

[1] The steadfast and unfailing Polestar.
[2] Learned man.
[3] Spiritual guide; religious teacher.

He threw my crumbs away,
Scrubbed the bowl with sand,
Rinsed it with water,
Cleansed it of the filth of learning.

translated by Khushwant Singh

MAITHILI SHARAN GUPTA

NOW, THOSE DAYS ARE GONE FOR GOOD

Now, those days are gone for good.
    Though heart's sap swells in us still,
It is body's once stout trunk
    that, drained so, lacks will.

Rains rode by and left their stamp of lightning;
    winter withdrew and left us with its chill;
Leaving behind their sulky heats for remembrance,
    how many springs have crossed the barren hill?

Only God knows whether
    the gaming meant gain or loss for our skill,
but who can gainsay one win?
    Songs gone for good, their echoes lift us still.

translated by L. E. Nathan

UMASHANKAR JOSHI

THE WASHERMAN

Strolling on the bank of the Sabarmati
the Scientist and the Poet approached
a washerman, who in beating clothes on a stone-slab
was not aware of their august presence.

The poet said: As he is beating the clothes,
what beauty unfolds itself in the water-spray!
My heart leaps up as I behold the rainbow . . .
Ah me! Were I born a century ago
I would have been a Wordsworth.

The Scientist: Eh, before Newton
there lived not even a washerman,

who could discover this simple truth
that light as it passes through water
must split itself into seven colours?

The Poet said: Washermen? What would you
expect from them? Here's one.
Rama!—he cried to the man and asked
as he stood with his mouth agape:
Do you ever care to stop and look
rapt in joy at the rainbow
in the spray with its seven colours?

The Washerman stood aghast.
He looked to his right and left.
Why on earth such important men
should find it worthwhile to talk to him.
Mabap! [1] if I indulged in such antics,
my children at home would perish.

The Poet: To have a glimpse of Beauty
do spare a moment for the colours seven.
If I did that, when should I finish this heap?

And unmindful of the kindly visitors,
looking downward, he began to beat
the clothes. To save himself from the spray
the Scientist moved and mumbled:
Look! to no purpose did Newton live.
His discoveries—it is the same to this man
whether they are there or not.
The poet smiled wryly: The heart
of this man does not leap up.
In vain did Wordsworth sing.

translated by the author

AGYEYA (SACHCHIDANANDA VATSYAYAN)

BORROW IN THE MORNING, LEND AT NIGHT

When I woke to morning, I saw a wealth of sun,
As a birdsong faded, its singing just done.

Sunlight I asked: Can you spare a spark of your heat?

[1] Ma—mother; bap—father.

Bird I asked: Can you lend a sweet note of your song?
Grass I inquired of: Can I beg a blade of new green?
Conch weed I conjured: Can I share one beam of your open-
ing brightness?
Wind I pleaded with: Can I take from your flowing a shadow
of breath?
Wave I questioned: Can I have a hair's width of your heady
leap?
Sky I asked: Can I borrow your boundlessness for the space
of one wink?

All, I asked for a share and all gave,
And I live, for living, in fact, adds only to these:
Warm sweetness, fragrant green opening brightness, heady,
resilient flowing

In boundless being, aware
Of all such borrowed goods.

Dark in the desolate night, I woke from a dream
Of an Unseen Shapeless who had questioned me closely:
Your life, he said, is a heap of happenings,
Such a wide wealth,
Can't you lend me, therefore, a little of love which I swear
I'll have back with a hundredfold interest,
A hundred times that, whenever I return?

I replied: Love? Division?
My tone was tangled, for the deal
Figured far ahead of my having lived it.

That Unseen Shapeless cried: Yes,
For truly these things together form love:
This being alone, this anguish, this wanting,
This labyrinth, this lack of having been through,
This hunting, this doubleness, this helpless hurt of divorce,
This rising in dark to recognize finally
Whatever you own is owned at once by another.
It is yours, all yours,
So lend me a little
Who desire it so direly.

But in that midnight pitch of the dark, I was dumb,
Leery of lending
This Unseen Shapeless anything.
Who can tell
What this beggar may be?

translated by L. E. Nathan

MOHAN SINGH

EVENING

The sun horse panting and snorting
Reaches the shores of evening
Kicking his hoofs and flicking red dust
His vermilion mane wet with perspiration
He throws red foam from his mouth

The mellow-colored Evening comes
And places her hand between his pricked ears
Her long fingers
Feel the hot breath from his nostrils
And take off the bridle from his mouth

The restive animal
Tamed and quietened
Walks behind the Evening slowly
And goes into the stable of darkness

translated by Balwant Gargi

BACHCHAN (HARIVANSH RAI)

MY GARDEN PLANT

My garden plant, my friend, my likeness,
Plant of my garden,
You bear within you the plant of my being,
Friend of my being.

     My being's beloved sowed you,
     My garden thrived on the wealth of your being,
     My garden plant, my friend, my likeness,
     Friend of my being,
     Emblem of him I have loved.
     Ah how shall I water you now?
     My pitcher of love is empty,
        My likeness, my friend,
     My garden plant, my friend, my likeness,
        Plant of my being,
     Plant of my love, my likeness, my being,
        My garden friend.

Now is the month of the great monsoon,
But he I have loved is away, is away,
All I have been is passing away,
    My garden plant, my friend, my likeness,
    Plant of my garden.
How dry your leaves now, your stalk
How dry, how hardened;
The song in my throat now hurts, being hardened and dry,
    My garden plant, my likeness, my friend.
May the last of my being be laid
In the shade of your being,
May God endow me with power to endure past love,
    My garden plant, my friend, my likeness,
    Plant of my garden,
    Who bear within you the plant of my being,
    Friend of my being.

translated by M. Halpern

G. S. SIVARUDRAPPA

KRISHNA

In the darkness
a rain-wrought cage!
The God-Elephant swayed
behind the bars of the Evil One!

Red lips nourished on butter
and flutes!
With love,
the *gopi's* heartbeat galloped!

The Jumna quickened
for dreams come true,
and Brindavan's bamboo forest
was flute to that breath!

The flute left its song in the air
and made way for the Kingdom's glory;
in a Mathura palace,
it nursed the light.

In that smiling boy's
flute-holding finger grew
the thunder of Arjuna's chariot

and in that fluting breath
the conch-shell trumpet of war!

In the bewilderment of war
hear the Lord's own song:
Here I come, I come again
in age after age of need!

Again, again the darkness
and the rain-wrought cage.
And there! again, swaying
his trunk, the God-Elephant!

translated by A. K. Ramanujan

This twentieth-century poem draws on a long accumulation of myths about the popular god Krishna, regarded as the eighth incarnation of the preserver god Vishnu. In an effort to prevent the incarnation, the half-demon Kansa imprisoned the predestined parents, setting the elephant and other animals as guards. But Krishna was born, was "nourished on butter," and grew to be both the amorous flute-playing companion of the cowgirls (*gopis*) and the astute spiritual adviser to Arjuna, champion of the Pandavas in the great battle over the Ganges River Valley that is the basis for the *Mahabharata* and the *Bhagavad Gita*.

PAKISTAN

Going from the literature of India to that of Pakistan, we pass over national lines that did not exist until the postcolonial political partition of India and Pakistan in 1947; in fact, nine hundred miles of India lie between the two parts of Pakistan. In terms of language and culture we sometimes find no division line at all. West Pakistani poets of the Punjab area express themselves in Urdu, as do their Indian counterparts just east of the border. The medium of expression of the poets of East Pakistan is Bengali, as it is of the poets of West Bengal in India.

Nevertheless, Pakistan is now an independent nation with

twenty years' accretion of tradition and culture. In the consideration of Pakistani literature and art, the most significant divergence from that of India rests in their different religious orientations. Pakistan is an Islamic state. India's government is officially purely secular, but a great preponderance of her people are Hindu, and her culture is largely Hindu-centered, although millions of Indians are Muslims with Islamic mores.

India's sculptures and paintings are, for the most part, sensuous in the Hindu manner, with gods, goddesses, and the beloved figures of mythology represented in frank, if somewhat overblown, physical detail. The sculpture and painting of Pakistan, on the other hand, are more closely akin to the art forms of Persia, the original homeland of the early Aryan conquerors of India. Emphasis is on the nonhuman elements of nature and an ingenious use of stylized design, most highly developed in the intricate mosaics and inlay-work.

In general, Pakistan in her poetic conventions, as well as in her visual arts, looks back toward Persia more than toward India, her closer neighbor.

Muhammad Iqbal (1873–1938) may be considered the father of Pakistani poetry, as he is of the political state of Pakistan, in spite of the fact that he died nine years before the realization of the independent Islamic nation. In the first place, Iqbal was a master poet in both Persian and Urdu, the first official language of Pakistan (Bengali in recent years has also won recognition as a political medium for the State). In the second place, his philosophy is said to have led to the dream that was to become Pakistan. His friend and disciple, M. Shuja Namus, says that Iqbal always considered himself to be an Indian of the India of his day. However, he believed the two distinct traditions of Hinduism and Islam could never unite and flow together as one stream and therefore enunciated the idea of "two nations in one India," as Namus puts it. Whether Iqbal any more than Tagore would be content with the present distinct political separation of the two "traditions" is a moot question.

The translations in the present selection are chiefly from Iqbal's Urdu writing. Namus considers them inferior to his poems in Persian, whereas V. G. Kiernan declares that "in Urdu, Iqbal is allowed to have been far the greatest poet of this century" and was "the first prominent Urdu poet who was a native of the Panjab." In any event, Urdu is the language of a major portion of present-day Pakistan and therefore should logically introduce our poetry of her people.

Included are a number of fine *ghazals*. The *ghazal* form is probably the nearest approximation in the Persian-Urdu tradition to the sonnet with its strict form and rhyme scheme. Both Persian and Urdu provide seemingly limitless rhyme possibilities, of which the feminine form is most usual. In general, the Kiernan translations make no effort to reproduce either meter or ryhme.

Iqbal injected into the *ghazal*—traditionally in earlier Persian literature a light love poem—a seriousness of purpose and depth of philosophy that marked his verse in general. The form must be from seven to seventeen lines long and permits a certain freedom in selecting from among a number of recognized meters, but it demands a prevailing rhyme scheme, such as *aabacada*.

Ghazal No. 16, which Kiernan calls one of Iqbal's greatest, may well be considered by fervent Pakistanis to be the call to the founding of Pakistan "by men whose eyes see far and wide." And note how in "Jehad" and other poems Iqbal sets aside the conquest by sword that marked earlier Islamic extension.

N. M. Rashed (1910–   ), considered to be one of Pakistan's foremost poets, has also established a reputation in international affairs. During International Cooperation Year in 1965 he served as his nation's Information Officer at the United Nations.

"Sheba in Ruin," with its overtones of implication for today's world, stands as a companion piece to "Near the Balcony," which begins like a quiet tone poem and ends in the discordancy of contemporary life, for which religion apparently has no saving grace.

Taufiq Rafat (1927–   ) has written in English in a completely modern idiom. One brief example is included here.

Unlike their brothers of West Pakistan, the Pakistanis of East Bengal retain strong ties of cultural pride with their predominantly Hindu neighbors of West Bengal in India. In an early search for a common Pakistani tradition, poets of East Bengal sprinkled their writing with many words taken from Arabic, Persian, and Urdu, but this has slackened off in recent years. The Bengalis—East as well as West—are a naturally fervent and lyrical people whose expression even the more restrictive laws of Islam have not been able to suppress. In general, then, we note a freer and less didactic quality in the Bengali poetry of Pakistan than in the Urdu.

Abdul Ghani Hazari (1925–   ) in 1964 was granted the Asian Poetry Award of the International P.E.N. Society for

his poem "Some Bureaucrats' Wives." Less bitter and iconoclastic, but nevertheless thoroughly contemporary in tone, is
"At the Death of a Friend's Son." The poem has been translated into sensitive English by Hazari himself.

MUHAMMAD IQBAL

GHAZAL NO. 7

Lovely, Oh Lord, this fleeting world; but why
Must the frank heart, the quick brain, droop and sigh?
Though usury mingle somewhat with his godship,
The white man is the world's arch-deity;
His asses graze in fields of rose and poppy:
One wisp of hay to genius You deny;
His Church abounds with roasts and ruby wines:
Sermons and saws are all Your mosques supply.
Your laws are just, but their expositors
Bedevil the Koran, twist it awry;
Your paradise no one has seen: in Europe
No village but with paradise can vie.
—Long, long have my thoughts wandered about heaven;
Now in the moon's blind caverns let them sty!
I, dowered by Nature with empyreal essence,
Am dust—but not through dust does my way lie;
Not East nor West my home, nor Samarkand,
Nor Ispahan nor Delhi; in ecstasy,
God-filled, I roam, speaking what truth I see—
No fool for priests, nor yet of this age's fry.
My folk berate me, the stranger does not love me:
Hemlock for sherbet I could never cry;
How could a weigher of truth see Mount Damavand
And think a common refuse-heap as high?
In Nimrod's fire faith's silent witness, not
Like mustard seed in the grate, burned splutteringly,—
Blood warm, gaze keen, right-following, wrong-forswearing,
In fetters free, prosperous in penury,
In fair or foul untamed and light of heart—
Who can steal laughter from a flower's bright eye?
—Will no one hush this too proud thing Iqbal
Whose tongue God's presence-chamber could not tie!

translated by V. G. Kiernan

GHAZAL No. 9

Fabric of earth and wind and wave!
    Who is the secret, you or I,
Brought into light? or who the dark
    world of what hides yet, you or I?
Here in this night of grief and pain,
    trouble and toil, that men call life,
Who is the dawn, or who dawn's prayer
    cried from the minaret,[1] you or I?
Who is the load that Time and Space
    bear on their shoulder? Who the prize
Run for with fiery feet by swift
    daybreak and sunset, you or I?
You are a pinch of dust and blind,
    I am a pinch of dust that feels;
Through the dry land, Existence, who
    flows like a streamlet, you or I?

translated by V. G. Kiernan

GHAZAL No. 10

Hill and vale once more under the poppy's lamp are bright,
In my heart the nightingale has set new songs alight;
Violet, violet, azure, azure, golden, golden mantles—
Flowers, or fairies of the desert, rank on rank in sight?
On the rose spray, dawn's soft breeze has left a pearl of dew,
Now the sunbeam turns this gem a yet more glittering white.
Town or woodland, which is sweeter, if for her unveiling
Careless beauty love towns less than where green woods invite?

Delve into your soul and there seek out life's buried tracks;
Will you not be mine? then be not mine, be your own right!
World of soul—the world of fire and ecstasy and longing:
World of sense—the world of gain that fraud and cunning
    blight;
Treasure of the soul once won is never lost again:
Treasured gold, a shadow—wealth soon comes and soon takes
    flight.

---

[1] The faithful are called to prayer at dawn by the *muezzin*, whose cries from the eminence of the minaret ring out over village or city street.

In the spirit's world I have not seen a white man's Raj,[1]
In that world I have not seen Hindu and Muslim fight.
Shame and shame that hermit's saying poured on me—You forfeit
Body and soul alike if once you cringe to another's might!

translated by V. G. Kiernan

GHAZAL No. 16[2]

By men whose eyes see far and wide new cities shall be founded:
Not by old Kufa or Baghdad is my thought's vision bounded!

Rash youth, newfangled learning, giddy pleasure, gaudy plume,—
With these, while these still swarm, the Frankish wineshop is surrounded.

Not with philosopher, nor with priest, my business; one lays waste
The heart, and one sows discord to keep mind and soul confounded;

And for the Pharisee—far from this poor worm be disrespect!
But how to enfranchise Man, is all the problem I have sounded.

The fleshpots of the wealthy are for sale about the world;
Who bears love's toils and pangs earns wealth that God's hand has compounded.

I have laid bare such mysteries as the hermit learns, that thought,
In cloister or in college, in true freedom may be grounded.

No fastings of Mahatmas[3] will destroy the Brahmins' sway;
Vainly, when Moses holds no rod, have all his words resounded!

translated by V. G. Kiernan

[1] Rule; sovereignty. In India the British Colonial Government was referred to as the Raj.

[2] Kiernan considers this "one of Iqbal's greatest *ghazals*." Is the new civilization the poet envisions, the Islamic state of Pakistan?

[3] Divine incarnations, or "great souls." However, this undoubtedly refers specifically to Mahatma Gandhi, whose periodic fasts protested various social evils, from caste discrimination to foreign domination.

RUBA'IYAT

Faith is like Abraham at the stake: to be
Self-honoring and God-drunk, is faith. Hear me,
You whom this age's way so captivate!
To have no faith is worse than slavery.

Music of strange lands with Islam's fire blends,
On which the nation's harmony depends;
Empty of concord is the soul of Europe,
Whose civilization to no Mecca bends.

Love's madness has departed: in
The Muslim's veins the blood runs thin;
Ranks broken, hearts perplexed, prayers cold,
No feeling deeper than the skin.

translated by V. G. Kiernan

JEHAD[1]

This is an age, our canonist's new dictum
Assures us, of the pen: in our world now
The sword has no more virtue.—Has it not reached
Our pious oracle's ear, that in the Mosque
Such sermonizing nowadays has grown
Rhymeless and reasonless? Where, in a Muslim's hand,
Will he find dagger or rifle? and if there were,
Our hearts have lost all memory of delight
In death. To one whose nerves falter at even
An infidel cut down, who would exclaim
"Die like a Muslim!" Preach relinquishment
Of such crusades to him whose bloody fist
Menaces earth! Europe, swathed cap-a-pie
In mail, mounts guard over her glittering reign
Of falsehood; we enquire of our divine,
So tender of Christendom; if for the East
War is unhallowed, is not war unhallowed
For Western arms? and if your goal be truth,
Is this the right road—Europe's faults are all glossed,
And all Islam's held to so strict an audit?

translated by V. G. Kiernan

[1] Muslim holy war, or crusade for or against a belief.

Two Planets

Two planets meeting face to face,
One to the other cried "How sweet
If endlessly we might embrace,
And here forever stay! how sweet
If Heaven a little might relent,
And leave our light in one light blent!"

But through that longing to dissolve
In one, the parting summons sounded.
Immutably the stars revolve,
By changeless orbits each is bounded;
Eternal union is a dream,
And severance the world's law supreme.

translated by V. G. Kiernan

N. M. RASHED

Near the Balcony

Wake up, winsome bedroom's Light;
Wake up from your bed of velvet dream,
Though you still cling to night's delights.
Come to this window;
Morning's lights
Caress minarets
Whose heights
Mirror my desires.
Open those drowsy eyes
That awaken love in my heart;
Look at the minarets
Basking in the dawn.
Do you recall beneath their shadows
A shabby *mullah* [1]
Drowsing in a dark basement,
Like his idle god,
A demon, sorrowful,
A sign of three hundred years' shame,

[1] Religious teacher; often both interpreter and enforcer of Islamic law.

A shame without cure?
Look: as if jungle spirits with torch in hand
Had left their lairs to prowl,
The crowd in the market rushes madly—
Like a flood.
Somewhere, in each of these men's hearts
Flickers—bride-like—
A spark of soul.
But not one has the power to burst
Into a raging flame.
Among them wallow the diseased, the poor,
Nourishing cruelty beneath the sky.
I am but a beast of burden, tired, old,
On whom Hunger, hefty and strong, rides;
And like other city folk
After passing a night of pleasure,
I too go out to pick up rags and trash
Beneath that fickled sky.
At night, I too return to a shack.
Look at my helplessness!
Again and again I return to this window
To look at the minarets
When evening gives them a departing kiss.

translated by M. H. K. Qureshi and Carlo Coppola

SHEBA IN RUIN

Solomon sits, head on knees.
The land of Sheba is ruined;
Sheba, laid waste,
A haunted land, a heap of agony,
Without flower, without shrub.
There, dry winds thirst for rain;
Birds bend beaks under wing;
Men with parched gullets writhe.

Solomon sits, head on knees,
Dour, dishearted, with disheveled hair.
Was cunning, might, the bounding of a deer?
Love, a flame's sudden leap?
Desire, a rise without scent?
These are life's ways;
The less said of them the better.

Sheba is ruined;
Nothing remains but marauders' tracks;
Neither Sheba nor her fair queen remains.

Solomon sits, head on knees.
From where shall good fortune's messengers come?
From where shall wine
For the cup of age come?

translated by M. H. K. Qureshi and Carlo Coppola

TAUFIQ RAFAT

POEM 4

The time to love
is when the heart says so.

Who cares
    if it is muddy august
    or tepid april?—
for Love's infallible feet
    step daintily
    from vantage to vantage
    to the waiting salt-lick.

If Spring
has any significance,
it is for us,
    the rhymesters,
    who need
    a bough to perch on
    while we sing.

Love is a country
with its own climate.

ABDUL GHANI HAZARI

AT THE DEATH OF A FRIEND'S SON

At the noon of the first spring
                we several men

became all soul,
in three-dimensional bosom of earth
we placed the color of petunia
before the spring breeze blew.

Come, let us pray
for the future of his saddened bones
and for the unborn dream;
let us forget Sakhina's stifled sobs
                    in the flesh's greenroom.

Ah! again, once again,
yet another time remove
the cover on that silenced face
(aha! the body cold stiff)
what a costly effort with
                    inexpensive yarn.
The hunger of seventeen winters of
                    the earth
killed at the eager threshold of
                    spring—
shouldn't I see his face once?

Look, look look
on the sleeping bathed petals
the sun's knocks are baffled
and the heat of his skull now
radiates into our bones,
and Sakhina's wailing offstage
obstructs Time's way.

In the yard outside
                    the undertaker's cart,
the cars of the friends come one by one
dozing like heartless asses,
and the proud material heart of
                    the father now
stumbles at the
                    steps of seventeen memories.
Alas, the heart—
heavier than the tears
and the pull of an invisible earth
                    at the bottom of life.

Let us all pray,
those of us who are nobody,

let us make a
                    beautiful solace.
But our prayer never rises high enough;
it scatters around
                    on the mossy walls
                    on the wild flowers of
                    the burial ground,
in the expectant lilt
                    of the Quran readers
                    under the *kamini* tree,
in the dank smell of the
                    much-dug earth,
in the curious eyes of the
                    urchins on the wall,
in the parade of dead names
                    inscribed on the simple tin plate pieces,
in the inexistent eyes of
                    the brittle skulls
                    coming up to receive the newest guest
and on those
                    god-seeking worms
                    walking over the damp
                    exhumed earth.

Yet, let us pray,
let us go soul's way.
For the warmth of seventeen winters
and the killed expectation
                    of a spring
is evolved today into
                    the carefulness of the diggers' spades,
                    in the laborers' sweat
and in the tremulous
monotone of the
                    expectant *moulana*.

And let us tell Sakhina:
our flesh is an event only
and the bones history—
immortal like god
and deathless like the
                    urge to pray.

                              translated by the author

NEPAL

A separate political entity, Nepal nevertheless has close cultural ties with India. Both Hinduism and Theravada Buddhism[1] have been guiding religious philosophies. However, since the Buddha is said to have been born in what is present-day Lumbini, Nepal, Buddhism—strongly interlarded with ancient animism and shamanism—now predominates.

Balakrishna Sama (1903–   ) of Nepal is a painter and dramatist, as well as a respected poet in a nation of poets. He reverts to pre-Buddhistic sources in his poem in praise of his patron god Krishna. "The Song," written in English, uses something of the same conceit as does Elizabeth Barrett Browning's "The Great God Pan."

BALAKRISHNA SAMA

The Song

Krishna played on the charmingly juicy flute.
In the town of Mathura,
In every house
In every room
In every fold of the heart
The air began to tremble in concord with the flute.
Krishna played on the charmingly juicy flute.

The grasses fell down from the chewing mouth of the cows,
The fishes came out of water.

[1] "School of the Elders" branch (popularly called Hinayana, or "Small Vehicle," by non-Theravadists), a more strict and personally dedicated commitment than the Mahayana, or "Large Vehicle," now prevalent in China, Korea, Japan, and Hawaii.

The peacocks were lost in meditation,
So they dropped down their feathers on the Lord,
And the cuckoos and the nightingales,
Tearing off their breasts with their own nails
Fell down on the branches of the trees in concord with the
    flute.
Krishna played on the charmingly juicy flute.

The milkmaids began to weep bitterly in happiness,
After some time like the golden images they remained
    motionless,
The river of adoration was profusely flowing,
And Krishna began to smile,
The whole universe dozed in ecstasy,
The Heaven and the Earth kissed each other,
The eyelashes of the milkmaids began to be entangled in con-
    cord with the flute.
Krishna played on the charmingly juicy flute.

The poet here skillfully intertwines two separate elements of the
Krishna legend. At one period in his youth Krishna, the eighth
avatar of the preserver god Vishnu, was the amorous cowherd
whose artistry on the flute charmed all living things. In a later
period, lured to Mathura by his enemy, Kansa, he met and conquered every obstacle and foe by his wit and his skill in battle craft.

The Poetry of
Southeast Asia

Southeast Asia, roughly extending from the eastern boundaries of India to and including the Philippine Islands, is a multifarious area. Physical, religious, and cultural influences of India and China are intermingled in varying degrees.

THAILAND

Half Chinese and half Tibetan, the Thai people have been staunchly independent of the European colonization that surrounded their small monarchy. Earliest religious and cultural influences accompanied the importation of Hinduism from India. This later gave way to Buddhism, which holds sway today and has inspired some of the world's most unique artistic expression.

In "The White Lotus" by *Prince Phanuphan Yukhon* (1883–1932) the significance of the lotus—in both Hinduism and Buddhism a symbol of the unsullied purity that may be realized from, and rises above, the contaminated mire of this world—implies the purity of Buddhist belief. The con-

temporary poet *Chayasi Sunthonphiphit* (1934–   ) makes
the religious reference frankly explicit in "Till Heart's End."

H.R.H. PRINCE PHANUPHAN YUKHON

THE WHITE LOTUS

A white lotus, gleaming in the wide
Circle of the pond,
Its petals pure to my eye:
The clear water flows, splashes; there are fish
Gliding in and out and all around. Watching them,
My heart goes soft inside me.
Droves of butterflies arch back and forth,
Hanging over the lotus, inhaling its breath,
Drinking from its center.
The small boat shuffles by
And the lotus slowly drifts out of sight.

translated by James N. Mosel and Burton Raffel

CHAYASI SUNTHONPHIPHIT

TILL HEART'S END

My mind glows,
Knows no fear of the darkness and its tight web
Though the stars blur, and the moon's dim rays
Are sucked into nothingness,
And the oneness of man still cannot be found;

Though the sky splits and crackles,
Drops no gentle music,
Though a rooster's hurried cackle jars my ears,
And a frightened dog goes whimpering up and down.

This clear light inside me
Pushes the wild, heavy night back:
It will never flicker, it can never change,
Neither pain nor sorrow can reach it.

The earth swings in circles:
Soon, light must break through, dawn

Hanging golden and clear over all the world, men
Living like men.

In the lonely night I lie listening to my own heart,
The darkness so thick I could lose my way
Except for the faint, echoing chant
Of the most precious words ever written—

Words like drops from heaven
Falling like wisdom, strength, peace, beauty, into my waiting
    heart.
These two small hands will move as this mind leads them,
Will carry Buddha's divine Law
Here to this earth, until this heart no longer beats.

                    translated by James N. Mosel and Burton Raffel

INDONESIA

Contemporary developments naturally come to mind
when one thinks of Indonesia, a comparatively new nation
formed of the vast course of islands lying between the
Indian and Pacific oceans like stepping-stones from the
great landmass of Asia to the continent of Australia. But
ships from Europe brought influences that are evident from
the start in modern Indonesian poetry. The Dutch government fostered a program of translation of Western authors
into some of the major languages of the countries that then
formed the Netherlands Indies.

Literature of the classical period, which reached its apex
about 1500, was largely based on Hindu sources. That from
the postclassical time to the twentieth century was marked
by a rather debilitating romanticism.

In 1933 a group of daring writers, under the leadership
of Takdir Alisjahbana, initiated *Pudjangga Baru* (*The New
Writer*), a journal devoted to the work of Indonesian authors
writing in *bahasa Indonesia*, which, in the 1920's, had been

accepted as a national language. Although it was based chiefly on Malay, the mother tongue of a small minority, the new *lingua franca* was sufficiently close to the regional languages to be adopted fairly easily. Burton Raffel in the introduction to his *Anthology of Modern Indonesian Poetry* asserts that this was the first periodical to publish exclusively in *bahasa Indonesia,* the first given entirely to Indonesian life and literature, and the first to be edited exclusively by Indonesians.

In his discussion of the problems facing the translation of Indonesian poetry into English, Raffel states that *bahasa Indonesia* is especially rich in rhyme, which the local poet uses to the full. He believes the translator does better by not attempting to reproduce the rhyme in English. Raffel also points to differences in sound and syntax for which equivalents cannot be found in English.

During the Japanese occupation of the islands, 1942–45, the indigenous literature, in order to survive, had to go into hiding. Instead of discouraging authorship, apparently this gave it new life. Coteries met *sub rosa,* reading new works in manuscript form and passing them on to other small groups.

J. E. Tatengkeng (1907–) is cited by Raffel as one of the few *Pudjangga Baru* poets still writing and the only one to adopt the innovations introduced by the postwar poets. Tatengkeng was privileged to have received a good education in Dutch and for a time taught Dutch in a missionary school. His early poetry reveals more of his Christian belief than does his later, which reflects the influence of Chairil Anwar and his associates.

Apart from structures adopted from Western traditions, Raffel testifies to the continuing popularity and to the adaptability of two indigenous forms. The *pantun* he calls the "principal" medium of poetic expression. It is, he says, "a four-line, closely rhymed little poem divided into two self-contained and often very different couplets." The next most prevalent poetic form, according to Raffel, is the proverb, so brief that it can often be expressed in only two words. Although rhyme is always in the *pantun,* it is not strictly adhered to elsewhere.

"Traveler First Class," of the Anwar school, offers dramatic contrast to the earlier "On the Shore: Twilight," though both have the island-sea setting. (The reader is, by the way, almost constantly aware of the archipelago environment of all Indonesia's writers.)

Amir Hamzah (1911–1946) was one of the founders of

the *Pudjangga Baru* and generally considered to be the finest poet of the prewar period. Raffel refers to him as "the first great summit in modern Indonesian poetry," whose reputation can be challenged only by Chairil Anwar. His two volumes of verse—*Njanji Sunji* (*Songs of Loneliness*) and *Buah Rindu* (*Fruits of Longing*)—show Islamic fervor and little Western influence, at least insofar as themes are concerned.

Much of Amir's poetry is autobiographical in nature, the *Songs of Loneliness* dwelling especially on his love for a girl of whom his family did not approve and whom he did not marry. However, there is often an ambiguous undercurrent that implies God may be the beloved. "Because of You" has a sense of fatalism and a use of metaphor that suggest the possibility of direct influence from Omar Khayyam. The reader is referred to Omar's "For in and out, above, about, below / 'Tis nothing but a Magic Shadow-show" and his " 'Tis all a Chequer-board of Nights and Days / Where Destiny with Men for Pieces plays."

Chairil Anwar (1922–1949), although living only to the age of twenty-seven and producing no more than seventy poems of twenty or fewer lines each, became a major influence in Indonesian letters. In verse charged with personal emotion, written in a colloquial language, and departing from the traditional four-word line, Anwar revolutionized the poetic customs of a people. In imbuing the vernacular with literary dignity he might be compared with Dante and Chaucer. His technical competence revealed an awareness of poetic trends in other cultures. In fact, Anwar was a translator of such stature that it is recognized that his name would have endured in Indonesian letters on this reputation alone even though he had written no original verse.

Although Anwar was a recognized influence in his lifetime, no collection of his poetry was published until after his death. A posthumous volume, *Deru Tjampur Debu* (*Noise Mixed with Dust*), gives some indication of the unromantic contemporaneity of his writing.

Note the similarity in theme but the contrasting sentiment in "My Love's on a Faraway Island" and "My Love Far in the Islands." "At the Mosque" has a curious juxtaposition of Islamic fervor and modern revolt. Anwar frequently used the traditional *pantun* for surprisingly modern purposes.

Sitor Situmorang (1924–   ), having lived for some years in Paris, shows a more direct Western influence, especially in his imagery. Whereas Anwar was solely the poet, Sitor is a versatile writer who has published dramas, essays, and short stories, as well as verse. He is considered to be the major inheritor of Anwar's poetic legacy, adding to it his own deeper sensuousness and intellect.

Asrul Sani (1926–) is also a many-faceted writer, having established a reputation as critic, short-story writer, essayist, and poet. He has written and directed motion pictures, translated Western writers, and served for a period as director of the National Theatrical Academy. He has studied in Europe and the United States.

Toto Sudarto Bachtiar (1929–) is another poet who is not only a poet. During the struggle for independence, Bachtiar served in the army. Later he studied law at the University of Indonesia and edited an official publication of the Indonesian Air Force. He has also held other editorial posts.

For those who have known the vitality and color of Djakarta, Bachtiar's "Djakarta in the Evening" has a nostalgic impact that involves all the senses.

W. S. Rendra (1935–) is judged by Raffel to be a remarkably endowed young poet who is opening new possibilities unexplored by Chairil Anwar and his followers. The Rendra poem included here was inspired, Raffel says, by Rendra's marriage.

J. E. TATENGKENG

Traveler First Class

Before I was thirty
I was never more than a deck passenger.
Thanks to the efforts of my friends
And the transfer of sovereignty
I'm now a traveler first class.

I'm one of the army
of inspection officials
Wandering
From island to island
Building up the country.

Every evening I play bridge in the salon
And drink my beer
And rage at the waiter.

I've never written a report.

I disembark
And give half a rupiah
For the workers on the first of May.

translated by James S. Holmes

ON THE SHORE: TWILIGHT

The small waves break with a splash,
The great sun flickers.
It's a quiet, pleasant day,
With blue-red mountains all around.

The fishermen's boats sail along in clusters,
Out from the bay, into the shallows:
The sailors sing melancholy songs
Of old loves, lost loves.

The sun looks down the other side of the mountains,
The moon slips grinning into its place,

And this poet goes off into musing
And praise—and gathers in a poem.

The emptier, the lonelier the world
The more yearningly the Soul sings on . . .

translated by Burton Raffel and Nurdin Salam

AMIR HAMZAH

BECAUSE OF YOU

Flowers burst into bloom,
Loving life because of You:
Love spreading like flowers in my heart
Filled it with the fragrance of blossoms, and their dust.

Life is a dream, something
Played behind a screen, and I,
Now dreamer, now dancer, am pulled
In and out of existence.

So the bright leather puppet shines

His shadow on the screen, bringing us a world
Of emotions. The longing heart follows;
Two souls join, fuse.

I am a puppet, you are a puppet,
To please the puppeteer as he runs through his song;
We glance at each other, out on the open screen,
For as long as the one melody lasts.

Other bright-colored dolls take their turn;
You and I are laid in our box.
I am a puppet, you are a puppet,
To please the puppeteer running out his rhymes.

translated by S. T. Alisjahbana, Sabina Thornton, and Burton Raffel

The metaphor here is that of the Indonesian shadow drama in which leather figures, intricately cut out and brilliantly decorated, are projected against a white screen. For generations the favorite stories have been those of the classical epics of India, the *Mahabharata* and the *Ramayana*.

CHAIRIL ANWAR

AT THE MOSQUE

I shouted at Him
Until He came.

We met face to face.

Afterwards He burned in my breast.
All my strength struggles to extinguish Him.

My body, which won't be driven, is soaked with sweat.

This room
Is the arena where we fight,

Destroying each other,
One hurling insults, the other gone mad.

translated by Burton Raffel and Nurdin Salam

MY LOVE'S ON A FARAWAY ISLAND

My love's on a faraway island,
A sweet girl, doing nothing for lack of anything better.

The *prau* slides quickly along, the moon gleams,
Around my neck I wear a charm for my girl;
The wind helps, the sea's clear, but I know
I'm not going to reach her.

In the calm water, in the gentle wind,
In the final sensation, everything goes swiftly.

Fate takes command, saying:
"Better steer your *prau* straight into my lap."

Hey! I've come this way for years!
The *prau* I'm in is going to crash!
Why is Fate calling
Before I have a chance to hug my girl?

My sweet on a faraway island,
If I die, she'll die for lack of anything better.

translated by Burton Raffel and Nurdin Salam

MY LOVE FAR IN THE ISLANDS

My love far in the islands,
     Loving girl,
Now passing the time alone.

The boat sails on, the moon is cool,
I carry a present round my neck,
The wind helps, the sea is clear,
Yet I know that I shall never reach her.

In the clear water, in the moaning wind,
In the feeling I have that all passes,
My death is speaking queenly words
"My lap must be your boat's harbor."

Why! how many years have I sailed
In my boat as fragile as me?
Why must my death begin to call me
Before I have kissed my love again?

My loving girl far in the islands,
        If I should die,
Will die passing the time alone.

translated by Derwent May

SITOR SITUMORANG

SWIMMING POOL

For Rulan

The child and I are stretched out
Carelessly on the edge of the pool,
Examining clouds in the blue sky
As if to find some special sign.

Reflected in the clear pool
I see the calm clarity of a face
Long since silenced and gone
But not yet pronounced dead.

Then the child asks of his own accord
If men go to heaven
When they die.

And because I know for sure
I nod quietly
And the child immediately understands.

translated by Jean Kennedy and Burton Raffel

ASRUL SANI

REMEMBER FATHER, REMEMBER FATHER

"Let us take the north road!"
    "Brother, that is not the north."
"Ah, then my child has been taken to the south."

Gone on horseback to the south,
Racing, racing, racing through the black night.
Even while we were all as close as brothers
My child was carried away
And I was killed.

"Let us take the south road!"
    "No, brother, that is not the south."
"Ah, then, my loved one has been taken southeast."

You know the love of every father
And what he hopes for his children.
Now all hope and love are gone.
The wind from the sea has blown with a far-off sadness.

"Bring all the troops to the southeast!"
    "My friend, that is not the way."
"Ah, where, where have you taken my child?"

You!—you who were my loved one!
Who is there to guide you,
To show you that shadows are not substance,
That the sun is not God,
And that to hope is to acquiesce.

Listen, listen, here is the suffering of man!
He asks for good fortune
And yet curses, curses at whoever has sinned . . .
Yes, friend, I have damned my own brother,
Because love
Knows no brother.

I take all my curses back:
Let my brother pass in peace.
And to you who heard what I said
I confess: "I was not killed by my brother,
I killed myself."

"Brother, where is the right, where is the left, where is the
          middle road?"
    "Yes, the three run in all directions."
"I want to follow them, everywhere."

Peace, peace be with you, brother,
Galloping, galloping down the shining street.
And you, little one, on your mother's knee,
If grow you will,
Play carefully with your glass beads;
As soon as you know how to laugh
Then remember father—remember father . . . !

translated by Jean Kennedy

TOTO SUDARTO BACHTIAR

DJAKARTA IN THE EVENING

Earning my daily living, and daily living
With mud-caked coolies and women bathing naked
In the river I love, O city of my heart.
Bells on the trams and motor horns competing.
Air weighing on the long and twisting road.

Buildings and heads, lost in the dusk, breaking apart.
Kites like coal in the southwest sky.
        O city I love,
Press me into the center of your heart,
Into the heart of your noise and of your suffering.

I look up as though I dreamed at a white moon
Swimming in a sky of young clouds.
        The pure wells
Lie hidden. Earth has its coat of dust.
And hand and word restrain the breath of the free spirit
Waiting to be taken by death.

I know nothing.
      But outside, all is simple.
Longing songs that play with their own sadness
Wait for the silence surprised at the door at dawn
And the dreams of men go on forever.

Constantly changing place, the noises of bell and horn,
In the earning one's daily living, and daily living,
Among the coolies returning along the roads,
And women climbing the banks of the river I love.

The children swimming and laughing in their innocence,
In reflections of the palace seized by cramp.
The evening kites soaring out of sight
In the black night that suddenly leaps out.

The pure wells irretrievably hidden.
The constant coat of dust upon the earth.
Weapon and hand restraining the free spirit.
O city that I love, after the dusk,
City that I live in, and of my longing.

translated by Derwent May

W. S. RENDRA

LITTLE SISTER NARTI

I'm writing this letter
While the sky drips down
And two small wild ducks
Are making love in the pond
Like two naughty children,
Funny and nice,
Two flapping ducks
Making their feathers shake.
Hey, little sister Narti,
I want you for my wife!

Twelve angels
Have descended,
In this time of drizzling rain:
In front of the window-mirror
They stare and wash their hair
For the celebration.
Hey, little sister Narti,
In my fancy bridegroom clothes,
Covered with flowers and wearing a sacred sword,
I ache to lead you to the altar
And marry you.

I'm writing this letter
While rain drips
From the sky;
A sweet, spoiled child
Cries for her toys;
Two mischievous little boys
Are having fun in the ditch
And the jealous sky is watching.
Hey, little sister Narti,
I want you
To be the mother of my children!

translated by Burton Raffel

PHILIPPINES

The Republic of the Philippines is an anomaly in the Asian context. Not only have her peoples brought a cultural mixture from earlier homelands in Malaya and China, but Western influence has permeated the life of the peoples for so many centuries that it is often difficult to determine what is indigenous and what imported. From the Spanish conquest in 1571, through the United States hegemony from 1898 to 1945 and the Japanese occupation of World War II years, the archipelago, especially the urban areas, came under outside pressures. The most literate composition was first in Spanish and then in English, and in each there has been publication worthy of consideration. However, there was, of course, an early folk expression. In recent years Tagalog literature has burgeoned as the national language and has become increasingly the language of instruction. Eight other regional vernaculars have also served as literary media, notably Ilocano, Bisayan, and Cebuano, the latter vying most strongly with Tagalog for publication.

José Rizal (1861–1896), in his own writing, exemplifies the language paradox of the Philippines. The final publication price for Rizal's novels of Filipino self-respect was no less than the author's life. Yet the *Noli me Tangere,* subtitled "A Tagalog Novel," and the later *El Filibusterismo* were written and first published in Spanish. More about Rizal, the man and author, introduces the excerpts from his major novel.

The first stanza of "My Last Farewell," which introduces the Filipino poetry in this volume, is printed on the flyleaf of the most recent English translation of the *Noli.* Asuncion David-Maramba, writing in his *Philippine Contemporary Literature,* comments on Rizal as a poet: "The permanent value of Rizal's prose is still controversial, but few will deny the literary quality of his verse. It was a

genuine poet who, on the eve of execution, could indulge
the poetic whimsy that after his death he would sing to his
beloved country."

Rizal's style in meter and rhyme may be sampled in the
first stanza of the Spanish original:

> Adiós, Patria adorada, región del sol querida,
> Perla del Mar de Oriente, nuestro perdido edén,
> A darte voy, alegre, la triste, mustia vida;
> Y fuera más brillante, más fresca, más florida
> También por ti la diera, la diera por tu bien.

Rafael Zulueta da Costa (1915–   ) uses the name R.
Zulueta da Costa as a writer and Rafael Zulueta as a busi-
nessman. Although he has achieved eminence in various
fields—education, business, aeronautics, and theatrics—
Zulueta da Costa's first love was poetry. He began writing
verse as a school lad at the age of thirteen, had his work
published in a literary review shortly thereafter, and at
the age of twenty-five became the first recipient of the
coveted Commonwealth Literary Award for his collection,
Like the Molave and Other Poems. The title poem, included here, not only calls upon Rizal but is a contemporary
echo of the struggle from oppression, which the earlier
patriot so forcefully represented in his prose and verse.

Zulueta da Costa began writing poetry in Spanish. Later
he turned to English, in which "Like the Molave" was
written. He has now published three volumes of verse in
English. Critics acknowledge his recognizable indebtedness
to Whitman and other free-verse writers.

In recent years Zulueta da Costa has won recognition for
his translations of opera librettos into English and for his
creative sponsorship of the performing arts.

Bienvenido N. Santos (1911–   ), a native of Manila,
writes in English. He spent several years studying and
traveling in the United States, where he recently became the
first visiting lecturer from the Philippines under the State
University of Iowa Foundation in Creative Writing. He is
a poet but also a novelist, short-story writer, and magazine
editor. He was a winner in an international short-story con-
test sponsored by the New York *Herald Tribune* and of
the Palanca literary prize for the short story.

Santos's "March of Death" speaks directly to many Western readers, especially Americans, who remember the infamous Death March of Bataan in World War II.

Nick Joaquin (1917–   ), a versatile author, is considered one of the best writers of fiction, drama, poetry, and critical essays. He himself records that he began writing poetry when he was "fourteen or fifteen" and started writing prose when he was eighteen. He began his first novel in Hong Kong after the war, he says, "continued writing it in Europe and America during the 1950's, and finished it in Manila where it was finally published." It won the first Stonehill Award. He has since published a collection of short stories, a book of poems, and the play "A Portrait of the Artist as Filipino," which has been produced on the stage and made into a motion picture.

Joaquin represents the ultramodern in Filipino poetry and fictional prose. His "Six P.M.," written in English, embodies something of the existentialist view of life so prevalent in present-day Filipino writing.

JOSÉ RIZAL

MY LAST FAREWELL

Land that I love: Farewell: O Land the sun loves
Pearl in the sea of the Orient: Eden lost to your brood!
Gaily go I to present you this hapless hopeless life:
Were it more brilliant: had it more freshness, more bloom:
Still for you would I give it: would give it for your good!

In barricades embattled, fighting in delirium,
Others give you their lives without doubts, without gloom.
The site nought matters; cypress, laurel, or lily;
Gibbet or open field; combat or cruel martyrdom
Are equal if demanded by Country and home.

I am to die when I see the heavens go vivid,
Announcing the day at last behind the dead night.
If you need color—color to stain that dawn with,
Let spill my blood: scatter it in good hour;
And drench in its gold one beam of the newborn light.

My dreams when a lad, when scarcely adolescent:
My dreams when a young man, now with vigor inflamed:
Were to behold you one day: jewel of eastern waters:
Griefless the dusky eyes: lofty the upright brow;
Unclouded, Unfurrowed, Unblemished, and Unashamed!

Enchantment of my life: my ardent avid obsession:

To your health! cries the soul, so soon to take the last leap:
To your health! O lovely: how lovely: to fall that you may
    rise!
To perish that you may live! to die beneath your skies!
And upon your enchanted ground the eternities to sleep!

Should you find someday somewhere on my gravemound,
    fluttering
Among tall grasses, a flower of simple fame:
Caress it with your lips and you kiss my soul:
I shall feel on my face across the cold tombstone:
Of your tenderness, the breath; of your breath, the flame.

Suffer the moon to keep watch, tranquil and suave, over me:
Suffer the dawn its flying lights to release:
Suffer the wind to lament in murmurous and grave manner:
And should a bird drift down and alight on my cross,
Suffer the bird to intone its canticle of peace.

Suffer the rains to dissolve in the fiery sunlight
And purified reascending heavenward bear my cause:
Suffer a friend to grieve I perished so soon:
And on fine evenings, when someone prays in my memory,
Pray also—O my land! that in God I repose.

Pray for who have fallen befriended by no fate:
For all who braved the bearing of torments all bearing past:
For our poor mother piteously breathing in bitterness:
For widows and orphans: for those in tortured captivity
And yourself: pray to behold your redemption at last.

And when in dark night shrouded obscurely the graveyard lies
And only, only the dead keep vigil the night through:
Keep holy the peace: keep holy the mystery.
Strains, perhaps, you will hear—of zither, or of psalter:
It is I—O land I love—It is I, singing to you!

And when my grave is wholly unremembered
And unlocated (no cross upon it, no stone there plain);
Let the site be wracked by the plow and cracked by the spade
And let my ashes, before they vanish to nothing,
As dust be formed and part of your carpet again.

Nothing then will it matter to place me in oblivion!
Across your air, your space, your valleys shall pass my wraith!
A pure chord, strong and resonant, shall I be in your ears:
Fragrance, light, and color: whisper, lyric, and sight:
Constantly repeating the essence of my faith!

Land that I idolize: prime sorrow among my sorrows:
Beloved Filipinas, hear me the farewell word:
I bequeath you everything—my family, my affections:
I go where no slaves are—nor butchers: nor oppressors:
Where faith cannot kill: where God's the sovereign Lord!

Farewell, my parents, my brothers—Fragments of my soul:
Friends of old and playmates in childhood's vanished house:
Offer thanks that I rest from the restless day!
Farewell, sweet foreigner—my darling, my delight!
Creatures I love, Farewell! To die is to repose.

translated by Nick Joaquin

RAFAEL ZULUETA DA COSTA

LIKE THE MOLAVE [1]

Poem 1

Not yet, Rizal, not yet. Sleep not in peace:
There are a thousand waters to be spanned;
There are a thousand mountains to be crossed;
There are a thousand crosses to be borne.
Our shoulders are not strong; our sinews are
Grown flaccid with dependence, smug with ease
Under another's wing.

                    Rest not in peace;
Not yet, Rizal, not yet. The land has need
Of young blood—and, what younger than your own.
Forever spilled in the great name of freedom,
Forever oblate on the altar of
the free?

            Not you alone, Rizal.
            O souls
And spirits of the martyred brave, arise!
Arise and scour the land! Shed once again
Your willing blood! Infuse the vibrant red
Into our thin anaemic veins; until
We pick up your Promethean tools and, strong,
Out of the depthless matrix of your dream

[1] Notable for its strength and utility, the molave is the national tree of the Philippines.

And from the silent cliffs of freedom, we
Carve out forever your marmoreal dream!
Until our people are become like the molave,
Rising on the hillside, unafraid,
Strong of its own fiber; yes, like the molave!

Poem 2

The building is a landmark of progress.
The last stone has been laid, the last bolt riveted.
The big boss beams; the architect, the engineer smile.
Handshakes. Pretty speeches. The noble dedication.
    The shining placard: Erected A.D. 1940.

Who records the history of an edifice?
Who tells the story from cornerstone to ceremony?
Who peers into the humanity of daily-wage earners?
Who rehearses the drama of diggers, piledrivers, riveters,
    masons, woodworkers, and painters?
Who investigates into their motives?
Who speaks the Babel tongue of myriad interpretation?

    The government builds for progress.
    The capitalist builds for more capital.
    The architect builds for achievement.
    The engineer builds for enterprise.
    The holy one builds for the glory of God.
    What does the worker build for?

In the years before Christ there were whips.
In the year of our Lord there are also whips
    Other than leather.

Poem 3

They say the molave is extinct,
But they are blind or will not see.

Stand on the span of any river, and lo!
Eternally to and fro, cross and recross, molave!

Yes, molave strikes roads into the darkest core!
Yes, molave builds seven-thousand bridges in blood!

    Bagumbayan planted the final seed.
    Balintawak nurtured the primal green.

Molave, uprooted and choked, will not be destroyed.
Molave presses on and will not be detained.

Let Spain speak.
Let America speak.

Poem 4

Not yet, Rizal, not yet.
The glory hour will come.
Out of the silent dreaming,
From the seven-thousandfold silence,
We shall emerge, saying: *We are Filipinos,*
And no longer be ashamed.

Sleep not in peace.
The dream is not yet fully carved.
Hard the wood, but harder the blows.
Yet the molave will stand;
Yet the molave monument will rise,
And gods walk on brown legs.

BIENVENIDO N. SANTOS

THE MARCH OF DEATH

Were you one of them, my brother,
Whom they marched under the April sun
And flogged to bleeding along the roads we knew and loved?

> *March, my brother, march!*
> *The springs are clear beyond the road*
> *There is rest at the foot of the hill.*

We were young together,
So very young and unafraid;
Walked those roads, dusty in the summer sun,
Brown pools and mud in the December rains;
Ran barefoot along the beaten tracks in the canefields,
Planted corn after the harvest months.

Here, too, we fought and loved
Shared our dreams of a better place
Beyond those winding trails.

> *March, my brother, march!*
> *The springs are clear beyond the road*
> *At the foot of the hill is rest.*

We knew those roads by heart
Told places in the dark
By the fragrance of garden hedge
In front of uncle's house;
The clatter of wooden shoes on the bamboo bridge,
The peculiar rustling of the bamboo groves
Beside the house where Celia lived.

Did you look through the blood in your eyes
For Celia sitting at the window
As the thousands upon thousands of you
Walked and died on the burning road?
If you died among the hundreds by the roadside
It should have been by the bamboo groves
With the peculiar rustling in the midnight.

No, you have not died; you cannot die!
I have felt your prayer touch my heart
As I walked alone the crowded streets of America.

And we would walk those roads again one April morn,
Listen to the sound of working men
Dragging tree trunks from the forests,
Rebuilding homes—laughing again—
Sowing the fields with grain, fearless of death
From cloudless skies.

You would be silent, remembering
The many young bodies that lay mangled by the roadside;
The blood-soaked dust over the bloody rage of men;
The agony and the moaning and the silent tears;
The grin of yellow men, their blood-stained blades opaque
     in the sun;
The many months of hunger and torture, and waiting.

I would be silent, too, having nothing to say.
What matters if the winters were bitter cold
And loneliness stalked my footsteps on the snow?

> *March, my brother, march!*
> *The springs are clear beyond the road*
> *Rest, at the foot of the hill.*

And we would walk those roads again one April morn
Hand in hand like pilgrims marching
Towards the church on the hillside,
But there would be no hillside;

Only a little nipa house beside the bamboo groves
With the peculiar rustling in the midnight.

Or maybe I would walk them yet,
Remembering . . . remembering . . .

NICK JOAQUIN

Six P.M.

Trouvère at night, grammarian at morning,
ruefully architecting syllables—
but in the afternoon my ivory tower falls.
I take a place in the bus among people returning
to love (domesticated) and the smell of onions burning
and women reaping the washlines as the angelus tolls.

But I—where am I bound?

My garden, my four walls
and you project strange shores upon my yearning:
Atlantis? The Caribbeans? or Cathay?
Conductor, do I get off at Sinai?
Apocalypse awaits me: urgent my sorrow
towards the undiscovered world that I
from warm responding flesh for a while shall borrow:
conquistador at night, clockpuncher tomorrow.

The Poetry of
China and Korea

CHINA

Perhaps more than in any other culture, some knowledge of the early roots of poetry is necessary for a satisfactory consideration of the poetry of present-day China. Up until the most recent times schoolchildren were required to commit to memory all "The 300," as the Chinese familiarly call the *Shih Ching* (*Book of Songs*). Since the *Shih Ching* is an anthology of verse that is generally thought to cover the period 1000 to 700 B.C., we can see how traditions from very early times would have permeated contemporary poetic expression.

As the title of the collection indicates, the poems of the *Shih Ching* are essentially songs; indeed, the titles of many of them are also the titles of early Chinese melodies. So we recognize the initial bond between verse and music in China as we do in India.

Also, as in India, the earliest poetic expression is agreed to have been religious in nature, although recent poetry has not remained so, as it has in India. However, since Confucius interpreted all "The 300"—whether folk songs, love lyrics, secular celebration songs, hymns, or ritualistic verses —as having religious or moral implications, the sacred element continues to be an important one.

China's unusually extensive hoard of verse writing preserved from the earliest time, combined with her unique emphasis on poetic ability for government qualification, has produced a people with a reverence for verse and (again, until very recent times) a scorn for prose used for anything other than moralistic or didactic purposes.

We have referred to the initial affinity between Chinese poetry and music and song. In this respect the poetic tradition is similar to India's and to the origins of poetry in many other cultures. In another, however, it is vastly different and is unique—except for the later traditions of Korea and Japan. Because of the pictographic nature of the written language and the close relationship between Chinese calligraphy and art, the poetry of China has the power to appeal to the eye, as well as to the ear and mind.

The scroll that adorns the wall of the scholar's study or the family room of a Chinese home may often be, not a picture, but a familiar verse in a calligraphy that has been rendered with all the care of the highest visual art. The calligrapher's selection and preparation of his brushes, the mixing of his ink on the stone mortar, the assessment of shape and texture of paper or fabric on which the verse is to be set down, constitute an almost ritualistic ceremony in which the visual artist communes with the soul of the poet seeking to present the spirit of the verse as faithfully as possible to the eye. Furthermore, the fact that Chinese characters are brush-painted rather than written harshly by pen means that the verse so inscribed has a fluidity and movement analogous to that of the recited poem.

While all this is true, Chinese poetry is further enriched when it is read or recited, for color and variety are added by the tonal language. Literary historian Lai Ming holds that the four tonal differences of the Chinese language were clearly defined when the first attempts were made to translate Buddhist *sutras* into Chinese. As poets began to give more attention to tonal harmony, poetry was completely revolutionized.

Eunice Tietjens, in her *Poetry of the Orient*, judges that the rules governing the tonal scheme as well as the rhyme scheme of Chinese verse are absolute. The first tone, called *ping*, is "low and even." The other three are referred to as *tseh*: (2) "sharp and ascending," (3) "clear and far-reaching," (4) "straight and abruptly finished." Miss Tietjens quotes the metric chart of a stanza by Ch'en Hao:

Tseh tseh ping ping tseh tseh ping
Ping ping tseh tseh tseh ping ping

Ping ping tseh tseh ping ping tseh
Tseh tseh ping ping tseh tseh ping

In addition to this tonal pattern, the stanza has a definite rhyme scheme with the first, third, and last lines in agreement.

To this variation in tone James J. Y. Liu (*The Art of Chinese Poetry*) adds the music that is brought out in the "contrast between long and short syllables" and in the end rhyme. "On the whole," he writes, "Chinese verse has a stronger but perhaps less subtle music than English verse. The variation of tones creates a singsong effect characteristic of Chinese, and in fact most Chinese readers *chant* rather than merely *read* verse aloud." All the oral elements, Liu says, contribute to "a *staccato* effect, unlike the more flowing, *legato* rhythms of English or French verse."

Tone is, of course, more than a matter of aesthetic appeal, since a shift in pitch will effect radical change in meaning. Ch'ên Shou-yi cites as an example the word *fang*, which "in its highest pitch would mean 'direction,' in its lowest pitch would mean 'chamber,' and in the middle pitch would mean 'set free.'"

To these visual, tonal, and rhyme elements the poets of China added a fourth, meter. Although the natural rhythm of the language has been produced in lines of varying length, there have been several metrical patterns that have proved popular in different periods. Unlike English verse, the meter of Chinese poetry is based on quantity rather than on accent. Ancient poets of the North delighted in the four-character line, while their counterparts in the South used long and irregular lines. In a later period a five-syllable line was popular, giving way in the Medieval Period to that of seven syllables. Variety was brought in by Li Po (*ca.* A.D. 701–762) when he adopted as his basic pattern a verse form in which the stanza was composed of two three-syllable lines followed by one of seven syllables.

From the above it will be seen that the brief poem has been preferred by the Chinese poet and reader. In fact, a perennial favorite has been the so-called "stop short" of only four lines. Although verse of some length is included in the earliest literature, the tendency has always been toward brevity. It is interesting to note that China and Japan, so deeply influenced by Chinese culture, have no poetic epics such as are found in most other literary heritages.

Similes and metaphors, repetitions and refrains, as well

as parallelism—the last three especially marked in the poetry of early periods—which are found in other cultures, should also be added to these peculiarly Chinese elements.

Any discussion of poetry of the contemporary period would not be complete—at least insofar as the People's Republic is concerned—without attention to the influences of Communist ideology. Although Mao Tse-tung still expresses himself occasionally in the *shih* and *t'zu*,[1] in speeches and writings he strikes out against these traditional forms. He urges the development of a "revolutionary literature and art" that will "help the masses to propel history forward" (see pages 223–228). So contemporary poets of mainland China have freed themselves from the old modes of expression in order to give themselves fully to expression of the desirable point of view.

Chou Yang, in a contemporary literary critique, calls a "folk art gem" this poem which he includes in his *People's New Literature:*

> Chi Chen Taoist Temple
> Is a fine place.
> Fir and pine trees grow in the stone courtyard.
> Rip up the stone flagging and look,
> They are growing on the backs of the poor.

In translation, at least, it would appear from this sample that early poetic traditions have been abandoned completely. In the original, however, visual appeal of calligraphy would probably still be an element in the written work and tonal appeal in the recited.

Since so many excellent translations of Chinese verse of the traditional classical school are available, none is included in this volume.

Hu Shih (1891–1962) opens the selections, as it was he who opened the floodgates through which would pour the cascade of poetry in the vernacular that represents the mainstream of Chinese verse expression today. Hu's *Book of Experiments* proved that he meant what he said when in July of 1916 he told American friends his poetic efforts from that time forward would be expressed in *pei-hua,* the

---

[1] *Shih*—the earliest known poetic form. Nearest to the lyric or song, it generally employed regular five- or seven-character lines. *T'zu*—a "new verse" emphasizing form and color that reached its zenith in the Sung Dynasty (960–1279) and continued as the most popular medium for opera arias. *T'zu* was marked by irregular lines, controlled rhyme patterns, and fine tonal variations.

"vulgar" tongue. That he held no brief for his ability as a poet is apparent in his reference to the *pei-hua* collection as "experiments." As he himself put it, he stumbled and walked as awkwardly in the new form as a Chinese woman would on her bound feet. The important thing to him was that he was blazing a trail in which poets of greater stature would follow.

We recognize, too, of course, that Hu Shih's vocation was not poetry. In fact, it would be difficult to specify any one interest as predominant in his crowded life. Scholar, statesman, historian, philosopher, critic, author, lecturer, we could not expect him to be the complete poet, too. Nevertheless, his "Dream and Poetry" does present in acceptable verse the vision he had caught of a new world of poetry that would be opened to the Chinese people once the old, stultifying strictures had been put aside and new songs sung in the living language of the day.

Wen Yi-tuo (1899–1946) became a leader of the Crescent School of poets, founded by Hsü Chih-mo in 1923. Employing the vernacular and reflecting the influence of Western poets, especially those of the Romantic Era, Wen and the other Crescent writers skillfully welded the elements of modern and traditional versification. Wen, who was steeped in Chinese learning, was especially mindful of his people's cultural wealth and had no intention of abandoning it for an alien heritage. However, he approved of the freer poetic expression of the West and believed that in showing similar independence in choice of themes and forms, the poets of China could be a vital force in helping to liberate the minds of the people. He deeply influenced the poets who were to follow him.

Wen was also a skilled painter who had been educated in American art schools. He carried his modern ideas into expression in the visual arts as well. On the other hand, his sense of beauty in calligraphy prompted him to esteem the age-old emphasis on the identification of the poem's calligraphic form and its essential thought. So we see Wen Yi-tuo as a link between the traditions of the past and the exciting challenges of the future.

Such a coupling of old and new may be observed in his poetry itself. For instance, at the same time as Wen's poem "Forget Her" employs the folk-type refrain reminiscent of an ageless past, his "Dead Water" metaphorically protests the stultifying effects of passive acquiescence to outmoded tradition. Though Wen believes that the "ditch of hopelessly dead water may still claim a touch of something bright," nevertheless he warns that "beauty can never reside" there and it holds no promise of providing a world for today.

Feng Chih (1905–) is another poet deeply affected by Western thought and expression. Feng once studied in Germany and he gives indications of the education's having been a sound one. He is especially noted for his adaptation of the sonnet form to Chinese prosody. Yet Feng's verse, too, is an exciting bringing together of old and new. Though he is generally agreed to be basically Western in thought, nevertheless he reveals a respect for early traditions (witness his loving eulogy to the eighth-century poet Tu Fu) and Taoist philosophy. In fact, much of his writing in its metaphysical imagery is reminiscent of the thought and expression in the Taoist "bible," the *Tao Te Ching*.

"Sonnet XV" and "Sonnet XVI" are both marked by the Taoist concept of the unity of all life in the eternal Tao (Way, Creative Principle). The Tao, being eternal, cannot be brought into our lives or taken out, because we live our lives in it:

> Nothing can be brought over from afar, and
> Nothing can be taken away from here, either.

Likewise, in the Tao, man is one with all other aspects of nature:

> Our births, our growth, and our sorrows
> Are the lone pine standing on a mountain,
> Are the dense fog blanketing a city.

While in "Han Po Chops Wood" Feng gives us a recreation of a folk tale that reveals early oppressions of the peasantry by unscrupulous landlords, "I Sing of Anshan Steel" envisions the poor man's liberation through the miracles of modern industry and technology.

Pien Chih-lin (1910–) is coupled by Robert Payne with Tien Ch'ien as one of the "two outstanding poets of the new age." Born in Kiangsu Province, Pien studied European literature at the National University of Peking. A competent translator of French poetry, Pien has also translated his own poems into English. His early verse shows the influence of the French symbolist poets, especially Baudelaire.

Pien's essential independence of spirit is reflected in the freedom he exercises both in subject matter and in poetic form. Turning from traditional modes of expression, he adapts his colloquial speech to the natural rhythm of free verse. His first volume of poems, *Leaves of Three Autumns*, appeared in 1933, and he has been a regular contributor to literary periodicals.

Of the poems given here, "A Monk," despite its iconoclastic attitude toward religion, presents an almost nostalgic image of ritualistic forms. "The First Lamp," with its praise of "the first lamp that opens a new world," succinctly summarizes Pien's attitude toward life and art.

Ai Ch'ing (1910–　) , whose given name is Chiang Nai-ch'eng, is—like Wen Yi-tuo—painter as well as poet. Prominent among the group of poets that flowered during the Sino-Japanese War (1937–45), Ai's poems are frequently dark with death. Though in every sense modern in form and themes—the result of his firsthand acquaintance with Western literary movements during two years in France—his poems are also strangely reminiscent of some of the earliest anonymous songs preserved in the *Shih Ching*. For China three thousand years ago, even as today, was torn by war that brought with it suffering and tragic death far from loved ones. However, where the early bards accepted the day's hardship and injustice with confidence that, true to the principle of *yin* and *yang*, it would inevitably be followed by peace and justice, Ai Ch'ing in contemporary impatience bites back.

"Snow Falls on China" gives us at once a realization of Ai's love of the Chinese landscape, a sense of China's long history of predatory invasion, and the immediacy of this particular war confrontation here and now:

> Oh, pain and distress of China,
> Endless like the snowy night.

Ai Ch'ing has been one of the most influential of modern Chinese poets, his free-verse style greatly influencing his fellow-writers. He is not now, however, in a position for continuing influence in his homeland, having in 1958 been put on the blacklist of "bourgeois" writers. Perhaps this condemnation was inevitable in view of Ai's outspoken opposition to the suppression of free speech—in *On Poetry* (1940)—when he asserted poetry to be the "sound of freedom."

Tien Ch'ien (1914–　) is one of the most independent of contemporary poets in both form and matter. His songs of national and personal freedom are terse and set in lines even shorter than the four-character line favored by the old-time poets of the North. Poems on war and its attendant miseries are appropriately quick-paced, giving a sense of marching tempo. The poems' impression of martial purpose is best caught aurally, and so Tien's writings are favorites in mass poetry recitations. Although nationalism and freedom from foreign domination are his preferred themes, often, as in "Children's Festival," his concern with immediacies is bound to the loved traditions.

Mao Tse-tung (1893–   ), although older than some of the poets whose compositions precede his in this collection, as leader of the Communist Revolution and State, appropriately closes our introduction to contemporary Chinese poetry. He represents a paradox: as political leader he has brought his people to a course on who knows what unchartered seas; as a poet he has been almost completely faithful to the old standards. In his public pronouncements on the function of the arts in a communistic society he repudiates traditional standards (see the selection from "On Art and Literature," pages 223–228) and warns against adhering to traditional forms for the expression of revolutionary precepts. At the same time he himself writes in the forms he proscribes for others. Unlike the ideal Taoist sage-ruler, he apparently does not "practice what he preaches."

Mao's favorite verse forms are the ancient *shih* and *t'zu*, the former at its height of popularity in the Sung Dynasty (A.D. 960–1279). One might conjecture that the imperious stringency of these early types would have their natural appeal to the authoritarian mind. "To write *t'zu*, the poet had to fit his words to a definite musical pattern," Wu Hsiao-ju writes in a contemporary literary journal emanating from Peking. "Not only is the number of lines prescribed for each *t'zu* by its melody, but the tone of each word is also fixed. In general these rules are very strictly observed." Mao undoubtedly holds that the strict observance of rules is a good thing! Robert Payne, however, grants that Mao "succeeded in imposing upon these outworn patterns a new strength and a new vision."

In the same article from which the above remark is culled, Payne quotes Mao himself as saying: "Poems should, of course, be principally written in the new forms. It does no harm to write a little in the old style, as long as it is not set as an example for the young. This ancient style puts fences around the imagination. . . ."

The poems included here illustrate the union of ancient and modern in Mao's verses. After viewing China through the perennial snows of winter and noting the Great Wall, symbol of a previously unimpregnable past, he comes to the conclusion that it is the men of today who hold the promise for a great China. "After Swimming Across the Yangtze River" offers special interest in the light of Mao's continued river-swimming, even as an old man. "The Long March" presents a poetic record of man's amazing stamina when embued by a political ideal linked to the human will to survive.

HU SHIH

DREAM AND POETRY

It's all ordinary experience,
All ordinary images.
By chance they emerge in a dream,
Turning out infinite new patterns.

It's all ordinary feelings,
All ordinary words.
By chance they encounter a poet,
Turning out infinite new verses.

Once intoxicated, one learns the strength of wine,
Once smitten, one learns the power of love:
You cannot write my poems
Just as I cannot dream your dreams.

translated by Kai Yu Hsu

OLD DREAM

From the green foliage below the hill
Emerges a corner of flying roof.
It awakens an old dream, and causes
Tears to fall within me.

For it I sing a song of old,
In a tune no one understands,
Ah, I am not really singing,
Only reviewing an old dream.

translated by Kai Yu Hsu

WEN YI-TUO

FORGET HER

Forget her, as a forgotten flower—
    That ray of morning sun on a petal
    That whiff of fragrance from a blossom—
Forget her, as a forgotten flower.

Forget her, as a forgotten flower,
    As a dream in the wind of spring,
    As in a dream, a bell's ring.
Forget her, as a forgotten flower.

Forget her, as a forgotten flower.
    Listen, how sweetly the crickets sing;
    Look, how tall the grass has grown.
Forget her, as a forgotten flower.

Forget her, as a forgotten flower.
    No longer does she remember you.
    Nothing now lingers in her memory.
Forget her, as a forgotten flower.

Forget her, as a forgotten flower.
    Youth, what a charming friend,
    Who makes you old overnight.
Forget her, as a forgotten flower.

Forget her, as a forgotten flower.
    If anyone should ask,
    Tell him she never existed.
Forget her, as a forgotten flower.

Forget her, as a forgotten flower.
    As a dream in the wind of spring,
    As in a dream, a bell's ring.
Forget her, as a forgotten flower.

translated by Kai Yu Hsu

DEAD WATER

Here is a ditch of hopelessly dead water.
No breeze can raise a single ripple on it.
Might as well throw in rusty metal scraps
or even pour leftover food and soup in it.

Perhaps the green on copper will become emeralds.
Perhaps on tin cans peach blossoms will bloom.
Then, let grease weave a layer of silky gauze,
and germs brew patches of colorful spume.

Let the dead water ferment into jade wine
covered with floating pearls of white scum.
Small pearls chuckle and become big pearls,
only to burst as gnats come to steal this rum.

And so this ditch of hopelessly dead water
may still claim a touch of something bright.
And if the frogs cannot bear the silence—
the dead water will croak its song of delight.

Here is a ditch of hopelessly dead water—
a region where beauty can never reside.
Might as well let the devil cultivate it—
and see what sort of world it can provide.

translated by Kai Yu Hsu

I WANTED TO COME HOME

I wanted to come home
While your little fists were like the orchids yet to open;
While your hair still remained soft and silken;
While your eyes shone with that spirited gleam;
I wanted to come home.

I did not come home,
While your footsteps were keeping cadence in the wind;
While your little heart was beating like a fly against the
        windowpane;
While your laughter carried that silver bell's ring,
I did not come home.

I should have come home,

While a spell of blur covered your eyes;
While a gust of chilly wind put out a fading light;
While a cold hand snatched you away like a kite;
    I should have come home.

translated by Kai Yu Hsu

FENG CHIH

SONNET XV

Look at those packhorses, one train after another,
Bringing in loads of goods from afar.
Water could also carry over some dirt and sand
From faraway places with unknown names.

From thousands of miles away the wind would
Sweep over the sighs of a distant country:
We have traveled over numerous rivers and hills,
Staying with them for a moment, but leaving them all the
    time.

We are like birds that soar in the sky,
And control the space any time and all the time,
And yet all the time feel totally dispossessed.

What is this thing called our reality?
Nothing can be brought over from afar, and
Nothing can be taken away from here, either.

translated by Kai Yu Hsu

SONNET XVI

We stand together on top of a towering mountain
Transforming ourselves into the immense sweep of view,
Into the unlimited plain in front of us,
And into the footpaths crisscrossing the plain.

Which road, which river is unconnected, and
Which wind, which cloud is without its response?
The waters and hills we've traversed
Have all been merged in our lives.

Our births, our growth, and our sorrows

Are the lone pine standing on a mountain,
Are the dense fog blanketing a city.
We follow the blowing wind and the flowing water
To become the crisscrossing paths on the plain,
To become the lives of the travelers on the paths.

translated by Kai Yu Hsu

HAN PO CHOPS WOOD

A DIALOGUE BETWEEN A MOTHER AND HER SON

The nineteenth of the first lunar month,
It had been raining several days and nights.
Suddenly it stopped after midnight,
Leaving a waning moon in the sky.

Moonlight filled the whole room
The old woman was startled from her dream,
She woke up her son and said,
"There is a man's shadow outside."

The son said, "So late at night,
How could there be anybody?"
"You young people don't know," said she,
"This is the spirit of Han Po.

"Han Po was a woodcutter.
All day long he chopped wood in the mountain,
He owed his landlord more usurious debt
Than he could expect ever to pay back.

"He chopped wood all his life
So that his landlord might cook and eat;
He chopped wood all his life
So that his landlord could keep warm with a fire.

"But he himself never
Ate or wore enough;
No matter how bad the weather was,
He never ceased chopping for a day.

"As it is now, it was that year,
The rain had lasted several days and nights,
By the nineteenth of the first lunar month,
The rain had turned into heavy snow.

"He was frozen to death
For many days afterwards nobody bothered,
Later even the tatters on his body
Were rotten in the storm.

"But his spirit after death
Still had to continue working;
Since he was stark naked he could
Come out only late at night.

"Every year on the day of his death
There was always moonlight after midnight,
To shine on the deep valleys,
Turning them as bright as day.

"Our spring rain here
Falls one whole month in a stretch;
Only on this special occasion
It would stop for half a night."

She told this story, sending
Chills down others' spines;
Outside, in the moonlight, there
Seemed really to be a man's shadow.

Her son said, "Mother,
Han Po's death was really sad,
But this was a story of the old days,
It is not our present time.

"In the past in our village
Everyone was a Han Po
But now among all of us
There is not a single one like him.

"So many Han Pos in the past
Died in cold and hunger;
And we expressed our sympathy
Only through a half night's moonlight.

"In the moonlight now perhaps
There is still the spirit of Han Po;
But he is coming out not to chop wood
Rather, to avenge his old grievance.

"Tomorrow we'll struggle against the landlords,
He will also clear his account with them;

No longer will he be timid,
He will appear in broad daylight."

translated by Kai Yu Hsu

I SING OF ANSHAN STEEL

I sing of Anshan steel.
Because of many wishes, I sing of Anshan steel.
When the train reaches the riverside, we wish for a bridge;
When the survey team arrives in wild mountains, it seeks
    deeper ore deposits;
For all these wishes, I sing of Anshan steel.

For much happiness, I sing of Anshan steel;
The farmers can have the proper tools they need;
And better looms weave more clothes;
For much happiness, I sing of Anshan steel.

For one famous saying, I sing of Anshan steel.
"What we don't understand we must learn."
The insight of this suggestion is proven here.
For one famous saying, I sing of Anshan steel.

For the many exemplars of man, I sing of Anshan steel.
Man tempers steel, and steel tempers man:
Heroes of a new order emerge without stop.
For the many exemplars of man I sing of Anshan steel.

For the many marvelous sights, I sing of Anshan steel.
Molten iron flows from the furnaces, thick smoke surges
    towards the sky,
All day long ceaselessly, and every night the sky is red.
For the many marvelous sights, I sing of Anshan steel.

For a lasting peace, I sing of Anshan steel.
As the harvest of steel increases, so grows the strength of
    peace.
Let the brave white dove soar ever higher and farther.
For a lasting peace, I sing of Anshan steel.

translated by Kai Yu Hsu

FOR TU FU

You suffered starvation in deserted villages,
Always you saw ahead of you a gutter death,
And yet you were incessantly singing
Of the glorious events that occurred each day.

Soldiers died, lay wounded on battlefields;
Stars fell down the sky,
A thousand horses vanished in scudding clouds,
To all these your life was a sacrifice.

Your poverty still glitters and shines
Like the rags of a deceased saint,
And the least tatter that remains

Is endowed with magic powers.
Their crowns and purples in this light
Are shoddy when compared with yours.

translated by Robert Payne

PIEN CHIH-LIN

A MONK

Striking his bell day after day
A monk remains in his pale-gray deep dream.
The traces and shadows of so many past years
Appear in memory like a patch of incense smoke
That spreads everywhere in the old temple.
The remains of sorrow stay in the censer
Together with the grief of devout men and women.
Boredom meanders perpetually round and round in the sutras.

Sleepy words trickle from his mouth, a man talking in his
    dream,
His head nods along with his knocking of the wooden fish,

Both so empty yet so heavy.
Stroke after stroke, the hills and rivers are lulled to sleep.
The hills and rivers sleep lazily in the afterglow,
As he finishes tolling the funeral bell of another day.

translated by Kai Yu Hsu

THE FIRST LAMP

Birds engulf hard pebbles to grind the grain in their crops.
Beasts fear fire. Men keep fire, and so arises civilization.
Blessed are those who arise at sunrise and sleep at sunset.
Yet I praise the first lamp that opens a new world.

translated by Robert Payne

TO THE YOUNG PIONEERS OF THE NORTHWEST

You have arranged a rendezvous with the rising sun:
Let's meet on the hilltop three miles from here.
A troop of hoes cuts through the lingering night,
Racing to be the first to greet the dawn.

Squeezing fat out of a deserted and barren land,
You demand that the yellow earth produce grains.
With their winter clothes of blackened grass torn open
One thousand mountains all change their color.

You arrange the individual colors and lines of each crop
Into the overall design of the fields.
You observe nature's ways to enrich nature
With the fullest force man can muster.

To let you taste a bit of sweetness in the midst of hardships
The earth yields flavorful grassroots, splendid!
All hands, once so tender, have grown callous,
When they shake hands with a girl, she might scream.

No need to worry that the hoe is too primitive,
Step by step it will open up a tomorrow.
You face the real and the present, and
"Hope" thus acquires many smiling faces.

translated by Kai Yu Hsu

AI CH'ING

SNOW FALLS ON CHINA

Snow falls on the Chinese land;
Cold blockades China. . . .

The wind like an old woman with many grievances
Closely follows behind
And stretches out her claws,
Tugs at clothes.
Her words are as old as the earth,
Complaining, never ceasing.

From the forests
Driving their carts
Come the farmers of China,
Wearing their fur caps—
Where do they want to go?

I tell you, I too
Am a descendant of farmers;
Like you, my face
Is etched with pain,
So deeply do I know
Those months, those years of labor,
Knowing how people live in the plains,
Passing hard days.
No, I am not happier than you.
—Lying in the river of time,
Often the tides of distress
Have entirely overwhelmed me.
In exile and in prison cells
I spent my most precious youth.
My life
Like yours
Is haggard.

Snow falls on the Chinese land;
Cold blockades China. . . .

Along the rivers of a snowy night
A small oil flame drifts slowly
In a ragged boat with a black sail.

Facing the lamp and hanging her head,
Who sits there?

O you
Snot-haired and dirty-faced young woman,
Is this your warm house,
A warm and happy nest and cave,
Burned out by the invader?
On such a night as this
You lost your husband's protection.
In terror of death you were teased
Utterly
By the enemy's bayonets.

Aiee, on so cold a night
Numerous old mothers
Crouch in homes not theirs,
Like strangers
Not knowing
Where tomorrow's wheels will take them.
The roads of China
Are as rugged as theirs.

Snow falls on the Chinese land;
Cold blockades China. . . .

Throughout the snowy pasture in the long night
Are lands bitten by the beacons of war.
Numerous men of tillage
Live in the village of Absolute Despair.
The cattle they fed are robbed,
The fat rice fields plundered.
Over the hungry earth,
Facing the dark sky,
They hold out shivering hands
Asking for succor.

Oh, pain and distress of China,
Endless like the snowy night.

Snow falls on the Chinese land;
Cold blockades China. . . .

O China
On this lampless night,
Can my weak lines
Give you a little warmth?

translated by Robert Payne

TIEN CH'IEN

FREEDOM IS WALKING TOWARD US

A sad
Nation, ah,
We must fight!
Beyond the window, in autumn,
In the field
Of Asia,
Freedom, ah . . .
Is walking toward us
From beyond the blood pools,
From beyond the dead bodies of our brothers—
A wild storm,
A swooping sea swallow.

translated by Kai Yu Hsu

CHILDREN'S FESTIVAL

O my young brothers,
You,
In the morning,
What roads did you come through?

Do you see
The soldiers walking in the streets,
Machine guns
Piled on their shoulders?

Help them,
Bring comfort to them;
They will fight,
They will die,
They will bleed. . . .

O my younger brothers,
Do not fear them;
Forbear,
For a little while.

Stretch hands to them.
Say:
Long live China!

translated by Robert Payne

MAO TSE-TUNG

THE LONG MARCH

None in the Red Army feared the distresses of the Long
   March.
We looked lightly on the ten thousand peaks and ten thousand
   rivers.
The Five Mountains rose and fell like rippling waves,
In the vast darkness we walked through the muddy hills.

Warm were the precipices where Gold Sand River dashed
   into them.
Cold were the iron chains of the Tatu Bridge.
Delighting in the thousand snowy folds of the Ming Moun-
   tains,
The last pass vanquished, the Three Armies smiled.

translated by Robert Payne

THE SNOW

All the scenery in the north
Is enclosed in a thousand li of ice,
And ten thousand li of whirling snow.
Behold both sides of the Great Wall—
There is only a vast confusion left.
On the upper and lower reaches of the Yellow River
You can no longer see the flowing water.
The mountains are dancing silver serpents,
The hills on the plains are shining elephants.
I desire to compare our height with the skies.
In clear weather
The earth is so charming,
Like a red-faced girl clothed in white.
Such is the charm of these rivers and mountains,
Calling innumerable heroes to vie with each other in pursuing
   her.

The emperors Shih Huang and Wu Ti were barely cultured,
The emperors Tai Tsung and Tai Tsu were lacking in feeling,
Genghis Khan knew only how to bend his bow at the eagles.
These all belong to the past—only today are there men of
    feeling!

translated by Robert Payne

SIXTEEN-SYLLABLE STANZA

What hills!
I sped my steed over them without dismounting.
Looking back with a start
I saw them only three feet three from the sky.[1]

translated by Kai Yu Hsu

ON THE LIU-P'AN MOUNTAIN

Light clouds on clear sky,
My eyes follow the southbound swan to the horizon.
He who fails to reach the Great Wall is not a man,
We have, as I count on my fingers, traveled 20,000 li.

The towering peaks on the Liu-p'an,
The banner unfurling in the western wind,
Today the long cord is in hand [2]
When shall I tie up the Yellow Dragon?

During the Long March, September 1935

translated by Kai Yu Hsu

[1] Author's note: A folk song says:
          The K'u-lou Mountain above
          The Pa-pao Mountain below,
          Only three feet three from the sky.
          Man passing over them must duck his head,
          And the horse must shed its saddle.

[2] "Long cord" refers to the petition received by an Emperor of the
Han Dynasty from General Chung Chün for a long cord with which the
general pledged to tie the chieftain of the invading "barbarians."

AFTER SWIMMING ACROSS THE YANGTZE RIVER

Having just drunk the water of Changsha
Now I eat the fish of Wuchang.
Crossing the ten-thousand-li-long Yangtze River
I gaze at the unlimited sky of the southland.
Let the winds and waves batter me,
Still it is better than strolling in a quiet garden,
Now that I have found freedom in space.
Did not Confucius say when on a river:
"Such is that which passes and is gone!"

The sails stir
But the Snake and Tortoise hills remain still.
Here a grand scheme takes shape.
A bridge flying across
Turning into a broad road Heaven's Moat that used to
    separate the north from the south.
Building a stone wall to the west
Will cut off the rain fallen on the Wu Mountain,
To create a towering dam above a mirror-like lake,
The goddess of the Wu Mountain should be unchanged,
But only startled by the changed world.

May 1956

translated by Kai Yu Hsu

KOREA

    Korean literature, like that of Japan, has been deeply
influenced by China. Early poets were not only steeped in
the traditions of Chinese poetry, but even expressed themselves in Chinese. Incantations, prayers, and songs of religious experience were the earliest verse, passed on orally
from generation to generation.

By the thirteenth century, however, poems in the native language had been published in the *Saenaennorae (Poems of the East)*, the title of which designated the contents as being in the mother tongue. The *Saenaennorae* were marked by an increase in personal expression and may be recognized as truly lyrical outpourings of the poets' inner emotions, which was to be true of Korean poetry from that time onward. In contrast to the formalized structure and themes of Japan's *haiku*, poetry in Korea was from the earliest times remarkably unfettered.

However, there were, of course, certain patterns that became favorites. One such early Korean verse form was composed of three stanzas: the first two, with four lines each, developed an idea or set a theme, and a final stanza of two lines commented on or summarized what had been stated. The Western reader is reminded of a similar pattern followed in the octet and sestet of the Petrarchan sonnet.

The long poem with interspersed refrains was called the *changga* and was usually sung to a musical accompaniment. It was a favorite with women and commoners.

The most famous of all Korean poetry forms, however, and one of the most fixed and demanding, is the *sijo*, the first of which is attributed to U T'ak, a poet of the early fourteenth century. It, too, became a favorite of the ordinary people and a vehicle for every mood and emotion.

The anonymous *sijo* poems of the nineteenth century are on the theme of love, which Peter H. Lee says is the subject of most of the poems in this genre.

Korean literature of the modern period shows two overwhelming influences—the Japanese occupation from 1910–1946 and the impact of the West. During the military subjugation of Korea by Japan, repressive governmental measures increased. By 1930 all education was in the Japanese language, and Koreans were forbidden to speak their mother tongue and were forced to take Japanese names. Writing in Korean slackened off but never fully ceased. Poetry especially—always considered the literature closest to the hearts of the people—continued, but it "went underground." The early fervor and spontaneity, however, was replaced by a pervading sadness and pessimism that continues today in a Korea divided against herself.

As in other areas of Asia, Western influence came as the result of early translation (from about 1880) of French, German, English, and American poets. Experimentation in symbolism, free verse, and other forms that preoccupied the

West entered Korean poetry almost a generation later than their initiation in the West.

Han Yong-un (1879–1944) wrote under the pen name Manhae. Peter Lee refers to this Buddhist priest and Korean patriot as "one of the most original Korean poets of this century."

Kim Chŏng-sik (1903–1934), pen name Kim Sowŏl, wrote in the folk-song tradition, as is indicated in the selection "Wild Flowers of the Mountains," and many of his poems have been set to music.

Sim Hun (1904–1937) was a novelist and journalist as well as poet. He seems in "When That Day Comes" to look forward to Korea's liberation from foreign rule. Unfortunately, Sim died nine years short of the accomplishment.

Yu Ch'i-hwan (1908–1967) published his first volume of poems in 1939, although his verse had appeared in literary magazines from 1931. He was a prolific writer of poetry and serious prose. Through years of exile in Manchuria during the Japanese occupation, Yu continued to write and to develop a philosophy of an impersonal universe of which man is an integral part. He was killed in a traffic accident in Pusan early in 1967.

Sŏ Chŏng-ju (1915–　) is presently a professor of poetry at Tongguk University. Earlier he spent a number of years as a wanderer, getting as far north as Manchuria. He is said now to be resigned to the vagaries of life, and this appears to be endorsed in his autobiographical "Self-Portrait."

Yi Sang-hwa (1900–1943) was a member of a group of poets who founded the literary journal *Paekcho* (*White Tide*). Teacher as well as poet, Yi experienced years of wandering in China toward the end of his life. He died in 1943 "under pressure from the Japanese police," according to Peter H. Lee. His conflict with Japanese occupation forces is reflected in his poem "Does Spring Come to Stolen Fields?" Fellow-writers have commemorated him in a monument erected by them in 1948—a unique act in Korean literary life.

Pak Tu-jin (1916–　) is a poet of the nature school. Each of his several volumes of poetry marks a period of experience in his life—from *Hae* (*The Sun*), 1949, reflecting the years immediately following the lifting of the Japanese yoke, to *The Human Jungle,* his most recent volume (1963), reflecting the bitterness of his country's present ironic impasse. "River of Solitude" dwells on the irony of a people liberated from one oppression only to fall prey to another.

Pak Mok-wŏl (1917–　) began appearing in print in the

late 1930's and has continued to publish quietly but continually ever since. His second poetry collection, *The Clear and the Cloudy*, came out in 1964. One of Pak's most famous poems is "The Wayfarer," a long lyrical work which he compares with W. B. Yeats's "Lake Isle of Innisfree." He is at present chairman of the Department of Korean Language and Literature at Hanyang University.

Cho Chi-hun (1920–), with Pak Tu-jin and Pak Mok-wŏl, first published in *The Green Deer Anthology*, to which each poet contributed fifteen poems. "Ancient Temple" appears as a half-humorous memory of his years of meditation and writing in a Buddhist temple in Kangwon Province. He is recognized as being imbued with the Zen spirit. Cho has published four books of poems and several critical works. He is now teaching Korean literature at Korea University.

ANONYMOUS

SIJO POEMS

Alas, they deceived me—
The autumn moon and the spring breeze.
Since they came around in every season
I believed they were sincere and sure.
But they left me graying hair,
And followed the boys and went away.

The incense is burnt out in the censer;
The water clock tells us night is deep.
Where have you been half the night,
In what cheerful company?
You return to sound me on my sorrow,
When the moon climbs up the railing.

I reviewed my heart one day, and
Found a piece of it missing.
I have not fasted nor wept,
But—was it taken off of itself?
Think, love, you produced this sickness;
You can cure me, you alone can.

Mind, let me ask you how it is
You're still so young?

When I am well on in years
You, too, should grow old.
Why, if I followed your lead, Mind,
People would laugh me to scorn.

———————————

They say in this world, we have
Many remedies and brilliant swords.
But no sword to cut off this love,
No remedies that make me forget him.
I'll not forget until I am dead,
Cut off this tie, forever bury him.

translated by Peter H. Lee

MANHAE (HAN YONG-UN)

I DO NOT KNOW

Whose footstep is that paulownia leaf that falls silently in the windless air, drawing a perpendicular?

Whose face is that piece of blue sky peeping through the black clouds, chased by the west wind after a dreary rain?

Whose breath is that unnamable fragrance, born amid the green moss in the flowerless deep forest and trailing over the ancient tower?

Whose song is that winding stream gushing from an unknown source and breaking against the rocks?

Whose poem is that twilight that adorns the falling day, treading over the boundless sea with lotus feet and caressing the vast sky with jade hands?

The ember becomes oil again.

Ah, for whose night does this feeble lantern keep vigil, the unquenchable flame in my heart?

translated by Peter H. Lee

KIM SOWOL (KIM CHONG-SIK)

WILD FLOWERS OF THE MOUNTAINS

AFTER A FOLK SONG

In the mountains are blowing flowers,
There the flowers blow;
Autumn, spring, and summer through,
There the flowers blow.

In the mountains far and near,
In the mountains everywhere,
There the flowers bloom and blow,
So lovely, wild, and fair.

In the mountains are singing birds,
Where the flowers blow;
There they sing the seasons through
Because the flowers blow.

In the mountains are blowing flowers,
And there the flowers wilt;
Autumn, spring, and summer through,
There the flowers wilt.

translated by Lee In-soo

SIM HUN

WHEN THAT DAY COMES

When that day comes
Mt. Samgak will rise and dance,
the waters of Han will rise up.

If that day comes before I perish,
I will soar like a crow at night
and pound the Chongno bell with my head.
The bones of my skull
will scatter, but I shall die in joy.

When that day comes at last
I'll roll and leap and shout on the boulevard

and if joy still stifles within my breast
I'll take a knife

and skin my body and make
a magical drum and march with it
in the vanguard. O procession!
Let me once hear that thundering shout,
my eyes can close then.

translated by Peter H. Lee

YU CH'I-HWAN

FLOWERS

Autumn has come, and from somewhere the children
bring home flower seeds.
They count them over, arrange them
one by one:
balsam, cockscomb, smartweed,
morning glory.
　　After homework,
when they are ready for sleep,
even in bed they talk about seeds:
If only we had a garden to plant them.
Meanwhile, night deepens; and when their mother
covers them up with straw mats,
these poor tired flowers fall asleep, each embracing
a fabulous flower bed.

translated by Peter H. Lee

SO CHONG-JU

SELF-PORTRAIT

Father was a serf, seldom came home at night.
At home my grandmother, old as
The shriveled root of leek,
And a blossoming date tree.
Big with child, mother wanted just one apricot.

I was a mother's son with dirty fingernails
Under a lamp by the mud wall.

With bushy hair and staring eyes
I am said to resemble grandpa on mother's side
Who in 1894 went to sea and never returned.

For twenty-three years the wind has reared two-thirds of me,
And the world has become a more embarrassing place.
Some have read a convict in my eyes,
Others an idiot in my mouth.
Yet I will repent nothing.

At each dawn brightly assailing,
The dews of poetry settled on my brow,
Mixed with drops of blood.
And I have come this far panting
Like a sick dog with his tongue hanging out
In the sun and in the shade.

translated by Peter H. Lee

YI SANG-HWA

DOES SPRING COME TO STOLEN FIELDS?

The land is no longer our own.
Does spring come just the same
to the stolen fields?
On the narrow path between the rice fields
where blue sky and green fields meet and touch,
winds whisper to me, urging me forward.
A lark trills in the clouds
Like a young girl singing behind the hedge.
O ripening barley fields, your long hair
is heavy after the night's rain.
Light-headed, I walk
lightly, shrugging my shoulders, almost
dancing to music the fields are humming—
the field where violets grow, the field
where once I watched a girl planting rice, her hair
blue-black and shining—
    I want
a scythe in my hands, I want
to stamp on the soil, soft as a plump breast,
I want to be working the earth and streaming with sweat.

What am I looking for? Soul,
my blind soul, endlessly darting
like children at play by the river,
answer me: where am I going?
Filled with the odor of grass, compounded
of green laughter and green sorrow,
I walk all day, lamely, as if possessed
by the spring devil:
for these are stolen fields, and our spring is stolen.

translated by Peter H. Lee

PAK TU-JIN

RIVER OF SOLITUDE

In the reflection:
A flowing river of blood.
The night is brilliant fireworks:
Set adrift in solitude.

Endless quid pro quo demanded
Between beast and beast;
Toward tomorrow's
End.

Before a blue-honed knife;
Lie Peace and Liberty
On the chopping block:
Unable to move.

The fire-touched eyes
Of a cat,
The bloody record
Spewed from the throat
Of a crow;
Stand witness of this night
For distant tomorrow.

The wind becomes wine:
The sunlight, tears.
And the elderly Master,
For this world and the next,
Is now silent.

The last bouquet
To decorate both tomb and wedding:
Is already the trampled
Sleet of despair.

How comfortable is this night . . .
So refined is the
Domesticated colonial intellect!

The standard, once unfurled
But now retired:
Cloud and wind rebel above
The field.

At the solitary riverside
Where a dove once called its mate
And fell,

An old blind bronze horse
Neighs tremulously to
The distant dusk.

translated by Marshall Pihl and Paik Syeunggil

PAK MOK-WOL

THE WILD-PEACH BLOSSOM

The hill is
Kugang-san,
A purple stony hill;

One or two
Wild-peach blossoms
Begin to blow,

To the stream,
Jade-clear,
Flowing with melted spring snow,

A deer
Comes down
To wash her feet.

translated by Kim Jong-gil

On a Certain Day

The word 'Poet' is an article
That always comes before my name.
With this worn hat
On my head,
I've wandered through the rainy streets.
This is something too awkward
To be my own perfect cover;
Or too absurd for a shelter
For my little ones,
Who have nobody else to look up at.
Yet, how could a man
Be safe from wet all his life?
To keep my hair dry . . .
That is enough
For grateful tears.

translated by Kim Jong-gil

CHO CHI-HUN

Ancient Temple

Overcome by a stealthy slumber,
A blue boy in the upper seat,

With the wooden fish in his hands,
Closes his eyes and nods.

While Amitabha and Bodhisattva
Smile, smile without words,

Along the western borders,
Under the blinding red sky,
Peonies fall, peonies fall.

translated by Peter H. Lee

POETRY OF JAPAN

As we move from the poetry of China to that of Japan, we acknowledge Japan's indebtedness to Chinese civilization and at the same time take care not to overemphasize it. We look back to Japan's early reverence for Chinese mores and culture, and we cannot deny the tremendous sway the mainland has had over her island neighbor. In fact, the Great Reform instituted by Emperor Tenshi in A.D. 645 formalized and deepened an influence that had begun as much as a century before.

From early in the eighth century, Japanese poets were writing in Chinese. The *Kaifūsō* in 751 brought together a collection of such indigenous poetic expression in the foreign tongue, and Fujiwara no Teika, in his twelfth-century "Guide to the Composition of Poetry," exhorted would-be poets to read and reread the collected works of Po Chü-i and to imitate his style, as well as the style of the early Japanese poets largely based upon Po.

However, we cannot stop at such evidences and conclude that Japanese poetry is little more than imitation of the Chinese. Even without recognition of the native ingenuity of the Japanese people, there are differences in language and in environment that require certain originality in poetic expression in the Japanese language.

Let us consider first the remaining similarities. We have noted the close affinity that Chinese poetry has with music and song. This was true of early Japanese verse and remains true today. One can appreciate the traditional *haiku* only when one hears it chanted against the background of the flute and koto and with the dramatic effects of the wooden clappers.

Japanese poetry has the visual appeal of calligraphic writing, as has the Chinese. It likewise follows the Chinese tradition in often linking poetry and painting. As in China, also, the Japanese poem is controlled by line length rather than by the metrical patterns that govern Western verse. Also, like Chinese poetry, it is closely linked to religious thought. This will be discussed more fully later.

The standard intercultural elements of verse, such as simile, metaphor, and parallelism, are also found in the Japanese product. In general, however, the verbal economy of the favorite brief forms dictates a more frequent use of metaphor than of simile. Metaphors early became fixed as traditional symbols to which the accustomed reader reacts automatically, as, for instance, the cherry blossom, a symbol of spring, representing beauty, with an emphasis on its fragile and ephemeral qualities.

The other element, parallelism, is not always fully drawn; more often it is subtly implied. Such a typical implication is found in the clear, yet undefined, parallel between the individual and surrounding nature in this verse by the thirteenth-century priest Jakuren:

> One cannot ask loneliness
> How or where it starts.
> On the cypress-mountain,
> Autumn evening.

Both the Chinese and the Japanese apparently have an ingrained preference for the brief and often cryptic verse form. In view of the many other influences of Chinese poetry, it would not seem unreasonable to see in the three-line *haiku* some influence of China's loved four-line "stop short." Makoto Ueda, however, in commenting unfavorably on changing the uneven line number of the *haiku* when it is translated into English, notes that the "three-line form . . . embodies a feeling of unbalance and inconclusiveness" that is an essential intention of the Zen-oriented *haiku* poet.

Two essential elements of Chinese poetry that the Japanese cannot share are tone and rhyme. The Japanese language does not have the tone levels that make spoken Chinese almost a continuous song. Although traditional verse is still chanted to musical accompaniment, the deliberate nonaccentuation of Japanese results in a flatness of tone that is almost the antithesis of oral Chinese.

For the Chinese poet, rhyme presents the technical challenge that it does to his English counterpart. However, since most Japanese words end in vowel sounds, rhyme is more usual than unusual and therefore does not offer the poet the challenge that it does in so many other cultures. In lieu of accent and rhyme, the Japanese poet sets a quantitative meter based upon syllable count, thus:

> Na-tsu gu-sa ya
> tsu-wa-mo-no do-mo ga
> yu-me no a-to.

The syllables have been set off by hyphens here in order to indicate clearly that each syllable ends in a vowel. (The vowels, by the way, are pronounced much as they are in Italian: a—ah; u—oo, not yew; e—ā, as in hay; the consonants as in English, except that the "g" is always given the hard sound.)

In connection with the syllable count, it might be noted that the poet often inserts certain words or syllables whose purpose is to assist in the proper recitation of the poem rather than to contribute to meaning. These are used more frequently by the old masters than by the contemporary *haiku* poets. In the poem quoted above, for instance, the *ya* at the end of line one is an exclamation that marks a division in the poem. *Kana* at the end of poems is simply a poetic end-word with no particular meaning, as *selah* is thought to be in early Hebrew poetry.

The poem quoted above was written by *Matsuo Basho* (1644–1694), Japan's most famous poet in the *haiku*, Japan's most famous verse form. Harold G. Henderson translates it as follows:

> Summer grass
> of stalwart warriors' splendid dreams
> the aftermath.

This leads us into a brief discussion of some of Japan's traditional poetic forms and the impact upon them in recent years by Western literature.

The *Manyōshū*[1] (*Collection of 10,000 Leaves*), the oldest anthology of Japanese poetry, compiled in the eighth century, treats a great variety of themes. Many of the poems achieve considerable length, and we do not yet find the emphasis on

---

[1] The line over a vowel indicates a prolongation in pronunciation practically the equivalent of another vowel.

brevity and ellipsis that will be so marked at later periods. Nevertheless, even the longer poems have within them—or, more properly, attached to them—brief verses of summary and comment that are essentially the later popular *tanka*, or *waka*.[1] These *envois* are generally in the five-line arrangement of thirty-one syllables that is distinctive of the *tanka*. Together with the briefer *haiku*, the *tanka* persists as a favorite poetry form, as is attested each year by its use in the Emperor's poetry contests, which thousands of amateur poets enter.

The poetry of the *Manyōshū* used a refined, literary language that kept it the special preserve of court circles. It was not until the introduction of *haikai* in the fifteenth century that the colloquial tongue was used. In the following century *haikai*, meaning "lighthearted" or "free," verse was raised to the level of literature. Previously it had been regarded as largely humorous and unworthy as literature. Attention is given here to this now obsolete medium because it served as a stepping-stone to *haiku*. Matsuo Bashō, who in the seventeenth century developed and perfected the *haiku*, carried over into this even more demanding form the use of the vernacular and the freedom of theme and expression that were the hallmarks of *haikai*. Both innovations helped to make *haiku* the poetry of the masses.

Where the *tanka* expresses an emotion or impression in five lines totaling only thirty-one syllables, the *haiku* cuts the lines to three and the syllables to seventeen. Obviously, such brevity does not permit the full delineation of an idea nor can a seventeen-syllable expression philosophize. This does not mean that *haiku* is slight or elementary. Actually, it probably makes more demands upon the reader than does any other literary medium. The poet records an impression that the reader is expected to carry through into thought or give universal relevance.

In its brevity and in its concern with the fleeting moment, *haiku* is recognized as an aspect of Zen Buddhism. Zen, like Taoism, emphasizes the world in its natural state, with man an integral part of nature. An appreciation of the "suchness" of things comes, not through deep philosophizing or protracted formal study, not through verbal explication, but in immediate perception of the passing moment. Emphasis is on the here and now, which must be lived and appreciated to the full; it represents the totality of life, and yet, even

---

[1] Designations for the same verse form: *tanka* meaning "short poem"; *waka*, "Japanese poem."

as we are aware of it, it is gone into the past and we are already involved in another fleeting event.

Although early in its development Japan had turned toward the continent, especially China, for cultural inspiration and political wisdom, her initial contacts with the West proved so traumatic that for two centuries (1640–1853) her rulers sealed the country off in every respect from the outside world. Japanese life during this long period, then, was free to concentrate on the development of her native cultural attributes, undisturbed by foreign conflicts or influences. It was not until after the island empire was shocked out of her isolationism by the entrance of the American fleet into Uraga Bay in 1853 that Western culture was to have any real impact. From then on, however, the literature and arts of Japan were never again to be as free from external effects as they had been during those two hundred years of national seclusion, a unique phenomenon in the cultural record of world civilizations.

The first collection of English and American poems in Japanese translation was published in 1882. Earlier, however, individual poets had been aware of the developments at work among their fellow-poets in Europe and America. More and more they adapted Keats's sonnet, Whitman's free verse, and all varieties of longer forms to express their modern thoughts and emotions. Donald Keene claims that Western literature first entered China and other areas of Asia by way of these Japanese translations—an interesting reversal of the earlier China-to-Japan migration.

Despite the initial excitement of poetic experimentation in the early years of influence and among the *avant-garde,* one has only to note the scores of poetry magazines today devoted entirely to the traditional *tanka* and *haiku* to realize that the older indigenous expression still holds the hearts of the masses. Nevertheless, once the door has been opened, it can never again be fully closed. Even the *tanka* and *haiku* of the contemporary period show a freedom in topic and outlook that sets them apart from their progenitors.

The poems in the traditional brief forms are given here both in Romaji and in translation. Romaji uses the Roman letters to give a phonetic representation of the calligraphic *kanji* in which the poems would be printed for the Japanese reader. Through the Romaji the Western reader can get some sense of the sound of the original and can note the linear arrangement of syllables: in the *tanka,* five lines of 5, 7, 5, 7, and 7; in *haiku,* three lines of 5, 7, and 5. Although ama-

teurs writing *tanka* and *haiku* in English are inclined to feel
iron-bound by a strict syllable arrangement, we observe that
the mature poet may take liberties, as do Shakespeare and
Milton in their creative use of the iambic pentameter line.
Ryōkan's second line would require a syllable-length pause
after the "m" preceding the two-count "popo," thus providing the required seven syllables. In the second line of the
poem by Ōkuma Kotomichi, the "u" in "yūbe" is indicated
as being of two-syllable duration. It is, of course, often
impossible to render both meaning and exact syllable representation into an English translation that will have appeal
and literary quality. Although Donald Keene usually attempts
to reproduce the appearance of the five-line original, in this
Ōkuma poem he abandons the original form in the interests
of quality translation.

The four *tanka* quoted here have been selected to show the
sort of evolution in tone and subject matter that occurred
within the strictures of the thirty-one conventionally arranged
syllables of the old poetry form.

Ryōkan (1757–1831) represents himself as an itinerant
monk paying homage to the Buddha in orthodox fashion.
However, his offering is not the usual rice or other simple
foods but violets, delicate blossoms of untrammeled and
hidden places, and dandelions, gaudy blooms of the open
field and common life. Mingled in the begging bowl, they
give a sense of past and present merging in Ryōkan's poem.

Ōkuma Kotomichi (1798–1868), in his straightforward,
unsentimental expression of loneliness, offers direct contrast
to *Tachibana Akemi* (1812–1868), in whose writing we find
the acme of blunt description of contemporary work activity,
getting about as far from the ultra-refinement of the early
court *tanka* as it is possible to come.

Kobayashi Issa (1763–1828), much of whose life was impoverished and unhappy, is said to be the best loved of
Japan's poets. He speaks directly to the common people of
everyday life and emotions.

The next selection of *haiku* brings us to the war generation. *Mizuhara Shūōshi* (1892–) sketches a scene reminiscent of his nation's years of peaceful isolation. *Nakamura
Kusatao* (1901–) and *Kāto Shūson* (1905–), on the
other hand, emotionally shatter their verse form even while
remaining formally within it. Somehow the compression of
the *haiku* increases its power to seize the reader with the
traumatic experience.

When we leave the indigenous Japanese verse forms, we

enter into a world that frankly acknowledges the influence
of the West.

Shintaishi, or poetry in the "modern style," dates from
the volume of translations of English and American poets
published in 1882, referred to earlier. Seven years later another such collection appeared. Each included a number of
experimental *shintaishi*. It is interesting to note, however,
that both the translations and the original poems held to
the traditional five- to seven-syllable line, much as Pope
translated Homer's free-flowing unrhymed lines into the
heroic couplets that, in eighteenth-century England, were
considered the only acceptable form.

"A Mouse" by *Yosano Akiko* (1874–1941) is composed in
the Western style, but the poet's empathy with a fellow living
creature of the lowest order is imbued with Zen compassion.
Both Akiko and her husband, Yosano Tekkan, wrote in *shintaishi* and in what they called the "rejuvenated" *tanka*. They
gathered about them a considerable coterie of young poets of
the early twentieth century.

Kitahara Hakushū (1885–1942) was one of the disciples
of the Yosanos. Living for a time in Nagasaki, where Roman
Catholicism had its first and deepest influence, Kitahara in
his earliest work reflects acquaintance with the foreign culture and religious beliefs. "Secret Song of the Heretics" was
published in 1909 in *Jashūmon* (*The Heretical Religion*), as
Christianity was called during the Tokugawa period. Regarded as one of the most versatile of contemporary poets,
Kitahara is noted for his serious verse, as well as for his folk
poems and nursery rhymes which have been set to music as
popular songs. "Secret Song of the Heretics" gives the Western Christian reader the impression of looking into a mirror
and of being startled by a darkly distorted yet recognizable
reflection of a familiar self.

Hagiwara Sakutarō (1886–1942) was a theorist and essayist, as well as a creative poet. Where "Night Train" is thoroughly modern in both content and expression, "Harmful
Animals" pours age-old superstition into the new mold of
shintaishi.

Nakahara Chūya (1907–1937) is given credit by Geoffrey
Bownas for being the first to use true "colloquial style."
Nevertheless, Bownas says, he was little recognized by his
contemporaries. In Nakahara's "Hour of Death" the reader
gets a sense of the despair that permeates the society and
the individual soul bereft of familiar faith.

Nakano Shigeharu (1902–   ) calls upon present-day poets

of Japan to abandon the old symbols and formalities and
sing songs relevant to the twentieth century. His "Song"
might well be regarded as a succinct lecture against the topics
and forms that were set for the traditional *tanka* and *haiku*.
Kitagawa Fuyuhiko (1900–   ) in "Early Spring" has a similar message, but in more personal terms than those of the
Marxist-oriented Nakano. And Kitagawa finds that, despite
the present-day assurance implicit in the humming of steelworks, it is in the ancient promise of the earth that man
still has faith.

Tanikawa Shuntarō (1931–   ), the youngest of the poets
whose works are represented here, is a prolific and multifaceted author. The half-dozen volumes of his work comprise
essays and dramas, as well as poetry ranging from free verse
to romantic chansons and poems in the formal genres of both
Japan and the West. Tanikawa uses the English sonnet here
in an original line arrangement to express an existential sense
of suffering and estrangement.

Takamura Kōtarō (1883–1956) chronologically precedes
several of the aforementioned poets, but his poem "My
Poetry" seems a most fitting conclusion to a collection of
Japanese poetry showing Western influence. This sculptor and
poet, whose life began contemporaneously with the birth of
the *shintaishi* movement, reminds us that no matter how the
Japanese poet may appear to be influenced by poets of the
West, by the nature of his birth and the conditioning of his
culture, he expresses something basically Japanese; "the traffic" of his poetry necessarily moves along a non-Western
path.

TANKA

Hachi no ko ni	In my begging bowl [1]
Sumire tampopo	Violets and dandelions
Kokimazete	Are mixed together:
Sanze no hotoke ni	These will be my offering
Tatematsuriten	To the Buddhas of Three Worlds.

Ryōkan
translated by Donald Keene

[1] Itinerant Buddhist monks go from door to door with bowls, begging
for their single daily meal.

Kurehatsuru It were better not to call
Haru no yūbe no Than to leave me in the loneliness
Sabishiki ni Of the late spring afternoon.
Kaeraba towanu
Hito ya masaramu

> *Ōkuma Kotomichi*
> *translated by Yokuo Uyehara and*
> *Marjorie Sinclair*

Akahada no Stark naked, the men
Danshi mureite Stand together in clusters;
Aragane no Swinging great hammers
Marogari kudaku They smash into fragments
Tsuchi uchifurite The lumps of unwrought metal.

> *Tachibana Akemi*
> *translated by Donald Keene*

Tanoshimi wa It is a pleasure
Kami wo hirogete When, spreading out some paper,
Toru fude no I take brush in hand
Omoi no hoka ni And write far more skillfully
Yoku kakeshi toki Than I could have expected.

> *Tachibana Akemi*
> *translated by Donald Keene*

Tanoshimi wa It is a pleasure
Momohi hineredo When, after a hundred days
Naranu uta no Of twisting my words
Futo omoshiroku Without success, suddenly
Idekinuru toki A poem turns out nicely.

> *Tachibana Akemi*
> *translated by Donald Keene*

Tanoshimi wa It is a pleasure
Sozoro yomiyuku When, in a book which by chance
Kaki no naka ni I am perusing,
Ware to hitoshiki I come on a character
Hito wo mishi toki Who is exactly like me.

> *Tachibana Akemi*
> *translated by Donald Keene*

Tanoshimi wa
Yo ni tokigataku
Suru kaki no
Kokoro wo hitori
Satorieshi toki

It is a pleasure
When, without receiving help,
I can understand
The meaning of a volume
Reputed most difficult.

Tachibana Akemi
translated by Donald Keene

HAIKU

Asagao no
hana de fuitaru
iori kana

A morning-glory vine,
all blossoming, has thatched
this hut of mine.

Kobayashi Issa
translated by Harold G. Henderson

Utsukushi ya
shōji no ana no
ama-no-gawa

A lovely thing to see:
through the paper window's hole
the Galaxy.

Kobayashi Issa
translated by Harold G. Henderson

Toshikasa wo
urayamaretaru
samusa kana

Now that I'm old
I am envied by people—
Oh, but it's cold!

Kobayashi Issa
translated by Harold G. Henderson

Isu yosete
Kiku no kaori ni
Mono wo kaku

Drawing up a chair
In the scent of chrysanthemums
I write my verses.

Mizuhara Shūōshi
translated by Donald Keene

Guntai no
Chikazuku oto ya
Shūfūri

The tramping sound
Of troops approaching
In the autumn wind.

Nakamura Kusatao
translated by Donald Keene

In the middle of the night there was a heavy air raid. Carrying my sick brother on my back I wandered in the flames with my wife in search of our children.

Hi no oku ni	In the depths of the flames
Botan kuzururu	I saw how a peony
Sama wo mitsu	Crumbles to pieces.

Kogarashi ya	Cold winter storm—
Shōdo no kinko	A safe-door in a burnt-out site
Fukinarasu	Creaking in the wind.

Fuyu kamome	The winter sea gulls—
Sei no ie nashi	In life without a house,
Shi no haka nashi	In death without a grave.

Katō Shūson
translated by Donald Keene

YOSANO AKIKO

A Mouse

In my attic dwells a mouse.
The creaking noise he makes
Reminds me of a sculptor who carves
An image all night long.

Again when he dances with his wife,
He whirls like a race horse, round.
Though the attic dirt and dust flutter down
On this paper as I write,
How would he know?
But I stop to think:
    I am living with mice.
    Let them have good food
    And a warm nest.
    Let them drill a hole in the ceiling and,
    From time to time, peep down on me.

translated by Shio Sakanishi

KITAHARA HAKUSHŪ

Secret Song of the Heretics [1]

I believe in the heretical teachings of a degenerate age, the
    witchcraft of the Christian God,
The captains of the black ships, the marvelous land of the
    Red Hairs,
The scarlet glass, the sharp-scented carnation,
The calico, arrack, and *vinho tinto* of the Southern Barbarians;

The blue-eyed Dominicans chanting the liturgy who tell me
    even in dreams
Of the God of the forbidden faith, or of the bloodstained
    Cross,
The cunning device that makes a mustard seed big as an
    apple,
The strange collapsible spyglass that looks even at Paradise.

They build their houses of stone, the white blood of marble
Overflows in crystal bowls; when night falls, they say, it
    bursts into flame.
That beautiful electrical dream is mixed with the incense of
    velvet
Reflecting the bird and beasts of the world of the moon.

I have heard their cosmetics are squeezed from the flowers of
    poisonous plants,
And the images of Mary are painted with oil from rotted
    stones;
The blue letters ranged sideways in Latin or Portuguese
Are filled with a beautiful sad music of heaven.

Oh, vouchsafe unto us, sainted padres of delusion,
Though our hundred years be shortened to an instant, though
    we die on the bloody cross,
It will not matter; we beg for the Secret, that strange dream
    of crimson:
Jesus, we pray this day, bodies and souls caught in the in-
    cense of longing.

                      translated by Donald Keene

[1] This poem is filled with curious old words dating back to the late
sixteenth century, when Portuguese and Spanish priests propagated
Christianity in Japan. The references in stanza two to the micro-
scope and telescope are, of course, anachronistic. The magic lantern of stanza three is puzzling, as is the "white blood of marble":
it seems likely that the poet was more interested in the exotic sound
of the words than the meaning.

HAGIWARA SAKUTARŌ

NIGHT TRAIN

The pale light of daybreak—
The fingerprints are cold on the glass door,
And the barely whitening edges of the mountains
Are still as quicksilver.
As yet the passengers do not awaken;
Only the electric light pants wearily.
The sickeningly sweet odor of varnish,
Even the indistinct smoke of my cigar,
Strikes my throat harshly on the night train.
How much worse it must be for her, another man's wife.
Haven't we passed Yamashina yet?
She opens the valve of her air pillow
And watches as it gradually deflates.
Suddenly in sadness we draw to one another.
When I look out of the train window, now close to dawn,
In a mountain village at an unknown place
Whitely the columbines are blooming.

translated by Donald Keene

HARMFUL ANIMALS

Particularly
When something like a dog is barking
When something like a goose is born a freak
When something like a fox is luminous
When something like a tortoise crystallizes
When something like a wolf slides by
All these things are harmful to the health of man.

translated by Donald Keene

THE NEW ROAD OF KOIDE

The road that has newly been opened here
Goes, I suppose, straight to the city.
I stand at a crossway of the new road,

Uncertain of the lonely horizon.
Dark, melancholy day.
The sun is low over the roofs of the row of houses.
The unfelled trees in the woods stand sparsely.
How, how, to restore myself to what I was?
On this road I rebel against and will not travel,
The new trees have all been felled.

translated by Donald Keene

NAKAHARA CHŪYA

THE HOUR OF DEATH

The autumn sky is a dull color
A light in the eyes of a black horse
The water dries up, the lily falls
The heart is hollow.

Without gods, without help
Close to the window a woman has died.
      The white sky was sightless
      The white wind was cold.

When she washed her hair by the window
Her arm was stemlike and soft
      The morning sun trickled down
      The sound of the water dripped.

In the streets there was noise:
The voices of children tangling.
But, tell me, what will happen to this soul?
Will it thin to nothingness?

translated by Donald Keene

NAKANO SHIGEHARU

SONG

Don't sing
Don't sing of scarlet blossoms or the wings of dragonflies
Don't sing of murmuring breezes or the scent of a woman's
   hair.

All of the weak, delicate things
All the false, lying things
All the languid things, omit.
Reject every elegance
And sing what is wholly true,
Filling the stomach,
Flooding the breast at the moment of desperation,
Songs which rebound when beaten
Songs which scoop up courage from the pit of shame.
These songs
Sing in a powerful rhythm with swelling throats!
These songs
Hammer into the hearts of all who pass you by!

translated by Donald Keene

KITAGAWA FUYUHIKO

EARLY SPRING

Midnight
A rain mixed with snow fell,
It trickled desolately on the bamboo thicket.
The dream dealt with another's heart.
When I awoke
The pillow was cold with tears.
—What has happened to my heart?
The sun shines in mildly from tall windows,
A humming rises from the steelworks.
I got out of bed
And poked with a stick the muck in the ditch;
The turbid water slowly began to move.
A little lizard had yielded himself to the current.
In the fields
I push open black earth.
The wheat sprouts greenly grow.
—You can trust the earth.

translated by Donald Keene

TANIKAWA SHUNTARŌ

SONNET

When I sing a song
The world is hurt inside the song.
I try to make the world sing,
But the world is silent.

My words
Are always poor, strayed children.
Like dragonflies, they sit on the objects
And tremble within many a silence.

Though they try to escape into the objects
My words
Are incapable of loving the world.

They, cursing me,
Are snatched away by the starry sky, and die.
—I put their bodies on sale.

translated by Makoto Ueda

SONNET

When I watch the blue of the sky
I feel as if I had a place to return to.
Yet the brightness which has come through the clouds
No longer goes back to the sky.

The luxurious sun endlessly wastes.
Even after nightfall we are busy picking up.
As all men are meanly born
They never enjoy abundant rest as trees do.

The windows cut off all that brims over.
I want no room smaller than the universe.
So I grow unfriendly with other men.

To be is to hurt space and time.
And the pain rather tortures me.
My health will return when I am gone.

translated by Makoto Ueda

TAKAMURA KŌTARŌ

MY POETRY

My poetry is not part of western poetry;
The two touch, circumference against circumference,
But never quite coincide . . .
I have a passion for the world of western poetry,
But I do not deny that my poetry is formed differently.
The air of Athens and the subterranean fountain of
  Christianity
Have fostered the pattern of thought and diction of western
  poetry;
It strikes through to my heart with its infinite beauty and
  strength—
But its physiology, of wheatmeal and cheese and *entrecôtes,*
Runs counter to the necessities of my language.
My poetry derives from my bowels—
Born at the farthest limits of the far east,
Bred on rice and malt and soya beans and the flesh of fish,
My soul—though permeated by the lingering fragrance of
  Gandhara [1]
And later enlightened by the "Yellow Earth" civilization [2] of a
  vast continent
And immersed in the murmuring stream of the Japanese
  classics—
Now marvels excitedly at the power of the split atom . . .
My poetry is no other than what I am,
And what I am is no other than a sculptor of the far east.
For me the universe is the prototype of composition,
And poetry is the composed counter-points.
Western poetry is my dear neighbor,
But the traffic of my poetry moves on a different path . . .

translated by Ninomiya Takamichi and D. J. Enright

[1] Ancient Gandhara in northwest India, with its Greco-Buddhist art.
[2] Northern Chinese civilization of the Han Dynasty.

DRAMA

As poetry had similar origins and purposes in all early cultures, whether East or West, so, too, did drama. Even from this remote distance (from the "peanut gallery" of the theater of time, we might say) we can almost see the way in which drama evolved from oral literary traditions. The intoner of cabalistic chants, imbued with mystic fervor, bows and beckons to his gods. The enthusiastic reciter of a people's great epics begins to mimic the valorous deeds he recounts. The bard, singing his sad songs of death, adds action to his laments. So simply and naturally did dramatic action grow out of orally transmitted literature.

Frequently made is the facile generalization that drama is a "universal language." Presumably this is because we have here an art form that depends as much upon the physical acting out of plot and character as verbal explication, and we are inclined to believe that what we *see* can be understood and believed. The premise may be true, but the argument does not necessarily follow.

From the time two thousand years ago when Aristotle in his *De Poetica* defined drama and dramatic poetry as imitative of human nature and human action, Western audiences have measured dramatic writings and performances by the degree to which they satisfactorily meet this requirement. We seek in tragedy the *katharsis*—the often violent cleansing of the emotions—that Aristotle enunciated as a supreme test of the tragic in drama. Obviously, if we are to be *purged* of our own pent-up emotions (not simply offered *escape* from them), we must identify ourselves sufficiently with the characters to feel pity for them and to feel fear for ourselves. "There, but for the grace of God, go I."

133

Even in our highly ornate opera, with its weight of artificially imposed music and its emphasis on an exaggerated showmanship, we expect human authenticity to be sufficient for us to become emotionally involved. Indeed, the musical score effectively emphasizes the tragic involvement of the characters. While the libretto would ask us to believe that Tristan and Isolde are bewitched by a magic love potion, Wagner's orchestration leaves no doubt that two human beings are enmeshed in a fateful and doomed passion that had its origins in the lovers' hearts and not in a shared cup.

Aristotle placed greatest value on human action and human character when he listed the several components of drama in their order of importance: plot (or action), character, thought, diction (the manner in which the characters express, not *their thoughts,* but the *dramatist's basic thought* or thesis), melody (music and dance), and spectacle (or the physical setting and accoutrements). As has been said, even in opera, which is the closest Western approximation to the dramatic productions of Asia, the Occidental has a propensity to find the essential human element in the spectacle, the melody, or the dramatist's thesis.

Apparently Asian audiences have remained closer to the ancient origins of drama than have those of the West, for as we view a dramatic performance of almost any area of the non-Western world, we find Aristotle's "pleasurable accessories"—melody and spectacle—moving up to first importance. Essentially, the traditional drama of Asia is *dance* drama. There is little concern for realism either in mode of presentation or in literary development of character and plot. Whether we attend a "monkey dance" in the natural "theater-in-the-round" formed by a forest glade in Bali or a production in Tokyo's Kabukiza, one of the largest and most modern theaters in the world, we enter a world of the theater that is sharply divorced from reality. Each subordinates literary composition to physical production.

In the traditional theater of Asia, then, we conclude that Aristotle's elements of drama are arranged in the following order of importance: melody, spectacle, thought, diction, character, plot. Elsewhere I have discussed this thesis fully;[1] here, only a brief substantiation will be given.

Since most of the traditional themes of Asia have their roots in religious or didactic works (the *Ramayana,* the

[1] "Asian Drama via Aristotle," *The Western Humanities Review,* Vol. XXI, No. 1, Winter 1967.

source for the Balinese monkey dance; loyalty and patriotism, themes for the most famous of the *Kabuki* plays), *thought* is high in the order of importance. Also, since the customary accompanying recitation or dialogue is expressed in verse, diction (or the mode of expression) is of concern. Characters and plots are already so well known to audiences that we might say the playwright need do little more than retell his stories to satisfy the theater-goer. He need not waste his inventive genius on devising new characters in new situations.

Above all, as we enter a theater of India, Japan, or China, we must be prepared to step out of the world of reality and not look for its re-creation on the stage. Our purpose in entering is to escape our customary human entanglements and not to exchange them for a too-realistic representation of the troubles of other persons of our own ilk.

What we have had to say here is, of course, chiefly applicable to Asian drama before the impact of Western influences. How does it apply to the present-day theater? Perhaps the most concrete way in which to tackle this question is to discuss representative modern dramas of India, Japan, and China against the background of their national traditions.

The Drama of India

Aristotle, the first great dramatic critic in the Western world, considered drama almost exclusively from the point of view of literature. For that reason he puts "melody" and "spectacle" last in his list of the essential elements of drama. He almost entirely loses sight of the representational elements in drama. To be sure, he rates "action" as the playwright's primary concern. However, his discussion makes clear that the action is more psychological or mental than it is physical. It is the sort of action that can be handled as well by the novelist as by the dramatist. Following Aristotle to the fullest extent of his argument, we come to such "plays" as T. S. Eliot's *Cocktail Party,* in which the theater audience merely listens to a dialogue that is carried on almost without physical movement.

Such a nonrepresentational play could not be found within the Indian tradition, unless it were an all-out aping of a modern Western convention. Throughout its long theatrical history India has always conceived of drama in its all-inclusive and multifaceted aspects. The great critical guide to Sanskrit dramaturgy deals as much with specifics of music, dance, acting, stage setting, and mechanics as it does with the literary product. The *Natyasastra* (roughly dated between 200 B.C. and A.D. 200), attributed to Bharata Muni, was addressed to the actor and the stage director, as well as to the dramatist, because their skills were considered to be equally important. Detailed instructions are given in all areas, from philosophy and aesthetics to problems of production. Indian drama is a whole made up of these indivisible parts.

Whereas Aristotle propounded the philosophy of *katharsis,*

136

Bharata Muni set down almost its exact opposite as the goal of the Indian dramatist. According to the theory of *rasa,* the dramatist seeks not to achieve a violent purgation of the emotion, but, rather, to develop a gentle, impersonal sentiment that will pervade his entire work so that his audience will leave the theater with spirits exalted and purified. All components of the drama—from the language of expression to the elements of production—should contribute to its *rasa.*

Rabindranath Tagore (1861–1941), who so profoundly influenced the various art forms of India during the late nineteenth and early twentieth centuries, epitomized the teachings of Bharata Muni concerning the role of drama and of the dramatist. Tagore deliberately turned his back on the heavily Westernized theater of his day and returned to early traditions.

In the original Bengali, *Bisarjan (Sacrifice)* is in blank verse. Many of the longer speeches, especially those by the priest Raghupati, were delivered in a declamatory style. Although this is not as obvious in *Bisarjan* as in such dance dramas as *Chitrangada,* music and dance often inject unrealistic elements.

Tagore wrote his plays, composed music and song for them, choreographed those that included dance, defined production details, and often directed them and acted in them. At the age of twenty-two, in the first production of his *Bisarjan,* Tagore acted the part of Kali's aged priest, Raghupati, in what was to prove to be one of his most successful roles. Tagore was, in effect, Bharata Muni's later-day ideal. The contemporary critic Balwant Gargi, in his *Theatre in India,* asserts that Tagore's plays "must be judged in terms of production and not only by their written texts."

So, as we read *Sacrifice* we should attempt to hear the cadence of blank verse (imagine a Shakespeare play), visualize the color and pageantry of the temple scenes, and accept the deliberately unrealistic declamatory speeches of the priest at the same time as we recognize the modernity of its theme—revolt against the old gods.

Among the scores of modern dramatists who have written plays in the fifteen major languages, and locally in some five hundred dialects, Rabindranath Tagore remains preeminent, despite the tendency of young contemporary playwrights to rebel against him. As he was versatile in his life in general, so was he versatile in his dramatic expression. His writing in the dramatic form extends from his earliest verse plays in the 1880's, through serious plays and light comedies on social issues, to the colorful and imaginative dance dramas of his later years.

If one Indian playwright is to be represented in a selection from Asian drama of the last two hundred years, this one should be Tagore. The chief difficulty is in deciding which of his treasury of dramatic expression is to be taken. *Sacrifice* was selected because it deals with contemporary India's attitudes toward her ancient religious beliefs. In this drama, centered in the temple of Kali, the goddess of destruction, Tagore presents a powerful denunciation of all religious superstition and bigotry, especially Kali's representation of blind forces of destruction. In the radical religious thought of *Sacrifice* we find Tagore—as in so many other respects—well in advance of the thinking of the time (1903).

RABINDRANATH TAGORE

SACRIFICE

Characters

> GUNAVATI, *the Queen*
> RAGHUPATI, *a priest*
> GOVINDA, *the King*
> JAISING, *the servant of the temple*
> APARNA, *a beggar girl*
> NAKSHATRA, *the prince; Govinda's brother*
> NAYAN RAI, *general of the army*
> CHANDPAL, *second in command of the army*
> DRUVA, *a boy*

Scene: *A temple in Tippera*

(*Enters* GUNAVATI, *the Queen.*)

GUNAVATI. Have I offended thee, dread Mother? [1] Thou grantest children to the beggar woman, who sells them to live, and to the adulteress, who kills them to save herself from infamy, and here am I, the Queen, with all the world lying at my feet, hankering in vain for the baby-touch at my bosom, to feel the stir of a dearer life within my life.

[1] Kali, the "Earth Mother," goddess of both production and destruction, who demands sacrificial (at one time, human) killings. The Kalighat Temple in Calcutta, which enshrines Kali, is one of the most ancient and most famous in India. Even today, often women seeking fertility pray and make sacrifice at Kali's temple.

What sin have I committed, Mother, to merit this,—to be banished from the mothers' heaven?

(*Enters* RAGHUPATI, *the priest.*)

O Master, have I ever been remiss in my worship? And my husband, is he not godlike in his purity? Then why has the Goddess who weaves the web of this world-illusion assigned my place in the barren waste of childlessness?

RAGHUPATI. Our Mother is all caprice, she knows no law, our sorrows and joys are mere freaks of her mind. Have patience, daughter, to-day we shall offer special sacrifice in your name to please her.

GUNAVATI. Accept my grateful obeisance, father. My offerings are already on their way to the temple,—the red bunches of hibiscus and beasts of sacrifice.

(*They go out. Enter* GOVINDA, *the King;* JAISING, *the servant of the temple; and* APARNA, *the beggar girl.*)

JAISING. What is your wish, Sire?

GOVINDA. Is it true that this poor girl's pet goat has been brought by force to the temple to be killed? Will Mother accept such a gift with grace?

JAISING. King, how are we to know from whence the servants collect our daily offerings of worship? But, my child, why is this weeping? Is it worthy of you to shed tears for that which Mother herself has taken?

APARNA. Mother! I am his mother. If I return late to my hut, he refuses his grass, and bleats, with his eyes on the road. I take him up in my arms when I come, and share my food with him. He knows no other mother but me.

JAISING. Sire, could I make the goat live again, by giving up a portion of my life, gladly would I do it. But how can I restore that which Mother herself has taken?

APARNA. Mother has taken? It is a lie. Not mother, but demon.

JAISING. Oh, the blasphemy!

APARNA. Mother, art thou there to rob a poor girl of her love? Then where is the throne before which to condemn thee? Tell me, King.

GOVINDA. I am silent, my child. I have no answer.

APARNA. This blood-streak running down the steps, is it his? Oh, my darling, when you trembled and cried for dear life, why did your call not reach my heart through the whole deaf world?

JAISING (*to the image*). I have served thee from my infancy, Mother Kali, yet I understand thee not. Does pity only belong to weak mortals, and not to gods? Come with me, my child, let me do for you what I can. Help must come from man when it is denied from gods.

(JAISING *and* APARNA *go out. Enter* RAGHUPATI; NAK-
SHATRA, *who is the King's brother; and the courtiers.*)

ALL. Victory be to the King!

GOVINDA. Know you all, that I forbid shedding of blood in the temple from to-day for ever.

MINISTER. You forbid sacrifice to the Goddess?

GENERAL NAYAN RAI. Forbid sacrifice?

NAKSHATRA. How terrible! Forbid sacrifice?

RAGHUPATI. Is it a dream?

GOVINDA. No dream, father. It is awakening. Mother came to me, in a girl's disguise, and told me that blood she cannot suffer.

RAGHUPATI. She has been drinking blood for ages.[1] Whence comes this loathing all of a sudden?

GOVINDA. No, she never drank blood, she kept her face averted.

RAGHUPATI. I warn you, think and consider. You have no power to alter laws laid down in scriptures.

GOVINDA. God's words are above all laws.

RAGHUPATI. Do not add pride to your folly. Do you have the effrontery to say that *you* alone have heard God's words, and not I?

NAKSHATRA. It is strange that the King should have heard from gods and not the priest.

GOVINDA. God's words are ever ringing in the world, and he who is willfully deaf cannot hear them.

RAGHUPATI. Atheist! Apostate!

GOVINDA. Father, go to your morning service, and declare to all worshipers that from hence they will be punished with banishment who shed creatures' blood in their worship of the Mother of all creatures.

RAGHUPATI. Is this your last word?

GOVINDA. Yes.

RAGHUPATI. Then curse upon you! Do you, in your enor-mous pride, imagine that the Goddess, dwelling in your land, is your subject? Do you presume to bind her with your laws and rob her of her dues? You shall never do it. I declare it,— I who am her servant. (*Goes.*)

NAYAN RAI. Pardon me, Sire, but have you the right?

---

[1] According to early legend, Kali killed the demon Raktavira. If his blood were spilled, every drop would produce another demon like him. To prevent this, Kali drank the blood. From then on she demanded fresh slaughter for her blood lust.

MINISTER. King, is it too late to revoke your order?

GOVINDA. We dare not delay to uproot sin from our realm.

MINISTER. Sin can never have such a long lease of life. Could they be sinful,—the rites that have grown old at the feet of the Goddess?

(*The King is silent.*)

NAKSHATRA. Indeed they could not be.

MINISTER. Our ancestors have performed these rites with reverence; can you have the heart to insult them?

(*The King remains silent.*)

NAYAN RAI. That which has the sanction of ages, have you the right to remove it?

GOVINDA. No more doubts and disputes. Go and spread my order in all my lands.

MINISTER. But, Sire, the Queen has offered her sacrifice for this morning's worship; it is come near the temple gate.

GOVINDA. Send it back. (*He goes.*)

MINISTER. What is this?

NAKSHATRA. Are we, then, to come down to the level of Buddhists, and treat animals as if they have their right to live? Preposterous!

(*They all go out. Enters* RAGHUPATI,—JAISING *following him with a jar of water to wash his feet.*)

JAISING. Father.

RAGHUPATI. Go!

JAISING. Here is some water.

RAGHUPATI. No need of it!

JAISING. Your clothes.

RAGHUPATI. Take them away!

JAISING. Have I done anything to offend you?

RAGHUPATI. Leave me alone. The shadows of evil have thickened. The King's throne is raising its insolent head above the temple altar. Ye gods of these degenerate days, are ye ready to obey the King's laws with bowed heads, fawning upon him like his courtiers? Have only men and demons combined to usurp gods' dominions in this world, and is Heaven powerless to defend its honour? But there remain the Brahmins,[1] though the gods be absent; and the King's throne will supply fuel to the sacrificial fire of their anger. My child, my mind is distracted.

JAISING. Whatever has happened, father?

---

[1] The Brahmins, the first of the four major castes, were the religious teachers and custodians of sacred scriptures. Traditionally they upheld the old forms of religious observance.

RAGHUPATI. I cannot find words to say. Ask the Mother Goddess who has been defied.

JAISING. Defied? By whom?

RAGHUPATI. By King Govinda.

JAISING. King Govinda defied Mother Kali?

RAGHUPATI. Defied you and me, all scriptures, all countries, all time, defied Mahākāli,[1] the Goddess of the endless stream of time,—sitting upon that puny little throne of his.

JAISING. King Govinda?

RAGHUPATI. Yes, yes, your King Govinda, the darling of your heart. Ungrateful! I have given all my love to bring you up, and yet King Govinda is dearer to you than I am.

JAISING. The child raises its arms to the full moon, sitting upon his father's lap. You are my father, and my full moon is King Govinda. Then is it true, what I hear from people, that our King forbids all sacrifice in the temple? But in this we cannot obey him.

RAGHUPATI. Banishment is for him who does not obey.

JAISING. It is no calamity to be banished from a land where Mother's worship remains incomplete. No, so long as I live, the service of the temple shall be fully performed.

(*They go out. Enter* GUNAVATI *and her attendant.*)

GUNAVATI. What is it you say? The Queen's sacrifice turned away from the temple gate? Is there a man in this land who carries more than one head on his shoulders, that he could dare think of it? Who is that doomed creature?

ATTENDANT. I am afraid to name him.

GUNAVATI. Afraid to name him, when I ask you? Whom do you fear more than me?

ATTENDANT. Pardon me.

GUNAVATI. Only last evening Court minstrels came to sing my praise, Brahmins blessed me, the servants silently took their orders from my mouth. What can have happened in the meantime that things have become completely upset,—the Goddess refused her worship, and the Queen her authority? Was Tripura a dreamland? Give my salutation to the priest, and ask him to come.

(ATTENDANT *goes out. Enter* GOVINDA.)

GUNAVATI. Have you heard, King? My offerings have been sent back from Mother's temple.

GOVINDA. I know it.

GUNAVATI. You know it, and yet bear the insult?

---

[1] Mahākāli, known popularly as Parvati, was the wife of Shiva, the god of destruction. Their son was Karttikeya, the warrior god.

GOVINDA. I beg to ask your pardon for the culprit.

GUNAVATI. I know, King, your heart is merciful, but this is no mercy. It is feebleness. If your kindness hampers you, leave the punishment in my hand. Only, tell me, who is he?

GOVINDA. It is I, my Queen. My crime was in nothing else but having given you pain.

GUNAVATI. I do not understand you.

GOVINDA. From to-day shedding of blood in gods' temples is forbidden in my land.

GUNAVATI. Who forbids it?

GOVINDA. Mother herself.

GUNAVATI. Who heard it?

GOVINDA. I.

GUNAVATI. You! That makes me laugh. The Queen of all the world comes to the gate of Tripura's King with her petition.

GOVINDA. Not with her petition, but with her sorrow.

GUNAVATI. Your dominion is outside the temple limit. Do not send your commands there, where they are impertinent.

GOVINDA. The command is not mine, it is Mother's.

GUNAVATI. If you have no doubt in your decision, do not cross my faith. Let me perform my worship according to my light.

GOVINDA. I promised my Goddess to prevent sacrifice of life in her temple, and I must carry it out.

GUNAVATI. I also promised my Goddess the blood of three hundred kids and one hundred buffalo, and I will carry it out. You may leave me now.

GOVINDA. As you wish. (*He goes out.*)

(*Enters* RAGHUPATI.)

GUNAVATI. My offerings have been turned back from the temple, father.

RAGHUPATI. The worship offered by the most ragged of all beggars is not less precious than yours, Queen. But the misfortune is that Mother has been deprived. The misfortune is that the King's pride is growing into a bloated monster, obstructing divine grace, fixing its angry red eyes upon all worshipers.

GUNAVATI. What will come of all this, father?

RAGHUPATI. That is only known to her, who fashions this world with her dreams. But this is certain, that the throne which casts its shadow upon Mother's shrine will burst like a bubble, vanishing in the void.

GUNAVATI. Have mercy and save us, father.

RAGHUPATI. Ha, ha! I am to save you,—you, the consort

of a King who boasts of his kingdom in the earth and in heaven as well, before whom the gods and the Brahmins must—Oh, shame! Oh, the evil age, when the Brahmin's futile curse recoils upon himself, to sting him into madness.

(*About to tear his sacrificial thread.*) [1]

GUNAVATI (*preventing him*). Have mercy upon me.

RAGHUPATI. Then give back to Brahmins what are theirs by right.

GUNAVATI. Yes, I will. Go, master, to your worship and nothing will hinder you.

RAGHUPATI. Indeed your favour overwhelms me. At the merest glance of your eyes gods are saved from ignominy and the Brahmin is restored to his sacred offices. Thrive and grow fat and sleek till the dire day of judgment comes. (*Goes out.*)

(*Re-enters* KING GOVINDA.)

GOVINDA. My Queen, the shadow of your angry brows hides all light from my heart.

GUNAVATI. Go! Do not bring a curse upon this house.

GOVINDA. Woman's smile removes all curse from the house, her love is God's grace.

GUNAVATI. Go, and never show your face to me again.

GOVINDA. I shall come back, my Queen, when you remember me.

GUNAVATI (*clinging to the King's feet*). Pardon me, King. Have you become so hard that you forget to respect woman's pride? Do you not know, beloved, that thwarted love takes the disguise of anger?

GOVINDA. I would die, if I lost my trust in you. I know, my love, that clouds are for moments only, and the sun is for all days.

GUNAVATI. Yes, the clouds will pass by, God's thunder will return to his armoury, and the sun of all days will shine upon the traditions of all time. Yes, my King, order it so, that Brahmins be restored to their rights, the Goddess to her offerings, and the King's authority to its earthly limits.

GOVINDA. It is not the Brahmin's right to violate the eternal good. The creature's blood is not the offering for gods. And it is within the rights of the King and the peasant alike to maintain truth and righteousness.

GUNAVATI. I prostrate myself on the ground before you; I beg at your feet. The custom that comes through all ages

---

[1] At puberty the Brahmin boy is invested with the sacred or sacrificial thread, his mark of caste distinction, which he is to wear at all times.

is not the King's own. Like heaven's air, it belongs to all men. Yet your Queen begs it of you, with clasped hands, in the name of your people. Can you still remain silent, proud man, refusing entreaties of love in favour of duty which is doubtful? Then go, go, go from me.

(*They go. Enter* RAGHUPATI, JAISING, *and* NAYAN RAI.)

RAGHUPATI. General, your devotion to Mother is well known.

NAYAN RAI. It runs through generations of my ancestors.

RAGHUPATI. Let this sacred love give you indomitable courage. Let it make your sword-blade mighty as God's thunder, and win its place above all powers and positions of this world.

NAYAN RAI. The Brahmin's blessings will never be in vain.

RAGHUPATI. Then I bid you collect your soldiers and strike Mother's enemy down to the dust.

NAYAN RAI. Tell me, father, who is the enemy?

RAGHUPATI. Govinda.

NAYAN RAI. Our King?

RAGHUPATI. Yes, attack him with all your force.

NAYAN RAI. It is evil advice. Father, is this to try me?

RAGHUPATI. Yes, it is to try you, to know for certain whose servant you are. Give up all hesitation. Know that the Goddess calls, and all earthly bonds must be severed.

NAYAN RAI. I have no hesitation in my mind. I stand firm in my post, where my Goddess has placed me.

RAGHUPATI. You are brave.

NAYAN RAI. Am I the basest of Mother's servants, that the order should come for me to turn traitor? She herself stands upon the faith of man's heart. Can she ask me to break it? Then to-day comes to dust the King, and to-morrow the Goddess herself.

JAISING. Noble words!

RAGHUPATI. The King, who has turned traitor to Mother, has lost all claims to your allegiance.

NAYAN RAI. Drive me not, father, into a wilderness of debates. I know only one path,—the straight path of faith and truth. This stupid servant of Mother shall never swerve from that highway of honour. (*Goes out.*)

JAISING. Let us be strong in our faith as he is, Master. Why ask the aid of soldiers? We have the strength within ourselves for the task given to us from above. Open the temple gate wide, father. Sound the drum. Come, come, O citizens, to worship her who takes all fear away from our hearts. Come, Mother's children.

(Citizens come.)
FIRST CITIZEN. Come, come, we are called.
ALL. Victory to Mother!
　(They sing and dance.)

The dread Mother dances naked in the battlefield,
　Her lolling tongue burns like a red flame of fire,
Her dark tresses fly in the sky, sweeping away the sun and
　　stars,
　Red streams of blood run from her cloud-black limbs,
And the world trembles and cracks under her tread.

JAISING. Do you see the beasts of sacrifice coming towards the temple, driven by the Queen's attendants?
　(They cry.)
Victory to Mother! Victory to our Queen!
RAGHUPATI. Jaising, make haste and get ready for the worship.
JAISING. Everything is ready, father.
RAGHUPATI. Send a man to call Prince Nakshatra in my name.
　*(*JAISING *goes. Citizens sing and dance.)*
GOVINDA. Silence, Raghupati! Do you dare to disregard my order?
RAGHUPATI. Yes, I do.
GOVINDA. Then you are not for my land.
RAGHUPATI. No, my land is there, where the King's crown kisses the dust. No! Citizens! Let Mother's offerings be brought in here.
　(They beat drums.)
GOVINDA. Silence! *(To his attendants.)* Ask my General to come. Raghupati, you drive me to call soldiers to defend God's right. I feel the shame of it; for the force of arms only reveals man's weakness.
RAGHUPATI. Sceptic, are you so certain in your mind that Brahmins have lost the ancient fire of their sacred wrath? No, its flame will burst out from my heart to burn your throne into ashes. If it does not, then I shall throw into the fire the scriptures, and my Brahmin pride, and all the arrant lies that fill our temple shrines in the guise of the divine.
　(Enter GENERAL NAYAN RAI *and* CHANDPAL, *who is the second in command of the army.)*
GOVINDA. Stand here with your soldiers to prevent sacrifice of life in the temple.
NAYAN RAI. Pardon me, Sire. The King's servant is powerless in the temple of God.

GOVINDA. General, it is not for you to question my order. You are to carry out my words. Their merits and demerits belong only to me.

NAYAN RAI. I am your servant, my King, but I am a man above all. I have reason and my religion. I have my King,— and also my God.

GOVINDA. Then surrender your sword to Chandpal. He will protect the temple from pollution of blood.

NAYAN RAI. Why to Chandpal? This sword was given to my forefathers by your royal ancestors. If you want it back, I will give it up to you. Be witness, my fathers, who are in the heroes' paradise,—the sword, that you made sacred with your loyal faith and bravery, I surrender to my King. (*Goes out.*)

RAGHUPATI. The Brahmin's curse has begun its work already.

(*Enters* JAISING.)

JAISING. The beasts have been made ready for the sacrifice.

GOVINDA. Sacrifice?

JAISING. King, listen to my earnest entreaties. Do not stand in the way, hiding the Goddess, man as you are.

RAGHUPATI. Shame, Jaising! Rise up and ask my pardon. I am your Master. Your place is at my feet, not the King's. Fool! Do you ask King's sanction to do God's service? Leave alone the worship and the sacrifice. Let us wait and see how his pride prevails in the end. Come away.

(*They go out. Enters* APARNA.)

APARNA. Where is Jaising? He is not here, but only you,— the image whom nothing can move. You rob us of all our best without uttering a word. We pine for love, and die beggars for want of it. Yet it comes to you unasked, though you need it not. Like a grave, you hoard it under your miserly stone, keeping it from the use of the yearning world. Jaising, what happiness do you find from her? What can she speak to you? O my heart, my famished heart!

(*Enters* RAGHUPATI.)

RAGHUPATI. Who are you?

APARNA. I am a beggar girl. Where is Jaising?

RAGHUPATI. Leave this place at once. I know you are haunting this temple to steal Jaising's heart from the Goddess.

APARNA. Has the Goddess anything to fear from me? I fear her. (*She goes out.*)

(*Enter* JAISING *and* PRINCE NAKSHATRA.)

NAKSHATRA. Why have you called me?

RAGHUPATI. Last night the Goddess told me in a dream that you shall become king within a week.

NAKSHATRA. Ha, ha, this is news indeed.

RAGHUPATI. Yes, you shall be king.

NAKSHATRA. I cannot believe it.

RAGHUPATI. You doubt my words?

NAKSHATRA. I do not want to doubt them. But suppose, by chance, it never comes to pass.

RAGHUPATI. No, it shall be true.

NAKSHATRA. But, tell me, how can it ever become true?

RAGHUPATI. The Goddess thirsts for King's blood.

NAKSHATRA. King's blood?

RAGHUPATI. You must offer it to her before you can be king.

NAKSHATRA. I know not where to get it.

RAGHUPATI. There is King Govinda.—Jaising, keep still.—Do you understand? Kill him in secret. Bring his blood, while warm, to the altar.—Jaising, leave this place if you cannot remain still.

NAKSHATRA. But he is my brother, and I love him.

RAGHUPATI. Your sacrifice will be all the more precious.

NAKSHATRA. But, father, I am content to remain as I am. I do not want the kingdom.

RAGHUPATI. There is no escape for you, because the Goddess commands it. She is thirsting for blood from the King's house. If your brother is to live, then you must die.

NAKSHATRA. Have pity on me, father.

RAGHUPATI. You shall never be free in life, or in death, until her bidding is done.

NAKSHATRA. Advise me, then, how to do it.

RAGHUPATI. Wait in silence. I will tell you what to do when the time comes. And now, go.

(NAKSHATRA goes.)

JAISING. What is it that I heard? Merciful Mother, is it your bidding? To ask brother to kill brother? Master, how could you say that it was Mother's own wish?

RAGHUPATI. There was no other means but this to serve my Goddess.

JAISING. Means? Why means? Mother, have you not your own sword to wield with your own hand? Must your wish burrow underground, like a thief, to steal in secret? Oh, the sin!

RAGHUPATI. What do you know about sin?

JAISING. What I have learned from you.

RAGHUPATI. Then come and learn your lesson once again

from me. Sin has no meaning in reality. To kill is but to kill,—
it is neither sin nor anything else. Do you not know that the
dust of this earth is made of countless killings? Old Time is
ever writing the chronicle of the transient life of creatures in
letters of blood. Killing is in the wilderness, in the habitations
of man, in birds' nests, in insects' holes, in the sea, in the
sky; there is killing for life, for sport, for nothing whatever.
The world is ceaselessly killing; and the great Goddess Kali,
the spirit of ever-changing time, is standing with her thirsty
tongue hanging down from her mouth, with her cup in hand,
into which is running the red life-blood of the world, like
juice from the crushed cluster of grapes.

JAISING. Stop, Master. Is, then, love a falsehood and mercy
a mockery, and the one thing true, from beginning of time,
the lust for destruction? Would it not have destroyed itself
long ago? You are playing with my heart, my Master. Look
there, she is gazing at me with her sweet mocking smile.
My bloodthirsty Mother, wilt thou accept my blood? Shall
I plunge this knife into my breast and make an end to my
life, as thy child, for evermore? The life-blood flowing in
these veins, is it so delicious to thee? O my Mother, my
bloodthirsty Mother!—Master, did you call me? I know you
wanted my heart to break its bounds in pain overflowing my
Mother's feet. This is the true sacrifice. But King's blood!
The Mother, who is thirsting for our love, you accuse of
bloodthirstiness!

RAGHUPATI. Then let the sacrifice be stopped in the temple.

JAISING. Yes, let it be stopped—No, no, Master, you know
what is right and what is wrong. The heart's laws are not the
laws of scripture. Eyes cannot see with their own light,—the
light must come from the outside. Pardon me, Master, pardon
my ignorance. Tell me, father, is it true that the Goddess
seeks King's blood?

RAGHUPATI. Alas, child, have you lost your faith in me?

JAISING. My world stands upon my faith in you. If the
Goddess must have King's blood, let me bring it to her. I
will never allow a brother to kill his brother.

RAGHUPATI. But there can be no evil in carrying out God's
wishes.

JAISING. No, it must be good, and I will earn the merit
of it.

RAGHUPATI. But, my boy, I have reared you from your
childhood, and you have grown close to my heart. I can
never bear to lose you, by any chance.

JAISING. I will not let your love for me be soiled with sin. Release Prince Nakshatra from his promise.

RAGHUPATI. I shall think, and decide to-morrow. (*He goes.*)

JAISING. Deeds are better, however cruel they may be, than the hell of thinking and doubting. You are right, my Master; truth is in your words. To kill is no sin, to kill brother is no sin, to kill king is no sin.—Where do you go, my brothers? To the fair at Nishipur? There the women are to dance? Oh, this world is pleasant! And the dancing limbs of the girls are beautiful. In what careless merriment the crowds flew through the roads, making the sky ring with their laughter and song. I will follow them.

(*Enters* RAGHUPATI.)

RAGHUPATI. Jaising.

JAISING. I do not know you. I drift with the crowd. Why ask me to stop? Go your own way.

RAGHUPATI. Jaising.

JAISING. The road is straight before me. With an alms-bowl in hand and the begger girl as my sweetheart I shall walk on. Who says that the world's ways are difficult? Anyhow we reach the end,—the end where all laws and rules are no more, where the errors and hurts of life are forgotten, where is rest, eternal rest. What is the use of scriptures, and the teacher and his instructions?—My Master, my father, what wild words are these of mine? I was living in a dream. There stands the temple, cruel and immovable as truth. What was your order, my teacher? I have not forgotten it. (*Bringing out the knife.*) I am sharpening your words in my mind, till they become one with this knife in keenness. Have you any other order to give me?

RAGHUPATI. My boy, my darling, how can I tell you how deep is my love for you?

JAISING. No, Master, do not tell me of love. Let me think only of duty. Love, like the green grass, and the trees, and life's music, is only for the surface of the world. It comes and vanishes like a dream. But underneath is duty, like the rude layers of stone, like a huge load that nothing can move.

(*They go out. Enter* GOVINDA *and* CHANDPAL.)

CHANDPAL. Sire, I warn you to be careful.

GOVINDA. Why? What do you mean?

CHANDPAL. I have overheard a conspiracy to take away your life.

GOVINDA. Who wants my life?

CHANDPAL. I am afraid to tell you, lest the news becomes

to you more deadly than the knife itself. It was Prince Nak-shatra, who——

GOVINDA. Nakshatra?

CHANDPAL. He has promised to Raghupati to bring your blood to the Goddess.

GOVINDA. To the Goddess? Then I cannot blame him. For a man loses his humanity when it concerns his gods. You go to your work and leave me alone.

(CHANDPAL *goes out*.)

GOVINDA (*addressing the image*). Accept these flowers, Goddess, and let your creatures live in peace. Mother, those who are weak in this world are so helpless, and those who are strong are so cruel. Greed is pitiless, ignorance blind, and pride takes no heed when it crushes the small under its foot. Mother, do not raise your sword and lick your lips for blood; do not set brother against brother, and woman against man. If it is your desire to strike me by the hand of one I love, then let it be fulfilled. For the sin has to ripen to its ugliest limits before it can burst and die a hideous death; and when King's blood is shed by a brother's hand, then lust for blood will disclose its demon face, leaving its disguise as a goddess. If such be your wish I bow my head to it.

(JAISING *rushes in*.)

JAISING. Tell me, Goddess, dost thou truly want King's blood? Ask it in thine own voice, and thou shalt have it.

A VOICE. I want King's blood.

JAISING. King, say your last prayer, for your time has come.

GOVINDA. What makes you say it, Jaising?

JAISING. Did you not hear what the Goddess said?

GOVINDA. It was not the Goddess. I heard the familiar voice of Raghupati.

JAISING. The voice of Raghupati? No, no! Drive me not from doubt to doubt. It is all the same, whether the voice comes from the Goddess, or from my Master.—(*He unsheathes his knife, and then throws it away*.) Listen to the cry of thy children, Mother. Let there be only flowers, the beautiful flowers for thy offerings,—no more blood. They are red even as blood,—these bunches of hibiscus. They have come out of the heartburst of the earth, pained at the slaughter of her children. Accept this. Thou must accept this. I defy thy anger. Blood thou shalt never have. Redden thine eyes. Raise thy sword. Bring thy furies of destruction. I do not fear thee.— King, leave this temple to its Goddess, and go to your men.

(GOVINDA *goes.*) Alas, alas, in a moment I gave up all that I had, my Master, my Goddess.

(RAGHUPATI *comes.*)

RAGHUPATI. I have heard all. Traitor, you have betrayed your master.

JAISING. Punish me, father.

RAGHUPATI. What punishment will you have?

JAISING. Punish me with my life.

RAGHUPATI. No, that is nothing. Take your oath touching the feet of the Goddess.

JAISING. I touch her feet.

RAGHUPATI. Say, I will bring kingly blood to the altar of the Goddess before it is midnight.

JAISING. I will bring kingly blood to the altar of the Goddess before it is midnight.

(*They go out. Enters* GUNAVATI.)

GUNAVATI. I failed. I had hoped that, if I remained hard and cold for some days, he would surrender. Such faith I had in my power, vain woman that I am. I showed my sullen anger, and remained away from him; but it was fruitless. Woman's anger is like a diamond's glitter; it only shines, but cannot burn. I would it were like thunder, bursting upon the King's house, startling him up from his sleep, and dashing his pride to the ground.

(*Enter the boy* DRUVA.)

GUNAVATI. Where are you going?

DRUVA. I am called by the King. (*Goes out.*)

GUNAVATI. There goes the darling of the King's heart. He has robbed my unborn children of their father's love, usurped their right to the first place in the King's breast. O Mother Kali, your creation is infinite and full of wonders, only send a child to my arms in merest whim, a tiny little warm living flesh to fill my lap, and I shall offer you whatever you wish. (*Enters* NAKSHATRA.) Prince Nakshatra, why do you turn back? I am a mere woman, weak and without weapon; am I so fearful?

NAKSHATRA. No, do not call me.

GUNAVATI. Why? What harm is in that?

NAKSHATRA. I do not want to be a king.

GUNAVATI. But why are you so excited?

NAKSHATRA. May the King live long, and may I die as I am,—a prince.

GUNAVATI. Die as quick as you can; have I ever said anything against it?

NAKSHATRA. Then tell me what you want of me.

GUNAVATI. The thief that steals the crown is awaiting you,—remove him. Do you understand?

NAKSHATRA. Yes, except who the thief is.

GUNAVATI. That boy, Druva. Do you not see how he is growing in the King's lap, till one day he reaches the crown?

NAKSHATRA. Yes, I have often thought of it. I have seen my brother putting his crown on the boy's head in play.

GUNAVATI. Playing with the crown is a dangerous game. If you do not remove the player, he will make a game of you.

NAKSHATRA. Yes, I like it not.

GUNAVATI. Offer him to Kali. Have you not heard that Mother is thirsting for blood?

NAKSHATRA. But, sister, this is not my business.

GUNAVATI. Fool, can you feel yourself safe, so long as Mother is not appeased? Blood she must have; save your own, if you can.

NAKSHATRA. But she wants King's blood.

GUNAVATI. Who told you that?

NAKSHATRA. I know it from one to whom the Goddess herself sends her dreams.

GUNAVATI. Then that boy must die for the King. His blood is more precious to your brother than his own, and the King can only be saved by paying the price, which is more than his life.

NAKSHATRA. I understand.

GUNAVATI. Then lose no time. Run after him. He is not gone far. But remember. Offer him in my name.

NAKSHATRA. Yes, I will.

GUNAVATI. The Queen's offerings have been turned back from Mother's gate. Pray to her that she may forgive me.

(*They go out. Enters* JAISING.)

JAISING. Goddess, is there any little thing that yet remains out of the wreck of thee? If there be but a faintest spark of thy light in the remotest of the stars of evening, answer my cry, though thy voice be the feeblest. Say to me, "Child, here I am."—No, she is nowhere. She is naught. But take pity upon Jaising, O Illusion, and for him become true. Art thou so irredeemably false, that not even my love can send the slightest tremor of life through thy nothingness? O fool, for whom have you upturned your cup of life, emptying it to the last drop?—for this unanswering void,—truthless, merciless, and motherless?

(*Enters* APARNA.)

Aparna, they drive you away from the temple; yet you

come back over and over again. For you are true, and truth cannot be banished. We enshrine falsehood in our temple, with all devotion; yet she is never there. Leave me not, Aparna. Sit here by my side. Why are you so sad, my darling? Do you miss some god, who is god no longer? But is there any need of God in this little world of ours? Let us be fearlessly godless and come closer to each other. They want our blood. And for this they have come down to the dust of our earth, leaving their magnificence of heaven. For in their heaven there are no men, no creatures, who can suffer. No, my girl, there is no Goddess.

APARNA. Then leave this temple, and come away with me.

JAISING. Leave this temple? Yes, I will leave. Alas, Aparna, I must leave. Yet I cannot leave it, before I have paid my last dues to the——— But let that be. Come closer to me, my love. Whisper something to my ears which will overflow this life with sweetness, flooding death itself.

APARNA. Words do not flow when the heart is full.

JAISING. Then lean your head on my breast. Let the silence of two eternities, life and death, touch each other. But no more of this. I must go.

APARNA. Jaising, do not be cruel. Can you not feel what I have suffered?

JAISING. Am I cruel? Is this your last word to me? Cruel as that block of stone, whom I called Goddess? Aparna, my beloved, if you were the Goddess, you would know what fire is this that burns my heart. But you *are* my Goddess. Do you know how I know it?

APARA. Tell me.

JAISING. You bring to me your sacrifice every moment, as a mother does to her child. God must be all sacrifice, pouring out his life in all creation.

APARNA. Jaising, come, let us leave this temple and go away together.

JAISING. Save me, Aparna, have mercy upon me and leave me. I have only one object in my life. Do not usurp its place. (*Rushes out.*)

APARNA. Again and again I have suffered. But my strength is gone. My heart breaks. (*She goes out.*)

(*Enter* RAGHUPATI *and* PRINCE NAKSHATRA.)

RAGHUPATI. Prince, where have you kept the boy?

NAKSHATRA. He is in the room where the vessels for worship are kept. He has cried himself to sleep. I think I shall never be able to bear it when he wakes up again.

RAGHUPATI. Jaising was of the same age when he came to

me. And I remember how he cried till he slept at the feet of the Goddess,—the temple lamp dimly shining on his tear-stained child-face. It was a stormy evening like this.

NAKSHATRA. Father, delay not. I wish to finish it all while he is sleeping. His cry pierces my heart like a knife.

RAGHUPATI. I will drug him to sleep if he wakes up.

NAKSHATRA. The King will soon find it out, if you are not quick. For, in the evening, he leaves the care of his kingdom to come to this boy.

RAGHUPATI. Have more faith in the Goddess. The victim is now in her own hands and it shall never escape.

NAKSHATRA. But Chandpal is so watchful.

RAGHUPATI. Not more so than our Mother.

NAKSHATRA. I thought I saw a shadow pass by.

RAGHUPATI. The shadow of your own fear.

NAKSHATRA. Do we not hear the sound of a cry?

RAGHUPATI. The sound of your own heart. Shake off your despondency, Prince. Let us drink this wine duly consecrated. So long as the purpose remains in the mind it looms large and fearful. In action it becomes small. The vapour is dark and diffused. It dissolves into water-drops, that are small and sparkling. Prince, it is nothing. It takes only a moment,—not more than it does to snuff a candle. That life's light will die in a flash, like lightning in the stormy night of July, leaving its thunderbolt for ever deep in the King's pride. But, Prince, why are you so silent?

NAKSHATRA. I think we should not be too rash. Leave this work till to-morrow night.

RAGHUPATI. To-night is as good as to-morrow night, perhaps better.

NAKSHATRA. Listen to the sound of footsteps.

RAGHUPATI. I do not hear it.

NAKSHATRA. See there,—the light.

RAGHUPATI. The King comes. I fear we have delayed too long.

(*King comes with attendants.*)

GOVINDA. Make them prisoners. (*To* RAGHUPATI.) Have you anything to say?

RAGHUPATI. Nothing.

GOVINDA. Do you admit your crime?

RAGHUPATI. Crime? Yes, my crime was that, in my weakness, I delayed in carrying out Mother's service. The punishment comes from the Goddess. You are merely her instrument.

GOVINDA. According to my law, my soldiers shall escort you

to exile, Raghupati, where you shall spend eight years of your life.

RAGHUPATI. King, I never bent my knees to any mortal in my life. I am a Brahmin. Your caste is lower than mine. Yet, in all humility, I pray to you, give me only one day's time.

GOVINDA. I grant it.

RAGHUPATI (*mockingly*). You are the King of all kings. Your majesty and mercy are alike immeasurable. Whereas I am a mere worm, hiding in the dust. (*He goes out.*)

GOVINDA. Nakshatra, admit your guilt.

NAKSHATRA. I am guilty, Sire, and I dare not ask for your pardon.

GOVINDA. Prince, I know you are tender of heart. Tell me, who beguiled you with evil counsel?

NAKSHATRA. I will not take other names, King. My guilt is my own. You have pardoned your foolish brother more than once, and once more he begs to be pardoned.

GOVINDA. Nakshatra, leave my feet. The judge is still more bound by his laws than his prisoner.

ATTENDANTS. Sire, remember that he is your brother, and pardon him.

GOVINDA. Let me remember that I am a king. Nakshatra shall remain in exile for eight years, in the house we have built, by the sacred river, outside the limits of Tripura. (*Taking NAKSHATRA's hands.*) The punishment is not yours only, brother, but also mine,—the more so because I cannot share it bodily. The vacancy that you leave in the palace will prick my heart every day with a thousand needles. May the gods be more friendly to you, while you are away from us.

(*They all go out. Enter* RAGHUPATI *and* JAISING.)

RAGHUPATI. My pride wallows in the mire. I have shamed my Brahminhood. I am no longer your master, my child. Yesterday I had the authority to command you. To-day I can only beg your favour. That light is extinct in me, which gave me the right to defy King's power. The earthen lamp can be replenished and lighted again and again, but the star once extinguished is lost for ever. I am that lost star. Life's days are mere tinsel, most trifling of God's gifts, and I had to beg for one of those days from the King with bent knees. Let that one day be not in vain. Let its infamous black brows be red with King's blood before it dies. Why do you not speak, my boy? Though I forsake my place as your master, yet have I not the right to claim your obedience as your father,—I who am more than a father to you, because father to an orphan? But that man is the most miserable of all beggars who has to beg for love. You are still silent, my child? Then let my knees bend to you, who were smaller than my knees when you first came to my arms.

JAISING. Father, do not torture the heart that is already broken. If the Goddess thirsts for kingly blood, I will bring it to her before to-night. I will pay all my debts, yes, every farthing. Keep ready for my return. I will delay not. (*Goes out.*)

(*Storm outside.*)

RAGHUPATI. She is awake at last, the Terrible. Her curses go shrieking through the town. The hungry Furies are shaking the cracking branches of the world-tree with all their might, for the stars to break and drop. My Mother, why didst thou keep thine own people in doubt and dishonour so long? Leave it not for thy servant to raise thy sword. Let thy mighty arm do its own work!—I hear steps.

(*Enters* APARNA.)

APARNA. Where is Jaising?

RAGHUPATI. Away, evil omen. (*Aparna goes out.*) But if Jaising never comes back? No, he will not break his promise. Victory to thee, Great Kali, the giver of all success!—But if he meet with obstruction? If he be caught and lose his life at the guards' hands?—Victory to thee, watchful Goddess, Mother invincible! Do not allow thy repute to be lost, and thine enemies to laugh at thee. If thy children must lose their pride and faith in their Mother, and bow down their heads in shame before the rebels, who then will remain in this orphaned world to carry thy banner?—I hear his steps. But so soon? Is he coming back foiled in his purpose? No, that cannot be. Thy miracle needs not time, O Mistress of all time, terrible with thy necklace of human skulls.

(JAISING *rushes in.*)

Jaising, where is the blood?

JAISING. It is with me. Let go my hands. Let me offer it myself (*entering the temple*). Must thou have kingly blood, Great Mother, who nourishest the world at thy breast with life?—I am of the royal caste, a Kshatriya. My ancestors have sat upon thrones, and there are rulers of men in my mother's line. I have kingly blood in my veins. Take it, and quench thy thirst forever.

(*Stabs himself, and falls.*)

RAGHUPATI. Jaising! O cruel, ungrateful! You have done the blackest crime. You kill your father!—Jaising, forgive me, my darling. Come back to my heart, my heart's one treasure! Let me die in your place.

(*Enters* APARNA.)

APARNA. It will madden me. Where is Jaising? Where is he?

RAGHUPATI. Come, Aparna, come, my child, call him with all your love. Call him back to life. Take him to you, away from me, only let him live.

(APARNA *enters the temple and swoons.*)

(*Beating his forehead on the temple floor.*) Give him, give him, give him—Give him back to me! (*Stands up addressing the image.*) Look how she stands there, the silly stone,—deaf, dumb, blind,—the whole sorrowing world weeping at her door,—the noblest hearts wrecking themselves at her stony feet! Give me back my Jaising! Oh, it is all in vain. Our bitterest cries wander in emptiness,—the emptiness that we vainly try to fill with these stony images of delusion. Away with them! Away with these our impotent dreams, that harden into stones, burdening our world!

(*He throws away the image, and comes out into the courtyard. Enters* GUNAVATI.)

GUNAVATI. Victory to thee, great Goddess!—But where is the Goddess?

RAGHUPATI. Goddess there is none.

GUNAVATI. Bring her back, father. I have brought her my offerings. I have come at last, to appease her anger with my own heart's blood. Let her know that the Queen is true to her promise. Have pity on me, and bring back the Goddess only for this night. Tell me,—where is she?

RAGHUPATI. She is nowhere,—neither above nor below.

GUNAVATI. Master, was not the Goddess here in the temple?

RAGHUPATI. Goddess?—If there were any true Goddess anywhere in the world, could she bear this thing to usurp her name?

GUNAVATI. Do not torture me. Tell me truly. Is there no Goddess?

RAGHUPATI. No, there is none.

GUNAVATI. Then who was here?

RAGHUPATI. Nothing, nothing.

(APARNA *comes out from the temple.*)

APARNA. Father!

RAGHUPATI. My sweet child! "Father,"—did you say? Do you rebuke me with that name? My son, whom I have killed, has left that one dear call behind him in your sweet voice.

APARNA. Father, leave this temple. Let us go away from here.

(*Enters the King.*)

GOVINDA. Where is the Goddess?

RAGHUPATI. The Goddess is nowhere.

GOVINDA. But what blood-stream is this?

RAGHUPATI. King, Jaising, who loved you so dearly, has killed himself.

GOVINDA. Killed himself? Why?

RAGHUPATI. To kill the falsehood that sucks the life-blood of man.

GOVINDA. Jaising is great. He has conquered death. My flowers are for him.

GUNAVATI. My King!

GOVINDA. Yes, my love.

GUNAVATI. The Goddess is no more.

GOVINDA. She has burst her cruel prison of stone, and come back to the woman's heart.

APARNA. Father, come away.

RAGHUPATI. Come, child. Come, Mother. I have found thee. Thou art the last gift of Jaising.

translated by the author

The Drama of Japan

Nō, the earliest of Japan's indigenous dramatic forms, remains closest to its original sources. *Nō* performances today attract an elect few who attend because they find in this esoteric theater an expression of Zen Buddhism, or because they enjoy a reversion to an art that has kept clear of Occidental contamination. Since we are dealing here with the theater of modern time, we will pass by *Nō,* which remains largely what it was at its inception some five hundred years ago, and come to modern developments.

Although *Shingeki,* or "new drama," has been of increasing importance in Japan, particularly in Tokyo, since its introduction early in the twentieth century, *Kabuki* continues to be the major attraction. The present repertoire consists of some four hundred plays and dances, most of which were written between the seventeenth and mid-nineteenth centuries. The plots and characters of the most popular productions are so well known that often only one or two scenes of a play will be given during a particular performance. The uninitiated observer may get the impression of a singularly disjointed program. In fact, the Western theater-goer must be prepared to check his critical norms at the door as he enters the *Kabuki* auditorium.

In Japan, as in India, music and dance appear at the top of Aristotle's dramatic elements. From the moment that the increasing tempo of the wooden clappers announces the beginning of a performance, sound effects are of the utmost importance.

Orchestral music helps to determine pace and to intensify emotion. Choral comment on the action is similar to the sort of comment or judgment that was passed by the chorus in Greek tragedy. In addition, the chorus occasionally takes over the lines of the characters. Also, the actors voice their lines with an artificiality of tone that successfully destroys any literal semblance of reality.

In fact, here again as in India, the audience is not looking to the stage for a slice of real life. Most elements are contrary to Western concepts of theater. In addition to the element of "melody" already mentioned, dances are frequently interpolated. A dance sequence may represent an arduous journey or a duel between adversaries. The climactic moment in a drama is often such a dance, as likely as not performed on the *hanamichi*, a runway extending from stage left through the theater, bringing the stage action into close relationship with the audience.

The element of spectacle, which Aristotle regarded as the least worthy of the dramatic components, is high in importance in *Kabuki*. Here it is the ornate costuming. Stage sets are marked by simplicity, often being no more than a backdrop representing the stylized pine tree of *Nō* drama. But against them the brilliant costumes stand out in glowing magnificence.

An unrealistic remnant of a previous era is the all-male casts in *Kabuki* performances. This is probably *Kabuki's* greatest obstacle to the Occidental audience. Yet female impersonators build enduring reputations and pass their art from father to son through several generations. The chief box-office attraction of a particular season may be a famous *onnagata*, or female impersonator, in a favorite role.

While the religiously oriented *Nō* drama has been subsidized through five centuries, first by nobility and more recently by interested clubs and groups, *Kabuki* has depended on popular appeal. Hence it has been subject to the pressures of public opinion and has adapted itself to changing tastes. Today's programs are no longer restricted to the great patriotic pieces of the samurai period, but include ghost stories (fast-paced adaptations from *Nō*) and often lighthearted social plays concerning the common people.

Action of a basic and exciting nature has the appeal that it would in any truly people's theater. But even here the Western viewer may have difficulty in discerning the stirring action when it comes. The long-awaited slaying of the villain, for instance, may be depicted in a dance sequence that may not be understood by the foreigner. Or the hero's moment of supreme triumph may be registered in a *mie,* a moment of inactivity held during the accelerated beating of the wooden clappers.

But of even greater importance than the *action* is the *actor.* In the dance, in the *mie,* in the interpretation by the *onnagata,* the audience is observing and assessing the art of the actor. The literary base from which the actor is launched may be almost totally disregarded. As the astute Spaniard comes just in time for the performance by his favorite matador, so the *Kabuki* connoisseur may attend only that portion of a long evening program in which his favorite actor interprets a noted scene. In such an attitude toward the theater we are a far cry from the experience of *katharsis* that Aristotle considered to be the desired result of dramatic tragedy.

The influence of Western drama, as has been said, entered the *Shingeki* theater early in this century. Its initial expression was in the translated works of such European and American dramatists as Shakespeare, Ibsen, and O'Neill. Performances were first by amateur groups or by small experimental companies. Later, young playwrights expressed themselves in terms of the dramatic conventions of the West.

To the present time, however, *Shingeki* has fought a losing financial battle against the ever-popular *Kabuki.* Although the new theater is beginning to attract larger audiences, it does so by holding to comparatively low admission fees, which result in low pay for actors.

Kikuchi Kan (1888–1948) was novelist and short-story writer, as well as dramatist. His reputation as a versatile and prolific author between World Wars I and II brought him the unofficial title of *Bundan no ōgosho,* or "Prince of the Literary World." Kikuchi's humble and impoverished youth is reflected in many of his works, especially in his championship of the common man.

Until his later years, when he began to pander to mass tastes and even to turn out government propaganda, Kikuchi Kan's writing was marked by meticulous craftsmanship and psychological insight.

Okujō no Kyōjin (*The Madman on the Roof*) first appeared as a short story in 1916 and was later adapted as a play by the author. Its initial production was at the Imperial Theatre, Tokyo, in 1920.

Although this drama is brief, it gives considerable insight into the life of the common people during a period of social change. The dichotomy of generations is dramatized in the conflict between the father and his younger son who rejects religious superstition and speaks in behalf of modern scientific methods. Nevertheless, an undercurrent of Zen thought may be sensed in the concluding emphasis on the soaring spirit of the "mad" elder brother and his apparent ability to communicate directly with the gods.

This is obviously a *Shingeki* play, yet there are several opportunities for the introduction of traditional methods of production. In his *Kabuki Theatre*, Earle Ernst points out that supposedly realistic dramas given in Japan's *Shingeki* theaters may still be so heavily influenced by the traditions of *Nō* and *Kabuki* that playing time is almost doubled. The *mie*, the dance, and other stylized methods can be introduced in a variety of ways. In a staging of *The Madman on the Roof* one can imagine the use of an effective dance sequence in the scene of the priestess's incantations, or of a *mie* performed by the younger brother when he breaks in upon this scene. In fact, Kikuchi Kan seems to prepare the way for the *mie* when, in his stage instructions, he says that Suejiro "stands amazed at the scene before him."

KIKUCHI KAN

THE MADMAN ON THE ROOF

Characters

KATSUSHIMA YOSHITARO, *the madman, twenty-four years of age*
KATSUSHIMA SUEJIRO, *his brother, a seventeen-year-old high-school student*
KATSUSHIMA GISUKE, *their father*
KATSUSHIMA OYOSHI, *their mother*
TOSAKU, *a neighbor*
KICHIJI, *a manservant, twenty years of age*
A PRIESTESS, *about fifty years of age*

Place: *A small island in the Inland Sea*
Time: *1900*

The stage setting represents the backyard of the KATSU-SHIMAS, *who are the richest family on the island. A bamboo fence prevents one from seeing more of the house than the high roof, which stands out sharply against the rich greenish sky of the southern island summer. At the left of the stage one can catch a glimpse of the sea shining in the sunlight.*

YOSHITARO, *the elder son of the family, is sitting astride the ridge of the roof, and is looking out over the sea.*

GISUKE (*speaking from within the house*). Yoshi is sitting on the roof again. He'll get a sunstroke—the sun's so terribly hot. (*Coming out.*) Kichiji! Where is Kichiji?

KICHIJI (*appearing from the right*). Yes! What do you want?

GISUKE. Bring Yoshitaro down. He has no hat on, up there in the hot sun. He'll get a sunstroke. How did he get up there, anyway? From the barn? Didn't you put wires around the barn roof as I told you to the other day?

KICHIJI. Yes, I did exactly as you told me.

GISUKE (*coming through the gate to the center of the stage, and looking up to the roof*). I don't see how he can stand it, sitting on that hot slate roof. (*He calls.*) Yoshitaro! You'd better come down. If you stay up there you'll get a sunstroke, and maybe die.

KICHIJI. Young master! Come on down. You'll get sick if you stay there.

GISUKE. Yoshi! Come down quick! What are you doing up there, anyway? Come down, I say! (*He calls loudly.*) Yoshi!

YOSHITARO (*indifferently*). Wha-a-at?

GISUKE. No "whats"! Come down right away. If you don't come down, I'll get after you with a stick.

YOSHITARO (*protesting like a spoiled child*). No, I don't want to. There's something wonderful. The priest of the god Kompira is dancing in the clouds. Dancing with an angel in pink robes. They're calling to me to come. (*Crying out ecstatically.*) Wait! I'm coming!

GISUKE. If you talk like that you'll fall, just as you did once before. You're already crippled and insane—what will you do next to worry your parents? Come down, you fool!

KICHIJI. Master, don't get so angry. The young master will not obey you. You should get some fried bean cake; when he sees it he will come down, because he likes it.

GISUKE. No, you had better get the stick after him. Don't be afraid to give him a good shaking-up.

KICHIJI. That's too cruel. The young master doesn't understand anything. He's under the influence of evil spirits.

GISUKE. We may have to put bamboo guards on the roof to keep him down from there.

KICHIJI. Whatever you do won't keep him down. Why, he climbed the roof of the Honzen Temple without even a ladder; a low roof like this one is the easiest thing in the world for him. I tell you, it's the evil spirits that make him climb. Nothing can stop him.

GISUKE. You may be right, but he worries me to death. If we could only keep him in the house it wouldn't be so bad, even though he is crazy; but he's always climbing up to high places. Suejiro says that everybody as far as Takamatsu knows about Yoshitaro the Madman.

KICHIJI. People on the island all say he's under the influence of a fox-spirit, but I don't believe that. I never heard of a fox climbing trees.

GISUKE. You're right. I think I know the real reason. About the time Yoshitaro was born, I bought a very expensive imported rifle, and I shot every monkey on the island. I believe a monkey-spirit is now working in him.

KICHIJI. That's just what I think. Otherwise, how could he climb trees so well? He can climb anything without a ladder. Even Saku, who's a professional climber, admits that he's no match for Yoshitaro.

GISUKE (*with a bitter laugh*). Don't joke about it! It's no laughing matter, having a son who is always climbing on the roof. (*Calling again.*) Yoshitaro, come down! Yoshitaro! When he's up there on the roof, he doesn't hear me at all —he's so engrossed. I cut down all the trees around the house so he couldn't climb them, but there's nothing I can do about the roof.

KICHIJI. When I was a boy I remember there was a gingko tree in front of the gate.

GISUKE. Yes, that was one of the biggest trees on the island. One day Yoshitaro climbed clear to the top. He sat out on a branch, at least ninety feet above the ground, dreaming away as usual. My wife and I never expected him to get down alive, but after a while, down he slid. We were all too astonished to speak.

KICHIJI. That was certainly a miracle.

GISUKE. That's why I say it's a monkey-spirit that's working in him. (*He calls again.*) Yoshi! Come down! (*Dropping his voice.*) Kichiji, you'd better go up and fetch him.

KICHIJI. But when anyone else climbs up there, the young master gets angry.

GISUKE. Never mind his getting angry. Pull him down.

KICHIJI. Yes, master.

    (KICHIJI *goes out after the ladder.* TOSAKU, *the neighbor, enters.*)

TOSAKU. Good day, sir.

GISUKE. Good day. Fine weather. Catch anything with the nets you put out yesterday?

TOSAKU. No, not much. The season's over.

GISUKE. Maybe it *is* too late now.

TOSAKU (*looking up at* YOSHITARO). Your son's on the roof again.

GISUKE. Yes, as usual. I don't like it, but when I keep him locked in a room he's like a fish out of water. Then, when I take pity on him and let him out, back he goes up on the roof.

TOSAKU. But after all, he doesn't bother anybody.

GISUKE. He bothers us. We feel so ashamed when he climbs up there and shouts.

TOSAKU. But your younger son, Suejiro, has a fine record at school. That must be some consolation for you.

GISUKE. Yes, he's a good student, and that is a consolation to me. If both of them were crazy, I don't know how I could go on living.

TOSAKU. By the way, a Priestess has just come to the island. How would you like to have her pray for your son? That's really what I came to see you about.

GISUKE. We've tried prayers before, but it's never done any good.

TOSAKU. This Priestess believes in the god Kompira. She works all kinds of miracles. People say the god inspires her, and that's why her prayers have more effect than those of ordinary priests. Why don't you try her once?

GISUKE. Well, we might. How much does she charge?

TOSAKU. She won't take any money unless the patient is cured. If he is cured, you pay her whatever you feel like.

GISUKE. Suejiro says he doesn't believe in prayers. . . . But there's no harm in letting her try.

(KICHIJI *enters carrying the ladder and disappears behind the fence.*)

TOSAKU. I'll go and bring her here. In the meantime you get your son down off the roof.

GISUKE. Thanks for your trouble. (*After seeing that* TOSAKU *has gone, he calls again.*) Yoshi! Be a good boy and come down.

KICHIJI (*who is up on the roof by this time*). Now then, young master, come down with me. If you stay up here any longer you'll have a fever tonight.

YOSHITARO (*drawing away from* KICHIJI *as a Buddhist might from a heathen*). Don't touch me! The angels are beckoning to me. You're not supposed to come here. What do you want?

KICHIJI. Don't talk nonsense! Please come down.

YOSHITARO. If you touch me the demons will tear you apart.

(KICHIJI *hurriedly catches* YOSHITARO *by the shoulder and pulls him to the ladder.* YOSHITARO *suddenly becomes submissive.*)

KICHIJI. Don't make any trouble now. If you do you'll fall and hurt yourself.

GISUKE. Be careful!

(YOSHITARO *comes down to the center of the stage, followed by* KICHIJI. YOSHITARO *is lame in his right leg.*)

GISUKE (*calling*). Oyoshi! Come out here a minute.

OYOSHI (*from within*). What is it?

GISUKE. I've sent for a Priestess.

OYOSHI (*coming out*). That may help. You never can tell what will.

GISUKE. Yoshitaro says he talks with the god Kompira. Well, this Priestess is a follower of Kompira, so she ought to be able to help him.

YOSHITARO (*looking uneasy*). Father! Why did you bring me down? There was a beautiful cloud of five colors rolling down to fetch me.

GISUKE. Idiot! Once before you said there was a five-colored cloud, and you jumped off the roof. That's the way you became a cripple. A Priestess of the god Kompira is coming here today to drive the evil spirit out of you, so don't you go back up on the roof.

(TOSAKU *enters, leading the* PRIESTESS. *She has a crafty face.*)

TOSAKU. This is the Priestess I spoke to you about.

GISUKE. Ah, good afternoon. I'm glad you've come—this boy is really a disgrace to the whole family.

PRIESTESS (*casually*). You needn't worry any more about him. I'll cure him at once with the god's help. (*Looking at* YOSHITARO.) This is the one?

GISUKE. Yes. He's twenty-four years old, and the only thing he can do is climb up to high places.

PRIESTESS. How long has he been this way?

GISUKE. Ever since he was born. Even when he was a baby, he wanted to be climbing. When he was four or five years old, he climbed onto the low shrine, then onto the high shrine of Buddha, and finally onto a very high shelf. When he was seven he began climbing trees. At fifteen he climbed to the tops of mountains and stayed there all day long. He says he talks with demons and with the gods. What do you think is the matter with him?

PRIESTESS. There's no doubt but that it's a fox-spirit. I will pray for him. (*Looking at* YOSHITARO.) Listen now! I am the messenger of the god Kompira. All that I say comes from the god.

YOSHITARO (*uneasily*). You say the god Kompira? Have you ever seen him?

PRIESTESS (*staring at him*). Don't say such sacrilegious things! The god cannot be seen.

YOSHITARO (*exultantly*). I have seen him many times! He's an old man with white robes and a golden crown. He's my best friend.

PRIESTESS (*taken aback at this assertion, and speaking to* GISUKE). This is a fox-spirit, all right, and a very extreme case. I will address the god.

> (*She chants a prayer in a weird manner.* YOSHITARO, *held fast by* KICHIJI, *watches the* PRIESTESS *blankly. She works herself into a frenzy and falls to the ground in a faint. Presently she rises to her feet and looks about her strangely.*)

PRIESTESS (*in a changed voice*). I am the god Kompira!

> (*All except* YOSHITARO *fall to their knees with exclamations of reverence.*)

PRIESTESS (*with affected dignity*). The elder son of this family is under the influence of a fox-spirit. Hang him up on the branch of a tree and purify him with the smoke of green pine needles. If you fail to do what I say, you will all be punished!

> (*She faints again. There are more exclamations of astonishment.*)

PRIESTESS (*rising and looking about her as though unconscious of what has taken place*). What has happened? Did the god speak?

GISUKE. It was a miracle.

PRIESTESS. You must do at once whatever the god told you, or you'll be punished. I warn you for your own sake.

GISUKE (*hesitating somewhat*). Kichiji, go and get some green pine needles.

OYOSHI. No! It's too cruel, even if it is the god's command.

PRIESTESS. He will not suffer, only the fox-spirit within him. The boy himself will not suffer at all. Hurry! (*Looking fixedly at* YOSHITARO.) Did you hear the god's command? He told the spirit to leave your body before it hurt.

YOSHITARO. That was not Kompira's voice. He wouldn't talk to a priestess like you.

PRIESTESS (*insulted*). I'll get even with you. Just wait! Don't talk back to the god like that, you horrid fox!

(KICHIJI *enters with an armful of green pine boughs.* OYOSHI *is frightened.*)

PRIESTESS. Respect the god or be punished!

(GISUKE *and* KICHIJI *reluctantly set fire to the pine needles, then bring* YOSHITARO *to the fire. He struggles against being held in the smoke.*)

YOSHITARO. Father! What are you doing to me? I don't like it! I don't like it!

PRIESTESS. That's not his own voice speaking. It's the fox within him. Only the fox is suffering.

OYOSHI. But it's cruel!

(GISUKE *and* KICHIJI *attempt to press* YOSHITARO'S *face into the smoke. Suddenly* SUEJIRO'S *voice is heard calling within the house, and presently he appears. He stands amazed at the scene before him.*)

SUEJIRO. What's happening here? What's the smoke for?

YOSHITARO (*coughing from the smoke, and looking at his brother as at a savior*). Father and Kichiji are putting me in the smoke.

SUEJIRO (*angrily*). Father! What foolish thing are you doing now? Haven't I told you time and time again about this sort of business?

GISUKE. But the god inspired the miraculous Priestess . . .

SUEJIRO (*interrupting*). What nonsense is that? You do these insane things merely because he is so helpless. (*With a contemptuous look at the* PRIESTESS *he stamps the fire out.*)

PRIESTESS. Wait! That fire was made at the command of the god!

(SUEJIRO *sneeringly puts out the last spark.*)

GISUKE (*more courageously*). Suejiro, I have no education, and you have, so I am always willing to listen to you. But this fire was made at the god's command, and you shouldn't have stamped on it.

SUEJIRO. Smoke won't cure him. People will laugh at you if they hear you've been trying to drive out a fox. All the gods in the country together couldn't even cure a cold. This Priestess is a fraud. All she wants is the money.

GISUKE. But the doctors can't cure him.

SUEJIRO. If the doctors can't, nobody can. I've told you before that he doesn't suffer. If he did, we'd have to do something for him. But as long as he can climb up on the roof, he is happy. Nobody in the whole country is as happy as he is—perhaps nobody in the world. Besides, if you cure him now, what can he do? He's twenty-four years old and he knows nothing, not even the alphabet. He's had no practical experience. If he were cured, he would be conscious of being crippled, and he'd be the most miserable man alive. Is that what you want to see? It's all because you want to make him normal. But wouldn't it be foolish to become normal merely to suffer? (*Looking sidewise at the* PRIESTESS.) Tosaku, if you brought her here, you had better take her away.

PRIESTESS (*angry and insulted*). You disbelieve the oracle of the god. You will be punished! (*She starts her chant as before. She faints, rises, and speaks in a changed voice.*) I am the great god Kompira! What the brother of the patient says springs from his own selfishness. He knows if his sick brother is cured, he'll get the family estate. Doubt not this oracle!

SUEJIRO (*excitedly knocking the* PRIESTESS *down*). That's a damned lie, you old fool. (*He kicks her.*)

PRIESTESS (*getting to her feet and resuming her ordinary voice*). You've hurt me! You savage!

SUEJIRO. You fraud! You swindler!

TOSAKU (*coming between them*). Wait, young man! Don't get in such a frenzy.

SUEJIRO (*still excited*). You liar! A woman like you can't understand brotherly love!

TOSAKU. We'll leave now. It was my mistake to have brought her.

GISUKE (*giving* TOSAKU *some money*). I hope you'll excuse him. He's young and has such a temper.

PRIESTESS. You kicked me when I was inspired by the god. You'll be lucky to survive until tonight.

SUEJIRO. Liar!

OYOSHI (*soothing* SUEJIRO). Be still now. (*To the* PRIESTESS.) I'm sorry this has happened.

PRIESTESS (*leaving with* TOSAKU). The foot you kicked me with will rot off!

(*The* PRIESTESS *and* TOSAKU *go out.*)

GISUKE (*to* SUEJIRO). Aren't you afraid of being punished for what you've done?

SUEJIRO. A god never inspires a woman like that old swindler. She lies about everything.

OYOSHI. I suspected her from the very first. She wouldn't do such cruel things if a real god inspired her.

GISUKE (*without any insistence*). Maybe so. But, Suejiro, your brother will be a burden to you all your life.

SUEJIRO. It will be no burden at all. When I become successful, I'll build a tower for him on top of a mountain.

GISUKE (*suddenly*). But where's Yoshitaro gone?

KICHIJI (*pointing at the roof*). He's up there.

GISUKE (*having to smile*). As usual.

> (*During the preceding excitement,* YOSHITARO *has slipped away and climbed back up on the roof. The four persons below look at each other and smile.*)

SUEJIRO. A normal person would be angry with you for having put him in the smoke, but you see, he's forgotten everything. (*He calls.*) Yoshitaro!

YOSHITARO (*for all his madness there is affection for his brother*). Suejiro! I asked Kompira and he says he doesn't know her!

SUEJIRO (*smiling*). You're right. The god will inspire you, not a priestess like her.

> (*Through a rift in the clouds, the golden light of the sunset strikes the roof.*)

SUEJIRO (*exclaiming*). What a beautiful sunset!

YOSHITARO (*his face lighted by the sun's reflection*). Suejiro, look! Can't you see a golden palace in that cloud over there? There! Can't you see? Just look! How beautiful!

SUEJIRO (*as he feels the sorrow of sanity*). Yes, I see. I see it, too. Wonderful.

YOSHITARO (*filled with joy*). There! I hear music coming from the palace. Flutes, what I love best of all. Isn't it beautiful?

> (*The parents have gone into the house. The mad brother on the roof and the sane brother on the ground remain looking at the golden sunset.*)

translated by Glenn Hughes and Yozan T. Iwasaki

The Drama of China

We get an immediate impression of Western reaction to old-style Chinese drama from the term "Chinese opera," which is the usual designation given by Western audiences to Chinese dramatic productions. We are struck first by the veritable cacophony of sound that precedes and accompanies Chinese plays. A significant production may be introduced by the setting off of strings of firecrackers at the theater entrance. The clash of gongs calls the noisily chattering audience to attention. Then, once the drama is launched, musical accompaniment and thunderous sound effects are in order.

As in the theater of Shakespeare's day, stage sets are apt to be more suggestive than realistic. A stool, for instance, may represent a mountain height, or a high-backed chair the Emperor's throne in a setting of imagined splendor. Here as in Japan, however, costumes are magnificent, wigs and faces brilliantly hued. Dialogue and monologue are carried on in high-pitched, nasal, singsong tones.

Action is equally unrealistic. The villain stamps, poses belligerently, and glares while he intones his evil intentions. The hero is at all times heroic in stance and action, arriving in the nick of time to save a lady in distress or to win a crucial victory. Tremendous distances on horseback are covered in a half-dozen swaggering paces across the stage, a horsehair switch spurring an imaginary charger to speed. High moments of tension are made obvious by the orchestra's mounting frenzy and by a repeated crashing of cymbals.

Characters are more stereotyped than human. The villain is so designated by his wig, his facial makeup, his costume, and his manner. Other stock characters are made equally unmistakable. We do not, then, have an Oedipus, whose personal tragedy arouses our compassion, but, rather, the ruler type, heroic but depersonalized.

Here, again, reality stops at the theater door. The ticket-purchaser leaves the cares of a mundane world behind and enters the never-never land of unadulterated imagination. He achieves his relief from the woes of life by simply ignoring them for a period. He does not seek the purgation of the emotions that Aristotle sought in tragedy.

All these are essential elements of Chinese drama as they were employed down until the first decades of this century, when Western-style drama was first introduced. However, it should be made clear that the traditional theater has not been completely abandoned for the new. Far from it. Cities of Europe and the United States continue to be visited by dramatic troupes from the People's Republic of China performing the old "Peking Opera." Theaters in Hong Kong and on Taiwan continue to offer the customary programs to packed houses.

New drama began in 1921 with the return of Hung Shen from the United States. His influence was felt through the Drama Association, which he organized. He was followed by Tien Han, who founded the Nan-Kuo Society. Both innovators wrote plays that dwelt on didactic themes dealing with women and marriage, war and poverty. The first professional drama troupe to produce plays in the Western style was the China Travelling Drama Company formed in 1934. This led to the establishment the following year in Nanking of the National School of Dramatic Arts.

Perhaps it is a natural accompaniment of didactic theater or perhaps it is a carry-over from the habit of so many earlier years, but dramas emanating from mainland China today present the same stereotyped characters as appeared in the old-style plays. Although devoid of wig and face paint and clothed in modern dress, the villain is still very much unadulterated evil and the hero unalloyed perfection. Only the setting and situations are different.

Cultural leaders in the People's Republic of China have been astute in their recognition of the power of the dramatic performance in the education of the masses. Hundreds of plays have poured from the pens of ideologically embued writers, have been produced by professional and amateur groups, and have been published and disseminated widely throughout the world. English-language versions, at least, are translations made at the source and emanate from the Foreign Language Press in Peking.

In his introduction to *The People's New Literature,* Emi Siao stresses the importance of revising the old literature still in circulation, especially the traditional drama, which has strong popular appeal. He asserts that at the time of the compilation of the book (1950), over two hundred plays were being revised or newly written and that "in Peking alone over a thousand [opera artists] are being re-educated." In a talk before delegates to the first All-China Conference on Writers and Artists in July 1949 Chou En-lai set the prerequisites for the ideological writer:

> When we write about the situation of the workers prior to the Liberation, for instance, we have to deal with the oppression of the bureaucratic capital; when we write about the present-day production, we have to stress our policy of benefiting the workers . . .; when we write about the peasants in the feudal villages, we have to expose the outrages of the landlords; when we write about the People's Liberation War, we have to expatiate on the reactionary officers of the Kuomintang troops and the Kuomintang soldiers, who sacrificed their lives for a worthless cause.

It is interesting—or depressing—to note how "stock" the situations and characters are in even those dramas that critics rate "superior." The first scene usually sets or recapitulates a situation that prevailed in prerevolutionary China, preferably an evil perpetrated by the Kuomintang. The remainder of the play is then devoted to an overcoming of the situation through the wise and humane action of the present government. Actions and characters are "black" or "white," with no allowances for gradations or for mixed intentions. Such humor as may be admitted is of a grimly satiric nature with the decadent landowner or the Kuomintang officer as the butt.

Despite these literary and artistic limitations, it seems advisable to include a contemporary drama of social consciousness as our selection representing the drama of modern China because of the obvious influence that such expression has had on mass thought.

Local producers and audiences apparently recognize an affinity between this type of modern theater and that of the old culture. *Thunderstorm* by Tsao Yu, said to be the most frequently produced modern play since its first appearance in 1934, has sometimes been adapted as opera with the addition of music and singing.

Shu Sheh-yu (1899–   ) was born in Peking. At the age

of twenty-five he went to England to lecture in Chinese at the School of Oriental Studies, London University. His first three novels were written there. Returning to China in 1930, he became a professor of Chinese literature at universities in Tsinan and Tsingtao. During the Sino-Japanese War (1937–45) he was in Chunking where he organized the National Writers and Artists Resistance Association.

In recent years Shu has served as deputy to the National People's Congress, vice-chairman of the Union of Chinese Writers, and chairman of the Peking Federation of Writers and Artists.

Shu is known best by his pen name, Lao Sheh, under which he has published a number of novels and plays. Probably his best-known work outside China is his novel that in 1940 appeared in English as *Rickshaw Boy*.

Dragon Beard Ditch, 1950, meets Chou En-lai's requirements perfectly. It dramatizes contrasting conditions under the rule of Chiang Kai-shek and that of the present regime. The setting is in a small, unimportant village among the common people. The dramatic situation revolves around the draining of a pestiferous ditch and the installation of modern plumbing facilities. The place and scene settings for Act I provide sufficient background for the reader to appreciate the dramatic contrast that is summed up in Act III, the play's conclusion.

LAO SHEH (SHU SHEH-YU)

DRAGON BEARD DITCH

Characters—RESIDENTS ON DRAGON BEARD DITCH

MR. LIU, *teashop proprietor*
OLD CHAO
THE TINGS:
      TING SZE, *head of the house*
      TING SZE-SAO, *his wife*
      KA-TSE, *their small son*
THE WANGS:
      MOTHER WANG, *a widow*
      WANG ERH-CHUN, *her unmarried daughter*
THE CHENGS:
      "MAD" CHENG, *the husband*
      CHENG NIANG-TSE, *his wife*
LITTLE NIU
RESIDENT A
RESIDENT B
YOUNG MAN, *Erh-chun's fiancé*
A POLICEMAN

Act I

Time: 1948, *the year before the liberation of Peking. A morning in early summer; it has rained during the night.*
Place: *Dragon Beard Ditch, a notorious ditch, east of the Bridge of Heaven.[1] The Ditch is full of muddy, slimy water, mixed with rubbish, rags, dead rats, dead cats, dead dogs and now and then dead children. The waste water from the nearby tannery and dyeworks flows into it and accumulations of night soil collect there to putrefy. The water in the Ditch is of various shades of red and green, and its stench makes people feel sick quite far away. Hence the district has earned the name of "Stinking Ditch Bank." On the two banks, closely packed together, there live laborers, handicraft workers—the multifarious toiling poor. Day in and day out, all the year round and all their lives, they struggle in this filthy environment. Their houses may tumble down at any moment; most of their yards have no lavatories, let alone kitchens. There is no running water; they drink*

---

[1] The center of a crowded district in the southern part of Peking.

bitter and rank-tasting well water. Everywhere there are swarms of fleas, clouds of mosquitoes, countless bedbugs and black sheets of flies, all spreading disease. Whenever it rains, not only do the streets become pools of mud, but water from the Ditch overflows into the yards and houses, which are lower than the street level, and thus floods everything.

Scene: *A typical small "courtyard" of the district; it contains only four tumbledown mud huts. Doors and windows are fixed anyhow; one is an old and broken lattice window, one is altered from a "foreign-style" window, another was probably originally a Japanese sliding door. Some have old and moldy newspaper pasted on; others just have broken wooden boards or pieces of old and tattered matting nailed on. Even if there is a small piece of glass anywhere, it is so covered with grime, soot, and dust that it hardly lets any light through.*

On the north side (i.e., the left-hand side of the audience) is the WANG *family's house. A large earthenware water-butt stands in front of the door, together with a few broken wooden boxes. There is an oblong table placed so that the sun, which is just breaking through the dark clouds, shines on it; a piece of cotton cloth used as a wrapper is spread out on the table to dry.* MOTHER WANG *is lighting the stove, which burns coal balls and is used both for soldering mirror frames and for cooking.*

On the east side there are two families, the TINGS *and the* CHENGS, *occupying one room each. The room on the left is the* TINGS' *house; the roof leaks and half a piece of tattered rush matting is tied on top of it, with a few broken bricks to keep it down; an old tire hangs under the eaves. A torn red curtain, covered with patches, hangs in the doorway. In front of the door there is hardly anything except a stove and a few broken pedicab parts. The room on the right is the* CHENGS' *house; an old bamboo curtain with the lower part half torn off hangs in the doorway. There are many cigarette cards pasted on the window. A stunted date tree grows near the door; a small trellis is supported by the tree and on the trellis climbs a morning glory. Under the trellis, at the top right-hand corner, is the wood-burning stove, built of mud and fixed to the ground.* CHENG NIANG-TSE *is lighting a fire with sticks which she has gathered. She is going to steam "wo-wo-tou"* [1] *for her husband's breakfast. (Most of*

---

[1] A kind of unleavened and steamed bread made of flour ground from coarse grain (especially maize), which until recently was a staple food of the poor in North China.

the people in this district have only two meals a day.) The corner of the wall behind the stove has fallen down, and through this gap can be seen distant houses, a few electric supply poles, and the lowering sky.

On the south side is the main gate of this courtyard, very low and narrow, so that one has to bend down when passing through. Outside the gate is a narrow lane, on the opposite side of which stands a large dilapidated house, with a board lettered in gold "Pawnshop" hanging from its top corner. On the west side of the main gate there is a broken-down wall, at the end of which stands OLD CHAO'S *house, consisting of a single room. The door is shut. In front of it lie a few of the bigger tools used by bricklayers. There are also a bench and a broken water-butt upside down. Some rubbish and brickbats are piled up behind the water-butt, and on these* NIANG-TSE *is drying her cigarette tray, tea, and other odds and ends of wares.*

Lines are strung across here and there on which the families have hung out their old and tattered clothes and bedding to dry. All is mud underfoot except for patches where ashes, cinders, broken bricks, or wooden boards have been laid down. The corners and the foot of the walls are mildewed and green with lichens. Overhead, dark clouds move slowly. The sun comes out one moment and goes in the next.

Curtain Rises: *Outside the main gate are heard the cries of peddlers selling vegetables, pigs' blood, donkey meat, bean curd, the cries of barbers and rag-and-bone men, and the voices of housewives arguing over prices. Nearby, there are also the sounds of the blacksmith's hammering, of handlooms, and of tin kettles and pans being beaten by the tinsmith.* CHENG NIANG-TSE *is sitting on a small bench in front of the stove and putting more sticks on the fire.* LITTLE NIU *is moving broken bricks from the foot of the wall by the gate, so as to make a path in the courtyard.* TING SZE-SAO *is using a broken basin to bail out the water which has flooded their room. The sun has just risen and* WANG ERH-CHUN *comes out of their room with wet clothes in her arms, looks at the sky, and hangs them on the line.* MOTHER WANG, *having lit the stove, looks up at the sky, and carefully gathers up the large cotton wrapper from the table and is going to take it into their room.* ERH-CHUN, *on her way back into the room, takes it from her mother and goes in.* MOTHER WANG *picks up the kettle, and walks towards the water-butt, but, feeling uneasy about the wrapper having been taken by her daugh-*

*ter, turns around and looks at her. Then she ladles water into
the kettle and puts it on the stove; she sits down and begins
to work.*

Act III

SCENE 1

Time: *1950, summer; small hours of the morning, before
dawn.*

Place: *The San Yuan, a small tea shop on higher ground
by the Ditch.*

Setting: *The tea shop consists of two rooms facing east,
with a door between. In summer, an extra shelter is put up
outside, consisting of old matting supported by poles. Under
this there is an earthen structure serving as a table, beside
which stands an oblong wooden table. On the latter are tea-
pots, cups, and small winepots, snacks to go with the wine,
cigarettes, and two or three glass jars containing little paper
packets of tea, shelled peanuts, etc.*

Curtain Rises: *It has rained during the early part of the
night and now has just stopped. Water is still heard dripping
from the matting. One or two cocks crow. The proprietor,*
MR. LIU, *lights a paraffin lamp, looks at the stove and kettles,
and then looks outside as if expecting somebody. A* POLICE-
MAN *walks into the shelter; his cape is soaking wet; he wears
galoshes but no socks, and his trousers are covered with mud;
he has a flashlight.*

POLICEMAN. Mr. Liu, you've taken a lot of trouble.

PROPRIETOR. Oh, it's nothing!

POLICEMAN. How are you getting on?

PROPRIETOR. Nearly ready now; when the neighbors arrive
there'll be hot tea and a comfortable place to sit.

POLICEMAN. That's good. The chief asks me to tell Uncle
Chao not to start digging yet; get the neighbors here first, in
case any house should collapse and somebody get hurt.

PROPRIETOR. That's new. It used to be nobody's business
if people were drowned or buried alive! Now the police have
even prepared a place for people to evacuate to, just in case
houses might collapse and crush people to death.

POLICEMAN (*as he listens, shines the flashlight into the
two rooms*). Yes, that's so. Everyone's helped this time,

luckily. If we'd had to depend on us few police and the construction gang, we couldn't have done it so quickly. I'm going now; when Uncle Chao comes with the neighbors, you look after them. Oh, here they are! (OLD CHAO *leads a group of people up.*) Is everyone here now, Uncle Chao?

OLD CHAO. One lot's here. The rest'll be here in a moment.

POLICEMAN. I'll leave it all to you now. I'm going to help dig. (*To all.*) Neighbors, you rest here. (*Exits.*)

OLD CHAO. Women and children go inside, there's a fire there, dry your feet first. (*Women and children go in; men stand about or sit.*) Erh-chun! Erh-chun! Isn't she here yet?

ERH-CHUN (*answering from outside*). Coming, Uncle Chao, I'm coming. (*She runs in, a torn raincoat on her shoulders, carrying a small bundle which she puts down, speaking as she takes off raincoat.*) Oh! I nearly fell down. It's awful slippery!

OLD CHAO. Don't talk; get to work!

ERH-CHUN. What shall I do?

OLD CHAO. First boil some water and make tea so that everyone can have a hot drink. Then heat more water and find a tub and see that the children soak their feet in hot water so they won't catch cold.

ERH-CHUN. Right! (*Picks up bundle and goes into the room.*)

(*A* YOUNG MAN *comes in carrying* MOTHER WANG *on his back, her arms full of things.*)

MOTHER WANG. Erh-chun, Erh-chun! Where are you? You don't care a bit about your mother! If I fell down and died I don't believe you'd even shed a tear!

ERH-CHUN (*to the* YOUNG MAN). Come in and rest a bit.

YOUNG MAN. I can't. I've got to carry more people here. (*Hurries out.*)

ERH-CHUN. Warm yourself by the fire inside, Ma. (*Starts to take things from her.*)

MOTHER WANG. I'm not staying here! (*She is unwilling to hand over things.*)

ERH-CHUN. Where are you going, then?

MOTHER WANG. Home, I've forgotten the iron.

OLD CHAO. Now don't be silly, Mother Wang. The iron won't be swept away by the flood! An old lady like you should set an example to the others and not make more bother for us.

MOTHER WANG. Oh dear! (*Sits down.*) I knew there'd be trouble. In the old days they always asked the astrologer for an auspicious day before starting work. Now, as soon as they say they're going to do it, they do it, without bothering to find out whether it's an auspicious day or not. No wonder we've got this flood if the Dragon King has been disturbed!

OLD CHAO. Erh-chun, get on with your work; let the old lady get it off her chest.

ERH-CHUN. Ma, make yourself comfortable here; don't grumble. Nowadays, whatever day the work is done is an auspicious day; you needn't bother about the Imperial calendar! (*Enters room.*)

(MAD CHENG *comes in, supporting* NIANG-TSE.)

NIANG-TSE. Let me go! Are you supposed to be helping me or pinching me?

MAD CHENG. Anything to please you, dear!

NIANG-TSE. What can I do, Uncle Chao?

OLD CHAO. You go and help Erh-chun inside. Mad Brother, you leave your things with Niang-tse; you'd better be a messenger, going backwards and forwards.

MAD CHENG. Yes, I can do that. Is there enough water here? I have the key to the water tap.

PROPRIETOR. It's all right, we've got plenty.

(MAD CHENG *goes out.*)

NIANG-TSE (*seeing* MOTHER WANG). Oh, why are you sitting here and not going inside, Old Lady?

MOTHER WANG. I won't go in. They are asking for trouble. They *would* go and dig the Ditch. Now they have dug up a mess, haven't they?

NIANG-TSE. You've forgotten; it was like this every time we had heavy rain.

OLD CHAO. Besides, after the Ditch has been remade, we'll never have any more trouble.

ERH-CHUN (*from the door*). Uncle Chao, Niang-tse, don't listen to her. Ma, if you're going to go on being so unreasonable, I'm going to get married straightaway and not look after you anymore!

MOTHER WANG. H'm! If you don't let me have a good look at him first, you needn't think of getting into the bridal chair!

ERH-CHUN. You've had a good look at him already!

MOTHER WANG. Me? Nonsense! When have I seen him?

ERH-CHUN. You've ridden on his back! (*Goes inside again.*)

MOTHER WANG. Was *that* him?

OLD CHAO }
NIANG-TSE } Ha! Ha! Ha!

NIANG-TSE. It's fixed up all right now, this marriage!

MOTHER WANG. I . . . I . . . I can't argue against all of you. I still want to go back home. Even a tumbledown home is worth a fortune. I can't sit around in a tea shop in the middle of the night!

NIANG-TSE. Never mind, Old Lady, this flood was no worse than those we had before, but the government and the police have taken precautions in case any house should collapse and bury people, and so they've brought us here. You'd better go in and have a rest.

ERH-CHUN (*from inside*). Come along! Tea's made. Who'll have some hot tea?

NIANG-TSE. Let's go and have some. (*Pulls* MOTHER WANG *in with her.*)

MAD CHENG (*calling from a distance*). Come this way, all come this way! Uncle Chao, another lot has arrived.

OLD CHAO (*running out*). This way, this way! (*A group of people enter, more men than women.*) Women go inside. Men put down your things, they won't be lost. Let's organize a bit. Let's send more people to help clean out water from houses and dig. We can't let the government people do all the heavy work while we just stand by and watch.

RESIDENT A. They're working so hard; we really ought to go back and help!

OLD CHAO. That's right. With Mr. Liu and me here you needn't worry about missing your people or losing anything. I suggest those over forty should clean out water and those under forty should dig; how's that?

RESIDENT B. That's right!

ALL. Let's go! (*Exeunt.*)

(SZE-SAO *runs in alone.*)

SZE-SAO. Uncle Chao, Uncle Chao, have you seen Ka-tse?

OLD CHAO. No; but he's too big to get lost.

SZE-SAO. That child never gives me a moment's peace of mind!

OLD CHAO. Where's Ting Sze?

SZE-SAO. Gone to dig.

OLD CHAO. Good chap, he's improved!

SZE-SAO. Improved? You wait and see! When he comes home tired, *I* have to suffer! He finds fault so, but he thinks *he's* done great deeds, and I ought to get down on my knees to welcome him back and see him off again!

OLD CHAO. Humor him a little and bear with him. Do as he wants. However you look at it, at least he's working for us all, and he *is* working very hard. It isn't easy for him.

NIANG-TSE (*calling from the door*). Sze-sao, come in and drink some hot tea!

SZE-SAO. Niang-tse, will you keep an eye on my things for

me? I must go and look for Ka-tse. For heaven's sake, he mustn't go after Little Niu . . . (*Exits.*)

(MAD CHENG *runs in.*)

MAD CHENG. Brother Ting is back.

(TING SZE *comes in, very tired, a shovel on his shoulder, his clothes covered with mud.*)

OLD CHAO. You're back, Ting Sze?

TING SZE. I'm dead tired. Why shouldn't I come back?

MAD CHENG. How's the Ditch getting on?

TING SZE (*sitting down*). Nearly dug through.

NIANG-TSE (*handing him tea*). Have a hot drink!

(*She hands tea to others.*)

MOTHER WANG (*coming out*). Ting Sze, what's really happening? Has the water gone down yet? Have any houses collapsed? When can we go back? Have they really moved the things on to the beds?

ERH-CHUN (*coming out*). Oh Ma! You can't talk without asking strings of questions! He's worked half the night. Let him rest now.

MOTHER WANG. I won't say another word. Treat me as if I were dumb. Will that be all right?

TING SZE. Don't squabble. If anyone wants to be kind, give me some water to wash my feet.

ERH-CHUN. I'll go! (*Goes inside.*)

TING SZE (*yawning*). Uncle Chao!

OLD CHAO. Yes, what is it?

TING SZE. Ever since they started remaking the Ditch, I've done my share, like you said. The government have played fair by us and we must play fair by them, isn't that right?

OLD CHAO. That's it! You're able-bodied; when they're rebuilding the Ditch for us, how could a young chap like you not get down to it?

TING SZE. But now, after sweating away the whole day, I have to get soaked at night. Even a plaster dummy goes to pieces in water, and I'm not made of plaster! I can't stand it. I'm going to give it up. I'll go back to my pedicab and leave this stinking place!

ERH-CHUN (*carrying water*). Soak your feet in this!

TING SZE (*putting his feet in basin*). I'm going to give it up!

ERH-CHUN. Give what up?

MAD CHENG. I'll wash your feet, Brother Ting! You're rebuilding the Ditch; you're as good as the government. I'm happy to wash your feet! Uncle Chao often says everyone who works for the community is a hero. *You're* a hero; I'm glad to wait on you, and you know *I'm* not at anyone's beck and call!

NIANG-TSE. Brother Ting, Mad Cheng is often muddle-headed, but this time he's right. Let him wash your feet for you.

TING SZE. Mad Brother, that would never do; I can't let you!

SZE-SAO (*running up*). No, certainly not! Get up, Mad Brother. I'll wash them for him. (*Squats down and washes his feet.*)

TING SZE. Where have you been?

SZE-SAO. I've been looking and looking for Ka-tse, and I still haven't found him!

TING SZE. Yes, if we lost our son too, that'd be a fine thing! I ought to leave this cursed place; nothing good ever happens here!

SZE-SAO. At it again? You're tired and sleepy and cross. After you're washed, I'll find a place for you to sleep. Ka-tse can't be lost; he's a big boy now.

OLD CHAO. Ting Sze, now you're digging the Ditch for us all, isn't everyone doing this? (*Thumbs up.*)

TING SZE. Oh yes? My feet are soaked till they're nearly rotted away; I should think they ought to say a good word for me!

(*A* POLICEMAN *comes in, carrying* KA-TSE, *fast asleep, on his back.*)

SZE-SAO (*turning towards them*). Ka-tse, where have you been?

POLICEMAN. He was so keen, he's been going around with me for hours. Now he can't keep his eyes open anymore, so I've brought him here.

KA-TSE (*opening eyes, gets down*). Ma, I was *so* sleepy!
(SZE-SAO *takes him into the room.*)

POLICEMAN. Mr. Chao, you must be tired, you've been going at it so hard. How's everything here now?

OLD CHAO. Fine! Have some tea; you're dead tired too.

ERH-CHUN. Here you are. (*Hands him tea.*)

POLICEMAN. Thank you. You've been working as hard as anyone! (*To* MOTHER WANG.) Madam, are you being put upon?

MOTHER WANG. Never mind whether I'm being put upon; what's really happening?

POLICEMAN. I'll tell you presently. Mad Brother, Niang-tse, you've had a tough time too!

NIANG-TSE. It's *you* who must be really worn out! Still, my old man hasn't done too badly as the messenger either!

POLICEMAN. You must have had about enough tonight, Ting Sze?

OLD CHAO. H'm! He's in a bad temper, talking about going back to his pedicab and not bothering anymore about our stinking business!

TING SZE. No, no, Uncle Chao, that's past! I'm all right again now. Comrade, you carried Ka-tse back here yourself, and I'll do whatever you tell me to! We're men; it's no use our acting like a lot of old women!

ERH-CHUN. Women! We aren't like you, sensible at one moment and muddleheaded the next!

POLICEMAN. All right, all right! Don't argue! Ting Sze, go and find a place to sleep.

TING SZE. Here's good enough; I'll just have a nap.

ERH-CHUN. Isn't he nice! When he stops being cross, he's more obliging than anyone!

(*Some of the men who went out earlier come in.*)

POLICEMAN. You must be tired, all of you. Is the Ditch through now?

ALL. Yes, it's through!

POLICEMAN. Are there any more people inside?

ERH-CHUN. Yes, the women and children are there.

POLICEMAN. Don't wake the children up. If the grownups want to hear about it, ask them to come out.

ERH-CHUN. I'll go and tell them. (*Runs to the door and calls.*)

POLICEMAN. Neighbors! (*Women, including* SZE-SAO, *follow* ERH-CHUN *out.*) Neighbors, please sit down. We're going to ask Uncle Chao to tell us about what happened last night. Some of you know about it already, but others aren't very clear. Uncle Chao, please tell us.

(*Some people sit down, others remain standing.*)

OLD CHAO. You sit down too. You've been at it half the night as well!

POLICEMAN. I'm all right. I can stand.

OLD CHAO. Neighbors, the plan was to make an underground drain first, and then fill in the old Ditch. You all know about this.

ALL. Yes.

OLD CHAO. When they started to dig out the Ditch, the engineers' department made careful plans to shore up the sides with props and boards, so as to prevent our houses and walls from falling down if the soil got loose underneath;

none of our houses here are very strong. You know about this too.

ALL. Yes.

OLD CHAO. But in spite of all these precautions we had this trouble last night. In the first place, nobody dreamed that such torrential rain would come so early in the season. In the second place, the earth dug out of the old Ditch, which there hadn't been time to move yet, blocked it up just where the new drain joins it. We were all taken by surprise, and some damage was done. The local authority and the police both feel very responsible about this. As soon as they heard the news, the district head and his fellow-workers all rushed here. The head himself carried people and saved things from the flood. The police chief is still cleaning water out from people's houses. Now, if any of you have anything to say, tell us, and we'll pass it on to the district head and police chief.

(*Nobody speaks.*)

POLICEMAN. Speak up; anything you've got to say, compliments or complaints, let's hear it. We're all one family here!

ERH-CHUN. It seems to me . . .

MOTHER WANG. Erh-chun, there are plenty of people here. Why should a girl like you speak first?

ERH-CHUN. All right, if *you've* anything to say, go ahead!

OLD CHAO. Speak up, Old Lady. Nowadays policemen are glad to listen to what we've got to say.

MOTHER WANG. I've nothing to say except this: Next time it rains, don't ask me to come out! It's terrifying to have to come out in the middle of the night.

POLICEMAN. The district head and police chief were afraid that some houses might collapse and kill people, Madam!

RESIDENT A. If they hadn't dug the underground drain, we shouldn't have had all this trouble, should we?

ERH-CHUN. You are talking nonsense!

RESIDENT A. Anyone who likes can talk here, can't they?

ERH-CHUN. Yes, but not nonsense! Without digging the drains how could the Ditch be filled up, and without doing away with the Ditch, however do you think we can get rid of the filth and stink?

NIANG-TSE. Besides . . .

RESIDENT B. Ha! The Women's Army! [1] (*Laughter.*)

---

[1] The expression here translated (literally) as "The Women's Army" could equally well be translated as "The Ladies' Army." It is a double joke: (a) at the expense of the women in general, who are doing all the talking, and (b) at the expense of Niang-tse in particular, who is so full of ideas. It is also a historical allusion, to the Princess of Ping-

NIANG-TSE. What I say is, weren't we flooded out by torrents of rain last year, the year before, every year? People were drowned and buried alive, and who cared? Let's be fair; this time it certainly isn't any worse and yet the district head himself gets soaked from head to foot rescuing us! We ought to thank them!

SZE-SAO. Never mind about anything else, just look at that husband of mine. (*Points to* TING SZE, *fast asleep with his head on the table.*) If it weren't for the Ditch being rebuilt, how could he ever have become a worker, doing something useful for all of us? Just think, when it's all finished, and people have changed for the better too, how wonderful it'll be then!

ERH-CHUN. Well said, Sze-sao!

(*Applause.*)

POLICEMAN. Tell us some more, Uncle Chao.

ALL. Yes, Uncle Chao, go on!

OLD CHAO. All right, I'll say a little more. The government hasn't repaired Wangfuching Street or the West Arch; they're rebuilding our Ditch first. That's something quite unheard-of. And now that this has happened, the government has taken special care of us. In all my sixty years I've never seen anything like it! Besides, when the new drain is finished we'll never have any more trouble, shall we? Kindness deserves kindness. The government cares for us, we must care for them. Isn't that right, neighbors?

ALL. That's right!

MAD CHENG. If there hadn't been this trouble, we shouldn't have realized what a good government we've got!

POLICEMAN. I just want to add this. Nobody was hurt this time; it might have been much worse. We moved as many of your things on to the beds as we could. Now it's stopped raining and it's light. Those who want to go home and see what things are like can go; for those who want to rest we've reserved two small inns on the west side. You can all do as you please.

OLD CHAO. Those who go home and find they can't rest or sleep there can still go to the inns, can't they?

POLICEMAN. That's right. The inns are the Dragon and the Phoenix. Erh-chun, you take the girls and the old ladies to the Dragon and look after them. Uncle Chao, you go with the men comrades to the Phoenix.

---

yang, who led an army known as "The Ladies' Army" and, by defeating the last of her father's opponents, enabled him to become the first emperor of the T'ang Dynasty (A.D. 618–906).

ERH-CHUN. Ma, Niang-tse, Sze-sao, everybody, let's go.

NIANG-TSE. I'll just get my things. (*Enters room followed by a few other women.*)

SZE-SAO (*coming out with* KA-TSE). This gentleman (*pointing to* TING SZE) is still asleep. We'd better not wake him up; let him sleep. (*She puts a jacket over his shoulders.*)

ERH-CHUN. Come on, Ma.

MOTHER WANG. I've never in my life stayed in an inn! I'm not going, I'm going home!

ERH-CHUN. The room's still full of water!

MOTHER WANG. I'd rather be in my own home, even if it's soaking wet!

ERH-CHUN. You're out to make trouble! You really are the limit, Ma!

SZE-SAO. Ka-tse, go with Granny Wang. If it isn't fit to stay there, then take her to the inn. Do you understand? Carry her things for her.

KA-TSE. Granny Wang, if I walk too fast, don't scold me!

MOTHER WANG. When did I ever scold anyone? You little demon!

POLICEMAN. Mother Wang, are you going? Walk slowly; it's very slippery.

MOTHER WANG (*turning back*). I've lived in Dragon Beard Ditch for years; you think I don't know how to walk carefully?

ERH-CHUN (*to the women*). Shall we go now?

ALL. Let's go. (*To* POLICEMAN.) Comrade, give our thanks to the district head and police chief. (*They go out.*)

OLD CHAO (*to the men*). Shall we go too?

RESIDENT A. Let's give a cheer for those who dug the Ditch!

ALL (*including those women who haven't yet gone*). Hurrah! Hurrah!

SCENE 2

Time: *1950, end of summer. The new drain is finished and a road built over it.*

Place: *The same courtyard as in Act. I.*

Setting: *The courtyard is very clean; the broken-down wall has been repaired, and the rubbish has all gone. The flower trellis is covered with pink and purple morning glory. A vase of fresh flowers stands on the water-butt in front of OLD CHAO's door. There is a new water-butt outside the TINGS' window. The whole courtyard is bathed in sunshine.*

Curtain rises: MOTHER WANG *is sitting on the small bench outside her room, sewing a jacket of patterned cloth for* ERH-CHUN. *A sewing basket is on the ground by her.* SZE-SAO *comes out of her room, looking at her own appearance, especially her new shoes and stockings.*

MOTHER WANG (*seeing* SZE-SAO *come out, starts to grumble*). Sze-sao! That wretched creature Erh-chun's gone gadding off somewhere again today! I'm making this new jacket for her, and I can't get hold of her even to try it on!

SZE-SAO. She's busy. You know there's going to be a big meeting today to celebrate the finishing of our new drain; it's like a wedding celebration! She says you and I and Niang-tse must all go. That's why I've put on my new shoes and stockings. Look how well these shoes fit!

MOTHER WANG. I'm not going to any meeting. I can't understand what people say.

SZE-SAO. There's nothing difficult to understand. It's all about building the drain, anyway. Building the drain's a good thing, and we must clap our hands for any good thing, and clapping our hands can't be wrong, can it, Old Lady?

MOTHER WANG. H'm! You're just like Erh-chun, smiling the whole day long just because of the new drain!

SZE-SAO. I've got something to smile about! Everyone used to urge Ting Sze to get a proper job, but he wouldn't listen. When the work on the Ditch started, the Ditch moved him!

MOTHER WANG. When did the stinking Ditch ever speak to *him?*

SZE-SAO. It's a manner of speaking. The Ditch seemed to say, "I stink, what will you do to me? I drowned your child, what will you do to me?" But when the government started to rebuild the Ditch it was Ting Sze who seemed to say, "Yes, you stink, and you drowned my child, and now I'm filling you in, you devil!"

(NIANG-TSE *comes in with her basket.*)

SZE-SAO. Niang-tse, how did you come to finish so early?

NIANG-TSE. Have you forgotten the meeting's today! This is something that doesn't happen once in a hundred years. I'm taking a half-day off to go to it. Ah! You're dressed up already, Sze-sao! I must put on a clean jacket myself. It's like celebrating our Dragon Beard Ditch's birthday. The new drain's finished, and the old Ditch is finished too!

MOTHER WANG. Seeing's believing! The old Ditch is still yawning there, not filled in yet!

NIANG-TSE. But it's going to be filled in! What on earth

should we keep it for? You don't take an active enough interest in local affairs, Old Lady!

MOTHER WANG. What do you mean by "an active interest"? I keep to myself certainly. I don't flatter people, and
I don't go looking for trouble.

SZE-SAO. I know why you're feeling down; it's because
Erh-chun's wanting to get married. You've got this worry on
your mind, so nothing suits you; that's it, isn't it?

MOTHER WANG. It's true, I shouldn't stop you all being
happy just because of my own worries. It's quite right, you
should be happy. Why, even Mad Brother has work to do.
Who would have thought it possible?

NIANG-TSE. Don't mention him. He'll be the death of me!

MOTHER WANG }
SZE-SAO   } Why?

NIANG-TSE. Ever since he got this wonderful job of looking after the water he wakes me up several times every
night. He keeps on asking me, "Niang-tse, hasn't the cock
crowed yet?"

MOTHER WANG. He's really active!

NIANG-TSE. Then a little while later, "Niang-tse, isn't it
light yet?" Looking after the water, he acts as if he were
the Imperial Minister of War, always afraid of holding up
His Majesty's business!

SZE-SAO. Don't grumble, Niang-tse. If it weren't for his
single-mindedness, always doing what he says he'll do, they
wouldn't have chosen him for this job. It seems to me, as
he hasn't the strength to fetch and carry, this job really suits
him!

NIANG-TSE. That's true; whatever we say, at least he's got
a job and nobody calls him useless anymore! I am glad
really, but it would be even better if he wouldn't disturb me
at night!

SZE-SAO. You can't have everything perfect; you're not
doing too badly. It's just the same with that husband of mine.
No one outside calls him "Ting Sze" anymore, they call him
"Mister Ting." Why, he can't stop smiling! And when he
gets back home he's as pleased as a dog with two tails!

NIANG-TSE. I should say so! There's any amount of work
for men in his trade. In our own district alone there's the
big ditch leading to the Yungting Gate, and the one by the
East Market; these will take months to do. The Communist
Party really gets things done! They say, the Palace Lakes,
Back Lake, and Shih Cha Lake, as well as the whole city
moat, are all to be dug out and new stone embankments

built. Then all the roads will be repaired in turn. *He'll* never have to worry about being out of a job! As for Ka-tse, he's going to do even better. When he finishes school he'll start in a factory; if he does well he may end up as a factory manager for all you know!

SZE-SAO. You are in a hurry! But, anyway, we shan't have to wait long for better times. Oh, I haven't sewed that collar on Ka-tse's jacket yet. (*Goes into her room to get her work.*)

MAD CHENG (*outside, singing*).

> Water I'm selling, sweet and bright,
> Drink it and the devils in your belly won't fight;
> Water I'm selling, bright and sweet,
> At a farthing a bucketful, I call it cheap.

NIANG-TSE. Look at that lunatic! Mother Wang, I'm going in now to change my dress. (*Exit.*)

MAD CHENG (*enters, still singing*).

> Fresh and fragrant, the tea you brew,
> Not like it used to be, brown as stew.
> For washing clothes or washing your face,
> It's easy on the soap, and of dirt it leaves no trace!

SZE-SAO (*coming out with her work, sews*). Mad Brother, why are you home and not looking after the water?

MAD CHENG. Mother Wang, Sze-sao, I've come back to practice that *shu-lai-pao*. I'm going to sing it at the big meeting. Ka-tse is looking after the water for me. He can read and write now; he's even more business-like than I am!

SZE-SAO. You're a smart pair, I'll say!

MAD CHENG. Sze-sao, don't look down on us. Whenever we sit down together we discuss problems.

SZE-SAO. Just you two?

MAD CHENG. Listen, just now I said, "Ka-tse, we've got two drains now, the new one in front of our yard and the old Ditch at the back. The new one is underground, its pipes are laid and it's all finished; and on top of it there's a fine level road." And he said, "When the old Ditch is all filled in, there'll be another road." And I said, "Then there'll be two roads, one in front of our houses and one behind. What shall we do when the roads are finished?" He's really clever, Sze-sao. He said, "We must plant trees," and he asked me, "What trees shall we plant?" "Willows," I said, "weeping willows, how beautiful!" And he said, "Pooh!"

SZE-SAO. Really! what a bad boy!

MAD CHENG. He says we must plant peach trees, so we can have big honey-peaches to eat. Isn't he clever!

NIANG-TSE (*inside room*). Don't chatter anymore! Hurry up and make up your rhymes!

MAD CHENG. There's plenty of time. I'm just coming to the most important part. Sze-sao, I've gone into it with Ka-tse. We must have a park here. He proposed that we should change the Goldfish Pond into a park with trees all round it, and a swimming pool and some pavilions as well. It would be wonderful!

NIANG-TSE (*coming out in a new dress*). Don't waste time dreaming!

SZE-SAO. He isn't just dreaming. Who'd have thought we'd have a fine road outside our gate, and proper clean lavatories, and running water? Why shouldn't we have a park here too?

MAD CHENG (*in the Peking Opera recitative style*). Sze-sao's words are weighty indeed! Mother Wang, Sze-sao, Niang-tse, for the present I take my leave! (*Enters his room.*)

SZE-SAO. No wonder children love him! He's like a Granny to them!

NIANG-TSE. Don't praise him; he's like a child, the more he's praised the more unbalanced he gets!

(TING SZE *comes in, very gay, carrying a new blue cotton jacket and trousers under his arm.*)

TING SZE. Mother Wang, Niang-tse, look at my new suit!

(*They surround him;* MOTHER WANG *feels the cloth for its quality;* NIANG-TSE *looks at the length of the trousers;* SZE-SAO *examines the stitching.*)

TING SZE (*seeing his wife's new shoes and stockings*). Ha! You're a stranger below the waist!

SZE-SAO. Don't be so silly! (*Holding up the jacket.*) Put it on and see if the length's right.

TING SZE (*putting it on*). How does it look?

NIANG-TSE. Fine! It's a very good fit.

MOTHER WANG. I'm afraid it will shrink in the wash, though.

TING SZE. You're always an optimist, aren't you!

MOTHER WANG. It isn't that! If you men can all do the shopping, what will there be left for us women to do?

SZE-SAO. Never mind how much it shrinks. Enjoy it today while it's new!

MOTHER WANG. If you don't mind my saying so, that's not the way to manage. *You* should have bought the cloth, and let us all help to make the suit for him; then one suit would have lasted as long as two like this!

TING SZE. But, Mother Wang, there are some things even

you don't know about. The man who sold it to me only asked four-fifty for this suit, and no bargaining either.

NIANG-TSE. Yes, there's no bargaining at all now. Prices are fixed.

TING SZE. I put the suit down and had a chat with him. I bragged a bit. I said, "I'm buying this for the big meeting; I've helped to build the drain and I can't stay away from the opening ceremony, can I?" Then I said, "In that blazing heat, the upper half of my body was grilled and the lower half soaked in black mud, the old Ditch stinking beside me, flies and mosquitoes biting me the whole time, and rank sweat streaming down into my shoes!" Well, before I could finish, what do you think he did? He pushed the suit into my hands and said, "Take it, give me four yuan. If I'm not losing fifty fen on the deal you can bury me in the old Ditch when you fill it up!" Mother Wang, would you ever have thought this kind of thing could happen?

MOTHER WANG. Oh, that's really cheap! I'm going to buy a new dress too!

TING SZE. Have you worked on the drain?

MOTHER WANG. That's right! Me work on the drain! Wouldn't it look nice! I give it up; I can't talk to you people. (*Returns to her sewing.*)

(ERH-CHUN *runs in with a red silk badge inscribed "steward" on her lapel, and her hair done up with a silk ribbon.*)

ERH-CHUN. Ting Sze, why are you still here? Your mates are assembling already!

TING SZE. I must change my trousers first! (*Runs into room.*)

MOTHER WANG. Erh-chun, quick! Come and try your jacket on! (*Holds it for her to try on.*)

ERH-CHUN (*trying it on*). Ma, it's going to be grand today! The Mayor and a comrade from the municipal Party committee are coming! Are you going?

MOTHER WANG. No, I'm not going; I'll stop at home and look after things.

ERH-CHUN. Still the same as ever! There's no need at all for you to stop at home! A policeman will be coming soon to look after all the street. Go and put your new dress on, for the Mayor to see!

NIANG-TSE. Come on, Old Lady! Dragon Beard Ditch doesn't have such a big do every day, you know!

SZE-SAO. Do come! I'll look after you!

MOTHER WANG. All right, I'll go. (*Enters room.*)

SZE-SAO. Put that small red pomegranate flower in your hair!

ERH-CHUN. Niang-tse, Sze-sao, we must be prepared. There'll be people from the newspapers coming to see us soon. They may photograph us. Niang-tse, if they ask you what are your impressions about the reconstruction of the Ditch, what will you say?

NIANG-TSE. What are "impressions"?

MOTHER WANG (*from inside room*). Don't *press* her. The more you press her, the less she'll be able to think what her "impressions" are!

ERH-CHUN. "Impressions"—I suppose it means what you think about it.

TING SZE (*rushing out from his room*). See you at the meeting! (*Runs out, happily singing "The Sky in the Liberated Areas Is Bright."*)

NIANG-TSE. Would it be all right if I said, "When the work on the Ditch was started, even my crazy husband had work to do, and I'm grateful to the government"?

ERH-CHUN. All right! How about you, Sze-sao?

SZE-SAO. If they ask me, I'll say, "If the government goes on like this, Dragon Beard Ditch will soon be one big garden! But there's one thing, when it is a garden, they must still let us go on living here!"

ERH-CHUN. You're quite a speaker, Sze-sao! Don't worry, we lived here when the Ditch stank; we'll go on living here when it smells sweet! . . . Ma! Aren't you ready yet?

MOTHER WANG. Don't hurry me. (*Comes out, pointing to her dress.*) Does it look all right?

ERH-CHUN (*looking her mother up and down*). It's all right! . . . Ma! What will *you* say if they ask you?

MOTHER WANG. I . . .

ERH-CHUN. Go on, what will you say?

MOTHER WANG. Now the new drain is finished, my married daughter can come back here and visit me!

ERH-CHUN. Is that all?

MOTHER WANG. I don't know what to say when I meet strangers. (*Suddenly remembering something.*) Erh-chun, I'm not going to have my photograph taken. Every time we have a photograph taken, we lose a soul!

ERH-CHUN. Ma, you do bring up old tales, don't you!

NIANG-TSE. I'll take your place, I'm not afraid of losing my soul! Let them take my photograph, so that people everywhere will know there's a Cheng Niang-tse in Peking! I've got another idea too. Let's all subscribe a little money to put up a stone, and have the words "There used to be a stinking Ditch here; the people's government made it into a fine road" carved on it.

ERH-CHUN. That's a really good idea; I must tell Uncle Chao. We'll all subscribe to it.

SZE-SAO. Yes, so we can let our children and grandchildren know about it too. I'll contribute!

(*The distant sound of waist drums is heard.*)

ERH-CHUN. The waist drummers are coming! Let's go!

KA-TSE (*rushes in carrying a small red flag*). Commander Uncle Chao is coming! Get into line!

(OLD CHAO *enters, very dignified, in a new suit, with a red silk badge on his breast.*)

ERH-CHUN. Look at Uncle Chao, just like a Commander-in-Chief!

OLD CHAO (*laughing*). You minx!

ERH-CHUN. Uncle Chao, you must be prepared. The press reporters are sure to come to interview you!

OLD CHAO. As if I needed you to tell me! I prepared three days ago!

ERH-CHUN. Well, let me be a reporter then. (*Mimicking.*) What are your impressions about the reconstruction of the Ditch?

OLD CHAO. Briefly or in detail?

ERH-CHUN (*mimicking*). Briefly, please.

OLD CHAO. As the saying goes, the Five Blessings have come to our door.

ERH-CHUN. Which Five Blessings?

OLD CHAO. In front of our gate, there's the underground drain; at the back the old Ditch is going to be filled in; that's the first. Fine roads at front and back, that's the second. The running water is the third. Later, when handicraft industry is established here, everybody will have work and livelihood; that's the fourth. And then, when the Goldfish Pond has been turned into a park where we can relax after the day's work, that'll be the fifth. Five Blessings!

ERH-CHUN
SZE-SAO   (*together with* OLD CHAO). Five Bless-
NIANG-TSE   ings!
MOTHER WANG

(*The neighbors, like those living in the courtyard, have all put on new clothes, and are going past the gate to the meeting. A* POLICEMAN *comes in and greets everyone. Some of the crowd wait outside the gate; others come in. Military music and waist drums sound in the distance.*)

POLICEMAN. Come to the meeting! It's nearly time to start! (MOTHER WANG *turns round to lock her door, but* SZE-SAO *and* NIANG-TSE *hasten to stop her. As they are pulling her towards the gate,* MAD CHENG *runs out of his room, a pair of bamboo castanets in his hand.*)

MAD CHENG. Wait a moment please, all of you! I've made up a new ballad, and I want to try it out on you first!

ALL. Yes, yes! Sing it for us!

MAD CHENG. Listen, then!

To all you people, I joyfully state,
The People's Government is truly great.
Is truly great, for it mended the Ditch,
And took great pains for us though we're not rich.
Think well of this, I beg you all,
East Arch, West Arch, Drum Tower tall,
Five Altars, Eight Temples, old Altar of Grain,
Summer Palace too needed mending again.
All needed repairing, I grant you this,
But why should they first mend Dragon Beard Ditch?
Simply because it was dirty, it stank,
When the Government saw it their very heart sank.
A first-rate Government, loving all poor men,
Help us to stand up proudly again.
They repaired the Ditch, made a road besides,
Help us to stand straight and march with great strides.
To march with great strides, and go laughing on,
All workers must strive with their hearts as one.
Must strive together, and work without cease,
Then our land will be great, the people happy,
And the world at peace!

ALL. Peace for us all!

(*Outside joyful shouts of "Long live Chairman Mao!" The crowd pours out of the gate. A military band strikes up.*)

Slow Curtain

translated by the Foreign Language Press, Peking

THE ESSAY
AND OTHER
EXPOSITORY PROSE

We have noted that the poetic and dramatic genres were the earliest to take conscious literary form. The elements of verse made it enjoyable, impressive, and mnemonic. Drama added the physical representation that brings the literary experience into living reality. For the East as for the West, prose as a species in the evolution of literature came later. This is understandable. The first uses of prose were for simple oral communication in the realm of mundane human affairs. Prose was not considered suitable for petition to or worship of the gods; for this, the beauty of poetry was felt to be most appropriate.

The most recent manifestation, then, in the realm of literature is prose. And the earliest uses of prose were didactic and expository.

Although the prose form distinguished as the essay appears late in the literary history of the West, there are collections of such prose expositions in China dating from as early as the fourth century B.C. Even so, it should be emphasized that in China prose did not challenge poetry's position as highest in literary regard until the twentieth century.

The term "essay," and the idea implicit in that term, did not come into the West until the sixteenth century when Michel Montaigne called his informal reflections *essais,* or first attempts or trials. His style was personal and informal. He was more interested in recording his subjective reactions to ideas and events than he was in teaching or preaching. The form which he introduced so delightfully was to be made formal and didactic by Francis Bacon in the next century. Today, the essay may be considered to embrace virtually all relatively brief explanatory and interpretive prose as distinguished from the imaginative or fictional.

Included in the expository prose here are selections from philosophical thought, autobiographical reflection, nostalgic recollection, literary argument, national asseveration, the highly subjective essay, and the personal diary. All are bound together by their authors' consciousness of recording thought with a sense of literary structure and form but in an essentially nonfictional manner. Some studiously avoid imaginative embellishments, while others delight in them. Taken together they give us a sense of the cross-cultural range of the essay and also offer especially attractive vantage points for seeing cultures "from the inside out."

Essays of India
and Ceylon

Swami Vivekānanda (1863–1902) was given the name of
Narendranāth Datta when born into a family of the Kāyastha
(writers) caste in Calcutta. Until he met the great religious
leader Sri Rāmakrishna, his intention had been to follow in
the family pattern and study in England for the law. Instead,
at the Rāmakrishna Mission on the banks of the Hooghly
River on the outskirts of Calcutta, he entered into a dozen
years of rigorous religious discipline. He emerged from the
ascetic experience as the persuasive voice of his mystical and
visionary religious teacher, his guru.

To have even an elementary understanding of Vivekānanda and his writing, one must know something of his
master. From early childhood Rāmakrishna had been subject to religious seizures, moments of spiritual ecstasy in
which he would feel his oneness with God. The son of a village priest serving the goddess Kali, Rāmakrishna had more
opportunity for spiritual development than for formal education. He was self-tutored, however, in the beliefs and forms
of India's other sects. It is said that he worshiped God in accordance with Buddhist, Jain, and Muslim custom, as well as
in his own Hindu manner. He was acquainted, also, to some
extent, with Judeo-Christian doctrines. Although Rāmakrishna voiced chiefly the distinctively Hindu concept of
a Divine Mother, of whom Kali was a major manifestation, he drew also on the God-insights offered by Christ, Buddha, Muhammad, and others. One is constantly aware of this
eclectic atmosphere as one walks about the Rāmakrishna
Mission on the Hooghly branch of the sacred Ganga or when

one attends meetings in any of the centers scattered from Colombo to London, Paris, and New York.

But it is Swami Vivekānanda who must be given chief credit for this world outreach. His natural talent and his good education continued to make him the vocal medium for the uneducated, though religiously inspired, Rāmakrishna. The Swami's missionary career began in Chicago in 1893 with a talk before the First World Parliament of Religions and continued through four years of lecturing in America and England. The final years of his brief life were spent at the Rāmakrishna Mission, where he worked hard to develop a center for social service as well as for religious experience.

Vivekānanda's concern for the future of his countrymen, as they were brought more and more under the influence of the West, burns in his writing, notably in "Modern India," the essay included here. The admonition to guard against blind acceptance of other culture values could come from no more authoritative a source than this devoted religious scholar, who was so fully aware of the advantages and disadvantages in the ways of life both of his native India and of the West.

Santha Rama Rau (1923–   ), contemporary writer in English, has spent more of her life abroad than in her native land. Years in England and America have been interspersed with brief periods at home. This gives her the peculiar ability to experience Indian life with the adventurous excitement of a newcomer, yet with an awareness and appreciation of the nuances of ancestral culture.

Santha, or Vasanthi Rama Rau Bowers as she is known in private life, was born to a wealthy family in the southern Tamil city of Madras. At the age of six she accompanied the family to London where the father represented his country in a series of conferences on India's future. There was a brief return home four years later and then further years in England until Santha was sixteen. During this second period the father was serving in London as Deputy High Commissioner for India. From that international eminence, the family was well aware of the growing threat of Nazism on the Continent. The home served as a haven of refuge for escapees from Dachau and other concentration camps. However, before World War II began, Rama Rau was sent as High Commissioner to South Africa (he was later to serve as his nation's first High Commissioner to Japan). The mother and daughters, after several months touring throughout Africa, returned to India.

Later, Santha spent four years at Wellesley College except

for vacations given to working in Washington in the Office of War Information. It was during this period that her first book was written and that she determined to be a writer. The year the war ended she returned to Bombay and began her search for a "job" on a magazine, much to her grandmother's horror —women just don't do such work!

"On Learning To Be an Indian" is a perceptive autobiographical vignette from *Home to India,* which records the return from abroad and some two years of travel throughout India as the mother guides her Europeanized daughters in an often traumatic experience of reacquaintance with their heritage. The excerpt stands as a finely expressed informal essay that offers a sharp contrast to that by Swami Vivekānanda.

J. Vijayatunga (1902–1950) was born near Galle, Ceylon, and was educated in universities in Ceylon and India. From the time of his first visit at the age of sixteen he considered India his second home, and later he transferred his citizenship to that country. In 1928 he accepted the invitation of Rabindranath Tagore to teach English in his forward-looking international school, Santiniketan, near Calcutta. A year later he set out on an extensive lecture tour that took him from India to England and the United States.

Vijayatunga was a poet, as well as a prose writer. His published works include six books of prose and two volumes of verse. *Grass for My Feet,* from which our essay is taken, presents informal pictures of life in the isolated southern village in which the author spent his early years. The view is light and entertaining, yet marked by keen insight and a wealth of intimate detail. The accounts range from fishing and jungle excursions, through village festivals, to scandal and tragedy, concluding with the family's leaving the village for the port town of Galle, where the first contact with Western culture will be experienced.

Although written in the early 1930's while Ceylon still lived under the rule of the British Raj, Vijayatunga's picture of a small Sinhalese village remains essentially true for today in those isolated areas into which Occidental influence has not penetrated. The author writes in English and his style is light, intimate, and impeccable.

SWAMI VIVEKĀNANDA

MODERN INDIA

It has been said before that India is slowly awakening through her friction with the outside nations, and, as the result of this little awakening is the appearance, to a certain extent, of free and independent thought in modern India. On one side is modern Western science, dazzling the eyes with the brilliance of myriad suns, and driving in the chariot of hard and fast facts collected by the application of tangible powers direct in their incision; on the other are the hopeful and strengthening traditions of her ancient forefathers, in the days when she was at the zenith of her glory—traditions that have been brought out of the pages of her history by the great sages of her own land and outside, that run for numberless years and centuries through her every vein with the quickening of life drawn from universal love, traditions that reveal unsurpassed valor, superhuman genius, and supreme spirituality, which are the envy of the gods—these inspire her with future hopes. On one side, rank materialism, plenitude of fortune, accumulation of gigantic power, and intense sense-pursuits, have through foreign literature caused a tremendous stir; on the other, through the confounding din of all these discordant sounds, she hears, in low yet unmistakable accents, the heartrending cries of her ancient gods, cutting her to the quick. There lie before her various strange luxuries introduced from the West—celestial drinks, costly well-served food, splendid apparel, magnificent palaces, new modes of conveyance—new manners, new fashions, dressed in which moves about the well-educated girl in shameless freedom; all these are arousing unfelt desires in her; again, the scene changes and in its place appear, with stern presence, Sita, Savitri,[1] austere religious vows, fastings, the forest retreat, the matted locks and orange garb of the semi-naked

[1] Sita and Savitri are famed as paragons of Hindu womanhood. Sita —wife of Rama, whose abduction by the Demon Ravana brings the central action of the epic *Ramayana;* an incarnation of the god Vishnu's wife Lakshmi. Savitri—famed in Indian legend for having saved her doomed husband from Yama, the God of Death; an episode in the *Mahabharata.*

Sannyasin,[1] Samadhi,[2] and the search after the Self. On one side, is the independence of Western societies based on self-interest; on the other, is the extreme self-sacrifice of the Aryan society. In this violent conflict, is it strange that Indian society should be tossed up and down? Of the West, the goal is—individual independence, the language—money-making education, the means—politics; of India, the goal is—*Mukti*,[3] the language—the Veda,[4] the means—renunciation. For a time, modern India thinks, as it were: I am running this worldly life of mine in vain expectation of uncertain spiritual welfare hereafter, which has spread its fascination over me; and again, lo! spellbound she listens: "Here, in this world of death and change, O man, where is thy happiness?"

On one side, New India is saying: "We should have full freedom in the selection of husband and wife; because, the marriage in which are involved the happiness and misery of all our future life, we must have the right to determine, according to our own free will." On the other, Old India is dictating: "Marriage is not for sense enjoyment, but to perpetuate the race. This is the Indian conception of marriage. By the producing of children, you are contributing to, and are responsible for, the future good or evil of the society. Hence, society has the right to dictate whom you shall marry and whom you shall not. That form of marriage obtains in society, which is conducive most to its well-being; do you give up your desire of individual pleasure for the good of the many."

On one side New India is saying: "If we only adopt Western ideas, Western language, Western food, Western dress, and Western manners, we shall be as strong and powerful as the Western nations"; on the other, Old India is saying: "Fools! By imitation, other's ideas never become one's own —nothing, unless earned, is your own. Does the ass in the lion's skin become the lion?"

On one side, New India is saying: "What the Western nations do are surely good, otherwise how did they become so great?" On the other side, Old India is saying: "The flash of lightning is intensely bright, but only for a moment; look out, boys, it is dazzling your eyes. Beware!"

---

[1] One who has renounced the world.

[2] The *yogi*'s realization of oneness with the Brahman, Creative Force of the universe.

[3] *Mukti*, or *moksha*—liberation from the bondage of existence; spiritual union with the Brahman.

[4] Religious doctrine and knowledge.

Have we not then to learn anything from the West? Must we not needs try and exert ourselves for better things? Are we perfect? Is our society entirely spotless, without any flaw? There are many things to learn, we must struggle for new and higher things till we die—struggle is the end of human life. Sri Rāmakrishna used to say: "As long as I live, so long I learn." That man or that society which has nothing to learn is already in the jaws of death. Yes, learn we must many things from the West, but there are fears as well.

A certain young man of little understanding used always to blame Hindu Shastras [1] before Sri Rāmakrishna. One day he praised the *Bhagavad Gita,* on which Sri Rāmakrishna said: "Methinks some European pandit [2] has praised the *Gita,* and so he has also followed suit."

O India, this is your terrible danger. The spell of imitating the West is getting such a strong hold upon you, that what is good or what is bad is no longer decided by reason, judgment, discrimination, or reference to the Shastras. Whatever ideas, whatever manners the white men praise or like, are good; whatever things they dislike or censure are bad! Alas! What can be a more tangible proof of foolishness than this?

The Western ladies move freely everywhere—therefore, that is good; they choose for themselves their husbands—therefore, that is the highest step of advancement; the Westerners disapprove of our dress, decorations, food, and ways of living—therefore, they must be very bad; the Westerners condemn image-worship as sinful—surely then, image-worship is the greatest sin, there is no doubt of it!

The Westerners say that worshiping a single Deity is fruitful of the highest spiritual good—therefore, let us throw our Gods and Goddesses into the river Ganges! The Westerners hold caste distinctions to be obnoxious—therefore, let all the different castes be jumbled into one! The Westerners say that child-marriage is the root of all evils—therefore, that is also very bad, of a certainty it is!

We are not discussing here whether these customs deserve countenance or rejection; but if the mere disapproval of the Westerners be the measure of the abominableness of our manners and customs, then it is our duty to raise our emphatic protest against it.

The present writer has, to some extent, personal experi-

---

[1] Esoteric sacred texts, once considered open only to Brahmins, the caste of religious teachers; contain many restrictive marriage laws.

[2] Scholar; learned man.

ence of Western society. His conviction resulting from such experience has been that there is such a wide divergence between the Western society and the Indian as regards the primal course and goal of each, that any sect in India, framed after the Western model, will miss the aim. We have not the least sympathy with those who, never having lived in Western society and, therefore, utterly ignorant of the rules and prohibitions regarding the association of men and women that obtain there, and which act as safeguards to preserve the purity of the Western women, allow a free rein to the unrestricted intermingling of men and women in our society.

I observed in the West also, that the children of weaker nations, if born in England, give themselves out as Englishmen, instead of Greek, Portuguese, Spaniard, etc., as the case may be. All drift towards the strong, that the light of glory which shines in the glorious may anyhow fall and reflect on one's own body; *i.e.*, to shine in the borrowed light of the great is the one desire of the weak. When I see Indians dressed in European apparel and costumes, the thought comes to my mind—perhaps they feel ashamed to own their nationality and kinship with the ignorant, poor, illiterate, downtrodden people of India! Nourished by the blood of the Hindu for the last fourteen centuries, the Parsee [1] is no longer a "Native"! Before the arrogance of the casteless, who pretend to be and glorify themselves in being Brahmans, the true nobility of the old, heroic, high-class Brahman melts into nothingness! Again, the Westerners have now taught us that those stupid, ignorant, low-caste millions of India clad only in loincloths are non-Aryans! They are therefore no more our kith and kin!

Oh India! With this mere echoing of others, with this base imitation of others, with this dependence on others, this slavish weakness, this vile detestable cruelty, wouldst thou, with these provisions only, scale the highest pinnacle of civilization and greatness? Wouldst thou attain, by means of thy disgraceful cowardice, that freedom deserved only by the brave and the heroic? Oh India! Forget not that the ideal of thy womanhood is Sita, Savitri, Damayanti; [2] forget not that the God thou worshipest is the great Ascetic of ascetics, the all-

---

[1] Parsees, or Parsis—Zoroastrians; descendants of seventh- and eighth-century refugees from Persia (Iran) who fled Muslim persecution.

[2] Damayanti, celebrated in Indian legend for her devotion to her husband Nala.

renouncing Shankara, the Lord of Uma;[10] forget not that thy marriage, thy wealth, thy life are not for sense-pleasure, are not for thy individual personal happiness; forget not that thou art born as a sacrifice to the *Mother's* altar; forget not that thy social order is but the reflex of the Infinite Universal Motherhood; forget not that the lower classes, the ignorant, the poor, the illiterate, the cobbler, the sweeper, are thy flesh and blood, thy brothers. Thou brave one, be bold, take courage, be proud that thou art an Indian, and proudly proclaim: "I am an Indian, every Indian is my brother." Say: "The ignorant Indian, the poor and destitute Indian, the Brahman Indian, the Pariah Indian, is my brother." Thou too clad with but a rag round thy loins proudly proclaim at the top of thy voice: "The Indian is my brother, the Indian is my life, India's gods and goddesses are my God, India's society is the cradle of my infancy, the pleasure-garden of my youth, the sacred heaven, the *Vārānasi*,[11] of my old age." Say, brother: "The soil of India is my highest heaven, the good of India is my good," and repeat and pray day and night: "O Thou Lord of Gauri,[12] O Thou Mother of the Universe, vouchsafe manliness unto me! O Thou Mother of Strength, take away my weakness, take away my unmanliness, and— *Make me a Man!*"

SANTHA RAMA RAU

ON LEARNING TO BE AN INDIAN

My grandmother cannot speak English. I have never discovered whether this is from principle or simply because she has never tried, but she understands it perfectly. In England Mother had kept Premila and me familiar with Hindustani by speaking it to us sometimes when we were home for vacations, and by teaching us Indian songs. So during our first few weeks in Bombay we could both understand the language though we were still too out of practice to try speaking it. Consequently my grandmother and I spoke different languages to each other. But we got along very easily in spite of it.

10 A name of the wife of Shiva or Shankara (the Gracious One).
11 Banaras.
12 A name for the wife of Shiva.

I found after a few days that in her own indirect way she was trying to instill in me something of the traditional Hindu girl's attitude to the household, the rest of the family, and living in general. The servants were the first problem that came up. Whenever the telephone rang, one of the servants would run to answer it. They were unanimously terrified of the instrument and would hold the receiver well away from the ear and scream "Allo?"

Naturally unless the caller and the name of the person who was being called were both very familiar to the servant, nothing was understood or accomplished. After watching this procedure for some time, I began to sprint for the telephone, too, whenever it rang. As long as I won it was all right, but occasionally I would reach it at the same time as the houseboy. The first time this happened he grasped the receiver and ignored my outstretched hand. I asked him please to let me answer the phone in future if I were in the house—this in very polite if halting Hindustani. I used the formal form of "you" as I would have to any stranger.

Afterwards my grandmother called me into her room. In her own mysterious way she had overheard the conversation and wanted now to warn me against treating the servants in such a way again.

"They are not your equals, so do not treat them as such. It is not enough for the servants to be frightened of you; that fear must be founded on respect. This pandering to them is some unreasonable sentimentality you have picked up in the West. It embarrasses them as much as it irritates me. . . ."

She went on to explain that one could retain a feeling of equality (tinged all the same with condescension) for the cook, because he, after all, had to be a Brahmin—one of our own caste—as he handled the food. By all means we should give the servants medicines if they were sick, see that their children were well treated, visit their quarters and make sure that their rooms were kept clean, even give their children an education—which they would never get if it were left to their families—but we should always keep our social distance.

Then there was the matter of prayers in the mornings. My grandmother was always up by five o'clock and said her prayers, decorated the images in her shrine, and sang the hymns of the day at that time. She would light a little ceremonial fire, throw spices and something that smelled like incense on it; when the fire died she rubbed her fingers in the ash and smeared it on her forehead. This provided the white part of her caste mark for the rest of the day. The other women of

the house were expected to join her, though there was no expressed compulsion. After a few days of this I decided that if
I expected to be able to stay awake after nine at night I must
stop keeping these hours.

One afternoon I told my grandmother that the prayers
were meaningless to me except as a curiosity, that I could
make no sense of the hymns, which were sung in Sanskrit
(I'm pretty certain they were incomprehensible to her also),
and that I felt I was too old to be converted to Hinduism
now.

She assured me briskly that even if I wanted to, I could
not be reconverted to Hinduism, and that no such expectation had prompted her to suggest that I come to prayers with
her. I had been born a Hindu, but since I had crossed water,
eaten beef, neglected to wear my caste mark, and committed
innumerable other offenses, I had lost my right to both my
religion and my caste.

"But don't assume from that that you may marry anyone
outside the Brahmin caste!" The real reason, it turned out,
for this religious indoctrination had been to show me something of the values by which Indians live.

"Do you realize that you know nothing of a factor which
is vital to the lives of most of your countrymen? Do you always want to see India through the eyes of a visitor? The real
Indians are the villagers, the peasants. Poverty and the work
on the land is so much a part of their daily living that they
must have a tremendous, inclusive faith to make such living
possible. If you want to understand these people, you must
also understand something of Hinduism. It is the most rigid
of beliefs, the most realistic of philosophies, and it determines
for them everything from their food to their morals.

"We have been called pacifists," she continued, showing
for the only time that I can remember a consciousness of the
existence of contemporary politics, "but it is not ignorance
that makes us so. We could be the most highly educated
country in the world. We have all the prerequisites for intelli-
gent 'political consciousness'—*if that were an end.* But I, for
one, can only hope that the religion and philosophy of our
people will secure them against civilization, and what you call
'progress.' Bless you, my child, progress is a convenient term
for describing our journey from the great age of India."

If I had at the time been less scared of my grandmother, I
would have argued with her about her attitude toward conditions in India, which I thought hopelessly reactionary. Concepts which had always seemed to me self-evident she ig-

nored or nullified with her strange, kindly, patronizing attitude toward "those Indians less fortunate than ourselves." Equality of opportunity? Absurd!

"But I can see that you do not even know what I am talking about. Because we let politics pass us by, because we have evolved no way of writing down our music, because we do not preserve in a concrete form our art and our stories, the West considers that we have lost our culture. But it is in the oral traditions of the villages that the arts of India are really alive. The brief Western immortality of museums is pointless to people who have seen eternity in their earth. In comparison with this the people of the West are short-sighted, are they not?"

"I suppose so."

"And we are long-sighted—which is not the same as being far-sighted," she added.

I was growing impatient because I had invited a friend to tea, it was dangerously near tea time, and I had yet to change.

"Is it all right," I asked my grandmother casually, "if I have a friend to tea?" It was a very informal meal and Asha frequently had girls from her school to it, so I didn't think there would be any objections.

"Perfectly all right, my child, if she is a suitable friend."

"Well, it's a he. I should think he's suitable. He traveled over from South Africa with us. Mother liked him."

I have never seen anyone look as shocked as my grandmother did then.

"The more I see of you girls the more amazed I am at your mother for the extraordinary education she has given you, and above all for allowing such outrageous behavior from any girl in our family!"

"I don't think this concerns her at all," I said, surprised. "Because, she could scarcely have kept us in a vacuum during all those years in England—particularly when she was away so much of the time!"

"That is exactly what I told her. You should never have been taken to England. You should have been left here in our care."

"But we wanted—"

"Don't argue with me, my dear child. I will discuss this with your mother."

I turned to leave the room. "Well, shall I call him up and tell him not to come?"

"Of course you cannot do that. If you have invited him already, we are obliged to extend hospitality to him. But while I am the head of this house it will not happen again."

Upstairs I asked Mother what to do. I told her that my grandmother had not yet heard the whole story. I had promised John that I would have dinner with him. Mother looked at me despairingly. "Was it for this that I learned to be a diplomat's wife?"

"I don't see that I've done anything so awful."

"I suppose it never occurred to you that your grandmother never receives Englishmen in her house?"

"Why *would* it occur to me?" I asked.

"For obvious reasons. The situation being what it is in India, in her own inimitable way your grandmother makes a personal—or rather a social—issue of it."

"I thought she was supposed to be so detached from politics."

Then Mother began to think that the whole situation was funny. "But the really appalling thing is your dinner engagement with him! If you go out alone with him, and the family knows about it, you're as good as married to him."

"You mean I'm not supposed to be alone with any man until I decide I want to marry him?"

"I'm afraid that's right, as long as we stay in your grandmother's house."

"But *Mother*, doesn't that seem to you a little absurd?"

"Darling, I was never alone with your father until I was married to him."

"But *Mother*—"

"I know, I know, times are changing, *everybody* does it, but I'm sorry, dear, you'll have to break the dinner appointment."

"But *Mother*—"

"Let's not discuss it further, shall we?"

When John came we had tea in icy solitude on the front veranda. His first remark was, "You look pale. Do you feel all right?"

"I feel fine. I'm not allowed to wear make-up around here." I had had a brief argument with Mother about that, too.

"Never thought it would make so much difference."

"My grandmother doesn't approve of it."

"Damn right. Now you won't get lipstick all over the cups and the napkins."

As Mother came out to join us the curtains to the living

room swung behind her, and I saw that the family was gathered there. I don't know how anything immoral could have gone on with the gardeners as an audience and on an open veranda, but I suppose they just wanted to make sure. I was thankful that John was facing out toward the garden.

He asked Mother where the family, of whom he had heard so much, were.

"Oh, they went out."

"*All* of them?"

"Of course," Mother said, as if it were the most natural thing.

"Oh."

"They went to the tennis tournament." When Mother says something in that carefully explanatory way, as if it were absurd that anyone shouldn't know, nobody can say, "What tournament?"

I took John out into the garden to tell him I couldn't dine with him that evening. I thought it would be best to tell him the whole story. I don't think he had the least idea what it all meant, for he just looked very hunted and said, "But you *don't* want to marry me, do you?"

This incident, when I looked back on it, brought into sharp contrast for me the astonishing changes that have taken place within fifty years in the ordinary girl's life in India. My grandmother was married when she was nine years old. When I heard that, I was profoundly shocked. Child marriage in books was one thing, but such a barbarous thing in my own family was quite another. Apparently I too had been influenced by the sensational inaccuracies that have been put out about India in books like Katherine Mayo's *Mother India.*

When my grandmother says that she was married when she was nine, she means that a betrothal ceremony was performed between her and my grandfather. Perhaps "betrothal" indicates too weak a link, for she could not then have married any other man—even if my grandfather were to have died before the actual wedding ceremony. Her "husband's" family would have been obliged to clothe her and shelter her just as they would the widow of one of their sons. As soon as the betrothal was completed she went to live in her mother-in-law's home. She stayed there until her mother-in-law died and she, as the oldest woman in the house, became the head of the family.

Between the time when she first came to live at the house

and the time that the real marriage ceremony took place, about seven years later, she was carefully chaperoned by some member of her "husband's" family on all occasions when she had to appear socially or in the presence of any men. This, Mother assures me, is the traditional method, at least in our caste. She took her place at once in the daily life of the home. A Hindu girl's duties in her mother-in-law's home are specific and exacting. Their purpose is to train the girl to be, as nearly as possible, the perfect wife and mother.

It is practically a tradition among Hindu women that their mother-in-law is always a monster of efficiency and demands equal competence from them. She insists that the young bride must give no order to a servant which she cannot perfectly carry out herself. Consequently the bride must learn to cook, sew, clean, bring up children (and there are always several in the house on whom she can practice), run the family life, advise those younger than herself, keep the accounts of the household, and keep a careful check on the finances of each individual member of the family. I'm sure every Hindu wife of that generation can tell stories about having had to cook meals for twenty-five people single-handed, or of having had to rip out a seam fifteen times because it was not sewn finely enough.

In those days, half a century ago, the joint-family system still dominated the social life of Hindus. My grandmother's mother-in-law, for instance, presided over her family, with her husband as a sort of consort. All their sons lived in the house with them, and as the boys married brought their wives to live in the family home. The daughters lived there until they were married and then they, like my grandmother, went to live in the homes of their mothers-in-law. The children of the sons were educated in the house by tutors until they were old enough to go abroad to college. My grandmother learned to read and write along with her nieces and nephews after she was married, but that was the limit of her education. Besides these close members of the family, various cousins, and great-uncles left over from another generation, lived in the same house. It was a joint family of the most conservative type.

Originally this social unit had grown out of the fact that India was almost entirely an agricultural country, and wealth was measured only in land. The sons of any land-owning family, therefore, were compelled to live together for economic reasons, and because the laws for property division were so sketchy. As the system took root and grew, somehow the women seem to have taken charge. Their province—and this is true to a wide extent even today—was the home and there they were dictators. The wife of the oldest man in the house held and dispensed all the money in the household. Anything that any member earned was given to her and she drew from each according to his capacity and gave to each according to his need. So although she had no legal rights, she could, if she wanted, have absolute control over the members of her own family.

By the time my grandmother, as the wife of the oldest son, came to be head of the household, the system was already breaking down. Our family moved from the south, which is our home, to Bombay. My grandmother found that her sons showed a regrettable tendency to wander off to what she considered the less civilized parts of the world. One of them, Shivan, even married a Viennese girl, beautiful—but a foreigner. Grandmother found that she had no control either over whom her sons married or over the education of her grandchildren. But to look at her and the way in which she lived you would never suspect that the conditions which made her standards valid were vanishing from India.

One of the minor forms which my grandmother's continued autocracy took was the examination of the mail received by anybody living in the house. Asha told me that she used to censor, and sometimes entirely remove, letters from people of whom she did not approve. She did not know the people who wrote to me, and still had not gathered in her own way their respective life histories, so she would just question me closely about all my mail. From whom were the letters? Any of them from men? Where had I met them? Did my mother know their families? If the questions were not satisfactorily answered, she would say, "In my opinion you should not reply to that letter," or, "Surely a brief note will be sufficient answer."

To me even Mother's education—which seemed to her so progressive and enlightened—appeared incredibly narrow. Certainly she was not married at an appallingly early age—although her sisters were; she was given, on her own insistence and on the arguments of one of her brothers who was at an English university, a formal education at school and college. She had wanted to be a doctor and after endless arguments with her mother she was allowed to go to medical school in Madras. But unfortunately her mother heard that she was the only girl in her class and that every morning she would find notes on her desk from the men students—some expressing their view of women who broke the fine conventions of Indian womanhood by leaving their homes and entering a world of men, and some exclaiming poetically, "If I were Dante, you would be my Beatrice. . . ." She was taken out of the school immediately and continued, instead, more ladylike work in English literature in a women's college.

All the same, Mother defied two of the most rigid social conventions of the time before she was twenty-five. She earned a living by lecturing in English literature in a Madras college; and at twenty-five she was the first Kashmiri girl to marry outside her community. When we went back to Kashmir—more than twenty years after Mother's marriage—I met women who still would not receive Mother, and could scarcely be civil to her if they met her at somebody else's house, because of the shocking way in which she had broken their social rules when she was a girl. For at that time in India there was a prejudice not only against inter-caste marriages but against inter-community ones too. If your family or your ancestors came from Kashmir, your husband should come from there too.

Because Mother had to fight against the old standards, and because she was brought up to believe in them, she has an emotional understanding of them which my sister and I will never have. Brought up in Europe and educated in preparatory and public schools in England, we felt that the conventions were not only retrogressive and socially crippling to the country, but also a little ridiculous. We thought at the time that one needed the perspective of travel to see these things. But we were only flattering ourselves, for later we found many young Indians who had lived at home all their lives and had a far clearer picture of India's social problems and, moreover, were doing a great deal more toward solving them than we ever thought of doing.

J. VIJAYATUNGA

VILLAGE GOES TO TOWN

From time immemorial peasant and nomad have had their fairs and bazaars, where they come to barter and exchange, buy and sell. These fairs and bazaars are still, happily, a feature of the Oriental scene. In the mind of the villager the town is a bazaar, only with a more permanent group of shops. He accepts the town as a matter of course, but its effect on him is no greater than the effect of the fortnight's holiday (in August) on the modern city-dweller.

Our village has one or two stores, one run by an uncle of mine, the Headman, another, which is part Pharmacy and part Grocery, run by the eldest son of the village millionaire who died some time ago. Neither the topography of the village nor the temperament of the village folk has hitherto encouraged the development of a cluster of shops. But a mile away where the road from our village to Galle town is intercepted by the Baddegama-Udugama Road (along which you reach the Wanduramba Temple) is a regular hive of shops. Bicycles made in Birmingham lean against the shop verandas; pedal Singer Sewing Machines of American make are being industriously and rather spectacularly worked. Piles of Java Sarongs, Cheviot Tweeds, cheek by jowl with dried Maldive fish, Swadeshi salted fish, Japanese enameled washbasins, German aluminum pails; all these draw a constantly changing, vociferous, gesticulating throng of buyers and someday-would-be buyers. Outside on the road are groups of men— the local Headmen, smelling of toddy and arrack, looking important, their naked rotund bellies proudly exposed, the Sarong being tied quite low on the waist: around these Headmen, the ubiquitous henchmen and satellites, smelling only of toddy, arrack being costlier, but with a proper meekness in the very smell; and a solitary policeman from either the Police Station at Nagoda or Baddegama, in his blackish-blue uniform and pill-box cap, very self-conscious, trying to look both as if he were His Majesty's Government and His Majesty's Governed. There are other groups—of the local Beau Brummels, slender, lithe men dressed in Sarongs and half-sleeved Cameesa comparing notes about their latest fancies, or maybe planning for a cattle-lifting, or a night's debauch— of mild-looking men, advertising by their chastened demeanour and lusterless eyes, that wife and child and the accustomed hearth await them and that adventure and illicit pleasure are no longer for them—there are loud-voiced Tamils from the nearby tea plantations, and Tamil women, nonchalantly walking hither and thither, calling to each other across the street in their loud sing-song voices. This is the nearest we have to a Town.

It is hardly more than a rendezvous, and at best a place to buy luxuries. To sell—your coco-nuts, your areca-nuts, and your grain—you must go to Galle town. Galle, derived from *Gala* which means a resting place for cart bullocks, has always been the mart for the southern province. But nowadays Galle is not only a big mart of shops, it is also the place where the big people and the white people live, where the English schools are, where the hotels are, where the jail is, where the "Lunatic Asylum," simply designated so by Authority, is.

The village goes to Town to buy, to sell, to take the train for a pilgrimage, and above all to litigate. Both at Nagoda and at Baddegama there are Gansabhavas (Village Tribunals) presided over by an official magistrate. But the village folk never seem to enjoy attendance at the Gansabhava with half the zest with which they attend the Courts at Galle. Whatever the reasons that take my people to Galle, they never fail to buy. The town visitor not only buys for himself but also for the stay-at-home.

The double bullock cart belonging to my Headman uncle makes about two journeys a month to Galle in addition to journeys when it is specially hired to take a load of rubber. His carter is a squat, swarthy, muscular man from Wandurambha village. The cart starts about ten o'clock at night. All that evening the carter receives instructions from dozens of people. One housewife wants so much worth of *Jadee,* or salted fish; another wants one of those clay cooking pans made in Matara, a seaside town south of Galle; a fastidious man repeats over and over the special weave of Sarong he wants; more than one want hanks of Jaffna tobacco; there are different requests from different houses for as many different kinds of sea-fish; my mother usually asks him to buy some Murunga, a long, lean pithy vegetable called "Drum-sticks" by white people, and some *Beli.* All the orders are given orally and noted mentally. Rarely is anything forgotten by the carter.

More frequent and more popular than these cart journeys are the journeys of the villagers on foot. The distance to Galle is twelve miles, but by using certain shortcuts this can be reduced to about ten. The usual method is to form a party. These parties start at early dawn before cockcrow. Generally they are mixed parties. He whose house is farthest wakes up earliest, and collects the rest of the party at the appointed houses on the way. People of those villages still farther from Galle than ours start soon after midnight, so that by the time our village folk are afoot there are other parties on the way. Sometimes there are greetings between friends and acquaintances in the different groups, but generally each group walks by itself separated only by a bend of the road or

by a distance not greater than a quarter of a mile. From midnight till dawn on the road to Galle is a most exhilarating
experience. The air is as fresh as can be. The sun is, of
course, anticipated, and there is an earnest of it ever so
slightly though it is still night, but night which is half past.
Nothing, neither houses, nor hayricks, nor brick kilns, nor
cattle in their sheds, nor fowls, nor people, nothing is quite
awake yet except the travelers. And yet nothing is quite
asleep either.

Sometimes we leave the high road whose dew-sprayed dust
is sweetly soft to the feet and take a shortcut across the fields.
These paths across fields are narrow ridges so that everyone
must walk in single file, and what is more, one must remember to keep strictly to the middle of the ridge. Halfway across
the ridge you find a stream gurgling through its sluice with
half wakefulness. We plunge into the stream, raising our Sarongs above our knees and wade through with unhastened
steps, enjoying the feel of the water as it swirls around our
legs.

Presently the shortcut leaves the fields and goes through a
steep jungle. Here are numerous small rocks, right in the
middle of the path, but the path has been trodden so close to
the rocks that they seem friendly. Even in the half light you
can see that each rock is aware of your going past. When you
know them rocks can be very lively and friendly. A rock is
really an eye of Nature. A rock being limbless is all eye.
Once you help that eye to open it keeps open ever after. But
only you who helped it by your friendliness know this.

We emerge from the jungle footpath into the high road
once more, but on either side of the road are strange tall
trees, sentinel-wise, their identity lost in a shimmer of darkness and light. It is curious but it is true that, walking along
that forest-edged road in the early dawn, each traveler falls
into a silence, as it were in response to a command or the
suggestion of an affinity. After the chatter that kept us company crossing the field this sudden silence is almost a phenomenon as distinct as the vibrating silence of the forest.

Each of us seems to forget the fuss and preparations of the
journey, its purpose and errands. Those items, one, two,
three, four, that are to constitute our purchases have receded
into a limbo of their own. We walk on, the Village going to
Town, walking through an ancient forest, that was there
when our ancestors first plunged through it going out to
make for themselves a new village. Gradually the shadows
broaden out, leaving a narrowing perspective in the distance

we have already left behind. Somewhere ahead of us a cock crows.

Full daylight descends on us now, making us see each other as well as our surroundings with prosaic eyes. Our feet hasten their steps, the crowds on the road increase, our interest in our fellowmen decreases, carts flash by, more houses meet our eyes than we care for; there is a bend ahead, we turn it and come upon a row of Moorish tinkers' shops, their fronts overladen with all kinds of tin utensils. Here another road cuts into ours, a little farther on the railway line crosses it, and within the next half-hour we are right in the bosom of the town, at the "Gala," or stopping-place for all the carts that come from all the villages to the town. Here we meet the carter of my Headman uncle's cart, and the members of the party simulate a certain liveliness. Soon they separate, some to go to the Courts, some to hire professional "Petition" writers, others to sell their areca-nuts and coco-nuts.

Somehow the day passes quickly enough, it is nearing sunset when we meet each other again at the "Gala," but it seems only a few hours since we parted. Our faces are flushed, perspiring, and dirty, but we look really happy now that the day's business is over and we have met together safe and sound. Carrying our various parcels, we turn our feet Village-wards, and within half an hour we have forgotten the Town and are once again a convivial gang of villagers, each thinking, despite the subject of conversation, of the dinner that awaits him within the bosom of his family.

Essays of China

The essay form has had a long and honorable place in Chinese literary history. In fact, the *Lü-Shih Ch'un Ch'iu* (*The Spring and Autumn of the House of Lü*), compiled in 240 B.C., is composed of 160 skillful, creative pieces that may be regarded as essays.

In the eleventh century A.D., in the examination of applicants for civil-service positions, scholarly expository discussions of the Confucian classics replaced the earlier poetry exercises. In 1487 the Eight-Legged Essay was defined as the uncompromising form to be used for examination purposes. Each "leg," or section, had a set function and place from which the writer was not to deviate.

Although the Eight-Legged Essay was never highly regarded in the history of literature, its influence does not seem to have been confined to government circles. In the essay the use of a formal "literary" language, the regard for a well-defined structure, and the restriction to certain subjects for discussion (such as comments on the *Analects of Confucius* or panegyrics to the throne) may be by-products of the Eight-Legged form. And there was always the tendency to seek models of expression from earlier times; essayists' eyes turned to classical prose as the eyes of the poets had turned to classical verse.

However, abandonment of classical literary language for the vernacular has been attributed to Hu Shih, who, while he was still a student in the United States (1916–17), thus introduced a revolution in Chinese poetry. A tentative groping toward change had begun early in the nineteenth century, following the First Sino-Japanese War. From that time on, Western influences increased and imitation of the old ways gradually decreased. The first generally recognized break did not come, however, until 1905 when literary composition was finally dropped from the examination system. This departure from a tradition that had held for two thousand years or more opened the way for dignifying the vernacular to literary levels.

Hu Shih (1891–1962) gave voice to the new sound in Chinese literature in an essay, "A Preliminary Discussion of Literary Reform," that first appeared in 1917. The published expression consolidated thoughts Hu had expressed in several public addresses given earlier. Hu did more than preach reform. His poetry from that time, as well as his essays on the subject, demonstrated one of his major theses by using the vernacular as his medium.

Hu Shih's stature—as statesman, scholar, author, and critic —at home and abroad, helped promote his plea for complete literary regeneration, and the revolution that was to free Chinese writers from conformity to an ancient tradition was finally effected. The excerpts included here from *Constructive Literary Revolution: A Literature of National Speech—A National Speech of Literary Quality* summarize Hu's major theses.

Mao Tse-tung (1893–   ) is the chief voice of a later revolutionary movement in the literary life of China—that fostered by the Communist ideology. In a way, however, we may consider his pronouncements as, in certain respects, retrogressive. In the first place, where Hu Shih had sought to cut restrictive bonds, Mao sets up new prerequisites as constraining as the old. Writers must again confine themselves to certain themes expressed from the orthodox point of view.

Secondly, Mao himself apparently is bound by classical learning and is unable to cut himself loose from it. As we have seen, he prefers to write his verse in the traditional *shih* and *t'zu* forms. Even as he warns against the classics and the masters, he turns minds backward by referring to them, or he uses early folk stories to give point to his party propaganda. For instance, in 1957, the famous call for "a hundred flowers" to bloom—a unique, and quickly aborted, experiment in freedom of expression—refers back to an early story of a T'ang Dynasty (A.D. 618–906) empress who ordered a hundred flowers to bloom in her garden during the winter season. If listeners had taken to heart all the implications of impending disaster in this story—both for the unseasonal blooms and the tragic empress—the response to the call might have been more cautious than it was. Another interesting insight into Mao's acquaintance with China's traditions is his use of the Eight-Legged Essay form in one of his attacks on stereotyped writing. Using what he called "poison as an antidote to poison," Mao presented eight major indictments against reverting to stereotyped writing, which, he warns, "poisons the whole party and jeopardizes the revolution."

The selections given here present in substance Mao's theory of artistic expression as the tool of the state.

HU SHIH

A CHINESE LITERATURE OF NATIONAL SPEECH

The literary revolution we are promoting aims merely at the creation of a Chinese literature of national speech. Only when there is such a literature can there be a national speech of literary quality. And only when there is a national speech of literary quality can our national speech be considered a real national speech. A national speech without literary quality will be devoid of life and value and can be neither established nor developed. This is the main point of this essay.

I have carefully gone into the reasons why in the past two thousand years China has had no truly valuable and living classical-style literature. My own answer is that what writers in this period have written is dead stuff, written in a dead language. A dead language can never produce a living literature. . . .

Why is it that a dead language cannot produce a living literature? It is because of the nature of literature. The function of language and literature lies in expressing ideas and showing feelings. When these are well done, we have literature. Those who use a dead classical style will translate their own ideas into allusions of several thousand years ago and convert their own feelings into literary expressions of centuries past. . . . If China wants to have a living literature, we must use the plain speech that is the natural speech, and we must devote ourselves to a literature of national speech. . . .

Someone says: "If we want to use the national speech in literature, we must first have a national speech. At present we do not have a standard national speech. How can we have a literature of national speech?" I will say, this sounds plausible but is really not true. A national language is not to be created by a few linguistic experts or a few texts and dictionaries of national speech. To create a national speech, we must first create a literature of national speech. Once we have a literature of national speech, we shall automatically have a national speech. This sounds absurd at first but my readers will understand if they think carefully. Who in the world will be willing to learn a national speech from texts and dictionaries? While these are important, they are definitely not the effective means of creating a national speech. The truly effective and powerful text of national speech is the literature of national speech—novels, prose, poems, and plays written in the national speech. The time when these works prevail is the day when the Chinese national speech will have been established. Let us ask why we are now able simply to pick up the brush and write essays in the plain speech style and use several hundred colloquial terms. Did we learn this from some textbook of plain speech? Was it not that we learned from such novels as the *Shui-hu chuan, Hsi yu chi, Hung-lou meng,* and *Ju-lin wai-shi (Unofficial History of Officialdom)*? This type of plain speech literature is several hundred times as powerful as textbooks and dictionaries. . . . If we want to establish anew a standard national speech, we must first of all produce numerous works like these novels in the national speech style. . . .

A literature of national speech and a national speech of literary quality are our basic programs. Let us now discuss what should be done to carry them out.

I believe that the procedure in creating a new literature consists of three steps: (1) acquiring tools, (2) developing methods, and (3) creating. The first two are preparatory. The third is the real step to create a new literature.

1. *The tools.* Our tool is plain speech. Those of us who wish to create a literature of national speech should prepare this indispensable tool right away. There are two ways to do so:

(a) Read extensively literary works written in the plain speech that can serve as models, such as the works mentioned above, the *Recorded Conversations* of the Sung Neo-Confucianists and their letters written in the plain speech, the plays of the Yüan period, and the stories and monologues of the Ming and Ch'ing times. T'ang and Sung poems and *t'zu* written in the plain speech should also be selected to read.

(b) In all forms of literature, write in the plain speech style. . . . Not only those of us who promote the literature of plain speech should do this. I also advise those opposing this literature to do the same. Why? Because if they are not capable of writing in the plain speech style, it means that they are not qualified to oppose this type of literature. . . . I therefore advise them to do a little more writing in this style, write a few more songs and poems in the plain speech, and try to see whether the plain speech has any literary value. If, after trying for several years, they still feel that the plain speech style is not so good as the classical style, it will not be too late for them to attack us. . . .

2. *Methods.* I believe that the greatest defect of the literary men who have recently emerged in our country is the lack of a good literary method. . . . The "new novel" of today is completely devoid of a literary method. Writers do not have the technique of plot, construction, or description of people and things. They merely write many long and repulsive pieces which are qualified only to fill the space of the second section of a newspaper, but not qualified to have a place in a new literature. . . .

Generally speaking, literary methods are of three kinds:

(a) The method of collecting material. . . .

(b) The method of construction. . . .

(c) The method of description. . . .

3. *Creation.* . . . Only when we have mastered the tools and know the methods can we create a new Chinese literature. As to what constitutes the creation of a new literature, I had better not say a word. In my opinion we in China today have not reached the point where we can take concrete steps to create a new literature, and there is no need of talking theoretically about the techniques of creation. Let us first devote our efforts to the first two steps . . .

MAO TSE-TUNG

LITERATURE FOR THE MASSES

In the past, some comrades, to a certain or even a serious extent, belittled and neglected popularization and laid undue stress on raising standards. Stress should be laid on raising standards, but to do so one-sidedly and exclusively, to do so excessively, is a mistake. The lack of a clear solution to the problem of "for whom?" . . . also manifests itself in this connection. As these comrades are not clear on the problem of "for whom?", they have no correct criteria for the "raising of standards" and the "popularization" they speak of, and are naturally still less able to find the correct relationship between the two. Since our literature and art are basically for the workers, peasants, and soldiers, "popularization" means to popularize among the workers, peasants, and soldiers, and "raising standards" means to advance from their present level. What should we popularize among them? Popularize what is needed and can be readily accepted by the feudal landlord class? Popularize what is needed and can be readily accepted by the bourgeoisie? Popularize what is needed and can be readily accepted by the petit-bourgeois intellectuals? No, none of these will do. We must popularize only what is needed and can be readily accepted by the workers, peasants, and soldiers themselves. Consequently, prior to the task of educating the workers, peasants, and soldiers, there is the task of learning from them. This is even more true of raising standards. There must be a basis from which to raise. Take a bucket of water, for instance; where is it to be raised from if not from the ground? From midair? From what basis, then, are literature and art to be raised? From the basis of the feudal classes? From the basis of the bourgeoisie? From the basis of the petit-bourgeois intellectuals? No, not from any of these; only from the basis of the masses of workers, peasants, and soldiers. Nor does this mean raising the workers, peasants, and soldiers to the "heights" of the feudal classes, the bourgeoisie or the petit-bourgeois intellectuals; it means raising the level of literature and art in the direction in which the workers, peasants, and soldiers are themselves advancing, in the direction in which the proletariat is advancing. Here again the task of learning from the workers, peasants, and soldiers comes in. Only by starting from the workers, peasants, and soldiers can we have a correct understanding of popularization and of the raising of standards and find the proper relationship between the two.

In the last analysis, what is the source of all literature and art? Works of literature and art, as ideological forms, are products of the reflection in the human brain of the life of a given society. Revolutionary literature and art are the products of the reflection of the life of the people in the brains of revolutionary writers and artists. The life of the people is always a mine of the raw materials for literature and art, materials in their natural form, materials that are crude, but most vital, rich, and fundamental; they make all literature and art seem pallid by comparison; they provide literature and art with an inexhaustible source, their only source. They are the only source, for there can be no other. Some may ask, is there not another source in books, in the literature and art of ancient times and of foreign countries? In fact, the literary and artistic works of the past are not a source but a stream; they were created by our predecessors and the foreigners out of the literary and artistic raw materials they found in the life of the people of their time and place. We must take over all the fine things in our literary and artistic heritage, critically assimilate whatever is beneficial, and use them as examples when we create works out of the literary and artistic raw materials in the life of the people of our own time and place. It makes a difference whether or not we have such examples, the difference between crudeness and refinement, between roughness and polish, between a low and a high level, and between slower and faster work. Therefore, we must on no account reject the legacies of the ancients and the foreigners or refuse to learn from them, even though they are the works of the feudal or bourgeois classes. But taking over legacies and using them as examples must never replace our own creative work; nothing can do that. Uncritical transplantation or copying from the ancients and the foreigners is the most sterile and harmful dogmatism in literature and art. China's revolutionary writers and artists, writers and artists of prom-ise, must go among the masses; they must for a long period of time unreservedly and wholeheartedly go among the masses of workers, peasants, and soldiers, go into the heat of the struggle, go to the only source, the broadest and richest source, in order to observe, experience, study, and analyze all the different kinds of people, all the classes, all the masses, all the vivid patterns of life and struggle, all the raw materials of literature and art. Only then can they proceed to creative work. Otherwise, you will have nothing to work with and you will be nothing but a phony writer or artist, the kind that Lu Hsun [1] in his will so earnestly cautioned his son never to be-come.

Although man's social life is the only source of literature and art and is incomparably livelier and richer in content, the people are not satisfied with life alone and demand literature and art as well. Why? Because, while both are beautiful, life as reflected in works of literature and art can and ought to be on a higher plane, more intense, more concentrated, more

[1] Best-known pseudonym for Chou Yü-ts'ai (1881–1936), writer of fiction and essays; active in attempts to modernize China, culturally and politically.

typical, nearer the ideal, and therefore more universal than actual everyday life. Revolutionary literature and art should create a variety of characters out of real life and help the masses to propel history forward. For example, there is suffering from hunger, cold, and oppression on the one hand, and exploitation and oppression of man by man on the other. These facts exist everywhere and people look upon them as commonplace. Writers and artists concentrate such everyday phenomena, typify the contradictions and struggles within them, and produce works which awaken the masses, fire them with enthusiasm, and impel them to unite and struggle to transform their environment. Without such literature and art, this task could not be fulfilled, or at least not so effectively and speedily.

What is meant by popularizing and by raising standards in works of literature and art? What is the relationship between these two tasks? Popular works are simpler and plainer, and therefore more readily accepted by the broad masses of the people today. Works of a higher quality, being more polished, are more difficult to produce and in general do not circulate so easily and quickly among the masses at present. The problem facing the workers, peasants, and soldiers is this: they are now engaged in a bitter and bloody struggle with the enemy but are illiterate and uneducated as a result of long years of rule by the feudal and bourgeois classes, and therefore they are eagerly demanding enlightenment, education, and works of literature and art which meet their urgent needs and which are easy to absorb, in order to heighten their enthusiasm in struggle and confidence in victory, strengthen their unity, and fight the enemy with one heart and one mind. For them the prime need is not "more flowers on the brocade" but "fuel in snowy weather." In present conditions, therefore, popularization is the more pressing task. It is wrong to belittle or neglect popularization.

Nevertheless, no hard and fast line can be drawn between popularization and the raising of standards. Not only is it possible to popularize some works of higher quality even now, but the cultural level of the broad masses is steadily rising. If popularization remains at the same level forever, with the same stuff being supplied month after month and year after year, always the same "Little Cowherd" [1] and the same

---

[1] Reference to question-and-answer dialogue between the two characters of a popular Chinese folk opera.

"man, hand, mouth, knife, cow, goat," [3] will not the educators and those being educated be six of one and half a dozen of the other? What would be the sense of such popularization? The people demand popularization and, following that, higher standards; they demand higher standards month by month and year by year. Here popularization means popularizing for the people and raising of standards means raising the level for the people. And such raising is not from midair, or behind closed doors, but is actually based on popularization. It is determined by and at the same time guides popularization. In China as a whole the development of the revolution and of revolutionary culture is uneven and their spread is gradual. While in one place there is popularization and then raising of standards on the basis of popularization, in other places popularization has not even begun. Hence good experience in popularization leading to higher standards in one locality can be applied in other localities and serve to guide popularization and the raising of standards there, saving many twists and turns along the road. Internationally, the good experience of foreign countries, and especially Soviet experience, can also serve to guide us. With us, therefore, the raising of standards is based on popularization, while popularization is guided by the raising of standards. Precisely for this reason, so far from being an obstacle to the raising of standards, the work of popularization we are speaking of supplies the basis for the work of raising standards which we are now doing on a limited scale, and prepares the necessary conditions for us to raise standards in the future on a much broader scale.

Besides such raising of standards as meets the needs of the masses directly, there is the kind which meets their needs indirectly, that is, the kind which is needed by the cadres. The cadres are the advanced elements of the masses and generally have received more education; literature and art of a higher level are entirely necessary for them. To ignore this would be a mistake. Whatever is done for the cadres is also entirely for the masses, because it is only through the cadres that we can educate and guide the masses. If we go against this aim, if what we give the cadres cannot help them educate and guide the masses, our work of raising standards will be like shooting at random and will depart from the fundamental principle of serving the masses of the people.

To sum up: through the creative labor of revolutionary

[3] Simple character forms used in the child's first writing lessons.

writers and artists, the raw materials found in the life of the people are shaped into the ideological form of literature and art serving the masses of the people. Included here are the more advanced literature and art as developed on the basis of elementary literature and art and as required by those sections of the masses whose level has been raised, or, more immediately, by the cadres among the masses. Also included here are elementary literature and art which, conversely, are guided by more advanced literature and art and are needed primarily by the overwhelming majority of the masses at present. Whether more advanced or elementary, all our literature and art are for the masses of the people, and in the first place for the workers, peasants, and soldiers; they are created for the workers, peasants, and soldiers and are for their use.

translated by the Foreign Language Press, Peking

Essays of Japan

In Japan as in China, the essay form has had an enduring and distinguished history. Among the most delightful early manifestations are the *Makura-no Sōshi,* or *Pillow-Book,* by Sei Shōnogon, and the *Hōjōki,* or *Life in a Ten-Foot-Square Hut,* by Kamo no Chōmei. The former records irreverent reflections on life at the Imperial Court during the tenth century, made by a member of the circle that included the famous Lady Murasaki, author of the world's first known novel, *The Tale of Genji.* The *Hōjōki* consists of the meditations of a twelfth-century Thoreau, a Buddhist monk who withdrew from the world to live in a tiny hut in which he read, meditated, and wrote. G. L. Anderson calls the *Hōjōki* "one of the masterpieces in a great tradition of fugitive essays *(zuhitsu)* in Japanese literature."

Both are collections of essays in the diary or journal style, a genre that for centuries has been a favorite with the Japanese people. Sometimes the journal is recorded in a series of letters to a relative or friend. Among the most famous of recently published works in this form is *Looking at Life and Death,* the letters of a college student and a young girl facing death from cancer, which sold a million and a half copies.

Motoori Norinaga (1730–1801) led a literary revolt against the hold that for generations Chinese culture and Confucianist thought had had over the Japanese intelligentsia. He found in indigenous Shintoism and in the early legends and genealogical records of the *Kojiki (Record of Old Things),* the oldest chronicles of Japan, elements with which to develop pride in native origins and achievements.

Motoori is given credit for having drawn attention to Lady

Murasaki's *Tale of Genji* as a work of significant literary stature, rather than as a vehicle of either Buddhist or Confucianist preachment. In essays defining the underlying significance
of the novel, he resurrected from earlier literary criticism the
term *mono no aware*. This sense of the individual's awareness
of life's sadness and its evanescent beauty is now recognized
as being peculiarly Japanese, and the term has reentered the
country's literary lexicon.

One of the chief leaders in a national revival of Shinto,
Motoori spent thirty years attempting to establish the eighth-
century *Kojiki* as a basic scripture on which a sense of na-
tional pride, unity, and destiny might be based. From his
Tama kushige (*Precious Comb-box*) we take his essay, "The
True Tradition of the Sun Goddess."

Hirata Atsutane (1776–1834) carried to the extremes of
chauvinism Motoori's interest in Japan's indigenous culture.
Where Motoori loved and respected the products of his country's early civilization, Hirata worshiped them and refused to
acknowledge the contributions made by other cultures. In his
zeal for the native Shinto he ridiculed Buddhism and Confu-
cianism. Although he himself studied Western scientific
thought and Christian beliefs and even adapted them to his
own uses, he held them up to scorn. He seriously advanced
the theory that Japan's easternmost position was ordained of
the gods as a mark of special favor; since the sun rose first
on this nation, it was therefore first in the esteem of both the
gods and men.

From the groundwork in scholarship laid by Motoori and
others in their National Learning movement, Hirata developed a philosophy of national superiority that won a tremendous popular following, the effects of which were to be felt
fully more than a century later. "The Land of the Gods," from
Kodō Taii, shows the extremes to which Hirata's jingoism
carried him.

Lafcadio Hearn (1850–1904) may seem out of place in a
sampling of Japanese writings, and yet among the most
charming and most revealing essays on Japan are those by
this "adopted son." Many Japanese hail them as such and
also give Hearn credit for having ferreted out and got into
print scores of early folk stories that might otherwise have
been lost to modern readers.

Born in Scotland to an Anglo-Irish father and a Greek
mother, Hearn was destined to be a citizen of the world with
eclectic interests. In his youth he was sent to America by an
aunt and—as did so many eighteenth- and nineteenth-century

American authors—he got his first writing experience in the newspaper office. His early books included collections of folk stories of many lands. It was perhaps as a result of his interest in the folklore of China that Hearn also turned his attention to Japan.

When Hearn arrived in Japan in 1890, it was "love at first sight." Soon he was married to a Japanese woman, adopted from her family name the new name for himself, Koizumi Yakumo, and became a naturalized citizen. Although he could not read Japanese, Hearn was a patient listener and a keen observer. The retold folk stories and the sympathetic original essays that flowed from his pen imbued countless Western readers with a high regard for Japanese life and culture and contributed significantly to a "Japan fad" in interior decoration, home furnishings, art, and literature.

A trend that distressed Hearn was the rapid Westernization of the Old Japan he loved. An amusing reflection of this concern is found in his brief witty essay "Mosquitoes." Also, almost without being aware of it, the reader is introduced to a way of looking at life and death that is distinctive of Buddhistic thought and Japanese culture.

Hino Ashihei (1907–   ) served as a newspaper correspondent during the Sino-Japanese war of the 1930's. As a newsman he made no critical judgments concerning the ethics of Japan's position; he merely reported events and their human consequences to the best of his ability, which was considerable.

An excerpt from Hino's *Earth and Soldiers* is included here, for it is a brilliant example of contemporary expression in Japan's ever-popular journal form. Donald Keene refers to Hino's war diaries as "the most famous literary products of the 'China Incidents.'"

MOTOORI NORINAGA

THE TRUE TRADITION OF THE SUN GODDESS

The True Way [1] is one and the same, in every country and throughout heaven and earth. This Way, however, has

1 Carries a *double entendre:* "The Way of the Gods" of ancient indigenous Shinto; "The Way of Life" defined by both Confucius and Lao-tzu and later taken as an intrinsic part of Zen.

been correctly transmitted only in our Imperial Land. Its transmission in all foreign countries was lost long ago in early antiquity, and many and varied ways have been expounded, each country representing its own way as the Right Way. But the ways of foreign countries are no more the original Right Way than end-branches of a tree are the same as its root. They may have resemblances here and there to the Right Way, but because the original truth has been corrupted with the passage of time, they can scarcely be likened to the original Right Way. Let me state briefly what that one original Way is. One must understand, first of all, the universal principle of the world. The principle is that Heaven and earth, all the gods and all phenomena, were brought into existence by the creative spirits of two deities—Takami-musubi and Kami-musubi. The birth of all humankind in all ages and the existence of all things and all matter have been the result of that creative spirit. It was the original creativity of these two august deities which caused the deities Izanagi and Izanami to create the land, all kinds of phenomena, and numerous gods and goddesses at the beginning of the Divine Age. This spirit of creativity [*musubi*, lit., "union"] is a miraculously divine act the reason for which is beyond the comprehension of the human intellect.

But in the foreign countries where the Right Way has not been transmitted this act of divine creativity is not known. Men there have tried to explain the principle of Heaven and earth and all phenomena by such theories as the *yin* and *yang*,[1] the hexagrams of the Book of Changes,[2] and the Five Elements.[3] But all of these are fallacious theories stemming from the assumptions of the human intellect and they in no wise represent the true principle.

Izanagi, in deep sorrow at the passing of his goddess, journeyed after her to the land of death. Upon his return to the upper world he bathed himself at Ahagiwara in Tachibana Bay in Tsukushi in order to purify himself of the pollution

[1] The two necessary primal forces of creation and life: *yin*, female, evil, submissive, water, earth; *yang*, male, good, assertive, dominant, fire, Heaven.

[2] *I Ching* of early (*ca.* third century B.C.) China in which symbols are used for divination and to explain human events and physical phenomena; carried over later into Zen thought.

[3] The five components of the universe, according to Buddhism: form and matter, sensation, perceptions, psychic dispositions, and consciousness. Also, Buddhism defined the five personal elements of the individuality and the five "vital breaths."

of the land of death, and while thus cleansing himself, he gave birth to the Heaven-Shining Goddess who by the explicit command of her father-God, came to rule the Heavenly Plain for all time to come. This Heaven-Shining Goddess is none other than the sun in heaven which today casts its gracious light over the world. Then, an Imperial Prince of the Heaven-Shining Goddess was sent down from heaven to the middle kingdom of Ashihara. In the Goddess's mandate to the Prince at that time it was stated that his dynasty should be coeval with Heaven and earth. It is this mandate which is the very origin and basis of the Way. Thus, all the principles of the world and the way of humankind are represented in the different stages of the Divine Age. Those who seek to know the Right Way must therefore pay careful attention to the stages of the Divine Age and learn the truths of existence. These aspects of the various stages are embodied in the ancient traditions of the Divine Age. No one knows with whom these ancient traditions began, but they were handed down orally from the very earliest times and they refer to the accounts which have since been recorded in the *Kojiki* and the *Nihongi*. The accounts recorded in these two scriptures are clear and explicit and present no cause for doubt. Those who have interpreted these scriptures in a later age have contrived oracular formulae and have expounded theories which have no real basis. Some have become addicts of foreign doctrines and have no faith in the wonders of the Divine Age. Unable to understand that the truths of the world are contained in the evolution of the Divine Age, they fail to ascertain the true meaning of our ancient tradition. As they base their judgment on the strength of foreign beliefs, they always interpret at their own discretion and twist to their own liking anything they encounter which may not be in accord with their alien teachings. Thus, they say that the High Heavenly Plain refers to the Imperial Capital and not to Heaven, and that the Sun Goddess herself was not a goddess nor the sun shining in the heavens but an earthly person and the forebear of the nation. These are arbitrary interpretations purposely contrived to flatter foreign ideologies. In this way the ancient tradition is made to appear narrow and petty, by depriving it of its comprehensive and primal character. This is counter to the meaning of the scriptures.

Heaven and earth are one; there is no barrier between them. The High Heavenly Plain is the high heavenly plain which covers all the countries of the world, and the Sun Goddess is the goddess who reigns in that heaven. Thus, she is without a peer in the whole universe, casting her light to the very ends of heaven and earth and for all time. There is not a single country in the world which does not receive her beneficent illuminations, and no country can exist even for a day or an hour bereft of her grace. This goddess is the splendor of all splendors. However, foreign countries, having lost the ancient tradition of the Divine Age, do not know the meaning of revering this goddess. Only through the speculations of the human intelligence have they come to call the sun and the moon the spirit of *yang* and *yin*. In China and other countries the "Heavenly Emperor" is worshiped as the supreme divinity. In other countries there are other objects of reverence, each according to its own way, but their teachings are based, some on the logic of inference, and some on arbitrary personal opinions. At any rate, they are merely man-made designations and the "Heavenly Ruler" or the "Heavenly Way" have no real existence at all. That foreign countries revere such nonexistent beings and remain unaware of the grace of the Sun Goddess is a matter of profound regret. However, because of the special dispensation of our Imperial Land, the ancient tradition of the Divine Age has been correctly and clearly transmitted in our country, telling us of the genesis of the great goddess and the reason for her adoration. The "special dispensation of our Imperial Land" means that ours is the native land of the Heaven-Shining Goddess who casts her light over all countries in the four seas.[5] Thus our country is the source and fountainhead of all other countries, and in all matters it excels all the others. It would be impossible to list all the products in which our country excels, but foremost among them is rice, which sustains the life of man, for whom there is no product more important. Our country's rice has no peer in foreign countries, from which fact it may be seen why our other products are also superior. Those who were born in this country have long been accustomed to our rice and take it for granted, unaware of its excellence. They can enjoy such excellent rice morning and night to their heart's content because they have been fortunate enough to be born in this country. This is a matter for which they should give thanks to our shining deities, but to my great dismay they seem to be unmindful of it.

Our country's Imperial Line, which casts its light over this

---

[5] Actually, reference is to the entire known world. A phrase from the familiar Chinese maxim, "Within the four seas all men are brothers."

world, represents the descendants of the Sky-Shining Goddess. And in accordance with that Goddess's mandate of reigning "forever and ever, coeval with Heaven and earth," the Imperial Line is destined to rule the nation for eons until the end of time and as long as the universe exists. That is the very basis of our Way. That our history has not deviated from the instructions of the divine mandate bears testimony to the infallibility of our ancient tradition. It can also be seen why foreign countries cannot match ours and what is meant by the special dispensation of our country. Foreign countries expound their own ways, each as if its way alone were true. But their dynastic lines, basic to their existence, do not continue; they change frequently and are quite corrupt. Thus one can surmise that in everything they say there are falsehoods and that there is no basis in fact for them.

translated by Ryusaku Tsunoda, William Theodore de Bary, and Donald Keene

HIRATA ATSUTANE

THE LAND OF THE GODS

People all over the world refer to Japan as the Land of the Gods, and call us the descendants of the gods. Indeed, it is exactly as they say: our country, as a special mark of favor from the heavenly gods, was begotten by them, and there is thus so immense a difference between Japan and all the other countries of the world as to defy comparison. Ours is a splendid and blessed country, the Land of the Gods beyond any doubt, and we, down to the most humble man and woman, are the descendants of the gods. Nevertheless, there are unhappily many people who do not understand why Japan is the land of the gods and we their descendants. . . . Is this not a lamentable state of affairs? Japanese differ completely from and are superior to the peoples of China, India, Russia, Holland, Siam, Cambodia, and all other countries of the world, and for us to have called our country the Land of the Gods was not mere vainglory. It was the gods who formed all the lands of the world at the Creation, and these gods were without exception born in Japan. Japan is thus the homeland of the gods, and that is why we call it the Land of the Gods. This is a matter of universal belief, and is quite beyond dispute. Even in countries where our ancient traditions have not been transmitted, the peoples recognize Japan as a divine land because of the majestic effulgence that of itself emanates from our country. In olden days when Korea was divided into three kingdoms, reports were heard there of how splendid, miraculous, and blessed a land Japan is, and because Japan lies to the east of Korea, they said in awe and reverence, "To the East is a divine land, called the Land of the Rising Sun." Word of this eventually spread all over the world, and now people everywhere refer to Japan as the Land of the Gods, irrespective of whether or not they know why this is true. . . .

translated by Ryusaku Tsunoda, William Theodore de Bary, and Donald Keene

LAFCADIO HEARN

MOSQUITOES

With a view to self-protection I have been reading Dr. Howard's book, *Mosquitoes*. I am persecuted by mosquitoes. There are several species in my neighborhood; but only one of them is a serious torment,—a tiny needly thing, all silver-speckled and silver-streaked. The puncture of it is sharp as an electric burn; and the mere hum of it has a lancinating quality of tone which foretells the quality of the pain about to come,—much in the same way that a particular smell suggests a particular taste. I find that this mosquito much resembles the creature which Dr. Howard calls *Stegomyia fasciata,* or *Culex fasciatus:* and that its habits are the same as those of the *Stegomyia.* For example, it is diurnal rather than nocturnal, and becomes most troublesome during the afternoon. And I have discovered that it comes from the Buddhist cemetery,—a very old cemetery,—in the rear of my garden.

Dr. Howard's book declares that, in order to rid a neighborhood of mosquitoes, it is only necessary to pour a little petroleum, or kerosene-oil, into the stagnant water where they breed. Once a week the oil should be used, "at the rate of one ounce for every fifteen square feet of water-surface, and a proportionate quantity for any less surface." . . . But please to consider the conditions of *my* neighborhood.

I have said that my tormentors come from the Buddhist cemetery. Before nearly every tomb in that old cemetery there is a water-receptacle, or cistern, called *mizutame*. In the majority of cases this *mizutame* is simply an oblong cavity chiseled in the broad pedestal supporting the monument; but before tombs of a costly kind, having no pedestal-tank, a larger separate tank is placed, cut out of a single block of stone, and decorated with a family crest, or with symbolic carvings. In front of a tomb of the humblest class, having no *mizutame*, water is placed in cups or other vessels,—for the dead must have water. Flowers must also be offered to them; and before every tomb you will find a pair of bamboo cups, or other flower-vessels; and these, of course, contain water. There is a well in the cemetery to supply water for the graves. Whenever the tombs are visited by relatives and friends of the dead, fresh water is poured into the tanks and cups. But as an old cemetery of this kind contains thousands of *mizutame*, and tens of thousands of flower-vessels, the water in all of these cannot be renewed every day. It becomes stagnant and populous. The deeper tanks seldom get dry; the rainfall at Tokyo being heavy enough to keep them partly filled during nine months of the twelve.

Well, it is in these tanks and flower-vessels that mine enemies are born: they rise by millions from the water of the dead;—and, according to the Buddhist doctrine, some of them may be reincarnations of those very dead, condemned by the error of former lives to the condition of *Jiki-ketsu-gaki,* or blood-drinking pretas. . . . Anyhow, the malevolence of the *Culex fasciatus* would justify the suspicion that some wicked soul had been compressed into that wailing speck of a body. . . .

Now, to return to the subject of kerosene-oil, you can exterminate the mosquitoes of any locality by covering with a film of kerosene all stagnant water surfaces therein. The larvae die on rising to breathe; and the adult females perish when they approach the water to launch their raft of eggs. And I read, in Dr. Howard's book, that the actual cost of freeing from mosquitoes one American town of fifty thousand inhabitants, does not exceed three hundred dollars! . . .

I wonder what would be said if the city government of Tokyo—which is aggressively scientific and progressive— were suddenly to command that all water-surfaces in the Buddhist cemeteries should be covered, at regular intervals, with a film of kerosene-oil! How could the religion which prohibits the taking of any life—even of invisible life—yield to such a mandate? Would filial piety even dream of consenting to obey such an order? And then to think of the cost, in labor and time, of putting kerosene-oil, every seven days, into the millions of *mizutame*, and the tens of millions of bamboo flower-cups, in the Tokyo graveyards! . . . Impossible! To free the city from mosquitoes it would be necessary to demolish the ancient graveyards;—and that would signify the ruin of the Buddhist temples attached to them;—and that would mean the disparition of so many charming gardens, with their lotus ponds and Sanscrit-lettered monuments and humpy bridges and holy groves and weirdly-smiling Buddhas! So the extermination of the *Culex fasciatus* would involve the destruction of the poetry of the ancestral cult,—surely too great a price to pay! . . .

Besides, I should like, when my times comes, to be laid away in some Buddhist graveyard of the ancient kind, so that my ghostly company should be ancient, caring nothing for the fashions and the changes and the disintegrations of Meiji. That old cemetery behind my garden would be a suitable place. Everything there is beautiful with a beauty of exceeding and startling queerness; each tree and stone has been shaped by some old, old ideal which no longer exists in any living brain; even the shadows are not of this time and sun, but of a world forgotten, that never knew steam or electricity or magnetism or—kerosene-oil! Also in the boom of the big bell there is a quaintness of tone which awakens feelings, so strangely far-away from all the nineteenth-century part of me, that the faint blind stirrings of them make me afraid,—deliciously afraid. Never do I hear that billowing peal but I become aware of a striving and a fluttering in the abyssal part of my ghost,—a sensation as of memories struggling to reach the light beyond the obscurations of a million million deaths and births. I hope to remain within hearing of that bell. . . . And, considering the possibility of being doomed to the state of a *Jiki-ketsu-gaki*, I want to have my chance of being reborn in some bamboo flower-cup, or *mizutame*, whence I might issue softly, singing my thin and pungent song, to bite some people that I know.

HINO ASHIHEI

EARTH AND SOLDIERS

October 28, 1937
Aboard the (censored) Maru.

Dear Brother:

Again today, there is the blue sky and the blue water. And here I am writing this while lying on the upper deck of the same boat. I wish this were being written at the front, but not yet. All I can tell you is about the soldiers, lolling about the boat, the pine groves and the winding, peaceful line of the Japanese coast. What will be our fate? Nobody knows. The speculation about our point of disembarkation is still going on. Rumors that we are bound for Manchukuo are gaining strength.

Besides, there is a well-founded report that on the Shanghai front, where there has been a stalemate, our troops attacked and fought a ferocious battle. The story is that two days ago they advanced in force and rolled back the line for several miles, taking two important Chinese cities. They say that big lantern parades are swirling through the streets of Tokyo, in celebration. So the war is over! And we are to be returned, like victorious troops. That would be funny, in our case, but anyway, we are to be sent home soon!

Of course, this is nonsense, some absolutely ridiculous story. Yet we cannot avoid listening when someone talks in this vein. We cannot believe it and yet we do not wish to convince ourselves that it is not true.

This sort of life, while it is bad for the men because it is too easy, is even worse for the war horses, down in the hatch. They have been stabled belowdecks, in a dark and unhealthy hole. Sometimes, you can see them, clear down in the hold, standing patiently in the darkness. Some have not survived so well. They have lost weight. Their ribs are showing and they look sickly.

They have the best in food and water. Actually, they get better care than the men. Does it surprise you to know that, in war, a horse may be much more valuable than a man? For example, the horses get all the water they need. On the other hand, the supply of water for the men is limited, barely enough for washing, let alone the daily bath to which we are accustomed.

From that standpoint, the horses are much better off than we are. But the poor creatures have no opportunity for exercising, breathing fresh air, and feeling the sunlight. They are growing weaker. With my own eyes, I have seen a number of them collapse.

I never looked at a war horse, without thinking of poor Yoshida Uhei, who lives on the hillside, back of our town. In my memory, they are always together, just as they were before the war ever came. It is impossible to disassociate one from the other.

Perhaps you do not remember Uhei. He was a carter. He had a wagon, with which he did hauling jobs. His horse, Kichizo, drew it.

In all my life, I have never known such affection between man and animal. Kichizo was a big, fine chestnut, with great, wide shoulders and chest, and a coat like velvet. It used to shimmer in the sun and you could see the muscles rippling underneath the skin. Uhei cared for Kichizo like a mother with a baby.

I suppose this can be explained, at least in part, by the fact that Uhei had no children. He was already past forty, but his wife had never conceived. Undoubtedly, Uhei long ago gave up hope of having a child. So all his affection turned toward Kichizo, the horse. You have heard fathers brag about their sons? In a way, he did the same thing about Kichizo. "What strength!" he would say, "and yet how gentle he can be. He's a dear fellow, that Kichizo, even though he is so big and strong."

Then the war came. It came clear down to our little town, into the nooks and corners of the country, taking men and horses. Kichizo was commandeered by the army.

When he heard the news, Uhei was speechless with surprise for a while. I remember it very well. "The army needs your horse, Uhei," someone told him. "It is for the nation." Uhei looked at the speaker with dumb disbelief in his face. His eyes were frozen, uncomprehending. "Don't worry," they told him, "Kichizo will be all right. He isn't a cavalry horse. He won't be in any danger. They'll use him behind the lines, to pull wagons. It won't be anything different than what he does here. And the army takes good care of its horses. They're very important. Don't you worry about him."

Uhei turned away without speaking and began to run toward his home. He broke into a dead run, like a crazy man, and we saw him disappear behind the bend in the road. "He'll be all right," somebody said. "After all, it's only a horse."

That same afternoon, Uhei came back to town. He looked different then. He was smiling and his eyes were shining, and he swaggered around the streets. "Have you heard the news?" he kept saying. "Kichizo, my horse, is going to the war. They need big strong fellows for the army, so of course Kichizo was the first horse they thought about. They know what they're doing, those fellows. They know a real horse when they see one."

He went to the flagmaker and ordered a long banner, exactly like the ones people have when a soldier is called to the war.

"Congratulations to Kichizo on his entry into the army," this banner said, in large, vivid characters. Uhei posted a long pole in front of his house, high on the hillside, and attached this banner. It streamed out in the wind, where everyone could see. Uhei was bursting with pride. As soon as the banner was up, he took Kichizo out from the field and pointed up to where it floated gracefully above the house. "You see that, Kichizo," he said. "That's for you. You're a hero. You've brought honor to this village."

Meanwhile, Uhei's wife, O-shin, was carrying this human symbolism even further. She bought a huge piece of cloth and began preparing a "thousand-stitches belt" for the horse.[1]

This cloth that O-shin bought was big enough to cover four or five men. When she stood in the street, asking passersby to sew a stitch, they all laughed, but they did it. She had a needle that she borrowed from a matmaker to do such a big piece of work. When the stitches were all in, she herself worked all through one night, finishing the belt. It was very difficult, with such a big needle, but she finished it.

They put the good-luck belt around Kichizo's middle, just as though he were a soldier. At the same time, Uhei visited a number of different shrines in the neighborhood and bought lucky articles. O-shin sewed them into the belt.

And finally, he gave a farewell party and invited all the neighbors. Uhei was not a rich man and he couldn't afford it. If he had any savings, they were all spent that night. I was among those he invited. I took, as a gift, a bottle of wine.

[1] The "thousand-stitches belt" is a talisman, with red threads sewn by well-wishers for a Japanese soldier when he leaves for the front. It is supposed to protect him from wounds.

Most of the guests were already there, in Uhei's neat little house, by the time I arrived. They were in good humor, laughing and drinking. Uhei was excited and bustling around, seeing to everything. His eyes were glistening. "Yes, it's rare to find such a wonderful horse," he said. "You seldom find a horse with so much spirit and intelligence and at the same time so strong and vigorous. Oh, he'll show them! I'm so happy. Have a drink! Have many cups of wine for this happy occasion!"

There were tears rolling down his cheeks as he spoke and the bitter salt mingled with the wine he was drinking. Everyone was making a noise, laughing and talking and roaring jokes. O-shin kept hustling in and out of the kitchen, bringing hot food and warming the wine. She was a plain little thing, drab, I used to think. But that night, smiling and exuberant, she seemed transformed and almost beautiful.

When the party was at its height, Uhei suddenly jumped up from the table and ran outside. We heard the heavy clomp-clomp of a horse, walking through the front yard. And then, through an open window, Kichizo's long graceful neck came in. His head stretched all the way to the banquet table. He looked at us gravely; I again had the feeling that he knew all about this occasion, and knew it was for him, and what it meant.

Uhei ran into the room again and threw his arms around the horse's neck, and gave him boiled lobster and some octopus, and poured the ceremonial wine into his mouth. "To Kichizo," he cried. "Dear, brave Kichizo!" We all stood and drank and roared "Banzai!" three times. It must have seemed a little silly and sentimental. Yet, Uhei had inoculated us all with something of the love he had for that horse and it seemed natural enough to us.

In the later afternoon of the next day, I saw Uhei at Hospital Hill, returning from the army station. He had delivered Kichizo to them. I spoke to him, but he seemed not to recognize me, nor to have heard my voice, for he walked on a few paces. Then he turned and acknowledged the greeting in a distant, absent-minded sort of way. He looked haggard and sickly, as though he had lost his strength, and he left me hurriedly. All he said was "Kichizo has gone."

Later, someone told me how he brought the horse to the station. It was a terribly warm day. So Uhei took his own grass hat, cut two holes in the side for Kichizo's ears, and put it on the horse's head. Poor Kichizo, that heavy "thousand-stitches belt" must have been very warm and uncomfortable

in such weather. Besides, Uhei had decorated him with national flags, so that he looked like some sacred animal on the
way to dedication at a shrine. I suppose he felt just that way
about him.

O-shin accompanied them, holding the reins, as they
walked to the station. It was a curious and sad little trio, the
man and woman with that great sleek horse in its strange at-
tire, walking slowly down the hillside, through the village and
up the other side. Everyone watched silently. No one
laughed.

At the army station, a good many other horses were already gathered together in the yard. They had been examined
by the army veterinarians before being accepted. Now they
were merely waiting to be taken away on the train. No one
knew just when it would come.

O-shin left immediately, but Uhei stayed and stayed beside
Kichizo, patting its hip and running his fingers through its
mane. At first, the soldiers laughed, just as the people in the
village had done. But they soon saw how Uhei felt about his
horse and then they told him kindly, "Don't cry, Uncle. It's a
great promotion for your horse, isn't it? He's going to serve
the nation now, instead of pulling a cart around the village.
That's something, isn't it? Well, then, cheer up. Besides, he'll
get better care in the army than you could ever give him.
Don't you worry. He's going to be all right." So they tried to
console Uhei. Nevertheless, he stayed until dark.

Early the next day, he was back at the army station, fuss-
ing over Kichizo. Of course, there was nothing to be done.
The army grooms had already cared for and fed and watered
the horses, but the poor man wanted to see for himself. He
clucked around Kichizo like a hen with its chicks. Not that
day, nor for several days afterward, did the train come to
take the horses away.

It was quite a distance from Uhei's house to the army station, but he came every day, faithfully. He came early and
stayed until dusk.

At last the fatal day came. All the horses were loaded on
the train and taken to the harbor, where they went aboard
the transports. Uhei went along. He went as far as they
would let him and then the grooms again told him not to
worry, and promised they would take good care of Kichizo.
He bowed, eyes brimming with tears. He bowed and bowed,
and could only mumble, "Thanks, thanks, very much."

As the boat moved out of the harbor, he ran up to a bridge
overlooking the water. It was high above the water and he

stayed there until the very smoke from the steamer had vanished beneath the horizon. He waved his flag and shouted, "Kichizo," until he was hardly able to speak. And he kept his eyes riveted on the spot where the ship had disappeared.

This is all I know about the story. When I was called to the front, he was the first to come and wish me luck and help me with my preparations. On the day I left, he came again to the harbor and begged me to look out for Kichizo. "You know him," he said, eagerly. "You couldn't miss him among a thousand horses. Anyway, he has a small, white spot on his left side and, on the opposite hip, the character 'Kichi' is branded. You couldn't miss him."

"If I see him, I'll be sure and write to you," I said.

"Remember, he's a beautiful reddish chestnut," Uhei continued. "Yes, tell me if you see him. And please say something to him about me. That would seem strange to you, wouldn't it, talking to a horse? All right, but just pat him on the nose once or twice."

It seems cold and unkind of me, but only once have I asked about Kichizo since I came aboard this boat. The groom said he had not seen any such horse. Nor have I, although I have not tried to examine all the horses. But when I see one of them fall sick and die, and then go over the side to the small boat, I cannot help but recall Uhei. For his sake, I hope nothing like this has happened to Kichizo.

Speaking of the "thousand-stitches belt" reminds me of a recent episode that may give you a clear insight into our minds and hearts these days.

As you know, there is not a man aboard ship without one of these belts. They encircle every waist and each stitch carries a prayer for safety. Mine is of white silk and has a number of charms sewn into it. I do not understand the symbolism connected with each. Some are Buddhist and others Shinto. It makes no difference, of course. All are supposed to afford protection from wounds.

Mother gave me an embroidered charm bag, which contains a talisman of the "Eight Myriads of Deities," and a "Buddha from Three Thousand Worlds." In addition to those, I have an image of the Buddha, three inches in height, of exquisite workmanship. This was a present from Watabe, who lives on the hillside. When he gave it to me, he said it had been through three wars. "No bullet ever touched the man who wore it," he said. "It is a wonderful charm." Three different soldiers had carried it in the Boxer Rebellion, the first Sino-Japanese War, and the Russo-Japanese War. According to his story, they came through without a scratch.

All the men on this ship are loaded with tokens and amulets and belts and mementos from their family and friends. On warm days, when we take off our shirts, these articles are seen everywhere. I do not mean to scorn them, but it would be interesting to study them all, with the superstitions they embody. However, one cannot disregard the heartfelt sentiment connected with them.

There was one man who did scoff at them, and in no uncertain terms, either. He no longer does so. This man, Corporal Tachibana, is quite a character. He says he is an atheist. He likes to talk about his ideas and he deliberately provokes arguments, in which he stoutly defends the materialistic point of view. In these, he employs big, pedantic words that so puzzle the men that they cannot reply. Personally, I doubt that he himself understands the meaning of all the words he uses.

Particularly when he has had a little wine, Corporal Tachibana used to like to ridicule the men about their charms and talismans. "Absurd," he would say. "Absolutely ridiculous! If we could really protect ourselves with such things, there never would be anyone killed in war. The Chinese would use them, too, and so would every other kind of soldier. Then what kind of a war could you have, if nobody was killed? It is nonsense, and it is not befitting a member of the imperial army to do such things."

Of course, this was perfectly true and the men knew it. But still they believed in their pitiful little articles, the luck charms. To me, it seemed cruel and heartless of him. If he himself preferred not to place any stock in these ideas, very well. But why should he shake the faith of simple men who did? Strangely enough, however, he himself had a "thousand-stitches belt" around his middle.

One day recently, when it was very hot, we were all on the upper deck, lying in the shade. Suddenly, without a word, Corporal Tachibana jumped over the side and landed with a magnificent splash. He is not a good swimmer, and when the foam and spray disappeared, we saw him sink. Then he reappeared, churning the water with his arms and legs. Immediately, two of the men stripped and dived in after him. At the cry "Man overboard," a boat was lowered.

They pulled him into the boat and finally brought him up on deck again. His dripping hair was hanging over his face and his stomach heaved. In his right hand was his "thousand-stitches belt"!

As soon as he caught his breath, he explained that when he pulled off his shirt, his belt came with it and the wind blew it into the sea. When he saw it fluttering into the water, he jumped after it.

"Not because I was afraid of being shot if I lost it," he said, grinning. "I don't believe it can protect me in war. But my folks were so sincere about it that I couldn't just lose it in the ocean, this way. So I had to get it."

He must have thought we did not believe him, for he added, "The prayers of my people, reflecting on my brain, made me do it." Men who had been listening to him, with sly smiles on their faces, suddenly grew serious. The joking stopped. Inadvertently, it seemed to me, he had denied his own arguments and revealed a belief little different from that of the other men. Unconsciously, I put my hand on my own belt.

So much for today, I will write again soon.

translated by Baroness Shidzué Ishimoto

THE NOVEL

Very early in didactic prose writings we find evidences of imaginative expression that eventually was to evolve into a new type—fiction. The story told for purposes of teaching, or to make palatable a moral preachment, or to clarify the obscure, fades into the mists of prehistoric time. Such stories we see as early ancestors of today's novels and short stories.

However, it was not until imaginative prose came to exist for its own sake, rather than as a means to another end, that a new literary form was born. Or perhaps it might more accurately be said that it was not until fiction was written for reading pleasure, rather than solely for edification, that it came into its own; didactic or moral purpose may still be present but is no longer the primary creative cause.

In Asia as in the Occident, the novel, together with the short story, is peculiarly the product of the modern era. As such, we may expect to find these two recent modes of expression most subject to cross-pollination. In general, the prose fiction coming out of Asia today has been largely influenced by Western trends insofar as format and style are concerned. Subject matter, however, is another thing.

The very freedom of the novel form, which is so loosely defined and so subject to the winds of change, contributes toward a challenge in independence to both author and reader. This is especially true of the novel, it seems to me, for in the short story restriction in space and time tends to force a certain rigidity that often affects its content.

The novel, being, as Percy Lubbock puts it, "unusually exempt from the rules that bind" the other arts, can offer an unobstructed view of life as it actually is, rather than as it should be or is dreamed to be. Through the pages of the contemporary novel we participate in the social and political changes that lead to revolution; we enter into the everyday life of an Indian peasant family; or we become intimately involved in the psychology of a religious devotee bent upon the destruction of the acme of beauty that he so loves. In a realistic representation of actual life intended largely for a local reading public, we share the lives of fellow human beings caught up in victories and defeats universally human in nature but experienced in what may be fascinatingly unique settings and mores. Through narrative fiction we get something that all the texts in anthropology, geography, and history cannot give: we get the living essence rather than the filtered interpretation.

It is, of course, impossible to do justice to any novel through presentation of a chapter or bits and pieces of the total work. However, the genre should not be overlooked in a collection such as this, and extracts can give some sense of the author's style and at least a glimpse into the human lives and situations with which he deals.

Although, as Lubbock points out, the novel has enjoyed more freedom from artificial strictures than any of the other literary forms, it has undergone transformations and has been affected by changing tastes. The novels sampled here were, frankly, chosen chiefly for the insights they give into three very different modern cultures and for the recognized literary stature of their authors. However, they also represent stylistic types that are characteristic of the periods in which they were published.

José Rizal's *Noli me Tangere* reads like a Victorian novel. It is Dickensian in its social consciousness and, to a certain extent, in some of its humor and characterizations. But how different are the situations and environment!

In *Godan* Premchand gives us pretty much the realistic novel of the lower classes that ushered in the true modern novel. But, again, how different are the life patterns of the Indian peasant from the peasant of Europe or the workingman of America!

Kimitake Hiraoka brings us to the center of today in the psychological probing into character that is the focal core of his exciting *Temple of the Golden Pavilion*.

A Novel of the Philippines

José Rizal (1861–1896), of Tagalog parentage, Spanish and German educated, is today the national hero of the Philippines. It was his book *Noli me Tangere* (*Touch Me Not*), followed by its lesser sequel, *El Filibusterismo* (*The Subversive*), that set the torch of the conflagration that was to destroy more than three hundred years of Spanish domination of the Philippine Islands.

Even if Rizal had not made an enduring name for himself as the author of these revolution-provoking novels, he would have been a memorable figure in world culture. He was one of those rare prodigies who apparently recognize no mental limitations. His very life was, in a way, an affront to the Spanish rulers who governed on the premise that the Filipinos were an inferior people.

Completing his education in medicine at the University of Madrid, Rizal went on for further study in Germany. It was under the lowering skies of an inhospitable German winter that he began writing his *Noli,* obviously moved by nostalgia as well as by social concern for his fellow nationals. The book about Filipinos, subtitled "A Tagalog Novel," written in Spanish, was first published in Germany. (His *Fili* was to present a similar anomaly, being first published during his exile in Hong Kong.)

By profession Rizal was an eye specialist—one of the first to perform such delicate eye surgery as the removal of cataracts. (A moving account is given of his hesitancy to perform such an operation on his own mother when that need arose. However, he did have her come to Hong Kong where the surgery was successful.) Medicine, however, never completely dominated his life. He was a prolific writer of novels, stories, and poetry. He was an artist, both painter and sculptor. He was a linguist of such ability that it is said he could cope with any language within a few months of acquaintance with it and that he studied the dialects of remote peoples for no reason more utilitarian than just the joy of learning.

To a certain extent we may trace Rizal's life and thought in the character of Ibarra, the hero of his *Noli*. After years of study abroad, Ibarra returns to his homeland eager to share with his people the fruits of his superior education. He looks with a new perspective on the poverty and exploitation of the common folk by Jesuit priests and representatives of the Spanish government. However, even the unjust trial and subsequent execution of his father for treason do not cause him to abandon his original belief that reformation, not revolution, is the answer. With the exception of the incident concerning the father, this is Rizal, too. To the day of his death before a firing squad, Rizal was confident that if the Mother Church and the Mother Government in Spain could be made fully aware of the injustices being perpetrated in their names half the world away, they would intervene immediately to have them corrected. To the end, he pressed for reform, not revolution. He envisioned the Philippines as continuing under the political protection of the Spanish government, though with self-determination, and sheltered under the religious wing of the Roman Catholic Church. Ibarra's career departs from Rizal's when he joins the revolutionaries after listening to a grueling account of a lifetime of injustice suffered by the leader of a ragged band of insurrectionists.

The two Rizal novels were smuggled into the Philippines from abroad to be read at the risk of life itself, and after the Spanish period they were banned as being anti-Church. After this checkered career they have finally come into their own and are now even required reading in the Filipino public high schools.

Four chapters of the *Noli me Tangere* offer a fair sampling of the total work. Chapter 1 provides the setting and also gives a sample of Rizal's humor and satire. Chapters 10 and 11 describe the village atmosphere, define the political climate, and introduce some of Rizal's vividly portrayed characters. Chapter 51 describes the making of a revolutionary. It is after hearing the story of the rebel leader, Elias, that Ibarra abandons his middle course and joins the forces of violence.

JOSÉ RIZAL

Noli me Tangere

Chapter 1

A Party

Don Santiago de los Santos was giving a dinner party one evening towards the end of October in the 1880's. Although, contrary to his usual practice, he had let it be known only on the afternoon of the same day, it was soon the topic of conversation in Binondo, where he lived, in other districts of Manila, and even in the Spanish walled city of Intramuros. Don Santiago was better known as Capitan Tiago—the rank was not military but political, and indicated that he had once been the native mayor of a town. In those days he had a reputation for lavishness. It was well known that his house, like his country, never closed its doors—except, of course, to trade and any idea that was new or daring.

So the news of his dinner party ran like an electric shock through the community of spongers, hangers-on, and gate-crashers whom God, in His infinite wisdom, had created and so fondly multiplied in Manila. Some of these set out to hunt polish for their boots; others, collar buttons and cravats; but one and all gave the gravest thought to the manner in which they might greet their host with the assumed intimacy of long-standing friendship, or, if the occasion should arise, make a graceful apology for not having arrived earlier where presumably their presence was so eagerly awaited.

The dinner was being given in a house on Anloague Street which may still be recognized unless it has tumbled down in some earthquake. Certainly it will not have been pulled down by its owner; in the Philippines, that is usually left to God and Nature. In fact, one often thinks that they are under contract to the Government for just that purpose. The house was large enough, in a style common to those parts. It was situated in that section of the city which is crossed by a branch of the Pasig River, called by some the creek of Binondo, which, like all rivers of Manila at that time, combined the functions of public bath, sewer, laundry, fishery, waterway, and, should the Chinese water-peddler find it convenient, even a source of drinking water. For a stretch of almost a kilometer this vital artery, with its bustling traffic and bewildering activity, hardly counted with one wooden bridge, and this one was under repair at one end for six months, and closed to traffic at the other end for the rest of the year. Indeed, in the hot season, carriage horses had been known to avail themselves of the situation and to jump into the water at this point, to the discomfiture of any daydreamer in their vehicles who had dozed off while pondering the achievements of the century.

On the evening in question a visitor would have judged the house to be rather squat; its lines, not quite correct, although he would have hesitated to say whether this was due to the defective eyesight of its architect or to earthquake and typhoon. A wide staircase, green-banistered and partly carpeted, rose from the tiled court at the entrance. It led to the main floor along a double line of potted plants and flower vases set on stands of Chinese porcelain, remarkable for their fantastical colors and designs.

No porter or footman would have asked the visitor for his invitation card; he would have gone up freely, attracted by the strains of orchestra music and the suggestive tinkle of silver and china, and perhaps, if a foreigner, curious about the kind of dinner parties that were given in what was called the Pearl of the Orient.

Men are like turtles; they are classified and valued according to their shells. In this, and indeed in other respects, the inhabitants of the Philippines at that time were turtles, so that a description of Capitan Tiago's house is of some importance. At the head of the stairs the visitor would have found himself in a spacious entrance hall, serving for the occasion as a combination of music and dining room. The large table in the center, richly and profusely decorated, would have been winking delectable promises to the uninvited guest at the same time that it threatened the timid and naïve young girl with two distressing hours in close company with strangers whose language and topics of conversation were apt to take the most extraordinary lines. In contrast with these earthly concerns would have been the paintings crowded on the walls, depicting such religious themes as *Purgatory, Hell, The Last Judgment, The Death of the Just Man,* and *The Death of the Sinner,* and, in the place of honor, set off by an elegant and splendid frame carved in the Renaissance style by the most renowned woodworker of the day, a strange canvas of formidable dimensions in which were to be seen two old crones, with the inscription: *Our Lady of Peace and Happy Voyage, Venerated in Antipolo, Visits in the Guise of a Beggar the Pious and Celebrated Capitana Inés, Who Lies Gravely Ill.* This composition made up for its lack of taste and artistry with a realism that some might have considered extreme; the blue and yellow tints of the patient's face suggested a corpse in an advanced state of decomposition, and the tumblers and other receptacles which were about her, the cortège of long illnesses, were reproduced so painstakingly as to make their contents almost identifiable. The sight of these paintings, so stimulating to the appetite, and so evocative of carefree ease, might have led the visitor to think that his cynical host had formed a very shrewd opinion of the character of his guests; and indeed it was only to disguise his judgment that he had hung the room about with charming Chinese lanterns, empty birdcages, silvered crystal balls in red, green, and blue, slightly withered air plants, stuffed fishes, and other such decorations, the whole coming to a point in fanciful wooden arches, half Chinese, half European, which framed the side of the room overlooking the river, and gave a glimpse of a porch with trellises and kiosks dimly lighted by multicolored paper lanterns.

The dinner guests were gathered in the main reception room which had great mirrors and sparkling chandeliers. On a pinewood platform stood enthroned a magnificent grand piano, for which an exorbitant price had been paid, and which this night seemed more precious still because nobody was presumptuous enough to play on it. There was also a large portrait in oils of a good-looking man in a frock coat, stiff and straight, as well balanced as the tasseled cane of office between his rigid ring-covered fingers, who seemed to be saying: "See what a lot of clothes I have on, and how dignified I look!"

The furniture was elegant; uncomfortable, perhaps, and not quite suited to the climate, but then the owner of the house would have been thinking of self-display rather than the health of his guests, and would have told them: "Shocking thing, this dysentery, I know, but after all you are now seated in armchairs come straight from Europe, and you can't always do that, can you?"

The salon was almost full, the men segregated from the women as in Catholic churches and in synagogues. The few ladies were mostly young girls, some Filipinas, Spaniards the others, hastily covering their mouths with their fans when they felt a yawn coming on, and scarcely saying a word. If

someone ventured to start a conversation it died out in mono-
syllables, not unlike the night noises of mice and lizards. Did
the images of Our Lady in her various appellations, which
hung from the walls in between the mirrors, oblige them to
keep this curious silence and devout demeanor, or were
women in the Philippines in those times simply an exception?

Only one took the trouble of making the lady guests welcome; she was a kindly-faced old woman, a cousin of Capitan Tiago, who spoke Spanish rather badly. Her hospitality
and good manners did not extend beyond offering the Spanish ladies cigars and betel-nut chew on a tray, and giving her
hand to be kissed by her compatriots, exactly like a friar. The
poor old woman ended up by becoming thoroughly bored,
and, hearing the crash of a broken plate, hurriedly seized the
excuse to leave the room, muttering:

"*Jesús!* Just you wait, you wretches!"

She never came back.

The men, however, were already in higher spirits. In one
corner a number of cadets were vivaciously whispering to
one another, sharing scarcely muffled laughs as they glanced
about the room, sometimes pointing openly to this or that
person. On the other hand two foreigners, dressed in white,
went striding up and down the salon, their hands clasped behind them, and without exchanging a single word, exactly
like bored passengers pacing the deck of a ship. The center
of interest and liveliness seemed to be a group composed of
two priests, two laymen, and an officer, who were at a small
table with wine and English biscuits.

The officer was an aging lieutenant, Guevara by name, tall,
stern, with the air of a Duke of Alba left stranded in the
lower ranks of the Constabulary roster. He said little, but
what he said was heard to be sharp and brief. One of the
friars was a young Dominican, Father Sibyla, handsome, well
groomed, and as bright as his gold-rimmed glasses. He had
an air of premature gravity. Parish priest of Binondo, and
formerly a professor at the Dominican College of San Juan
de Letrán, he had the reputation of being a consummate ca-
suist, so much so that in other times, when members of his
Order still dared to match subtleties with laymen, the most
skillful debater among the latter had never succeeded in trap-
ping or confusing him; the agile distinctions of Father Sibyla
had made his antagonist look like a fisherman trying to catch
eels with a piece of string. The Dominican seemed to weigh
his words and they were few.

By way of contrast, the other friar, a Franciscan, was a

man of many words and even more numerous gestures. Although his hair was graying, his robust constitution seemed well preserved. His classic features, penetrating look, heavy jaws, and Herculean build, gave him the appearance of a Roman patrician in disguise, and recalled one of those three monks in the German story who in the September equinox would cross a Tyrolean lake at midnight, and each time place in the hand of the terror-stricken boatman a silver coin, cold as ice. However, Father Dámaso was not so mysterious as that; he was a jovial man, and if the tone of his voice was rough, like that of a man who has never held his tongue and who thinks that what he says is dogma and beyond question, his frank and jolly laugh erased this disagreeable impression; one could even forgive him when he thrust out toward the company a naked pair of hairy legs that would have made a fortune at the freak show of any suburban fair.

One of the civilians, Mr. Laruja, was a small man with a black beard whose only notable feature was a nose so large that it seemed to belong to an entirely different person. The other was a fair-haired young man, apparently a newcomer to the country, who was just then engaged in an excited discussion with the Franciscan.

"You'll see," said the latter. "A few more months in this country, and you'll be agreeing with me; it's one thing to govern from Madrid, and quite another to make do in the Philippines."

"But . . ."

"Take me, for example," Father Dámaso continued, raising his voice to keep the floor, "I've had twenty-three years of rice and bananas, and I can speak with authority on the matter. Don't come to me with theories and rhetoric; I know the natives. Listen, when I first arrived, I was assigned to a town, small it's true, but very hard-working in the fields. At that time I didn't know much Tagalog, but I was already hearing the women's Confessions; we understood one another, if you see what I mean. Well, sir, they came to like me so much that three years later, when I was transferred to a larger parish, left vacant by the death of a native priest, you should have seen all those women! They broke down and cried, they loaded me with presents, they saw me off with brass bands!"

"But that only goes to show . . ."

"Just a moment, one moment! Hold your horses! Now, my successor served a shorter time, and when he left, why, sir, he had an even greater escort, more tears were shed, more music played, and that in spite of the fact that he used to flog them more and had doubled the parish fees!"

"Permit me . . ."

"And that isn't all. Some time after, I served in the town of San Diego for twenty years; it's only a few months since I . . . left it." The recollection seemed to depress and anger him. "Well, twenty years! Nobody will deny that's time enough to know *any* town. There were six thousand souls in San Diego, and I couldn't have known each and every one of them better if I had given them birth and suck myself. I knew in which foot this little fellow limped, or where the shoe pinched that other little fellow, who was making love to that other dusky lady, and how many love affairs still another one had, and with whom, mind you, and who was the real father of this or that little urchin; all that sort of thing—after all, I was hearing the Confessions of each and every one of those rascals; they knew they had better be careful about ful-filling their religious duties, believe me. Santiago, our host, can tell you I'm speaking the honest truth: he has a lot of property there; in fact that is where we got to be friends. Well, sir, just to show you what the native is really like: when I left, there was scarcely a handful of old crones and lay members of our Order to see me off! That, after twenty years!"

"But I don't see the connection between this and the aboli-tion of the tobacco monopoly," complained the new arrival when the Franciscan paused to refresh himself with a glass of sherry.

Father Dámaso was so taken aback that he almost dropped the glass. He glared at the young man for some time, and then exclaimed with unfeigned shock:

"What? How's that? But is it possible that you can't see what's clearer than daylight? Don't you see, my dear boy, that all this is tangible proof that the reforms proposed by the Ministers in Madrid are mad?"

It was the young man's turn to be puzzled. Beside him Lieutenant Guevara deepened his frown, while Mr. Laruja moved his head ambiguously, uncertain whether to nod ap-proval or shake disapproval of Father Dámaso. The Domini-can, Father Sibyla, for his part, merely turned away from them.

"You believe . . ." the young Spaniard finally managed to blurt out, his face grave and inquiring.

"Believe it? Just as I believe in Holy Gospel! The native is so lazy!"

"Excuse me," said the new arrival, lowering his voice and drawing his chair closer. "What you have just said interests me very much indeed. Are the natives really *born* lazy? Or was that foreign traveler right who said that we Spaniards use this charge of laziness to excuse our own, as well as to explain the lack of progress and policy in our colonies? He was, of course, speaking of other colonies of ours, but I think the inhabitants there belong to the same race as these people."

"Rubbish! Pure envy! Mr. Laruja here knows the country as well as I do; ask him, go on, ask him if the ignorance and laziness of these fellows can be matched."

"Quite right," Mr. Laruja agreed promptly, "there is nobody lazier anywhere in the whole wide world than the native of these parts."

"None more vicious, or more ungrateful!"

"Or so ill-bred!"

The fair-haired young man looked uneasily around him.

"Gentlemen," he whispered, "I believe we are in the house of a native. Those young ladies . . ."

"Nonsense! you have nothing to worry about. Santiago does not consider himself a native; and in any case he is not around—and if he were, so what? Only newcomers have these crazy ideas. Let a few months pass; you'll change your mind when you have been to enough of their parties and dances, so called, and have slept on their bamboo cots, and eaten a lot of *tinola*."

"Is this *tinola* you speak about a fruit? Something like the lotus which makes men—what shall I say—forgetful?"

Father Dámaso burst out laughing. "Lotus, balotus! You're talking through your hat. *Tinola* is just a stew of chicken and squash. How long have you been here, anyway?"

"Four days," replied the young Spaniard, rather put out.

"Did you come out for a job?"

"No, sir. I came on my own account—to know the country."

"Well, sir, you are a rare bird indeed!" exclaimed Father Dámaso, studying him with amusement. "All this nonsense, and you're paying for it out of your own pocket too! You must be mad. There are so many books on the subject, and with a pinch of brains—let me tell you, sir, many famous books have been written with just that, a pinch of brains."

At this point Father Sibyla, the Dominican, abruptly cut short the exchange. "You were saying, Your Reverence, that you had served twenty years in the town of San Diego, and that you had left it. Was not Your Reverence happy there?"

The question was put in an easy, almost casual manner, but Father Dámaso lost his joviality immediately and stopped laughing.

"No," he grunted shortly, throwing himself back heavily in his armchair.

The Dominican went on, with even greater detachment:

"It must be painful to leave a town after twenty years, a town one knows as well as the clothes on one's back. As for myself, I was sorry to leave Kamiling, and I had been there only a few months. But my superiors were acting in the best interests of the Order, and, of course, also in my own."

Father Dámaso showed signs of being distraught. Unexpectedly, he smashed his fist on the arm of his chair and let out a great roar: "Either we have the Faith or we don't! Mark me, either priests are their own masters or they are not! The country is going to the devil! By God, it's gone already!"

And he smashed his fist down again.

Everyone in the salon was startled and turned to the little group. The Dominican raised his head and stared at the Franciscan from under the rim of his glasses. The two foreigners paused briefly, exchanged looks, showed their teeth momentarily, and then continued their promenade.

Mr. Laruja whispered in the newcomer's ear. "You've put him in a temper; you should have addressed him as Your Reverence."

Then the Dominican and the lieutenant, each after his own fashion, asked: "What does Your Reverence mean? What has come over you?"

"I say," cried the Franciscan, raising his heavy fists, "that the cause of all our troubles is that the Government takes the side of heretics against the ministers of God!"

"What do you mean, sir?" The officer half-rose from his chair.

"What do I mean?" the Franciscan echoed, in an even louder voice and facing the lieutenant challengingly. "I mean what I say, and I say what I like, and I say that when a priest throws the corpse of a heretic out of the parish cemetery, no one, not the King himself, has the right to meddle, and even less to impose penalties. Don't tell me that a tin-soldier general, a General Calamity . . . !"

"Sir," cried the lieutenant rising to his feet. "His Excellency is the Viceregal Patron of the Church!"

"Excellency, Viceregal Patron! Bah!" replied the Franciscan, also taking to his feet. "There was a time when he would have been dragged down the palace stairs; the Orders did it to that freethinker Governor Bustamante! *Those* were the days of faith!"

"I must warn you that I cannot allow such language. His Excellency stands in the place of His Majesty King Alfonso himself."

"King Thingumajigg! For us there is no King but the legitimate King!"

This reference to the Carlist pretender to the Throne of Spain was too much for the lieutenant.

"Enough!" he ordered in a parade-ground shout. "Either, sir, you withdraw what you have said, or I shall be obliged to report it to His Excellency as soon as possible tomorrow."

"Why don't you go now? Go on!" Father Dámaso challenged him, closing in with fists clenched. "Do you think that under my cassock I am less of a man? Get going! I'll even lend you my carriage," he added sarcastically.

The affair was becoming slightly ludicrous. Fortunately, the Dominican intervened.

"Gentlemen," he said with a ring of authority, in that nasal accent that suits friars so well. "Matters should not be confused, or offenses sought where none were given. We should distinguish between the statements of Father Dámaso as man, and his statements as priest. His statements as priest, by themselves, can never offend because, of course, they are based on absolute truth. In his statements as man we must make a subdistinction: those which he makes *ab irato*, that is to say, in anger; those which he makes *ex ore* but not *in corde*, that is to say, from the mouth but not from the heart; and finally those which he makes *in corde*, from the heart. Only the last can constitute an offense, and even then it would depend on whether they were premeditated for some reason or other, or whether they only arose *per accidens*, that is to say, without essential cause, and merely in the heat of discussion. If there should be . . ."

"*Per accidens* or perdition, I for my part know the reasons for those statements, Father Sibyla," the officer broke in. With all the growing jumble of distinctions, he was afraid he would end up being the one who was really at fault. "I know his reasons, and Your Reverence will perhaps be good enough to distinguish among them. Some time ago, when Father Dámaso was away from San Diego, his vicar allowed the Christian burial of a most honorable gentleman; a most honorable gentleman, sir, whom I had the honor to know on various occasions and whose hospitality I had enjoyed. But it was said he had never gone to Confession—so what? I don't go to Confession myself. But to announce that he was a suicide was, sir, a lie, a veritable calumny. A gentleman like that, with a son who was the object of all his love and hope; a man like that, who had faith in God, who knew his duties to society; a man honest and just—a man like that does not commit suicide! That's what I say, and I don't want to say here some other things I have in mind, for which," and here he turned to Father Dámaso, "Your Reverence should be grateful."

Then, turning his back on the Franciscan, he continued:

"Well, then, this priest, having returned to his parish and learning what had occurred, first turned his anger upon his unfortunate vicar, and then ordered the corpse of the gentleman in question to be dug up, thrown out of the cemetery, and buried I don't know where. The town of San Diego was too cowardly to protest; well, perhaps the truth is, very few learned about it; the dead man had no relatives, and his only son is in Europe. But His Excellency heard of it, and because he is a man with a good heart, he asked that the outrage be punished. It was: Father Dámaso was transferred—to a better parish! This is the whole story. Now, may it please Your Reverence to make your distinctions."

Having said this, he left the group.

"I am very sorry," Father Sibyla apologized to Father Dámaso, "that unwittingly I touched on such a delicate matter. Anyway, when all is said and done, you seem to have gained from the transfer. . . ."

"What is to be gained from such transfers?" Father Dámaso stammered, beside himself with rage. "And what about the losses? Papers . . . this and that . . . everything is mislaid . . . all sorts of things get lost. . . ."

But slowly the company regained its old tranquillity.

Other guests had arrived, among them an old Spaniard, lame, but with a mild and gentle face, who was leaning on the arm of an equally old Filipina, all curls and paint and European finery.

They were greeted cordially: Doctor de Espadaña and his wife, Doña Victorina, who by local custom shared his title and styled herself Madam Doctor. They soon took their places in a circle of acquaintances. There were also a number of journalists and merchants, who, after exchanging greetings, were seen to wander about aimlessly, not quite knowing what to do.

"Tell me, Mr. Laruja," said the fair-haired Spaniard,

"what's the owner of the house like? I still have to make his acquaintance."

"They say he's gone out; I've not seen him myself."

"Rubbish," interrupted Father Dámaso. "Don't worry about introductions in this house. Santiago is a good egg."

"He didn't invent gunpowder, certainly," added Mr. Laruja.

"You also, Mr. Laruja," Doña Victorina reproached him archly, in her particular version of Spanish. "How also can the poor dear invent gunpowder? They say," she added, fanning herself vigorously, "that it was invented by the Chinese many centuries yet."

"The Chinese? Are you crazy?" exclaimed Father Dámaso. "Don't be silly, ma'am. Gunpowder was invented by a Franciscan like myself, a certain Father Something-or-other Savalls, in the—the seventh century!"

"Oh, Franciscan! Well, maybe he was a missionary in China, this Father Savalls," replied the lady, who did not let her ideas go so easily.

"Madam, you must be referring to Schwartz," Father Sibyla observed distantly.

"But Father Dámaso said Savalls. I was quoting him only."

"Savalls, Suavarts, what does it matter? One letter won't make him Chinese," interjected Father Dámaso peevishly.

"And it was the fourteenth, not the seventh, century," added the Dominican magisterially, as if to take his colleague down another peg.

"Give one century, take another, that still doesn't make him a Dominican."

"Come now, Your Reverence should not lose his temper," smiled Father Sibyla. "So much the better that he should have invented it; he saved his brothers in your Order the trouble."

"And you say, Father Sibyla," asked Doña Victorina with a great show of interest, "that this was happening in the fourteenth century yet? But the fourteenth century before or after Christ?"

Fortunately for the Dominican two newcomers now entered the salon.

Chapter 10

The Town of San Diego

The town of San Diego lay near the shores of the Lake of Bai, surrounded by fields and meadows. It grew sugar, rice, coffee, and fruit, which were shipped directly to Manila, or else sold at throwaway prices to Chinese middlemen who exploited the credulity or vices of the farmers.

When on clear days the boys of the town climbed to the topmost story of the mossy, vine-covered church tower, they had below them a panorama of great beauty, although they were perhaps more interested in identifying their houses with rival shouts, in the jumble of nipa, tile, zinc, and palm roofs, each to be recognized among their orchards and gardens by their own special signs, this one by a certain tree, that one by a light-leaved tamarind, a third by a coconut tree laden with nuts, or a bamboo clump, a betel-nut palm, a cross. Beyond lay the river, like a great glass snake sleeping on the green fields, its back horned here and there by rocks. From afar it glided narrowly between steep banks to which contorted trees clung with naked roots, with a little house, barely to be descried, poised on the edge of an abyss, defying the winds and looking on its slender stilts like a heron watching the snake before pouncing on it. Nearer town, the river widened and moved more peacefully down a slight descent. The trunks of palms and other trees, the bark still on them, served as shaky bridges between the two banks, but if they were bad bridges, they were on the other hand, magnificent gymnastic machines on which to test a sense of balance, which was not to be sneezed at. The boys of the town, when they bathed in the river, found it amusing to watch some woman cross, balancing a basket on her head, or a tottering old man, feeling his way with a staff which more often than not slipped out of his grasp into the water.

But what always caught the eye was what might be called a peninsula of forest in that sea of cultivated fields. There might be found century-old trees with hollow trunks, which had died only when lightning struck their proud tops and set them afire; at such times, it was said, the fire had not spread, and had died on the spot. There also were enormous rocks which time and Nature had covered with velvety moss, and whose cracks the air had filled with layer upon layer of soil, packed in by the rains and fertilized by the birds. The vegetation of the tropics grew freely: bushes, thickets, interlaced creepers passing from tree to tree, hanging from the branches, clutching the roots on the ground and the ground itself. And, as if Nature were not yet content, plants grew on plants: moss and mushrooms in the crevices of tree trunks, aerial plants side by side with the leaves of the trees they climbed.

It was a forest that commanded respect. There were strange legends about it.

The most credible, and by the same token the least known and believed, was that when San Diego was only a miserable bunch of huts, and deer and wild pig roamed its grass-grown streets at night, there came to it one day an old Spaniard with deep-set eyes. He spoke Tagalog quite well, and, after going around the neighborhood, he asked for the owners of the forest and acquired it, presumably because it was known to have some hot springs, in exchange for clothes, jewelry, and a certain amount of money, which he handed over to pretenders who really had no title. Afterwards, no one knew how, he disappeared. The simple peasants were beginning to believe he had been the victim of an enemy's spell when a fetid odor from the forest called the attention of some herdsmen. They traced it to its source and found the body of the old man in a state of putrefaction hanging from the branch of a *balete* tree. If in life he had inspired fear with his deep cavernous voice, his sunken eyes, and soundless laughter, now, dead a suicide, he disturbed the sleep of the women. Some of the false vendors threw his jewelry into the river and burned the clothes they had received from him, and after the corpse was buried at the very foot of the *balete*, nobody ever dared pass by. Once a herdsman in search of his animals said he had seen mysterious lights there; those whom he called to help went so far as to hear lamentations. An unlucky lover who, to win the favor of his disdainful mistress, promised to pass the night under the tree and to prove it by tying a length of rattan around its trunk, died of a swift fever the day after the dare.

Months after, a young man, a Spanish half-breed to all appearances, arrived and said he was the son of the deceased. He established himself in those parts, dedicating himself to agriculture, especially the growing of indigo. Don Saturnino was taciturn, of a rather violent character, sometimes cruel, but very active and hardworking. He walled in the grave of his father and visited it from time to time. When he was getting on in years, he married a girl from Manila, by whom he had Don Rafael, the father of Crisóstomo Ibarra.

Don Rafael from an early age made himself loved by the peasants; agriculture, introduced and encouraged by his father, developed rapidly; new settlers came, and behind them many Chinese. The hamlet soon became a village with a native priest; then the village became a town, and when the native priest died, Father Dámaso took his place. But throughout these changes the old man's grave and its surroundings remained untouched. Sometimes the boys of the town, armed with sticks and stones, ventured to pick fruits nearby. But in the midst of their fun, or as they stared silently at the ancient rope swinging from the fatal branch, one or two stones would fall, coming from nobody knew where, and then they would cry out: "The old man, the old man!" and throw away fruits and sticks, jump down from the trees, scatter among the rocks and bushes, without stopping, until they were out of the forest, pale, some panting, others in tears, and very few in any mood for laughter.

Chapter 11

The Bosses

DIVIDE AND RULE

(THE NEW MACHIAVELLI)

Who ran the town of San Diego?

Not Don Rafael Ibarra in his lifetime, although he had the most money and lands, and almost everyone was under obligation to him. A modest man who depreciated whatever he did for the town, he never had partisans, and, when he was in trouble, everyone had turned against him.

Capitan Tiago?

It is true that his debtors welcomed him with orchestras, gave banquets in his honor, and showered him with gifts. The best fruit might always be found on his table; when a deer or wild pig was caught, he was given a quarter; if he admired a debtor's horse, it was in his stables half an hour later. But people laughed at him behind his back and called him Sacristan Tiago.

The Mayor perhaps?

This wretch did not command, he obeyed; he dared not reprimand, but was himself reprimanded; he made no decisions, they were made for him; yet had to answer to the Provincial Governor for whatever he had been ordered to do by the real masters of the town as if it had all been his own idea.

But let it be said to his credit that he had neither stolen nor usurped his office; it had cost him five thousand pesos and many humiliations, although, considering the income, it was cheap at that.

Was it God then?

Ah, the good God did not trouble the consciences or the sleep of the inhabitants of San Diego. At least He did not make them tremble, and, if they had been spoken to about Him in some sermon, they would surely have thought with a sigh: "If only there were indeed a God!" They did not bother much about Our Lord; the saints, male and female, gave them enough to do. In their eyes God had become one of those weak kings whose people pay court only to their favorites.

The truth was that San Diego was a kind of Rome; not the Rome of the calculating Romulus tracing her future walls with his plough; nor that later Rome, stained with blood, her own and others', that dictated laws to the world; but the Rome with which it was contemporaneous, the Rome of the nineteenth century, with the difference that, instead of marble monuments and a Colosseum, San Diego's monuments were made of plaited bamboo and its people gathered in a nipa cockpit. The parish priest was the Pope in the Vatican; the commanding officer of the garrison, the King of Italy in the Quirinal; all of this, of course, in terms of rattan and bamboo, but, in San Diego no less than in Rome, there were continuous quarrels, for each authority wanted to be sole master and found the other superfluous.

The parish priest was Father Bernardo Salví, the young and taciturn Franciscan who had replaced Father Dámaso. In his habits and manners he was very different from the usual run of members of his Order, even more so from his pugnacious predecessor. Father Salví was thin, sickly, almost constantly immersed in his own thoughts, strict in the performance of his religious duties, and careful of his good name. He made such an impression on his parishioners that barely a month after his arrival almost everyone in San Diego had joined the lay auxiliary of the Franciscan Order, the Tertiaries, to the discomfiture of the rival Confraternity of the Most Holy Rosary sponsored by the Dominicans. The pious heart leaped with joy to see around so many necks four or five scapulars, around so many waists a girdle of knotted rope, and over coarse cotton habits so many long-drawn faces. The head sacristan made quite a tidy fortune selling— perhaps it would be more correct to say, furnishing for a fee

—the necessary paraphernalia for the salvation of souls and the discomfiture of the Devil, who had once dared to contradict God face to face, doubting His very word, as may be found inscribed in the Book of Job, and who had carried Our Lord Jesus Christ across the skies, but who had now apparently become so susceptible that he shied away from a napkin painted with the crossed forearms of the Franciscan Order, and fled from its knotted cincture. But perhaps this proved only that progress had been made in such matters, and that the Devil was a reactionary, or at least a conservative like everyone who lives in darkness, the only alternative being that he had acquired the sensitivities of an adolescent girl.

In any case Father Salví was most assiduous; when he preached, and he was very fond of preaching, he caused all the doors of the church to be closed, like Nero who did not allow anyone to leave the theater while he sang; but Father Salví did it for the good, and Nero to the detriment, of souls. Father Salví punished the faults of his subordinates with fines, and flogged them only rarely, unlike Father Dámaso who had fixed everything with blows of his fist and stick, delivered with a guffaw and the best will in the world. One could not think badly of Father Dámaso because of this; he was convinced that one could deal with natives only with blows; a fellow-friar had said so in a book, and Father Dámaso believed it because he never contradicted the printed word, to the discomfort of many.

Although Father Salví used his stick only a few times, he made up for quantity with quality; yet one could not think of him badly because of that, either; fasting and abstinence had impoverished his blood and frayed his nerves, and, as the common people said, had gone to his head. As a result it did not make much difference to the backs of the church sacristans whether the parish priest feasted like Father Dámaso or fasted like Father Salví.

Since, according to the womenfolk, the Devil himself was keeping out of the priest's way after the great tempter had been caught one day, tied to the foot of the bed, flogged with the knotted cincture, and set free only after nine days, the only rival of the spiritual power (with tendencies toward the temporal) in San Diego was the commander of the local detachment of the Constabulary, who had the rank of second lieutenant.

Naturally, anyone who, after the Devil's painful experience, still had the temerity to clash with such a man as the parish priest deserved a worse reputation than the poor im-

prudent Devil himself, and it was generally agreed that the
commanding officer deserved whatever fate he should meet.
His wife, an old Filipina much painted and rouged, called
herself Doña Consolación; her husband and others had another name for her. The lieutenant, when he was not aveng-
ing his matrimonial misfortunes on his own person by getting
drunk like a lord, did it by drilling his soldiers up and down
in the noonday sun while he lolled in the shade, or, more
often, by beating up his wife. Perhaps she was no Lamb of
God taking away his sins, but she certainly gave him a fore-
taste on earth of the pains of Purgatory. They beat each
other up with gusto, giving their neighbors a free show which
might perhaps be described as a vocal and instrumental concert, a four-hand concerto with full pedal.

Whenever these scandalous happenings reached the ears of
Father Salví, he smiled, crossed himself, and said an Our Father; when the couple called him a hypocrite, a Carlist, and a
miser, he smiled again and prayed a little more. The lieutenant in turn lost no opportunity to warn the few Spaniards
who called on him:

"So you're going to the parish house to visit Father
Wouldn't-Hurt-A-Fly! Look out! If he offers you chocolate,
which I doubt, but anyway if he does offer it, keep your ears
open. If he calls the servant and tells him, 'So-and-so, make a
pot of chocolate, *hey*,' then you can rest easy; but if he says,
'So-and-so, make a pot of chocolate, *ha*,' then you'd better
pick up your hat and get away at a run."

"What!" his visitor would ask, taken aback. "He wouldn't
throw the pot at me would he? Good heavens!"

"My dear chap, he wouldn't go as far as that."

"Well, then?"

"Chocolate, *hey*, means really good chocolate; chocolate,
ha, means it will be very watery."

But this may have been merely malicious gossip on the
part of the commanding officer; the same story was told of
many a parish priest; indeed it may have been a practice of
the Order.

The lieutenant, prompted by his wife, had another trick up
his sleeve to play against the parish priest; he imposed a nine
o'clock curfew. Doña Consolación professed to have seen Father Salví, disguised in a native shirt and hat, stealing down
the streets at all hours. Father Salví took a saintly revenge.
Whenever he saw the lieutenant in church he unobtrusively
ordered the sacristan to close all the doors; then he took the
pulpit and preached until the very saints on the altar shut

their eyes and the wooden dove above him, symbol of the
Holy Ghost, begged for mercy. The commanding officer, like
all reprobates, was not thus to be reformed; he left when he
could, swearing, and at the first opportunity seized a sacristan
or servant of the priest, arrested him, beat him up, and set
him to washing down the floors of the barracks and his own
quarters, which thus acquired a brief respectability. The sacristan, fined for his absence by the friar, would tell the story;
Father Salví would hear him in silence, pocket the fine, and,
while he pondered a new subject for another sermon that
would be even longer and more edifying, would in the meantime let loose his goats and sheep to chew up the lieutenant's
garden. But, of course, these things did not prevent the parish
priest and the commanding officer from shaking hands when
they met, and conversing politely.

As for Doña Consolación, when her husband was sleeping
it off or having a siesta, and she could not pick a quarrel with
him, she stationed herself at her window; she could not stand
young girls and, in a blue flannel blouse, a cigar in her
mouth, she shouted out ribald nicknames for them as they
passed by, frightened, embarrassed, with downcast eyes, and
scarcely breathing. Doña Consolación had a great asset: to
all appearances she had never looked into a mirror.

These were the bosses of the town of San Diego.

Chapter 51

The Story of Elias

"About sixty years ago my grandfather lived in Manila,
working as a bookkeeper in the offices of a Spanish merchant. My grandfather was then very young but was already
married and had a son. One night the merchant's warehouse
caught fire from an unknown cause; the fire spread throughout the entire establishment, and then to many others. The
losses were very heavy; a scapegoat had to be found; and the
merchant brought charges against my grandfather. He protested his innocence in vain; he was poor and could not retain eminent counsel, and so he was condemned to be pa-
raded along the streets of Manila and publicly flogged. This
degrading punishment, a thousand times worse than death,
was still in use until not so long ago. My grandfather, for-
saken by all except his young wife, found himself bound to a
horse, followed by a sadistic crowd, and flogged at every
street corner, before the men who were his brothers and near
the many temples of a God of Love. When the wretch, con-

demned to perpetual infamy, had sated the vengeance of men with his blood, his sufferings, and his screams, they had to cut him loose from the horse for he had lost consciousness— would he had lost his life! In a refinement of cruelty, they set him free. His wife, who was then pregnant, went from door to door begging in vain for work or alms for her sick husband and helpless child. But who would trust the wife of a convicted arsonist? So she became a whore."

Ibarra started.

"Oh, don't let it disturb you. Prostitution was no longer dishonorable either for her or for her husband; honor and shame were no longer for the likes of them. The husband's wounds healed, and he came with his wife and child to hide in the mountains of this province. Here his wife gave birth to a deformed and diseased fetus that was fortunately dead. Here they lived a few months longer, miserable, isolated, hated and avoided by all. My grandfather, unable to bear his misfortunes, and less courageous than his wife, hanged himself; seeing his wife sick and deprived of all help and care drove him to despair. The corpse rotted before the very eyes of the son, who could scarcely take care of his ailing mother. The stench revealed it to the authorities. Charges were brought against my grandmother and she was found guilty of not notifying the police; the death of her husband was also blamed on her, and the charge was believed, for a felon's wife who had turned whore was thought to be capable of anything. If she said anything under oath, she was only perjuring herself; if she wept, she lied; if she called on God, she blasphemed. However, they took pity on her because she was pregnant again, and did not have her flogged until she had given birth. You know the friars propagate the belief that the only way to treat the natives is by beating them up; read what Father Gaspar de San Agustín has to say about it.

"Under such a judgment, a woman will curse the day her son is born; which is not only to lengthen her torment, but also to do violence to motherly love. Unfortunately, she was safely delivered of a son who, just as unfortunately, was born strong. Two months later the judgment was executed to the great satisfaction of men, who thus thought they had done their duty. No longer at peace in the mountains, she fled with her two sons to the neighboring province, and there they lived like wild beasts, hating and hated. The elder of the two brothers, who could still remember his happy childhood in the midst of such misery, turned bandit as soon as he was strong enough. Soon the sanguinary name of *Bálat* ran from province to province, the terror of the towns, for in his desire for vengeance he put everything to the torch and to the sword. The younger brother, who had a naturally good heart, had resigned himself to living in opprobrium beside his mother; they lived on what the forest yielded, and clothed themselves in the rags that were thrown to them by travelers. Her name had been forgotten, and she was known only as a slut and a convict who had been publicly flogged. He was known only as his mother's son, because the gentleness of his character made people doubt that he was the son of the arsonist, and because the morals of the natives were always subject to suspicion. In the end the famous *Bálat* fell into the hands of the law, and human justice, which had done nothing to teach him virtue, demanded a strict accounting of his crimes. One morning the younger brother was looking for his mother, who had gone into the forest to look for mushrooms and had not returned. He found her stretched out on the ground by the highway, under a cotton tree, her face turned to the sky, her eyes staring out of their sockets, her fingers dug convulsively into the bloodstained earth. He glanced upward following the dead woman's eyes and saw, hanging from a branch of the tree, a basket, and inside the basket the bloody head of his brother."

"My God!" exclaimed Ibarra.

"That is what my father said," continued Elias coldly. "Human society had dismembered the bandit's corpse; the trunk had been buried, but the limbs had been hung up in different towns. If you go some time from Kalamba to Santo Tomas you will still find the miserable *lomboy* tree where one of my uncle's legs hung rotting. Nature has cursed it and the tree neither grows nor gives fruit. The same thing was done with the other limbs, but the head, a man's best part, and the one most easily recognized, was hung near his mother's hut."

Ibarra lowered his head.

"The young man fled like one accursed," continued Elias. "He fled from town to town, over mountains and valleys, and when he thought that he would no longer be recognized, went to work in the house of a rich man in the province of Tayabas. His industry, and the sweetness of his character, won him the esteem of all those who did not know his past. By dint of hard work and thrift he managed to accumulate a little capital, and, since the bad days had gone, and he was young, he dreamed of happiness. His good looks, his youth, and his now comfortable means, won him the love of a girl in the town. He did not dare to ask her hand in marriage for fear that his past should be discovered. But love was stronger, and they succumbed to passion. To save the girl's honor, he risked everything and asked for her hand; and everything was discovered when the necessary documents were looked up. The girl's father was rich; he succeeded in having charges brought against the young man; the latter did not try to defend himself, but admitted everything and was sent to prison. The girl gave birth to a boy and a girl, who were brought up secretly in the belief that their father had died, which was not difficult since at a tender age they had seen their mother die, and did not bother much with looking into their parentage. Since our grandfather was rich our childhood was very happy. My sister and I started our schooling together. We loved each other as only twins can before they know other kinds of love. While still very young I went to study in the Jesuit school, and my sister was sent to board in the convent school of La Concordia so that we should not be wholly parted. Our brief schooling over—we only wanted to be farmers—we went home to take possession of our grandfather's estate. We lived happily for some time; the future smiled on us. We had many servants; our fields were fruitful; and my sister was on the eve of marrying a young man whom she adored, and who returned her love. Then, on some money matter and because of my then arrogant character, I antagonized a distant relative and one day he taunted me with my illegitimacy and my criminal descent. I thought it a calumny, and demanded satisfaction. Then the sepulcher in which lay so much rottenness was reopened, and the truth emerged to confound me. To our greater misfortune, we had had for years an old servant who endured all my caprices without ever leaving us, finding it enough to weep and sigh amid the scoffing of the other servants. I do not know how my relative found it out; the thing is that he had the old man haled into court and interrogated. The servant was our own father, who had clung to his beloved children. And I had beaten him up more than once! Our happiness vanished. I renounced our wealth; my sister lost her betrothed; and together with our father we left town. The thought that he had contributed to our misfortune shortened my father's days. I learned the sorrowful past from him. My sister and I were left alone.

"She wept much. In the midst of all the sorrows that piled up on us, she could not forget her love. Without a word of complaint she saw her betrothed marry another. I saw her waste away from day to day without being able to console her. One day she disappeared. I looked everywhere in vain for her; in vain made inquiries. Only six months later I learned that about that time, after a flood, the body of a girl, drowned or murdered, had been found on the beach of Kalamba. There was, it was said, a knife buried in her bosom. The town authorities issued notices of this discovery in the neighboring towns, but nobody came forward to claim the body. No girl was missing. But by the description they gave me afterwards, of her dress, her jewels, the beauty of her face, and her abundant hair, I recognized by poor sister. Since then I go from province to province. My name and my story are known to many. I am said to do many things, and sometimes it is not true. But I do not pay much heed to human society, and I go my way. Such is my story in a few words, and the story of one of society's judgments."

Elias stopped, and silently plied his paddle.

"I am beginning to believe you are not wrong when you say that the law should seek the common good by rewarding virtue and reforming the criminal," Crisóstomo murmured. "Only, such a thing is impossible. Utopian. Where would all the money come from, and all the officials?"

"What then is the use of all these priests who proclaim their mission of peace and charity? Is it more meritorious to pour water on a baby's head and touch his lips with salt in Baptism than to awaken in the darkened conscience of the criminal that spark given by God to every man to guide him to virtue? Is it more human to accompany the condemned man to the gallows than to accompany him along the straight path that leads from vice to virtue? Is there no money for informers, executioners, and soldiers? These things are not only degrading but also expensive."

"My friend, even though we wanted to do it, neither you nor I could achieve it."

"It is true that by ourselves we are nothing. But take up the cause of the people, join them, do not turn a deaf ear to their voice, give an example to the rest, give us an idea of what it is to have a country."

"What the people ask is impossible. It is necessary to wait."

"Wait! To wait is to suffer."

"If I were to ask for these reforms, they would laugh in my face."

"And if the people were behind you?"

"Never! I would never be the one to lead the mob to take by force what the Government believes inopportune. If I should ever see the mob in arms, I would take the side of the Government and fight against it because I would not recognize my country in such a mob. I want my country's good, that is why I am building the schoolhouse, but I seek it through education, through progress. We cannot find our way without the light of knowledge."

"Neither can freedom be won without a fight!" answered Elias.

"But I do not want that kind of freedom."

"Without freedom, there can be no light," retorted the boatman with spirit. "You say you know little about your country. I believe it. You see nothing of the struggle that is being prepared, or the clouds on the horizon: the struggle begins in the field of ideas, but will end in the bloodstained arena of action. I hear the voice of God: woe to those who would resist Him, history has not been written for them."

Elias was transfigured; he had stood up in the boat, and his manly face, uncovered and lighted by the moon, had some extraordinary quality. He shook his long hair and continued:

"Do you not see how everything awakens? Our people slept for centuries, but one day the lightning struck, and, even as it killed Burgos, Gomez, and Zamora, it called our nation to life. Since then new aspirations work on our minds, and these aspirations, now scattered, will one day unite under the guidance of God. God has not failed other peoples; He will not fail ours, their cause is the cause of freedom."

A solemn silence followed these words. Meantime, the boat, carried imperceptibly by the current, neared the shore. Elias was the first to break the silence.

"What shall I say to those who sent me?" he asked in a different tone.

"I have told you: that I deplore their condition, but that they should wait, for wrongs are not righted by other wrongs, and for our misfortunes all of us have a share of the blame."

Elias did not reply. He lowered his head, continued paddling and, having reached the shore, said good-bye to Ibarra:

"I thank you, sir, for your consideration to myself. In your own interest I ask you to forget me from now on and not to recognize me in whatever circumstances you may find me."

Having said this, he set out again, paddling towards a thicket farther on along the shore. During the long passage he remained silent; he seemed to see nothing but the thousands of diamonds that with his paddle he raised from and returned to the lake, where they vanished in mystery among the blue waves.

He arrived at his destination at last. A man left the thicket and approached him.

"What shall I tell the commander?" he asked.

"Tell him that Elias will keep his word," Elias answered sadly, "if he does not die sooner."

"When will you join us then?"

"When your commander believes that the hour of danger has come."

"Very well. Good-bye."

translated by León Ma. Guerrero

A Novel of India

Dhanpat Rai (1880–1936), the son of a poor village postal employee, originally aspired to become a lawyer. Instead, his education terminated at the ninth grade following his father's death. He was already married and, at the age of sixteen, had to provide for a wife and a stepmother and her two children. From conception to death, his life was bound by poverty. Even after several years of "successful" writing, he was to receive only five rupees (one dollar) for a short story.

However, Rai read widely and eclectically. Influences ranged from Tolstoy and Gorky to Thackeray and Gandhi. Later in life he was able to go to college. And so, by a circuitous route, he arrived at his writing career after resigning a minor government post.

It is generally acknowledged that the modern novel and short story began in India with this writer who is best known as Premchand. He was the first to turn from the traditional themes and from overblown romanticism to everyday life related in realistic terms. He first wrote in Urdu under the pseudonym of Nawab Rai. For a time after 1910 when the British burned all copies of his volume of short stories, *Sauz-e-Vatan,* because of their national independence themes, Rai was silent. Soon, however, he took the name of Premchand and began to express himself in Hindi. His first major novel, *Seva Sadan,* appeared in 1914. But *Godan (Cow Offering),* his last novel, was to be the masterpiece among all his writings, which eventually were to include some two hundred short stories, twelve novels, and several plays.

Godan deals with Premchand's favorite theme—the hard

and unrewarding life of the village peasant. The opening sentences of the book give a sense of setting, of village relationships, and of the personal problems of the peasant, Hori Ram, whose impoverished life is bound to the unproductive land:

> Hori Ram finished feeding his two bullocks and then turned to his wife Dhaniya. "Send Gobar to hoe the sugarcane. I don't know when I'll be back. Just get me my stick."
> Dhaniya had been making fuel-cakes, so her hands were covered with dung.[1] "First eat something before you leave," she said. "What's the big hurry?"
> A frown deepened the wrinkles on Hori's forehead. . . . "I have to worry that I may not even get to see the master if I reach there late. Once he starts his bathing and prayers I'll have to wait around for hours. . . . When someone's heel is on your neck, it's best to keep licking his feet."

Life, death, occasional too-fleeting joy, unremitting toil, heartbreak, increasing indebtedness, the ambition to own a cow, the desire to see his three remaining children realize more from life than he has—these are the elements of Hori Ram's life. The last two of the thirty-six chapters of *Godan* see Hori's bitter struggle to its pitiful conclusion.

PREMCHAND (DHANPAT RAI)

GODAN

Chapter 35

Hori's situation was deteriorating day by day. He'd been fighting a losing battle all his life but he had never lost heart, each defeat seeming to give him new strength to fight against fate. But now he had reached that final stage where he no longer had confidence even in himself. It would have been some consolation if he had been able to remain true to his conscience and his dharma,[2] but that was not the case. He'd violated his principles, failed in his duty, and done every kind of wrong imaginable. Despite that, not one of his ambitions

---

[1] Cow dung is collected fresh, patted into flat cakes, dried in the sun, and used for fuel.

[2] The Way; in Hinduism, especially the right way of life in respect to one's caste relationships.

in life had been fulfilled, and the prospect of better days had receded into the distance like a mirage until not even illusion remained. The lushness and glitter of false hopes had now faded away entirely. Like a vanquished ruler, he had shut himself up in the fortress of his two acres and was guarding it as though it were his life. He had endured starvation, suffered disgrace, and hired himself out as a common laborer, but he had held the fort.

Now even that fort was slipping from his hands. Three years' rent lay unpaid and Pandit Nokheram had filed eviction proceedings against him. There was no hope of getting the money anywhere. The land would be lost and he'd spend the rest of his days as a hired hand. Such was God's will. He couldn't very well blame the Rai Sahib, who had to make a living off his tenants. More than half the families in the village were facing eviction, so they were all in the same boat. If fate had ordained happiness for him, would he have lost his son that way?

Darkness had fallen and Hori was sitting brooding over these problems when Pandit Datadin appeared and spoke to him. "What's happened about your eviction notice, Hori? I'm not on speaking terms with Nokheram these days so I don't know anything. I hear you have fifteen days left."

Hori pulled out a cot for him to sit on. "He's the master. He can do what he likes. If I had the money, this mess would never have happened in the first place. It's not as though I'd gobbled up the money or thrown it around. If the land doesn't yield anything, or if what it does yield sells for a pittance, what's a farmer to do?"

"But you must save the property. How else are you going to live? This is all that's left of the inheritance from your forefathers. Lose that and where would you live?"

"That's in the hands of God. What control do I have over it?"

"There is one thing you could do."

Hori fell at his feet like a man just granted amnesty and said, "Blessings on you, maharaj.[1] You're my only hope. I had given up."

"There's no question of giving up. All you have to realize is that a man's duty is one thing in times of plenty and something quite different in times of trouble. In good days he gives out charity, whereas in bad, he even takes to begging. It

[1] "Prince"; here used, not literally, but in flattery of Hori's fellow-villager.

becomes his duty then. When we're in good health, we don't even touch water to our lips without the proper bathing and prayers, but when we're sick, we take food in bed without bathing or praying or changing clothes. It's the right thing to do at that particular time. There's a big gap between you and me here in the village, but when we go to the Jagannath temple in Puri,[1] that distinction disappears. The high and the low sit down in the same row and eat. In a time of crisis, the lord Rama ate wild berries polluted by the touch of Shabari and hid craftily to kill Bali. In times of distress, even the greatest of the great compromise their standards, not to speak of people like ourselves. You must know the man Ramsevak, don't you?"

"Yes, of course," Hori conceded.

"He's a patron of mine. He's very well off these days—lands on the one hand and moneylending on the other. I've never known a man with such power and influence. His wife died several months ago. They had no children. If you would be willing to marry Rupa to him, I could get him to agree. He'd never oppose my advice. The girl has come of age, and these are evil times. If anything should happen, your name would be mud. It's a very good opportunity for you. The girl will be married off and your land will be saved in the bargain. You'll be saved all the bother and expense of the wedding too."

Ramsevak was only three or four years younger than Hori, and the proposal to marry Rupa to a man like that was insulting. His Rupa, in full bloom, marry that withered old stump? Hori had suffered a lot of blows over the years, but this one struck deepest. He had now reached the point where someone could suggest selling his daughter and he lacked the courage to refuse. His head dropped in shame.

"Well, what do you say?" Datadin asked after a slight pause.

Hori refused to commit himself. "I'll have to think it over first."

"What's there to think over?"

"I should ask Dhaniya too."

"Are you agreeable or not?"

"Let me think a bit, maharaj. Nothing like this has ever happened in the family, and our honor has to be upheld."

"Let me have an answer within five or six days. Otherwise

[1] A festival in honor of the god Krishna is held here annually in Puri, Orissa, Krishna's image being carried on a heavy huge-wheeled cart.

the eviction is likely to go through while you're still thinking
it over."

Datadin went away. He had no worries about Hori. It was
Dhaniya he was concerned about, with her nose in the air.
She'd rather die than compromise the family prestige. If Hori
agreed, though, she'd come around too after much weeping
and wailing. After all, losing the land would damage their
prestige also.

Dhaniya came and asked, "What did the pandit come for?"

"Nothing special. We just talked about the eviction matter."

"He must have offered only sympathy—he certainly
wouldn't be offering a hundred-rupee loan."

"And I don't have the gall to ask for one at this point."

"Then why did he come in the first place?"

"To suggest a match for Rupiya."

"With whom?"

"You know Ramsevak? With him."

"How would I know him? Of course I've heard the name
for a long time. But he must be an old man."

"He's not old, but—yes, he is middle-aged."

"And you didn't tell the pandit off? If he'd talked to me,
I'd have given an answer he'd never forget."

"I didn't tell him off, but I did turn him down. He was saying the wedding wouldn't cost us anything and that we'd save
the fields besides."

"Why don't you come right out and admit he was suggest-
ing we sell the girl? The nerve of that old man!"

The more Hori thought about the matter, however, the
more his resistance weakened. He had no less pride about
family honor, but when a person is seized by an incurable
disease, he stops caring about what should and what should
not be eaten. Hori's attitude in front of Datadin could not
have been called compliance, but inwardly he had melted.
Age wasn't so important after all. Life and death were in the
hands of fate, and sometimes the young pass away while the
old remain. If happiness were written in Rupa's destiny, she
would find happiness even there. If sorrow were ordained,
she'd be unable to find happiness anywhere. And it was certainly not a question of selling his daughter. Anything he accepted from Ramsevak would be only a loan, to be repaid as
soon as he got hold of some money. There was nothing
shameful or humiliating about that. If he had the means, he
would certainly be marrying Rupa to some young man of
good family, giving a good dowry and sparing no expense to

entertain the marriage party. But since God had not granted him the wherewithal for that, what could he do but marry her off with only a tuft of sacred grass for a dowry? People would jeer at him, but there was no need for him to worry about people who just made fun without offering any help. The only trouble was that Dhaniya wouldn't agree. She was a real mule and would keep hanging on to that same old pride. This was no time to worry about family prestige. It was a chance to save their lives. If she was going to be so fussy about honor, all right—let her come up with five hundred rupees. Just where was she hoarding it?

Two days went by and no mention was made of the subject, although both of them talked about it indirectly.

"A marriage is only happy when the boy and girl are equally matched," Dhaniya would say.

"Marriage doesn't mean happiness, you fool," Hori would answer. "It means self-denial."

"Come off it. Self-denial?"

"Yes, and I'm the one to say so. What else can you call the state of being content with whatever circumstances God places you in?"

The next day Dhaniya came up with another angle on this question of marital happiness—"What fun is it to be in a husband's home with no father- or mother-in-law and with no brothers- or sisters-in-law? A girl should have the pleasure of being the new little bride for a while."

"That's not pleasure, it's punishment," Hori retorted.

"You have such queer ideas," Dhaniya snapped. "How's a bride going to manage all by herself in a house with no one else around?"

"Well, when you came to this house you had not one but two brothers-in-law, as well as a mother-in-law and a father-in-law. Tell me, what happiness did you get out of that?"

"You think people in all families are just like the ones who were here?"

"What else? You expect angels come down from the skies? The bride's alone in any case. The whole house orders her around. How can the poor thing please everyone? And anyone whose orders she ignores turns against her. Being alone is by far the best." [1]

---

[1] The foregoing discussion reflects the traditional "joint family" system still practiced in India, especially in the villages. The young wife joins her husband in his home and is expected to accommodate herself to the several generations resident under one roof or within one compound. She is especially subservient to her mother-in-law.

The discussion would always stop at this point, but Dha-niya was steadily losing ground. On the fourth day, Ramse-vak himself showed up, riding a big horse and accompanied by a barber and a manservant as though he was some great zamindar.[1] Though he was over forty and his hair was turn-ing gray, there was a certain brightness in his face and he had a sturdy physique. Hori looked really ancient alongside of him. Ramsevak was on his way to see about some court case and wanted to stop off for a while to avoid the noon heat. The sun was so fierce today and the wind so scorching! Hori got wheat flour and ghee [2] from Dulari's shop and spe-cial wheat cakes were prepared. All three guests were served. Datadin also turned up to give his blessings and a conversa-tion ensued.

"What sort of case is it, mahto?" Datadin inquired.

"Oh, there's always some case or other pending, maharaj," Ramsevak boasted. "Being meek as a cow doesn't get you anywhere in this world. The more you cringe, the more peo-ple put you down. The law courts and police and so forth are supposed to be for our protection, but no one really protects us. There's just looting all around. People are all ready and waiting to cut the throat of anyone poor and defenseless. God forbid that we be dishonest—that's a big sin. But not to fight for one's rights and for justice is an even bigger sin. Think about it—how long is a person to knuckle under? Ev-eryone around here considers the farmer fair game. He can hardly stay on in the village if he doesn't pay off the patwari.[3] If he doesn't satisfy the appetite of the zamindar's men, life is made impossible for him. The police chiefs and constables act like sons-in-law. Whenever they happen to be passing through the village, the farmers are duty-bound to entertain them royally and provide gifts and offerings lest they get the whole village arrested by filing a single report. Someone or other is always turning up—the head record-keeper or the revenue official or the deputy or the agent or the collector or the commissioner—and the farmer is supposed to attend him on bended knee. He has to make arrangements for food and fodder, for eggs and chickens, and for milk and ghee. You must know all about this yourself, maharaj. Every day some new officer is added to the list. Recently a doctor has started

[1] Landowner.

[2] Clarified butter; highly prized, both as a food delicacy and for an-nointing sacred images and funeral pyres.

[3] Revenue clerk.

coming to treat the water in the wells. Another doctor comes
around occasionally to look at the cattle, and then there's the
inspector who tests the schoolchildren. Lord knows all the departments these officers represent—there's a separate one for
towns, one for jungles, one for liquor, one for village welfare,
one for agriculture. . . . You want me to keep on naming
them? The padre shows up and even he has to be supplied
with provisions or he'll make a complaint. And anyone who
says that all these departments and officers do some good for
the farmers is talking through his hat. Just the other day, the
zamindar levied a tax of two rupees on every plough. He was
putting on a feast for some big official. The farmers refused
to pay so he just raised the rents of the whole village. And
the officers always side with the zamindar. It never occurs to
them that the farmer is also a human being, that he too has a
wife and family, and some honor and status to maintain.

"And this is all the result of our servility. I've had a drum-
mer announce throughout the village that no one should pay
the extra rent or let his land go. We're prepared to pay the
new rate if someone can convince us there's a good reason,
but if the zamindar was intending just to grind up and devour
the defenseless farmers, he was mistaken. The villagers went
along with me and they all refused to pay. When the zamindar saw that the whole village had united, he was forced to
back down. Confiscate all the land and who would work it?
In this day and age you have to be tough or no one pays any
attention. Even a child has to cry before he gets any milk
from his mother."

In midafternoon Ramsevak went on his way, having left an
indelible impression on Hori and Dhaniya. Datadin's spell
had worked. "Now what do you say?" he asked.

Hori pointed to Dhaniya. "You'd better ask her."

"I'm asking you both."

"Well, he is much older," Dhaniya replied, "but if you all
approve, I'm willing too. What's written in the stars will show
up in time, but anyway he's a good man."

As for Hori, he had the kind of confidence in Ramsevak
which the weak feel for men of spirit and courage. He had
begun building great castles in the air. With the support of a
man like this, he might pull through after all.

The date for the wedding was set. Gobar would also have
to be invited. It was up to them to write; whether he came or
not was up to him. At least he wouldn't be able to say he'd
not been invited. They'd have to send for Sona too.

"Gobar was never that way," Dhaniya said. "Now if Jhu-

niya will only let him come . . . Since going away, he's forgotten us so completely that there's been not a word from
him. No telling how they're getting along." Tears came to her
eyes as she spoke.

Gobar began preparing to leave as soon as he got the letter. Jhuniya didn't like the idea, but she couldn't object on an
occasion like this. For a brother not to attend his sister's
wedding would be unthinkable. Not going to Sona's had been
enough of a scandal.

"It's not right to be on bad terms with one's parents." Gobar's voice was thick with emotion. "Now that we're on our
own two feet, we can pull away from them or even fight
them. But it was they who gave us birth and brought us up,
so even if they give us a hard time now, we ought to put up
with it. They've been in my thoughts a lot recently. I don't
know why I got so angry at them that time. Because of you
I've had to leave even my mother and father."

"Don't dump the blame on my head," Jhuniya barked.
"The quarrel was all your doing. All that time I lived with
your mother, I never even breathed a harsh word."

"The fight was over you though."

"Well, what if it was? I gave up my whole home and family for your sake."

"No one loved you at your place anyway. Your brothers
were furious and their wives were spiteful. And if your father
had got hold of you, he'd have eaten you alive."

"All because of you."

"Well, from now on let's live in such a way that they'll get
some pleasure out of life too. Let's not do anything against
their wishes. My father's such a good man that he's never
even said an unkind word. Mother beat me a number of
times, but she would always give me something special to eat
afterwards. She'd thrash me, but then she'd have no peace of
mind until she had made me smile."

They both mentioned the matter to Malti. She not only allowed the time off but also gave them a spinning wheel and a
bracelet for the bride. She wanted to go herself, but she was
treating several patients who couldn't be left for even a day.
She did promise to come for the ceremony itself, though, and
brought out a pile of toys for Mangal. She kissed and fondled
him as though to compensate for all the time he'd be away,
but the child took no notice of her caresses in his delight at
going home—the home he had never even seen. In his child-
ish imagination, home was something better than heaven itself.

When Gobar reached home and saw its condition, however, he was so disheartened he felt like returning to the city
right away. Part of the house was about to fall down. Only
one bullock was tied up near the door and even it was on its
last legs. Dhaniya and Hori were beside themselves with delight, but Gobar was disturbed and dejected. What hope was
there of saving this home? He worked like a slave in the city
but at least he ate his fill—and he served only one master.
Here in the village everyone in sight was browbeating the
people. This was slavery with no compensation. Struggle to
raise a crop and then give its income to someone else, leaving
you to console yourself repeating the name of God. Only
people with hearts like his father's could put up with all this.
He couldn't have tolerated it for even a day.

And Hori was not the only one in this condition. The
whole village was in misery, and there was not a man but
wore an expression as gloomy as though suffering had
drained the life from him and was making him dance like a
wooden puppet. They moved about, did their work, were
crushed and suffocated only because this was written in their
fate. Life held neither hope nor joy, as though the springs of
life had dried up and all greenness had withered away. Being
June, there was still grain in the barns, but no happiness on
anyone's face. Most of the grain in the barns had been
weighed out and turned over to the moneylenders and the zamindar's agents, and even what was left was owed to others.

The future loomed darkly ahead with no path in sight, and
their spirits had become numbed. The mounds of garbage
piled up by the doors filled the air with stench, but no odor
reached their noses and no light their eyes. They ate whatever
scraps came their way like engines taking in coal. Their bullocks would sniff and poke around before putting their
mouths to the trough, but all the people wanted was to get
something in their stomachs. Flavor made no difference, as
they'd lost their sense of taste. And life had lost all flavor too.
For half a pice people could be made dishonest; for a handful of grain, the sticks would fly. They had reached the limits
of degradation where men forget all about dignity or shame.

The village had been in much the same state when Gobar
had known it as a child, but he had been accustomed to it. In
the four years away, however, he had seen a new world. Living in the midst of refined people in the city had stimulated
his mind. He had stood at the back of political meetings and
heard the speeches until they penetrated every part of him.
He had heard that men must carve out their own destiny,

that they must conquer their misery through their own insight and courage. No gods, no supernatural powers, would come to their rescue. Profound sympathies had been awakened within him. Where he had been headstrong and arrogant, he was now gentle and industrious, realizing that whatever one's situation, greed and selfishness would only make it worse. Threads of suffering had bound them all together, and men would be foolish to let petty self-interest break these sacred bonds of brotherhood. The ties uniting them must be strengthened. Such feelings had given wings to his humanity, and with the magnanimity which comes to the good at heart from observing the best and the worst in the world, he seemed poised to soar into the skies.

Whenever he saw Hori working now, Gobar would take over the job and do it himself, as though trying to atone for his previous behavior. "Father," he would say, "don't worry about a thing any more. Leave it all to me. From now on I'll send money for your expenses every month. You've been working yourself to death all this time. Take a rest now for a while. A curse on me, that you've had to suffer so when I could have helped."

Hori blessed the boy with every inch of his being, new inspiration filling his worn and aging body. How could he cripple Gobar's rising manhood with anxiety at this point by describing all his debts and obligations? Let the boy enjoy his meals in comfort and get some pleasure out of life. He, Hori, was willing to slog and slave. That had always been his life, and to sit around chanting prayers would be the death of him. He needed the ax and the hoe. Twirling a rosary would bring him no peace of mind.

"Just give the word," Gobar said, "and I'll arrange installments on all the debts and pay them off month by month. How much would they add up to?"

Hori shook his head. "No, son, why should you burden yourself down? You don't earn much yourself. I'll take care of everything. Times are bound to improve. Rupa's going away, so now all that's left is to pay off the debts. Don't you worry about it. Make sure you eat well. If you build up your body now, you'll live happily ever after. And me? Well, I'm used to killing myself with work. I don't want to tie you to the fields as yet, son. You've found a good employer. Serve her for a while and you'll become a man. She came here once, you know. A real live goddess."

"She's promised to come again the day of the wedding."

"We'll be happy to welcome her. Living alongside such

good people may mean less money but it increases one's wisdom and opens his eyes."

Just then Pandit Datadin beckoned to Hori. Leading him some distance away, he took two hundred-rupee notes from his waistband. "You did well to take my advice. Both things have been taken care of. You've done your duty to the girl and you've also saved the inheritance of your ancestors. I've done all I can for you. The rest is now up to you."

Hori's hands were trembling as they took the money and he was unable to raise his eyes or say a word. He felt as though he had fallen into a bottomless pit of shame and was still falling. After thirty years of struggling with life, he had finally been defeated, as defeated as though he had been stood up against the city gate with every passerby spitting in his face while he cried out, "I deserve your pity, my brothers. I didn't know what the wind of summer was like nor the rain of winter. Slash open this body and see for yourself how little life is left in it. Count the bruises and scars, the blows that have crushed it. Ask it if it has ever known rest and peace, if it has ever sat in the shade. And now this humiliation!" But he was still alive—cowardly, greedy, contemptible. All his faith, which had grown so infinite, so firm, so unquestioning, had been nibbled away.

"I must be leaving," said Datadin. "You should probably go see Nokheram right away."

"I'll go in a moment, maharaj," Hori murmured meekly, "but my honor is in your hands now."

Chapter 36

For two days the village rocked with revelry. Music rang out, songs filled the air, and finally Rupa departed with much weeping and wailing. Hori was never seen to leave the house, however, as though he were hiding in disgrace.

Malti's arrival had added to the excitement, and women had flocked in from the neighboring villages. Gobar's warmth and courtesy had charmed the whole village, and not a house was left unimpressed with the memory of his graciousness. Even Bhola fell at his feet,[1] and his wife offered betel,[2] gave

---

[1] Customary gesture of respect. In this instance this is an excessive tribute, since usually it is the young who bend and touch the feet of their elders.

[2] Aromatic and tangy leaves of the pepper plant, chewed by the peoples of Indian and Southeast Asia. The "chewing gum" of Asia is *pan*, composed of the nut of the betel palm, lime, sometimes a bit of to-

a parting gift of a rupee, and even asked his Lucknow address, saying she would certainly look him up if she ever got to the city. She made no reference to the money she had loaned Hori.

On the third day, as Gobar was making preparations to leave, Hori, in the presence of Dhaniya, came with tears in his eyes and confessed the guilt that had been burdening his heart for so long. "Son," he sobbed, "I took this load of sin on my head out of love for the land. No telling how God will punish me for it."

Gobar was not at all upset and his face registered no sign of irritation or anger. "There's no need to feel guilty, father," he said respectfully. "True, Ramsevak's money should be repaid. But what else could you have done? I've been an unworthy son, your fields aren't producing anything, and there's no money available anywhere. There's not enough food in the house to last even a month. Under such circumstances, there was no other way out. How could you live if the land were lost? When a man is helpless he can only resign himself to fate. No telling how long this rotten state of affairs will go on. Prestige and honor have no meaning when a man can't fill his stomach. If you'd been like the others, squeezing people by the throat and making off with their money, you too could have been well-off. You stuck to your principles and this is the punishment you get for it. If I had been in your position, I'd either be in jail or I'd have been hanged. I could never have tolerated my earnings going to fill up everyone else's houses while my own family sat by muzzled and starving."

Dhaniya was unwilling to let her daughter-in-law go with him, and Jhuniya herself wanted to stay a little longer. So it had been decided that Gobar would return alone.

Early the next morning Gobar took leave of everyone and set out for Lucknow. Hori accompanied him to the outskirts of the village, feeling more love for him than ever before. When Gobar stooped to touch his feet, Hori burst into tears as though he would never see his son again. His heart swelled with pride and happiness and confidence. The boy's affection and devotion had restored his spirit and heightened his stature. The weariness and gloom that had overwhelmed him a

---

bacco, wrapped in a betel leaf. Commoners and highborn alike enjoy *pan* and consider it conducive to good digestion. The wealthy spread their *pan* with gossamer strips of gold or silver foil.

few days before, making him lose his way, had changed to courage and light.

Rupa was happy in her new home. She had grown up in circumstances where money was the scarcest item, so all sorts of longings had remained stifled within her. Now she could begin to satisfy them. And Ramsevak, middle-aged though he was, had become young again. As far as Rupa was concerned, he was her husband. Whether he was young, middle-aged, or old made no difference to her womanly feelings, which depended not on her husband's looks or age but were rooted much deeper—in a pure tradition which could have been shaken only by a major earthquake. Engrossed in her own youthfulness, she prettied herself for her own sake, for her own delight. To Ramsevak she showed another side of herself, that of a housekeeper absorbed in the duties of the home. She didn't want to upset or embarrass him by flaunting her youthfulness. To her mind, there was now nothing lacking in life. With the barn full of grain, fields extending to the horizon and rows of cattle by the door, there was no room to feel any kind of deprivation.

Her greatest desire now was to see her own people happy. How could she ease their poverty? Still fresh in her memory was that cow which had appeared like a guest and then departed leaving them weeping. The memory had become even more poignant with time. Her identification with the new household was not yet complete. The old home was still the one where she belonged and the people there were her own people. Their sorrows were her sorrows and their joys her joys. The sight of a whole herd of cattle at the door here could not make her as happy as the sight of just one cow at the door there. That longing of her father's had never been fulfilled. The day that cow had appeared, he'd been as excited as though a goddess had descended from the heavens.[1] Since then he'd not had the means to get another, but she knew that his yearning was as strong as ever. The next time she went home, she'd take that prize one with her. Or perhaps she could have her husband send it. It was just a matter of asking him.

Ramsevak readily agreed, and the next day Rupa dispatched a herdsman with the cow, instructing him to tell Hori that she'd sent it to provide milk for Mangal.

[1] The cow is venerated among Hindus as life-sustaining and as a symbol of creation and motherhood. Also, as in many primitive societies, a farmer's wealth and status may be measured by the number of cows he owns.

Hori had also been concerned about getting a cow. There was really no hurry about it except that Mangal was there and he certainly had to have milk. The first thing he'd do when he got some money was buy a cow. The boy was more than his grandson and Gobar's son—he was also the favorite of Malti Devi and should be brought up accordingly. But where was the money to come from?

Fortunately a contractor just then started quarrying gravel from some barren land near the village to build a road. Hori hurried over as soon as he heard and began digging at eight annas a day. If the work lasted for even two months, he'd have enough money for the cow. After a full day's work in the scorching sun and wind, he'd come home nearly dead, but there was no hint of defeat. The next day he'd return to work as eagerly as ever. And after dinner at night, he'd sit in front of the dim lamp making twine, staying up until midnight or later. Dhaniya seemed to have gone crazy too. Instead of objecting to all this hard work, she'd sit down with him and join in the rope-making. A cow just had to be bought, and there was also Ramsevak's money to repay. Gobar had said so, and this drove her on.

It was past midnight one night and they were both still working. "If you're getting sleepy," Dhaniya spoke up, "you'd better go get some rest. You have to be at work again early in the morning."

Hori looked up at the sky. "I'll go, but it can't be more than ten o'clock now. You go get some sleep."

"I get a little sleep in the early afternoon."

"After a bite of lunch, I take a nap too, under a tree."

"The heat of the loo must be terrible."

"I don't feel a thing—it's a good shady spot."

"I'm afraid you might get sick."

"Oh, go on! The people who get sick are those who have time for it. My one concern is to have half Ramsevak's money paid back by the time Gobar comes back again. He'll bring some money with him too. If we can free our necks from that debt this year, it'll give me a new lease on life."

"I think of Gobar a lot these days. He's become so thoughtful and gentle."

"He touched my feet when he was leaving."

"Mangal was in such good shape when he arrived, but he's grown thin since coming here."

"He had milk and butter and everything there. Here it's a

big thing just to get chapaties.[1] Well, just let me get enough
money from the contractor and I'll buy a cow."

"We'd have a cow now if you had listened to me. You
couldn't even care for our own land and yet you took on the
burden of Puniya's."

"What else could I have done? Duty counts for something
too. Hira may have done us wrong but his family still had to
have someone to look after them. Tell me, who was there except me? Just imagine the state they'd be in if I hadn't helped
out. And in spite of all my efforts, Mangaru has sued her for
his money."

"When a person buries all her money and hoards it, creditors are bound to sue."

"What nonsense you're talking. It's hard enough just to
feed one's self off the land. As if anyone has money to bury!"

"Hira seems to have vanished off the face of the earth."

"Something tells me he'll be back some day or other."

They went to sleep. Early next morning Hori woke up and
saw Hira standing there—hair shaggy, clothes in shreds, face
withered, body shrunken to skin and bones. He ran up and
fell at Hori's feet.

Hori helped him up and hugged him. "You've melted away
to nothing, Hira! When did you get back? We were just
thinking about you last night! Have you been ill?"

The Hira he saw today was not the man who had soured
his life but the little boy with no mother or father to whom
he had given a home. The intervening twenty-five or thirty
years seemed to have disappeared without a trace.

Hira stood there sobbing and said nothing.

"Why are you crying, brother?" Hori said, taking his hand.
"It's only human to make mistakes. Where have you been all
this time?"

"What can I say?" Hira murmured. "It's enough to know
that I was spared to see you again. The killing haunted me and
I felt as though the cow were standing in front of me. It stood
there every moment, waking or sleeping, and wouldn't go
away.[2] I went insane and ended up in an asylum for five
years. I got out some six months ago and have been roaming

---

[1] Wheat cakes fried in oil or ghee.

[2] Hori had obtained a cow from the elderly widower Bhola in return for arranging his marriage, payment for the cow to be made at
some unspecified date. Hira, Hori's younger brother who had quarreled
with him, secretly poisoned the cow. However, the cow, living or dead,
had eventually to be paid for. The symbol of Hori's supposed prosperity thus became the cause of his destruction.

around begging. I wasn't brave enough to come back here. How could I show my face to anyone? At last I couldn't stand it, though, so I mustered up my courage and returned. You've looked after my wife and . . ."

"You ran away needlessly," Hori interrupted. "Why, it just meant paying a few rupees to the police chief, that's all."

"I'll be indebted to you as long as I live, dada."

"It's not as though I'm some stranger, brother."

Hori was exuberant. All life's misfortunes and disappointments seemed to roll away. Could anyone still say he's lost the battle of life? Was this pride, this joy, this bliss a sign of defeat? Those defeats had been his victory, and his dilapidated weapons had been banners of triumph. His chest swelled and his face grew bright. Hira's gratitude symbolized the success of his life. Even if he'd had a barn overflowing with ten tons of grain, or a thousand rupees buried in a pot, nothing could have brought him more ecstasy than this moment.

Hira looked him up and down. "You've grown very thin too, dada."

Hori laughed. "Is this any time for me to be fat? The only people who get fat are those with no worries about debts or prestige or honor. To be fat these days is downright shameful. A hundred men have to grow thin for one man to get fat. What happiness would that bring? Everyone would have to be fat before one could be happy. Have you seen Shobha yet?"

"I visited him last night. To think that you not only looked after your own family but also upheld the family honor and took care of those who spited you—while he sold off all his land and everything. God only knows what he's going to live on."

When Hori set off for work that morning, there was a heaviness in his body. He'd been unable to shake off the exhaustion of the previous day, but there was still vigor in his stride and confidence in his bearing.

The loo was already blowing by ten that morning, and as midday approached, the sun seemed to be raining down fire. Hori carried one basket of gravel after the other from the quarry to the road and loaded them on the carts there. When the noon break arrived, he could hardly catch his breath. Never had he been so exhausted—he could hardly lift his feet and he was burning up inside. Too tired to wash or eat, he spread out his shoulder cloth beneath a tree and tried to sleep, but his throat was parched with thirst. Knowing it was

bad to drink water on an empty stomach, he tried to control
the thirst, but the burning inside kept growing worse. He
couldn't bear it. A worker nearby had brought a bucket of
water and was eating his parched gram. Hori raised himself
up, drank a jugful of water, and then lay back down; but
within half an hour he threw up, and a deathly pallor spread
over his face.

"Are you all right?" the man asked.

Hori's head was in a whirl. "I'm all right. It's nothing," he
said.

With that he vomited again, and his hands and feet began
turning cold. Why was his head so dizzy? Darkness seemed to
be engulfing him. His eyes closed, and memories of the past
rose and flashed across his mind in jumbled succession—the
recent mixed with the distant past—as incoherent, distorted,
and disconnected as pictures in a dream. That happy childhood appeared when he had played at boyish games or gone
to sleep in his mother's arms. Then he saw Gobar coming
and touching his feet. The scene then changed to Dhaniya as
a young bride, dressed in her red wedding sari and serving
him food. Then the image of a cow rose before him, just like
the celestial cow which grants all wishes. He milked the cow
and was giving the milk to Mangal when the cow turned into
a goddess and . . .

"Time's up, Hori," the laborer nearby called out. "Come
pick up your basket."

There was no answer from Hori—his spirit was soaring
through other worlds. His body was burning and his hands
and feet were cold. He'd been struck down by the loo.

A man was sent racing to his house. An hour later Dhaniya came running. Shobha and Hira followed, carrying a cot
as a litter.

When Dhaniya felt his body, her heart seemed to stop and
the color drained from her face. "How do you feel?" she
asked, her voice trembling.

Hori's eyes flickered. "You've come, Gobar?" he murmured. "I've bought a cow for Mangal. Look, she's standing
over there."

Dhaniya had seen the face of death and she recognized it.
She had seen it creep up on tiptoe and she had seen it burst
like a storm. Before her eyes, her mother-in-law had died, her
father-in-law had died, two of her sons had died, and scores
of village people had died. A blow seemed to strike her heart.
The foundation on which her life had rested seemed to be
slipping away . . . but no, this was a time for courage, and

her fears were groundless. He'd only been knocked unconscious momentarily by the burning loo.

Checking the rush of tears, she said, "Look here. It's me.
Don't you recognize me?"

Hori returned to consciousness. Death had moved in close.
The smoke had cleared away and the coals were about to
burst into flame. He looked at Dhaniya tenderly and a tear
rolled from the corner of each eye.

"Forgive my mistakes, Dhaniya. I'm going now. The longing for a cow has had to remain a longing. And now that
money will go for the last rites. Don't cry, Dhaniya. How
much longer could you have kept me alive anyway? I've
suffered every possible misfortune. Now let me die."

His eyes closed again. Hira and Shobha came forward with
the litter. Lifting him onto it, they started back to the village.

The news had swept through the village like a great wind
and everyone had assembled. Lying there on the cot, Hori
perhaps saw everything and understood everything, but his
lips were sealed. Only the tears flowing from his eyes spoke
of the anguish of breaking the ties of worldly attachment.
The sorrow of things left undone—that is the source of attachment, not the tasks completed and the duties discharged.
The pain comes in making orphans of those to whom obligations could not be met, in the half-realized ambitions which
could not be fulfilled.

Although she understood full well, Dhaniya clung to the
dwindling shadow of hope. Tears were flowing from her eyes
but she dashed around like a machine, making a mango drink
one moment and massaging his body with wheat chaff the
next. If only there were money, she'd have sent someone for
a doctor.

"Make your heart strong, bhaabi," Hira said, weeping.
"Make the gift of a cow. Dada is leaving us now."

Dhaniya's eyes glowed resentfully. How much stronger
could she make her heart? And did she have to be reminded
of her duty to her husband? She'd been his partner in life—
obviously her duty was not just to mourn over him.

"Yes, make the *godan*," other voices called out. "Now is
the time." [1]

Dhaniya rose mechanically and brought out the twenty
annas earned that morning from the twine they had made.
Placing the money in the cold palm of her husband's hand,

----

[1] A cow given in charity might propitiate the gods and thus prevent
Hori's death.

she stepped forward and said to Datadin, "Maharaj, there is no cow nor calf nor money in the house. There are only these few coins. This is his *godan*, his gift of a cow."

And she collapsed on the ground, unconscious.

translated by Gordon C. Roadarmel

A Novel of Japan

Kimitake Hiraoka (1925–   ), writing under the pen name of Mishima Yukio, is one of the most recent of Japan's novelists in the Western tradition. In a way, however, he may be seen as a link between the most contemporary expression of his culture and the most ancient. He has written modern Western-style dramas and plays in *Nō*, Japan's ancient stage form. In the novel *Love in the Morning* he has fused ancient orthography and vocabulary with a shockingly modern theme. And a relationship may be found between the tenth-century Genji and his contemporary protagonist Mizoguchi in *The Temple of the Golden Pavilion.*

In the *Genji monogatari (The Tale of Genji)*, considered to be the world's earliest true novel, Murasaki Shikibu (late tenth and early eleventh centuries) depicts her central hero as being almost painfully aware of life's beauty, especially its ephemeral nature. Through all of Genji's amoral adventures there is the sense of *mono no aware,* the beauty and the sadness of the things of this life. To Genji, fleeting beauty is a painful, all-consuming passion lived out in terms of love.

Something of the same essence is found in Mishima's most ambitious novel, *Kinkakuji (The Temple of the Golden Pavilion).* Here the young acolyte, Mizoguchi, is also painfully aware of beauty, but unlike Genji, who is himself the acme of manly grace, Mizoguchi experiences life's harmony in bitter contrast to his own physical ugliness. Raised on his father's descriptions of the Golden Temple of Kyoto as an object of ethereal beauty, the boy reaches manhood with an obsession that ultimately leads to his destroying the temple as being too perfect for this world. Where the tenth-century

Genji is haunted by the transitory nature of perfection, twentieth-century Mizoguchi cannot bear to see the one physical representation of perfection remain in a crass and unfeeling society. The beauty of the Golden Temple, set against the drab disillusionment of a defeated Japan and against his own physical inadequacies, becomes more than Mizoguchi can bear. The temple must be destroyed.

Mishima has taken an actual criminal case as the basis for his compelling novel. In 1950 the Golden Temple of Kyoto was set afire by a young priest-in-training. The deed and later trial triggered a master writer's creative genius, resulting seven years later in the publication of *Kinkakuji*. The approach is similar to that taken by Dostoevsky in *Crime and Punishment*. The crime is seen "from the inside out," very much in the modern tradition of psychological probing into human motivations and character. The reader observes the forces at work in the life of both the child and the man that would lead to an act of seemingly wanton destruction.

In broader terms, one sees the novel as a revelation of a people's conflict between a culture-oriented past and a crassly materialistic present. From the rush and clatter and turmoil of a great city Mishima takes the reader to the fourteen-century temple, rising above the unruffled surface of its reflecting pool, set in deceptively simple gardens, where the quiet is disturbed only by the murmur of gentle streams or a breath of wind in miniature red maple trees. The journey either way— into the Temple Garden or out again—is itself traumatic. Mishima succeeds in focusing this sense of psychological shock within the life of Mizoguchi.

Mishima Yukio is a prolific young writer often referred to as the voice of Japan's "lost generation." In his forty-four years he has dealt consistently with themes that are challenging and controversial. He writes so steadily that facts concerning his literary output are outdated before they are put down. By 1965 he had published thirty-three plays, including a group in the ancient *Nō* tradition, seventy-four short stories, thirteen novels, a travel book, and numerous articles. His plays have been performed in several countries other than Japan; his novels have been translated into fifteen languages and have provided the substance for ten motion pictures. He published his first novel at the age of twenty-three, and the first of five national literary prizes was awarded him in 1954 when he was not yet thirty.

In addition to his writing, Mishima has found time to

travel widely in the United States and Europe and to take the title role in a gangster film.

From Chapter 1 of the novel we have excerpts that reveal the protagonist's childhood and early conditioning. The Golden Temple dominates from the very first sentence.

In accordance with his father's wishes, Mizoguchi becomes an acolyte—a priest-in-training—at the Golden Temple. His life goes on largely centered about the temple and its religious routine, but is touched occasionally by outside changes that disturb it much as a quiet pool is roiled by a stone tossed into it.

Mizoguchi becomes increasingly concerned that the temple will be destroyed by enemy bombs or will be consumed by fire. The thought of such possible destruction apparently takes over his subconscious. The temple escapes the ravages of war, but gradually Mizoguchi becomes possessed by the need to destroy the temple himself.

The last quarter of the book accelerates in pace as Mizoguchi lays plans for a threefold crime: the murder of the temple superior, the arson of the temple, and his self-destruction.

Chapter 10, which closes the book, relates the outcome of his designs.

MISHIMA YUKIO (KIMITAKE HIRAOKA)

THE TEMPLE OF THE GOLDEN PAVILION

Chapter 1

Ever since my childhood, Father had often spoken to me about the Golden Temple.

My birthplace was a lonely cape that projects into the Sea of Japan northeast of Maizuru. Father, however, was not born there, but at Shiraku in the eastern suburbs of Maizuru. He was urged to join the clergy and became the priest of a temple on a remote cape; in this place he married and begot a child, who was myself.

There was no suitable middle school in the vicinity of the temple on Cape Nariu. At length I left my parents' house and was sent to my uncle's home in Father's birthplace; while I lived there, I attended the East Maizuru Middle School, going to and fro on foot.

The sky in Father's hometown was very bright. But each

year in October and November, even on days when it did not
look as if there could be a single cloud, we would have several sudden showers. I wondered whether it was not here that
I developed my changeable disposition.

On spring evenings when I returned from school, I would
sit in my study on the second floor of my uncle's house and
gaze at the hills. The rays of the sinking sun shone on the
young leaves that covered the hillside and it looked as though
a golden screen had been set up in the midst of the fields.
When I saw this, the Golden Temple sprang into my mind.

Though occasionally I saw the real Golden Temple in pho-
tographs or in textbooks, it was the image of the Golden
Temple as Father had described it to me that dominated my
heart. Father had never told me that the real Golden Temple
was shining in gold, or anything of the sort; yet, according to
Father, there was nothing on this earth so beautiful as the
Golden Temple. Moreover, the very characters with which
the name of the temple was written and the very sound of the
word imparted some fabulous quality to the Golden Temple
that was engraved on my heart.

When I saw the surface of the distant fields glittering in
the sun, I felt sure that this was a golden shadow cast by the
invisible temple. The Yoshizaka Pass, which forms the
boundary between Fukui Prefecture and my own Kyoto Prefecture lay directly to the east. The sun rises directly above
this mountain pass. Though the actual city of Kyoto lies in
exactly the opposite direction, I used to see the Golden Temple soaring up into the morning sky amidst the rays of the
sun as it rose from the folds of those eastern hills.

Thus the Golden Temple was apparent everywhere. Insofar
as I could not actually set eyes on the temple, it was like the
sea. For though Maizuru Bay lies only three and a half miles
to the west of the village of Shiraku where I lived, the water
itself was blocked from view by the hills; yet there always
floated in the air a sort of presentiment of this sea: sometimes
the wind would bring with it a smell of the sea, sometimes in
rough weather flocks of gulls would swoop down into the
nearby fields to take refuge.

I had a weak constitution and was always being defeated
by the other boys in running or on the exercise bar. Besides, I
had suffered since my birth from a stutter, and this made me
still more retiring in my manner. And everyone knew that I
came from a temple. Some of the more ill-behaved children
used to make fun of me by imitating a stuttering priest as he
tried to stammer his way through the sutras. There was a

story in one of our books in which a stuttering detective appeared, and the boys used to read these passages to me in a specially loud voice.

My stuttering, I need hardly say, placed an obstacle between me and the outside world. It is the first sound that I have trouble in uttering. This first sound is like a key to the door that separates my inner world from the world outside, and I have never known that key to turn smoothly in its lock. Most people, thanks to their easy command of words, can keep this door between the inner world and the outer world wide open, so that the air passes freely between the two; but for me this has been quite impossible. Thick rust has gathered on the key.

When a stutterer is struggling desperately to utter his first sound, he is like a little bird that is trying to extricate itself from thick lime. When finally he manages to free himself, it is too late. To be sure, there are times when the reality of the outer world seems to have been waiting for me, folding its arms as it were, while I was struggling to free myself. But the reality that is waiting for me is not a fresh reality. When finally I reach the outer world after all my efforts, all that I find is a reality that has instantly changed color and gone out of focus—a reality that has lost the freshness that I had considered fitting for myself, and that gives off a half-putrid odor.

As can easily be imagined, a youth like myself came to entertain two opposing forms of power wishes. In history I enjoyed the descriptions of tyrants. I saw myself as a stuttering, taciturn tyrant; my retainers would hang on every expression that passed over my face and would live both day and night in fear and trembling of me. There is no need to justify my cruelty in clear, smooth words. My taciturnity alone was sufficient to justify every manner of cruelty. On the one hand I enjoyed imagining how one by one I would wreak punishment on my teachers and schoolmates who daily tormented me; on the other hand, I fancied myself as a great artist, endowed with the clearest vision—a veritable sovereign of the inner world. My outer appearance was poor, but in this way my inner world became richer than anyone else's. Was it not natural that a young boy who suffered from an indelible drawback like mine should have come to think that he was a secretly chosen being? I felt as though somewhere in this world a mission awaited me of which I myself still knew nothing. . . .

It is no exaggeration to say that the first real problem I

faced in my life was that of beauty. My father was only a simple country priest, deficient in vocabulary, and he taught me that "there is nothing on this earth so beautiful as the Golden Temple." At the thought that beauty should already have come into this world unknown to me, I could not help feeling a certain uneasiness and irritation. If beauty really did exist there, it meant that my own existence was a thing estranged from beauty.

But for me the Golden Temple was never simply an idea. The mountains blocked it from my sight, yet, if I should want to see it, the temple was always there for me to go and see. Beauty was thus an object that one could touch with one's fingers, that could be clearly reflected in one's eyes. I knew and I believed that, amid all the changes of the world, the Golden Temple remained there safe and immutable.

There were times when I thought of the Golden Temple as being like a small, delicate piece of workmanship that I could put in my hands; there were times, also, when I thought of it as a huge, monstrous cathedral that soared up endlessly into the sky. Being a young boy, I could not think of beauty as being either small or large, but a thing of moderation. So when I saw small, dew-drenched summer flowers that seemed to emit a vague light, they seemed to me as beautiful as the Golden Temple. Again, when the gloomy, thunder-packed clouds stood boldly on the other side of the hills, with only the edges shining in gold, their magnificence reminded me of the Golden Temple. Finally it came about that even when I saw a beautiful face, the simile would spring into my mind: "lovely as the Golden Temple." . . .

Chapter Ten

On the day after my visit to Gobancho I had already carried out an experiment. I had pulled out a couple of nails, which were about two inches long, from the wooden door at the back of the Golden Temple.

There are two entrances to the Hosui-in on the ground floor of the Golden Temple. Both are folding doors, one to the east, the other to the west. The old guide used to go up to the Golden Temple every night. First he would close the west door from the inside, then he would close the east door from outside and lock it. I knew, however, that I could enter the Golden Temple without a key. For there was an old wooden door at the back which was no longer in use. This door could easily be removed if one took out about half a dozen nails from the top and bottom. The nails were all loose and it was quite simple to pull them out with one's fingers. I had therefore taken out a couple of the nails as an experiment. I had wrapped them in a piece of paper and placed them carefully in the back of my drawer. A few days went by. No one seemed to have noticed. A week passed. There was still no sign that anyone had observed that the nails were missing. On the evening of the twenty-eighth I stealthily entered the temple and put them back in their former place.

On the day that I had seen the Superior crouching in the teahouse and had finally decided that I was not going to depend on anyone else's strength, I had gone to a pharmacy near the Nishijin police station in Chimoto Imaidegawa and bought some arsenic. First I was given a small bottle which could not have contained more than thirty pills. I asked for a larger size and finally paid one hundred yen for a bottle of a hundred pills. Then I went to an ironmonger's south of the police station and bought a pocketknife, which had a blade about four inches long. Together with the case it cost me ninety yen.

I walked back and forth in front of the Nishijin police station. It was evening and several of the windows were brightly lit. I noticed a police detective hurrying into the building. He was wearing an open-neck shirt and was carrying a briefcase. No one paid any attention to me. No one had paid any attention to me during the past twenty years and under present conditions this was bound to continue. Under present conditions I was still a person of no importance. In this country of Japan there were people by the million, by the tens of millions, who were tucked away in corners and to whom no one paid any attention. I still belonged to their ranks. The world felt not the slightest concern as to whether these people lived or died and for this reason there was something reassuring about them. The police detective was therefore reassured and did not bother to give me a second look. The red, smoky light of the lamp, illuminated the stone sign of the Nishijin police station; the character for *jin* had fallen out and no one had bothered to replace it.

On my way back to the temple I thought about the purchases which I had made that evening. They were exciting purchases. Although I had bought the drugs and the knife for the remote eventuality of having to die, I was so pleased with them that I could not help wondering whether this was not how a man must feel who has acquired a new house and who is making plans for his future life. Even after I had returned

to the temple I did not tire of looking at my two acquisitions.
I took the pocketknife out of its case and licked the blade.
The steel immediately clouded over and the clear coolness
against my tongue was followed by a remote suggestion of
sweetness. The sweetness was faintly reflected on my tongue
from within the thin steel, from within the unattainable essence of the steel. The clarity of form, the luster of iron like
the indigo color of the deep sea—it was they that carried this
limpid sweetness which coiled itself securely round the tip of
my tongue together with my saliva. Finally the sweetness
receded from me. Happily I imagined the day when my flesh
would be intoxicated by a great outburst of that sweetness.
Death's sky was bright and seemed to me like the sky of life.
My gloomy thoughts all left me. This world was now devoid
of agony.

After the war an automatic fire alarm of the latest model
had been installed in the Golden Temple. It was so designed
that when the temperature inside the temple reached a certain point, the warning bell would ring in the corridor of the
building where we lived. On the evening of June 29 something went wrong with the alarm. It was the old guide who
discovered the fault. I happened to be in the kitchen at the
time and I heard the old man report the matter to the deacon's office. I felt that I was listening to an encouragement
from heaven.

On the following morning, however, the deacon telephoned
the factory that had installed the equipment and asked them
to send a repairman. The good-natured guide went out of his
way to inform me of this development. I bit my lip. Last
night had been the golden opportunity for carrying out my
decision and I had missed it.

In the evening the repairman came. We all stood around
curiously watching him at work. It took a long time to carry
out the repairs. The man inclined his head to one side with a
vague air of discouragement and his audience began to leave
one by one. In due course I also left. Now I had to wait for
the repairs to be completed and for that signal of despair
when the alarm bell would ring out loudly through the temple buildings as the man tested it. I waited. The night pushed
its way up the Golden Temple like a rising tide, and I could
see the repairman's little light flickering inside the dark building. There was no sound of an alarm. The repairman gave up
and said that he would return on the following day to finish
the job.

He broke his word, however, and failed to come on July 1. The temple authorities were aware of no particular reason to speed up the repairs.

On June 30 I went once again to Chimoto Imaidegawa and bought some sweet bread and some bean-jam wafers. Since we were never given anything to eat between meals at the temple, I had occasionally come to this place and bought a few sweets out of my meager pocket money.

But my purchases on the thirtieth were not inspired by hunger. Nor did I buy the bread to help me swallow the arsenic. If I must give a reason, I should say that uneasiness caused me to buy that food.

The relationship between me and that full paper bag which I carried in my hand. The relationship between that perfect and isolated deed that I was about to undertake and the shabby bread in my bag. The sun oozed out from the cloudy sky and shrouded the old houses along the street like a sweltering mist. The perspiration began to run stealthily down my back as if a cold thread had suddenly been pulled along it. I was terribly tired.

The relationship between me and the sweet bread. What could it be? I imagined that when the time came and I was face to face with the deed, my spirit would be buoyed up by the tension and concentration of the moment, but that my stomach, which would be left in its usual state of isolation, would still demand some guaranty of this isolation. I felt that my internal organs were like some shabby dog of mine that could never be properly trained. I knew. I knew that however much my spirit might be enlivened, my stomach and my intestines—those dull, stolid organs lodged within my body —would insist on having their own way and would start dreaming some banal dream of everyday life.

I knew that my stomach was going to dream. It was going to dream about sweet bread and bean-jam wafers. While my spirit dreamed about jewels, my stomach would obstinately dream about sweet bread and bean-jam wafers. In any case, this food of mine would provide a fitting clue when people started to rack their brains about the reason for my crime. "The poor fellow was hungry," people would say. "How very human!"

The day came. July 1, 1950. As I have already mentioned, there was no prospect that the fire alarm would be repaired during the course of that day. This was confirmed at six o'clock in the evening. The old guide telephoned the factory once again and urged them to complete the repairs. The mechanic replied that he was unfortunately too busy to come that evening, but that he would finish the job on the following day without fail.

There had been about a hundred visitors at the temple during the day, but since the gates closed at half past six, the waves of human beings were already beginning to recede. When the old guide had finished telephoning, he stood at the entrance of the kitchen looking absently at the little field outside. He had completed his work for the day.

It was drizzling. There had been several showers since the morning. There was also a slight breeze and it was not too sultry for the time of year. I noticed the flowers of the pumpkin plants scattered here and there in the field under the rain. The soybeans, which had been planted in the previous month, had begun to sprout along the black, glossy ridges on the other side of the field.

When the guide was engaged in thinking, he used to bring his badly fitting false teeth together with a resounding clang. Every day he gave forth the same information to the temple visitors, but owing to his false teeth it was steadily becoming harder to understand him. He paid absolutely no attention to the various suggestions that he should have them repaired. The old man was muttering to himself as he gazed at the field. He paused for a moment and I could hear his dentures clattering. Then he started muttering again. He was probably grumbling about the delay in repairing the fire alarm. As I listened to his incomprehensible murmur, I felt he was saying that it was now too late for any repair—either to his teeth or to the fire alarm.

The Superior had an unaccustomed visitor that evening. It was Father Kuwai Zenkai, the head of the Ryuho Temple in Fukui Prefecture, who had been a friend during his seminary days. Since Father Zenkai had been a friend of the Superior's, he had also been friendly with my father.

The Superior was out when Father Zenkai arrived. Someone telephoned him and told him that he had a visitor; he said that he would be back in about an hour. Father Zenkai had come to Kyoto to spend a day or two at our temple.

I remembered that Father had always spoken happily about this priest and I knew that he had a very high opinion of him. He was extremely masculine both in appearance and in character and was a model of the rough-hewn type of Zen priest. He was almost six feet tall, with dark skin and bushy eyebrows. His voice was like thunder.

When one of my fellow apprentices came to tell me that Father Zenkai wanted to talk to me until the Superior returned, I felt rather hesitant. I was afraid that the priest's clear pure eyes would see through my plan, which was now so rapidly nearing the moment of execution.

I found him sitting cross-legged in the large visitors' hall in the main building. He was drinking saké, which the deacon had sensibly brought him, and munching some vegetarian tidbits. My fellow apprentice had been serving him until I arrived, but I now took his place and, sitting down formally in front of the priest, began to pour his saké for him. I sat with my back to the darkness of the silent rain. Father Zenkai therefore had two gloomy prospects before his eyes—the dark garden, which was sodden from the rainy season, and my face. But he was not a man to be enmeshed by this or anything else. Although it was our first meeting, he spoke brightly and without hesitation. One remark followed another. "You look just like your father." "You've really grown up, haven't you?" "How very sad that your father should have died!"

Father Zenkai had a simplicity that was alien to the Superior and a strength that my father had never possessed. His face was sunburned, his nostrils were extremely wide, the folds of flesh round the heavy brows of his eyes bulged toward each other, so that his face looked as if it had been modeled after the Obeshimi masks used for goblins in *Nō* plays.

He certainly did not have regular features. There was too much inner power in Father Zenkai. This power revealed itself just as it pleased and entirely destroyed any regularity that there might have been. His protruding cheekbones were precipitous like the craggy mountains depicted by Chinese artists of the Southern School.

Yet there was a gentleness in the priest's thundering voice that found an echo in my heart. It was not a usual sort of gentleness, but the gentleness of the harsh roots of some great tree that grows outside a village and gives shelter to the passing traveler. His gentleness was rough to the feel. As we talked, I had to be on my guard lest tonight of all nights my resolution should be blunted by contact with this gentleness. The suspicion occurred to me that the Superior might have asked Father Zenkai especially for my benefit, but I realized that he would hardly have had him come all the way from

Fukui Prefecture just for me. No, this priest was merely a peculiar guest, who by chance was going to be witness to a supreme cataclysm.

The white earthenware saké bottle held over half a pint, but Father Zenkai had already emptied it. I excused myself with a formal bow and went to the kitchen to fetch another bottle. As I returned with the heated saké, I was overcome by a feeling that I had never known until then. The desire to be understood by others had so far never occurred to me, but now I wished that Father Zenkai alone would understand me. He should have noticed that as I again knelt there before him pouring out his saké my eyes gleamed with a sincerity that they had not had a little while before.

"What do you think of me, Father?" I asked.

"Hm, I should say that you look like a good serious student. Of course I don't know what kind of debauchery you go in for on the sly. But there, I've forgotten. Things aren't like they used to be, are they? I don't suppose you young fellows nowadays have enough money for debauchery. When your father and I and the Superior here were young, we used to do all sorts of wicked things."

"Do I look like an ordinary student?" I asked.

"Yes," replied Father Zenkai, "and that's the best way to look. To look ordinary is by far the best thing. People aren't suspicious of you then, you see."

Father Zenkai was devoid of vanity. High-ranking prelates, who are constantly being asked to judge everything from human character to paintings and antiques, are apt to fall into the sin of never giving a positive judgment on anything for fear of being laughed at later in case they have been wrong. Then, of course, there is the type of Zen priest who will instantly hand down his arbitrary decision on anything that is discussed, but who will be careful to phrase his reply in such a way that it can be taken to mean two opposite things. Father Zenkai was not like that. I was well aware that he spoke just as he saw and just as he felt. He did not go out of his way to search for any special meaning in the things that were reflected in his strong, pure eyes. It made no difference to him whether there was a meaning or not. And what more than anything else made Father Zenkai seem so great to me was that when he looked at some object—at me for instance—he did not try to assert his individuality by perceiving something that he and no one else could see, but saw the object just as anyone else would see it. The mere objective world itself had no meaning for this priest. I understood what he was trying to tell me and gradually I began to feel at ease. So long as I looked ordinary to other people, I really was ordinary and, whatever strange actions I might bring myself to commit, this ordinariness would remain, like rice that has been sifted through a winnow.

Without any conscious effort, I had come to imagine myself as a quiet little bushy tree planted in front of Father Zenkai.

"Is it all right, Father," I said, "to act according to the pattern that people expect of one?"

"It's not always so easy. But if you start acting in a different way, people soon come to accept that as being normal for you. They're very forgetful, you see."

"Which personality is really lasting?" I asked. "The one that I envisage myself or the one that other people believe I have?"

"Both will soon come to an end. However much you may convince yourself that your personality is lasting, it is bound to cease sooner or later. While the train is running, the passengers stay still. But when the train stops, the passengers have to start walking from that point. Running comes to an end and resting also comes to an end. Death seems to be the ultimate rest, but there's no telling how long even that continues."

"Please see into me, Father," I said finally. "I am not the sort of person you imagine. Please see into my heart."

The priest put his saké cup to his mouth and looked at me intently. The silence weighed down on me like the great, black, rain-drenched roof of the temple. I shuddered. Then suddenly Father Zenkai spoke in a laughing voice that was extraordinarily clear: "There's no need to see into you. One can see everything on your face."

I felt that I had been completely understood down to the deepest recess of my being. For the first time in my life I had become utterly blank. Just like water soaking into this blankness, courage to commit the deed gushed up in me afresh.

The Superior returned to the temple. It was nine o'clock. As usual, a group of four set out to make the final inspection for the night. There was nothing out of the ordinary. The Superior sat drinking saké with Father Zenkai. At about half past twelve one of my fellow apprentices came to conduct the visitor to his bedroom. Then the Superior had his bath—or "entered the waters," as it was called in the temple—and by one o'clock on the morning of the second, when the night watch was finished, the temple was completely quiet. Outside it continued to rain silently.

My sleeping roll was spread out on the floor. I sat there by myself and contemplated the night that had settled on the temple. Gradually the night became denser and heavier. The large pillars and the wooden door of the little room where I sat looked austere as they supported this ancient night.

I stuttered silently inside my mouth. As usual, a single word appeared on my lips much to my irritation; for it was just like when one vainly searches for something in a bag and instead keeps on coming across some other object that one does not want. The heaviness and density of my inner world closely resembled those of the night and my words creaked to the surface like a heavy bucket being drawn out of the night's deep well.

It wouldn't be long now, I thought; I must just remain patient for a short while. The rusty key that opened the door between the outer world and my inner world would turn smoothly in its lock. My world would be ventilated as the breeze blew freely between it and the outer world. The well bucket would rise, swaying lightly in the wind, and everything would open up before me in the form of a vast field and the secret room would be destroyed. . . . Now it is before my eyes and my hands are just about to stretch out and reach it. . . .

I was filled with happiness as I sat there in the darkness for about an hour. I felt that I had never been as happy in my entire life. Abruptly I arose out of the darkness.

I made my way stealthily to the back of the library and put on the straw sandals that I had carefully placed there beforehand. Then in the drizzling rain I walked along the ditch behind the temple in the direction of the workroom. There was no lumber in the workroom, but the floor was strewn with sawdust whose rain-sodden smell wandered helplessly about the place. The workroom was also used for storing straw. It was usual to buy forty bundles of this straw at a time, but that night only three bundles remained from the last lot.

I picked up the three bundles and returned along the edge of the field. All was hushed in the kitchen. I made my way round the corner of the building and reached the rear of the Deacon's quarters. Suddenly a light shone in the lavatory window. I crouched down.

I could hear someone clearing his throat in the lavatory. It sounded like the Deacon. Then I heard him relieving himself. It seemed to go on forever.

I was afraid that the straw might get wet in the rain, and I protected it with my chest as I crouched there next to the building. The smell from the lavatory had been intensified by the rain and now it settled heavily over the clumps of ferns. The splashing in the toilet bowl stopped and then I heard a body bump against the wooden wall. Evidently the Deacon was not fully awake and he was still unsteady on his feet. The light in the window went out. I picked up the three bundles of straw and set out for the rear of the library.

My property consisted only of a wicker basket, in which I kept my personal belongings, and a small old trunk. I intended to burn all of it. Earlier in the evening I had packed my books, my clothes, my robes, and the various other odds and ends in these two pieces of luggage. I hope that people will recognize how carefully I went about everything. Such things as my mosquito-net rod that were apt to make a noise while I carried them, and also noninflammable objects, like my ashtray, my cup, and my ink bottle, which would leave evidence of my deed, I had packed between some soft cushions and wrapped up in a cloth. I had put these apart from my other possessions. In addition, I had to burn one mattress and two quilts. I moved all this bulky luggage piece by piece to the rear of the library and piled it up on the ground. Then I went to the Golden Temple to remove the back door that I mentioned earlier.

The nails came out one after another as easily as if they had been stuck in a bed of soft earth. I supported the slanting door with my entire body and the wet surface of the rotten wood swelled out to rub gently against my cheek. It was not as heavy as I had expected. Having removed the door, I laid it down on the ground next to the building. Now I could look into the interior of the Golden Temple. It was replete with darkness.

The door was just wide enough so that one could enter the temple sideways. I soaked my body into the darkness of the Golden Temple. Then a strange face appeared before me and made me tremble with fear. As I was holding a lighted match, my face was reflected on the glass case that contained the model of the temple.

This was hardly an appropriate time for such activities, but I now stopped and gazed intently at the miniature Golden Temple which stood inside its case. This little temple was illuminated by the moonlight of my match, its shadow flickered and its delicate wooden frame crouched there full of uneasiness. Almost immediately it was swallowed up by the darkness. My match had burned out.

Strangely enough, the red glow that dotted the end of the match made me nervous and I carefully stamped it out, just like that student whom I had once seen at the Myoshin Temple. Then I struck another match. I passed in front of the Sutra Hall and the statues of the three Buddhas and came to where the offertory box stood. The box had numerous wooden slats, between which the coins were dropped, and now as the light of my match flickered in the darkness the shadows of those slats rippled like waves. Inside the offertory box there was a wooden statue of Ashikaga Yoshimitsu, which was classed as a National Treasure. It was a sitting figure dressed in a priestly robe whose sleeves stretched out at both ends; a scepter rested in its hands. The eyes of the little shaven head were wide open and the neck was buried in the wide sleeves of the robe. The eyes of the statue glittered in the light of my match, but I was not afraid. It was really horrible, that little statue of Yoshimitsu. Though it was enshrined in a corner of the building that he had himself constructed, he seemed long since to have abandoned all ownership and control.

I opened the western door which led to the Sosei. As I have already mentioned, this was a hinged door which one could open from the inside. The rainy night sky was lighter than the inside of the Golden Temple. With a subdued grating sound the wet door let in the breeze-filled dark-blue night air.

Yoshimitsu's eyes, I thought as I bounded out of the door and ran back to the rear of the library. Those eyes of Yoshimitsu's. Everything would be performed in front of those eyes. In front of those unseeing eyes of a dead witness.

As I ran, I noticed that something was making a sound in my trouser pocket. It was the rattling of my matchbox. I stopped and stuffed a paper handkerchief under the lid of the box. This ended the rattle. No sound came from the other pocket, where my bottle of arsenic and my knife were securely wrapped in a handkerchief. Nor, of course, was there any sound from the sweet bread, the bean-jam wafers, and the cigarettes, which lay in the pocket of my jumper.

Then I embarked on some mechanical work. It took me four journeys to move all the things that I had piled up outside the library to their destination in front of the statue of Yoshimitsu in the Golden Temple. First I carried the mattress and the mosquito net, from which the rod had been removed. Then I took the two quilts. Next the trunk and the wicker basket, and after that the three bundles of straw. I piled all these things up in disorder, putting the straw bundles between the mosquito net and the bedding. The mosquito net seemed to be the most inflammable of all the objects and accordingly I stretched part of it over the rest of my luggage.

Finally I returned to the rear of the library and fetched the bundle in which I had wrapped the various things that were hard to burn. This time I took my load to the edge of the pond at the east of the Golden Temple. From here I could see the Yohaku Rock directly ahead of me. I stood under a cluster of pine trees and barely managed to protect myself from the rain.

The reflection of the night sky gave a dim whiteness to the surface of the pond. The dense duckweed made it look as if it were solid land and it was only from the occasional interstices between this thick covering that one could tell that water lay beneath. Where I stood it was not raining hard enough to make any ripples. The pond steamed in the rain and seemed to stretch out endlessly into the distance. The air was full of moisture.

I picked up a pebble and dropped it into the water. There was a splash of such exaggerated loudness that the air about me seemed to have cracked. For a while I crouched in the darkness without a sound, hoping by my silence to eradicate the noise that I had accidentally produced.

I put my hand into the water and the lukewarm duckweed clung to my fingers. First I let the mosquito-net rod slip into the water from my moist fingers. Then I entrusted my ashtray to the pond, as though I were rinsing it out. In the same way I dropped my cup and my ink bottle. That took care of all the things that had to be thrown into the water. All that remained beside me was the cushion and the cloth in which I had wrapped these objects. Nothing was left for me now but to take these two things in front of Yoshimitsu's statue and then finally to fire the temple.

The fact that at this moment I was abruptly overcome by hunger accorded too much with what I had expected and, far from gratifying me, made me feel that I had been betrayed. I was still carrying the sweet bread and the bean-jam wafers, which I had started eating on the previous day. I wiped my wet hands on the end of my jumper and devoured the food greedily. I was not aware of the taste. My stomach cried out loudly for food and did not care in the slightest about any sense of taste. It was a good thing that I was able to concentrate on stuffing the sweet bread hurriedly into my mouth. My heart was pounding. When I had finished swallowing the food, I scooped some water out of the pond and drank.

I was on the very threshold of my deed. I had completed all the preparations that led to the deed and now I was standing on the further edge of those preparations with nothing left to do but to hurl myself into the actual deed. With only the slightest effort I should be able to attain that deed.

I did not imagine for a moment that a gulf great enough to swallow my entire life was opening up between me and what I intended to do.

For at that moment I gazed at the Golden Temple to bid it a last farewell. The temple was dim in the darkness of the rainy night and its outline was indistinct. It stood there in deep black, as though it were a crystallization of the night itself. When I strained my eyes, I managed to make out the Kukyocho, the top story of the temple, where the entire structure suddenly became narrow, and also the forest of narrow pillars that surrounded the Choondo and the Hosui-in. But the various details of the temple, which had moved me so greatly in the past, had melted away into the monochrome darkness.

As my remembrance of the beauty grew more and more vivid, however, this very darkness began to provide a background against which I could conjure up my vision at will. My entire conception of beauty lurked within this somber, crouching form. Thanks to the power of memory, the various aesthetic details began to glitter one by one out of the surrounding darkness; then the glittering spread wider and wider, until gradually the entire temple had emerged before me under that strange light of time itself, which is neither day nor night. Never before had the Golden Temple showed itself to me in so perfect a form, never had I seen it glitter like this in its every detail. It was as though I had appropriated a blind man's vision. The light that emanated from the temple itself had made the building transparent, and standing by the pond I could vividly see the paintings of angels on the roof inside the Choondo and the remains of the ancient gold foil on the walls in the Kukyocho. The delicate exterior of the Golden Temple had become intimately mingled with the interior. As my eyes took in the entire prospect, I could perceive the temple's structure and the clear outline of its motif, I could see the painstaking repetition and decoration of the details whereby this motif was materialized. I

saw the effects of contrast and of symmetry. The two lower
stories, the Hosui-in and the Choondo, were of the same
width and, though there was a slight difference between them,
they were protected by the same extensive eave; one story
rested on top of its companion, so that they looked like a
pair of closely related dreams or like memories of two very
similar pleasures that we have enjoyed in the past. These twin
stories had been crowned by a third story, the Kukyocho,
which abruptly tapered off. And high on top of the shingled
roof the gilt bronze phoenix was facing the long, lightless
night.

Yet even this had not satisfied the architect. At the west of
the Hosui-in he had added the tiny Sosei, which projected
from the temple like an overhanging pavilion. It was as if he
had put all his aesthetic powers into breaking the symmetry
of the building. The role of the Sosei in the total architecture
was one of metaphysical resistance. Although it certainly did
not stretch very far over the pond, it looked as though it
were running away indefinitely from the center of the Golden
Temple. The Sosei was like a bird soaring away from the
main structure of the building, like a bird that a few moments before had spread its wings and was escaping toward
the surface of the pond, toward everything that was mundane. The significance of the Sosei was to provide a bridge
that led between the order which controls the world and
those things, like carnal desire, which are utterly disordered.
Yes, that was it. The spirit of the Golden Temple began with
this Sosei, which resembled a bridge that has been severed at
its halfway point; then it formed a three-storied tower; then
once more it fled from this bridge. For the vast power of sensual desire that shimmered on the surface of this pond was
the source of the hidden force that had constructed the
Golden Temple; but, after this power had been put in order
and the beautiful three-storied tower formed, it could no
longer bear to dwell there and nothing was left for it but to
escape along the Sosei back to the surface of the pond, back
to the endless shimmering of sensual desire, back to its native
land. Every time in the past that I had looked at the morning
mist or the evening mist as it wandered over the pond I had
been struck by this same thought—the thought that this was
the dwelling place of the abundant sensual power that had
originally constructed the Golden Temple.

And beauty synthesized the struggles and the contradictions and the disharmonies in every part of this building—
and, furthermore, it was beauty that ruled over them all! The

Golden Temple had been built with gold dust in the long, lightless night, just like a sutra that is painstakingly inscribed with gold dust onto the dark-blue pages of a book. Yet I did not know whether beauty was, on the one hand, identical with the Golden Temple itself or, on the other, consubstantial with the night of nothingness that surrounded the temple. Perhaps beauty was both these things. It was both the individual parts and the whole structure, both the Golden Temple and the night that wrapped itself about the Golden Temple. At this thought I felt that the mystery of the beauty of the Golden Temple, which had tormented me so much in the past, was halfway towards being solved. If one examined the beauty of each individual detail—the pillars, the railings, the shutters, the framed doors, the ornamented windows, the pyramidal roof—the Hosui-in, the Choondo, the Kukyocho, the Sosei—the shadow of the temple on the pond, the little islands, the pine trees, yes, even the mooring place for the temple boat—the beauty was never completed in any single detail of the temple; for each detail adumbrated the beauty of the succeeding detail. The beauty of the individual detail itself was always filled with uneasiness. It dreamed of perfection, but it knew no completion and was invariably lured on to the next beauty, the unknown beauty. The adumbration of beauty contained in one detail was linked with the subsequent adumbration of beauty, and so it was that the various adumbrations of a beauty *which did not exist* had become the underlying motif of the Golden Temple. Such adumbrations were signs of nothingness. Nothingness was the very structure of this beauty. Therefore, from the incompletion of the various details of this beauty there arose automatically an adumbration of nothingness, and this delicate building, wrought of the most slender timber, was trembling in anticipation of nothingness, like a jeweled necklace trembling in the wind.

Yet never did there come a time when the beauty of the Golden Temple ceased! Its beauty was always echoing somewhere. Like a person who suffers from ringing of the ears, I invariably heard the sound of the Golden Temple's beauty wherever I might be and I had grown accustomed to it. If one compared this beauty to a sound, the building was like a little golden bell that has gone on ringing for five and a half centuries, or else like a small harp. But what if that sound should stop?

I was overcome by intense weariness.

Above the Golden Temple that existed in the darkness I could still vividly see the Golden Temple of my vision. It had not yet concluded its glittering. The railing of the Hosui-in at the water's edge withdrew with the greatest modesty, while on its eaves the railing of the Choondo, supported by its Indian-style brackets, thrust out its breast dreamily towards the pond. The eaves were illuminated by the pond's reflection and the flickering of the water reflected itself uncertainly against them. When the Golden Temple reflected the evening sun or shone in the moon, it was the light of the water that made the entire structure look as if it were mysteriously floating along and flapping its wings. The strong bonds of the temple's form were loosened by the reflection of the quivering water, and at such moments the Golden Temple seemed to be constructed of materials like wind and water and flame that are constantly in motion.

The beauty of the Golden Temple was unsurpassed. And I knew now where my great weariness had come from. That beauty was taking a last chance to exercise its power over me and to bind me with that impotence which had so often overcome me in the past. My hands and my feet flinched from what lay before me. A few moments before, I had been only one step from my deed, but now once again I had retreated far into the distance.

"I had made all my preparations," I murmured to myself, "and was only one step from the deed. Having so completely dreamed the deed, having so completely lived that dream, is there really any need to act it out physically? Wouldn't such action be quite useless at this stage?

"Kashiwagi was probably right when he said that what changed the world was not action but knowledge. And there was also the type of knowledge that tried to copy the action to the utmost possible limit. My knowledge is of this nature. And it is this type of knowledge that makes the action really invalid. Does not the reason, then, for all my careful preparations lie in the final knowledge that *I would not have to act in earnest?*

"Yes, that's it. Action is now simply a kind of superfluity for me. It has jutted out of life, it has jutted out of my own will, and now it stands before me, like a separate, cold steel mechanism, waiting to be put in motion. It is as if there is not the slightest connection between me and my action. *Up to this point* it has been I, from here on it is not I. How can I dare to stop being myself?"

I leaned against the bottom of the pine tree. The wet, cool skin of the tree bewitched me. I felt that this sensation, this coolness was—myself. The world had stopped just as it was; no longer was there any desire and I, too, was utterly satisfied.

What should I do with this terrible weariness, I thought? Somehow I felt feverish and languid and my hands would not move where I intended. Surely I must be ill.

The Golden Temple was still glittering before me, just like the view of the Jissokan that Shuntokumaru had once seen. Within the black night of his blindness Shuntokumaru had seen the setting sun playing lambently on the Sea of Namba. He had seen Awaji Eshima, Suma Akashi, and even the Sea of Kii reflecting the evening sun under a cloudless sky.

My body seemed to be paralyzed and the tears flowed incessantly. I did not mind staying here just as I was until the morning came and I was discovered. I should not offer a word of excuse.

Until now I had been speaking at great length about how impotent my memory had been since the time of my childhood, but I must point out that a memory which is suddenly revived carries a great power of resuscitation. The past does not only draw us back to the past. There are certain memories of the past that have strong steel springs and, when we who live in the present touch them, they are suddenly stretched taut and then they propel us into the future.

While my body seemed benumbed, my mind was groping somewhere within my memory. Some words floated up to the surface and then vanished. I seemed to reach them with the hands of my spirit and then once again they were hidden. Those words were calling me. They were trying to approach me in order to put me on my mettle.

"Face the back, face the outside, and if ye meet, kill instantly!"

Yes, the first sentence went like that. The famous passage in that chapter of the *Rinsairoku*. Then the remaining words emerged fluently: "When ye meet the Buddha, kill the Buddha! When ye meet your ancestor, kill your ancestor! When ye meet a disciple of Buddha, kill the disciple! When ye meet your father and mother, kill your father and mother! When ye meet your kin, kill your kin! Only thus will ye attain deliverance. Only thus will ye escape the trammels of material things and become free."

The words propelled me out of the impotence into which I had fallen. All of a sudden my whole body was infused with strength. One part of my mind still kept on telling me that it was now futile to perform this deed, but my newfound

strength had no fear of futility. I must do the deed precisely because it was so futile.

I rolled up the cloth that lay beside me and tucked it under
my arm together with the cushion. Then I stood up. I looked
towards the Golden Temple. The glittering temple of my vision had begun to fade. The railings were gradually swallowed up in the darkness and the forest of slender pillars lost
its clarity. The light vanished from the water and its reflection on the back of the eaves also vanished. Soon all the details were concealed in the darkness and the Golden Temple
left nothing but a vague black outline.

I ran. I ran round the north of the temple. My feet became
accustomed to their task and I did not stumble. The darkness
opened up before me successively and guided me on my way.

From the edge of the Sosei I leaped into the Golden Temple through the hinged door at the western entrance, which I
had left open. I threw the cushion and the cloth onto the pile
that I had already prepared.

My heart was throbbing merrily and my wet hands were
trembling. Moreover, my matches were wet. The first one
wouldn't light. The second one was about to light when it
broke. The third one burst into flames and as I held out my
hand against the wind it illuminated the spaces between my
fingers.

Then I had to search for the bundles of straw. For, although I had dragged the three bundles in here myself and
placed them in different parts of the building, I had completely forgotten where I had put them. By the time that I
had found them, the match had burned out. I crouched down
by the straw and this time struck two matches together.

The fire delineated the complex shadows of the piles of
straw and, giving forth the brilliant color of the wild places,
it spread minutely in all directions. As the smoke rose into
the air, the fire hid itself within its white mass. Then, unexpectedly far from where I was standing, the flames sprang up,
puffing out the green of the mosquito net. I felt as if everything round me had suddenly become alive.

At this moment my head became completely clear. There
was a limit to my supply of matches. I ran to another corner
of the room, and, carefully striking a match, set fire to the
next bundle of straw. The new flames that sprang up heartened me. In the past when I had been out with my companions and we had made campfires I had always been particularly adept at the job.

Within the Hosui-in a great flickering shadow had arisen.

The statues of the Three Holy Buddhas, Amida, Kannon, and Seishi, were lit up in red. The wooden statue of Yoshimitsu flashed its eyes; and in the back its shadow fluttered.

I could hardly feel the heat. When I saw that the steadfast flames had moved to the offertory box, I felt that everything was going to be all right.

I had forgotten about the arsenic and the pocketknife. Suddenly I had the idea of dying in the Kukyocho surrounded by the flames. Then I fled from the fire and ran up the narrow stairs. It did not occur to me to wonder why the door leading up to the Choondo was open. The old guide had forgotten to close the second-story door.

The smoke swirled toward my back. As I coughed, I gazed at the statue of Kannon that was attributed to Keishin and at the music-playing angels painted on the ceiling. Gradually the drifting smoke filled the Choondo. I ran up the next flight of stairs and tried to open the door of the Kukyocho. The door would not open. The entrance to the third story was firmly locked.

I knocked at the door. It must have been a violent knocking, but the sound did not impinge on my ears. With all my might I knocked at the door. I felt that someone might open the door to the Kukyocho for me from the inside. What I dreamed of finding in the Kukyocho was a place to die, but since the smoke was already pursuing me I knocked impetuously at the door as though I were instead seeking a refuge. What lay on the other side of that door could only be a little room. And at that moment I poignantly dreamed that the walls of the room must be fully covered with golden foil, though I knew that in actual fact they were almost completely defoliated. I cannot explain how desperately I was longing for that radiant little room as I stood there knocking at the door. If only I could reach it, I thought, everything would be all right. If only I could reach that little golden room.

I knocked as hard as I could. My hands were not strong enough and I threw my whole body against the door. Still it would not open.

The Choondo was already filled with smoke. Beneath my feet I could hear the crackling sound of the fire. I choked in the smoke and almost lost consciousness. As I coughed, I kept on knocking. But still the door would not open.

When at a certain moment there arose in me the clear consciousness of having been refused, I did not hesitate. I dodged the stairs. I ran down to the Hosui-in through the swirling smoke; I must have passed through the fire itself. When finally I reached the western door, I threw myself out into the open. Then I started to run like a shot, not knowing where I was going.

I ran. It was fantastic how far I ran without stopping to rest. I can't even remember what places I passed. I must have left by the back gate next to the Kyohoku Tower in the north of the temple precincts, then I must have passed by the Myoo Hall, run up the mountain path that was bordered by bamboo grass and azalea, and reached the top of Mount Hidari Daimonji. Yes, it was surely on top of Mount Hidari Daimonji that I lay down on my back in the bamboo field in the shadow of the red pines and tried to still the fierce beating of my heart. This was the mountain that protected the Golden Temple from the north.

The cry of some startled birds brought me to my senses. Or else it was a bird that flew close to my face with a great fluttering of its wings.

As I lay there on my back I gazed at the night sky. The birds soared over the branches of the red pines in great numbers and the thin flakes from the fire, which were already becoming scarce, floated in the sky above my head.

I sat up and looked far down the ravine towards the Golden Temple. A strange sound echoed from there. It was like the sound of crackers. It was like the sound of countless people's joints all cracking at once.

From where I sat the Golden Temple itself was invisible. All that I could see was the eddying smoke and the great fire that rose into the sky. The flakes from the fire drifted between the trees and the Golden Temple's sky seemed to be strewn with golden sand.

I crossed my legs and sat gazing for a long time at the scene.

When I came to myself, I found that my body was covered in blisters and scars and that I was bleeding profusely. My fingers also were stained with blood, evidently from when I had hurt them by knocking against the temple door. I licked my wounds like an animal that has fled from its pursuers.

I looked in my pocket and extracted the bottle of arsenic, wrapped in my handkerchief, and the knife. I threw them down the ravine.

Then I noticed the pack of cigarettes in my pocket. I took one out and started smoking. I felt like a man who settled down for a smoke after finishing a job of work. I wanted to live.

translated by Ivan Morris

THE SHORT STORY

The brief story is probably as old as the human imagination. In recorded history it dates back even earlier than the semi-historical and semi-fictional gems of the early Hindus, Hebrews, and Buddhists. And yet it is as new as today's slick magazine. It may be as fruitful in allegorial implications as a parable spoken by Jesus to the multitude. It may be as directly moralistic as the prose and verse tales of India's second-century *Panchatantra*, or as amoral as the stories of *The Thousand and One Nights,* emanating from thirteenth-century Arabia. It may be as purely entertaining as the early anonymous fiction of China.

The story may be as indefinitely construed as Poe's definition that it have unity of mood and be brief enough to be read at "one sitting" (but how long is the twentieth-century "sitting"?); or it may be held strictly to the classical unities of time, place, and action, and to a similar logical construction that Aristotle demanded for dramatic tragedy, especially a clearly observable beginning, middle, and end.

No matter, however, what definition is adopted, most critics would agree that, as a *literary form,* the short story is the most recent in the evolution of literature. The general dating in the West is from the story masters Edgar Allen Poe of America and Nikolai Gogol of Russia. It is as though these two were born of a single literary constellation in 1809, developed their contributions in close spiritual conjunction, though widely separated in physical space, and moved on together—Poe in 1849, Gogol in 1852.

Since the short story is expected to be relatively brief (one critic strictly stipulates not more than twelve thousand words), it necessarily must observe certain formalities. The rule of thumb given in the *Reader's Guide to Literary Terms* appears to satisfy present-day demands: "A prose narrative briefer than the short novel, more restricted in characters and situations, and usually concerned with a single effect."

Probably because of its brevity and because its single mood and effect may be taken in by a reader "on the run," the short story is the most popular imaginative literature today. Having evolved from the completely fantastic tales of an earlier time and been worked upon by the contemporary demand for a relationship to reality, the short story affords an especially effective link between cultures. Although the good short-story writer is deprived of the time and space in which to give extended descriptions of settings and ways of life or to reveal character worked upon by culture patterns, he does have the opportunity to take the reader on a quick trip of discovery in a new environment.

The stories included in this volume have been selected, first, as pleasurable reading; secondly, as worthy examples of the short-story form; and, thirdly, for the glimpses they offer of the mores and ways of thought of the authors' countrymen. Again, it should be emphasized that we have here an expression that reveals, perhaps more than any other, the influences of the West, for the contemporary short story is a peculiarly Western product and not, in its modern conscious form, indigenous to Asia.

Short Stories of India

India's literary heritage includes some of the earliest stories known to man. It is thought that the most ancient were devised to emphasize moral teachings or—as in the animal fables of the *Panchatantra* and other collections—for the purpose of indirectly instructing rulers in ethical principles of government. The oldest tales were undoubtedly rendered in verse form for convenience in committing to memory and passing on by word of mouth from generation to generation. Later stories appeared in prose, but often with pithy passages interspersed with poetry.

Unlike China, India has had a respect for fictional prose that has assured the novelist and short-story writer an honorable place in literary circles.

Gaurishanker Goverdhanram Joshi (1892–   ) writes under the pseudonym Dhumektu. He is the author of more than forty-five published works, including plays, novels, biographies, travel books, and short stories. He has also written an autobiography. His recent writing has been confined almost exclusively to the short-story form.

Dhumektu is generally regarded as a leading writer in the Gujarati language, a major dialect of the Bombay area. One Indian critic refers to him as a "man of erudition and culture . . . a reflective thinker as well as an excellent storyteller."

"The Letter" is a poignant story of patience and parental love. Although it deals with universal human emotions and relationships, it's background and situation are peculiarly Indian. The story was translated into English by the author himself.

Khwaja Ahmad Abbas (1914–   ) is a writer in Urdu, the

Punjabi dialect that was derived from classical Persian. Grandson of the great Urdu poet Hali, Abbas's reputation has been established in prose writing. He has published more than twenty books that have been translated into a dozen languages, as well as into the major Indian dialects. He is also a magazine columnist, a writer of screen plays, and a director of *avant-garde* films. He is a member of India's National Book Trust.

Critics cite Abbas as one of a very few writers who have achieved stature in the Urdu novel.

In "The Sword of Shiva" an aged mother retells a village story that exalts the justice of Shiva, the destroyer god.

Khushwant Singh (1917–) is one of several younger writers of fiction who won recognition in the late 1930's and early 1940's. He is best known in the West for his *Train to Pakistan* (1956), a grimly realistic novel based on the mutual slaughter between Hindus and Muslims in the Punjab at the time of the partition of India when the British Colonial Government withdrew from the subcontinent. As a member of the Sikh religious community, Singh is able to observe the Hindu-Muslim friction with a certain objectivity.

K. R. Srinivasa Iyengar, writing of Singh, has called him an "anti-romantic . . . intolerant of cant and humbug, especially when they masquerade as wisdom and probity."

A lawyer and authority on Sikh culture, Singh is the author of several novels and short-story collections. His story "Riot" indicates how a petty incident may trigger a Hindu-Muslim riot of destructive proportions in present-day India. It was written in English.

DHUMEKTU
(GAURISHANKER GOVERDHANRAM JOSHI)

THE LETTER

In the gray sky of early dawn stars still glowed, as happy memories light up a life that is nearing its close. An old man was walking through the town, now and again drawing his tattered cloak tighter to shield his body from the cold and biting wind. From some houses standing apart came the sound of grinding mills and the sweet voices of women singing at their work, and these sounds helped him along his lonely way. Except for the occasional bark of a dog, the distant steps of a workman going early to work or the screech of a bird disturbed before its time, the whole town was wrapped in deathly silence. Most of its inhabitants were still in the arms of sleep, a sleep which grew more and more profound on account of the intense winter cold; for the cold used sleep to extend its sway over all things even as a false friend lulls his chosen victim with caressing smiles. The old man, shivering at times but fixed of purpose, plodded on till he came out of the town gate on to a straight road. Along this he now went at a somewhat slower pace, supporting himself on his old staff.

On one side of the road was a row of trees, on the other the town's public garden. The night was darker now and the cold more intense, for the wind was blowing straight along the road and on it there only fell, like frozen snow, the faint light of the morning star. At the end of the garden stood a handsome building of the newest style, and light gleamed through the crevices of its closed doors and windows.

Beholding the wooden arch of this building, the old man was filled with the joy that the pilgrim feels when he first sees the goal of his journey. On the arch hung an old board with the newly painted letters POST OFFICE. The old man went in quietly and squatted on the veranda. The voices of the two or three people busy at their routine work could be heard faintly through the wall.

"Police Superintendent," a voice inside called sharply. The old man started at the sound, but composed himself again to wait. But for the faith and love that warmed him he could not have borne the bitter cold.

Name after name rang out from within as the clerk read out the English addresses on the letters and flung them to the waiting postmen. From long practice he had acquired great speed in reading out the titles—Commissioner, Superintendent, Diwan Sahib, Librarian—and in flinging out the letters.

In the midst of this procedure a jesting voice from inside called, "Coachman Ali!"

The old man got up, raised his eyes to Heaven in gratitude and, stepping forward, put his hand on the door.

"Godul Bhai!"

"Yes. Who's there?"

"You called out Coachman Ali's name, didn't you? Here I am. I have come for my letter."

"It is a madman, sir, who worries us by calling every day for letters that never come," said the clerk to the postmaster.

The old man went back slowly to the bench on which he had been accustomed to sit for five long years.

Ali had once been a clever shikari. As his skill increased so did his love for the hunt, till at last it was as impossible for him to pass a day without it as it is for the opium eater to forgo his daily portion. When Ali sighted the earth-brown partridge, almost invisible to other eyes, the poor bird, they said, was as good as in his bag. His sharp eyes would see the hare crouching in its form. When even the dogs failed to see the creature cunningly hidden in the yellow-brown scrub, Ali's eagle eyes would catch sight of its ears; and in another moment it was dead. Besides this, he would often go with his friends, the fishermen.

But when the evening of his life was drawing in, he left his old ways and suddenly took a new turn. His only child, Miriam, married and left him. She went off with a soldier to his regiment in the Punjab, and for the last five years he had had no news of this daughter for whose sake alone he dragged on a cheerless existence. Now he understood the meaning of love and separation. He could no longer enjoy the sportsman's pleasure and laugh at the bewildered terror of the young partridges bereft of their parents.

Although the hunter's instinct was in his very blood and bones, such a loneliness had come into his life since the day Miriam had gone away that now, forgetting his sport, he would become lost in admiration of the green cornfields. He reflected deeply and came to the conclusion that the whole universe is built up through love and that the grief of separation is inescapable. And seeing this, he sat down under a tree and wept bitterly. From that day he had risen each morning at four o'clock to walk to the post office. In his whole life he had never received a letter, but with a devout serenity born of hope and faith he continued and was always the first to arrive.

The post office, one of the most uninteresting buildings in the world, became his place of pilgrimage. He always occupied a particular seat in a particular corner of the building, and when people got to know his habit they laughed at him. The postmen began to make a game of him. Even though there was no letter for him, they would call out his name for the fun of seeing him jump and come to the door. But with boundless faith and infinite patience he came every day— and went away empty-handed.

While Ali waited, peons would come for their firms' letters and he would hear them discussing their masters' scandals.

These smart young peons in their spotless turbans and creaking shoes were always eager to express themselves. Meanwhile the door would be thrown open and the postmaster, a man with a head as sad and inexpressive as a pumpkin, would be seen sitting on his chair inside. There was no glimmer of animation in his features; and such men usually prove to be village schoolmasters, office clerks, or postmasters.

One day he was there as usual and did not move from his seat when the door was opened.

"Police Commissioner!" the clerk called out, and a young fellow stepped forward briskly for the letters.

"Superintendent!" Another peon came; and so the clerk, like a worshiper of Vishnu, repeated his customary thousand names.

At last they had all gone. Ali too got up and, saluting the post office as though it housed some precious relic, went off, a pitiable figure, a century behind his time.

"That fellow," asked the postmaster, "is he mad?"

"Who, sir? Oh, yes," answered the clerk. "No matter what sort of weather, he has been here every day for the last five years. But he doesn't get many letters."

"I can well understand that! Who does he think will have time to write to him every day?"

"But he's a bit touched, sir. In the old days he committed many sins; and maybe he shed blood within some sacred precincts and is paying for it now," the postman added in support to his statement.

"Madmen are strange people," the postmaster said.

"Yes. Once I saw a madman in Ahmedabad who did absolutely nothing but make little heaps of dust. Another had a habit of going every day to the river in order to pour water on a certain stone!"

"Oh, that's nothing," chimed in another. "I knew one madman who paced up and down all day long, another who never ceased declaiming poetry, and a third who would slap himself on the cheek and then begin to cry out because he was being beaten."

And everyone in the post office began talking of lunacy. All working-class people have a habit of taking periodic rests by joining in general discussion for a few minutes. After listening a little, the postmaster got up and said:

"It seems as though the mad live in a world of their own making. To them, perhaps, we too, appear mad. The madman's world is rather like the poet's, I should think!"

He laughed as he spoke the last words, looking at one of

the clerks who wrote indifferent verse. Then he went out and the office became still again.

For several days Ali had not come to the post office. There was no one with enough sympathy or understanding to guess the reason, but all were curious to know what had stopped the old man. At last he came again; but it was a struggle for him to breathe, and on his face were clear signs of his approaching end. That day he could not contain his impatience.

"Master Sahib," he begged the postmaster, "have you a letter from my Miriam?"

The postmaster was in a hurry to get out to the country.

"What a pest you are, brother!" he exclaimed.

"My name is Ali," answered Ali absentmindedly.

"I know! I know! But do you think we've got your Miriam's name registered?"

"Then please note it down, brother. It will be useful if a letter should come when I am not here." For how should the villager who had spent three quarters of his life hunting know that Miriam's name was not worth a pice to anyone but her father?

The postmaster was beginning to lose his temper. "Have you no sense?" he cried. "Get away! Do you think we are going to eat your letter when it comes?" And he walked off hastily. Ali came out very slowly, turning after every few steps to gaze at the post office. His eyes were filling with tears of helplessness, for his patience was exhausted, even though he still had faith. Yet how could he still hope to hear from Miriam?

Ali heard one of the clerks coming up behind him and turned to him.

"Brother!" he said.

The clerk was surprised, but being a decent fellow he said, "Well?"

"Here, look at this!" and Ali produced an old tin box and emptied five golden guineas into the surprised clerk's hands. "Do not look so startled," he continued. "They will be useful to you, and they can never be so to me. But will you do one thing?"

"What?"

"What do you see up there?" said Ali, pointing to the sky.

"Heaven."

"Allah is there, and in His presence I am giving you this money. When it comes, you must forward my Miriam's letter to me."

"But where—where am I to send it?" asked the utterly bewildered clerk.

"To my grave."

"What?"

"Yes. It is true. Today is my last day: my very last, alas! And I have not seen Miriam, I have had no letter from her." Tears were in Ali's eyes as the clerk slowly left him and went on his way with the five golden guineas in his pocket.

Ali was never seen again and no one troubled to inquire after him.

One day, however, trouble came to the postmaster. His daughter lay ill in another town and he was anxiously waiting for news from her. The post was brought in and the letters piled on the table. Seeing an envelope of the color and shape he expected, the postmaster eagerly snatched it up. It was addressed to coachman Ali, and he dropped it as though it had given him an electric shock. The haughty temper of the official had quite left him in his sorrow and anxiety and had laid bare his human heart. He knew at once that this was the letter the old man had been waiting for: it must be from his daughter Miriam.

"Lakshmi Das!" called the postmaster, for such was the name of the clerk to whom Ali had given his money.

"Yes, sir?"

"This is for your old coachman Ali. Where is he now?"

"I will find out, sir."

The postmaster did not receive his own letter all that day.

He worried all night and, getting up at three, went to sit in the office. "When Ali comes at four o'clock," he mused, "I will give him the letter myself."

For now the postmaster understood all Ali's heart, and his very soul. After spending but a single night in suspense, anxiously waiting for news of his daughter, his heart was brimming with sympathy for the poor old man who had spent his nights for the last five years in the same suspense. At the stroke of five he heard a soft knock on the door: he felt sure it was Ali. He rose quickly from his chair, his suffering father's heart recognizing another, and flung the door wide open.

"Come in, brother Ali," he cried, handing the letter to the meek old man, bent double with age, who was standing outside. Ali was leaning on a stick and the tears were wet on his face as they had been when the clerk left him. But his features had been hard then and now they were softened by lines of kindliness. He lifted his eyes and in them was a light so unearthly that the postmaster shrank in fear and astonishment.

Lakshmi Das had heard the postmaster's words as he came towards the office from another quarter. "Who was that, sir? Old Ali?" he asked. But the postmaster took no notice of him. He was staring with wide-open eyes at the doorway from which Ali had disappeared. Where could he have gone? At last he turned to Lakshmi Das. "Yes, I was speaking to Ali," he said.

"Old Ali is dead, sir. But give me his letter."

"What! But when? Are you sure, Lakshmi Das?"

"Yes, it is so," broke in a postman who had just arrived. "Ali died three months ago."

The postmaster was bewildered. Miriam's letter was still lying near the door; Ali's image was still before his eyes. He listened to Lakshmi Das's recital of the last interview, but he could still not doubt the reality of the knock on the door and the tears in Ali's eyes. He was perplexed. Had he really seen Ali? Had his imagination deceived him? Or had it perhaps been Lakshmi Das?

The daily routine began. The clerk read out the addresses —Police Commissioner, Superintendent, Librarian—and flung the letters deftly.

But the postmaster now watched them as though each contained a warm, beating heart. He no longer thought of them in terms of envelopes and postcards. He saw the essential, human worth of a letter.

That evening you might have seen Lakshmi Das and the postmaster walking with slow steps to Ali's grave. They laid the letter on it and turned back.

"Lakshmi Das, were you indeed the first to come to the office this morning?"

"Yes, sir, I was the first."

"Then how . . . No, I don't understand . . ."

"What, sir?"

"Oh, never mind," the postmaster said shortly. At the office he parted from Lakshmi Das and went in. The newly-waked father's heart in him was reproaching him for having failed to understand Ali's anxiety. Tortured by doubt and remorse, he sat down in the glow of the charcoal sigri to wait.

translated by the author

KHWAJA AHMAD ABBAS

THE SWORD OF SHIVA

Come, son. Don't stand out there in the rain, or you will catch your death of cold. Come in. Stay a while in a poor old woman's hut till the rain stops. . . .

Strange are the ways of the gods, my son, aren't they? Look at this rain now—pit-a-pat, pit-a-pat—pouring down from the heavens all the time! It is this rain which puts life into the dead, dried-up earth. It is this rain which turns seed into seedling, seedling into plant. It is rain, indeed, which gives life to us. Without it we would all be dead, wouldn't we? But the rain takes life, too, when the floods come and the young crops rot under water, and whole villages are carried away by the angry mother Ganga.[1] The rain brings life, the rain brings death. It all depends upon our Karma,[2] son. The deed is the seed, and we reap what we sow. You can't sow millets and expect a crop of paddy, can you? The all-seeing eye of Lord Shiva[3] keeps watch on all that goes on in the world, and when Evil and Sin possess the very soul of men, the Destroyer's eye sends down arrows of wrath to end the reign of Evil. Thus was the mighty Ravana humbled and his Golden Lanka burnt to ashes by an army of mere monkeys.[4] Thus was the hefty tyrant Kansa killed by a mere slip of a boy. . . .[5]

The weapons of God are many and different, son. They say God's Big Stick is noiseless, and no one knows when it falls on an evil one's skull. But the most wondrous and terrible weapon of them all He has given in the keeping of god Indra, for isn't he the Lord of the Heavens, the king of all

[1] Ganges River.

[2] "Action," in light of the law of cause and effect; one's actions will have inevitable results which must be worked out in this incarnation or a subsequent one.

[3] The destroyer god; also, god of the cosmic order, of rhythm and the dance.

[4] In the epic *Ramayana,* Ravana was the evil demon king of Ceylon (Lanka), who abducted Rama's wife Sita. Sita was rescued and Ravana defeated by the monkey-king Hanuman and his army of monkeys.

[5] Son of a demon and tyrannical king of Mathura, Kansa was killed by the boy Krishna, eighth avatar of the preserver god Vishnu.

the gods and goddesses? It is Indra who has to lead the armies of God against the demon hordes of Evil. And to fight such frightful enemies he needs a frightful weapon.

Look yonder, through the window, at the heavens, son. You see the flash of lightning cutting through the black mass of clouds? This, the wise ones say, is the two-edged Sword of Shiva which the Destroyer has given to god Indra [1] to fight Evil and to destroy the sinful and the unclean. Haven't you seen how the evil and ungodly ones start trembling the moment they hear the drumbeats of thunder?

This Sword of Shiva is not made of iron or steel, my son. A sword of steel can become rusty and its blade can become blunt or get broken. But this weapon of God is made of the strangest and most wonderful substance. They say that once a very great Yogi did penance for so many years, sitting out in the open in the sun and the rain all the time, that his skin peeled off and his flesh melted away and he was reduced to a skeleton of dried-up white bones. It was from these sacred bones, hard and pure and sharp like diamonds, that Shiva fashioned his sword which you see flashing in the sky.

Son, you have doubtless heard that the lightning strikes the snakes. But have you wondered why? Because these poisonous, creeping, evil creatures, in their previous birth, were cruel and evil men who stung the innocent and poisoned them. So God punished them by giving them a new birth in this evil form. But lightning strikes not only the snakes but also the unclean and the ungodly, the evil and poisonous ones among the humans. Believe me, son, God's eye sees all, sees even through sevenfold walls of stones, and is not deceived by clean white clothes or princely turbans, or by all the riches of the world. God's eye sees right into the hearts of men, sees the evil and untruth and rottenness that may be hidden inside. And when the Sword of Shiva strikes, it cuts through the tallest and sturdiest tree, as if it was made of wax or butter, and reaches the necks of the guilty ones. I know, my son, I know because I have seen with mine own eyes. . . .

You, the young people of today, who go to schools and read big fat books will not believe what this ignorant old woman tells you. You say I am gone mad. Maybe I am. But I swear by God Shiva that what I tell you is the truth. And may the lightning strike me if I utter a single lie. . . .

I don't remember how many years ago—maybe twenty,

---

[1] God of the atmosphere and the heavens, who wages constant war against evil demons.

maybe twenty-five, maybe thirty, I have long since lost count of time—but there must be many in this village still alive who can tell you that the strange story I am about to narrate is not an invention of my crazy brain. If you want to see for yourself, go out of the village, behind the temple and beyond the tank,[1] and look at the stump of the neem tree that still stands there, right in the middle of the fields, like a huge and ugly scarecrow, with its warning finger raised to the heavens. Once this tree was so big and its leaves so thick that, even if twenty people stood under it, not a drop of rain would fall on them. But since that fateful day, no green leaves have ever smiled on its branches even in the season of spring, for that wretched tree was burn't to its very roots, when the Sword of Shiva smote down four men who stood under it, seeking shelter from the rain. . . .

It was a rainy day just like this. That year it had rained and rained and rained, till the tank was overflowing and the dusty track which connects our village with the Agra Road was lost under water. People had to come and go through the fields, which were like so many ponds. In this, our Untouchables'[2] quarter outside the village, the mud walls of many a hut had collapsed and a child, scarcely twenty days old, had been killed. . . .

Forgive me, son, I am old and my eyes often get sore and begin to run. . . . Don't think I am weeping. For a crazy old woman like me, what is there to weep about?

As I was saying, it was the season of the rains, but on that particular day the rain did stop just for a few hours, enough to lure many people out of the shelter of their homes and into the open on many different errands. Some went to hoe in their fields, some to that yonder village Rajapur, across the Agra Road, for it was the weekly market day. But all the while the sky was covered with thick black clouds and, towards the afternoon, it began to pour again. Those who hap-

---

[1] Well or reservoir containing the water supply for a village, often adjacent to the temple.

[2] The Panchamas—those so low as to be beyond the pale of caste. Orthodox Hindus have traditionally considered the touch or even the shadow cast by an Untouchable to be polluting. Untouchables live on the outskirts of the village, coming in only to perform tasks considered so degrading that others will not take them. They are barred from the village tank, the schools, the temples, and all association outside their own class. Gandhi worked in their behalf, calling them Harijans, or Children of God. Caste distinctions and untouchability have been outlawed by independent India's constitution, but change is a long time coming, especially in the non-urban areas.

pened to be somewhere near the village ran to the safety of
their homes. But there were four who had gone separately on
their different errands, who could not reach their homes, and,
one by one, they managed to reach the shelter of the big
neem tree. You may say it was their kismet [1] that brought all
of them there, on that fateful day.

You are not likely to have seen any one of these four; perhaps, you were not even born then. But you have heard of at
least one of them. He was the elder brother of the present
zamindar [2] of our village, Thakur Harman Singh—that was
his name. A very tall and handsome young man he was, with
a broad chest and big black moustaches. He was unmarried,
and many a landlord's daughter in our district was still hoping to be the lucky one to have him for a husband. When he
rode through the village, the girls would peep at him from
behind their doors and blush when they caught each other
doing so. He was also very sweet of tongue. When he talked
the one who listened was as if under a spell of magic. . . .

What's happened to my eyes today, I wonder? Maybe, it is
the smoke from the hearth. . . .

Harman Singh was a zamindar's son, but he always talked
sweetly and kindly to the royots.[3] He was also generous with
his money. They all respected him in the village, holding him
up as a model of what a zamindar should be. He was very
fond of hunting and that day, too, as soon as the rain had
stopped, he had set out to do some duck-shooting in the
swampy jheel.[4] But on the way his horse shied at a flash of
lightning and was so frightened by a peal of thunder that he
bolted, slipped in the mud, and fell, breaking one of his hind
legs. The Thakur who was just saved by a hair's breadth
could not bear to see the poor animal groan with pain and so
he shot him on the spot. He was returning to his bungalow
on foot when the downpour began and he ran to take shelter
under the big neem tree and found three men, all well known
to him, already standing there.

One of them was the village priest, Pandit Dharam Das, a
lean, skinny Brahmin, as always, with his sacred thread and
the big caste mark on his forehead prominently displayed. He
was reputed to be the wisest and most learned man of our
village. It was said that he knew all the holy books by heart.

[1] Fate.
[2] Landlord.
[3] Peasants.
[4] Lake.

And he had one great worry—how to keep the people of the village on the path of Faith. It was entirely due him that the reformers from the cities, who came sometimes preaching against caste and untouchability, got no hearing in our village. Dharam Das called them godless and lost no time in having them turned out of the village. The Brahmin was a widower himself but he was most concerned about the morals of the village boys and girls. If he saw a boy and a girl even standing together and talking, he got furious and asked the Panchayat [1] to severely punish the culprits. He used to say again and again: "We shall not allow our boys and girls to follow the evil ways of the city youth, meeting on the sly and having love talks, for it is these whisperings that sow the seed of sin." After that no boy dared to talk to a girl, at least not within sight or hearing of the Pandit.

But love has its strange ways, son, and you know perhaps that it doesn't listen to Pandits and priests. So there was at least one girl who managed to fall in what Pandit Dharam Das had so often called the bottomless pit of sin. She was Chanda, the daughter of Mooloo Ram, the silversmith. The village folk were shocked to find that this shameless one had not only sinned, but also borne the fruit of her sin. She, an unmarried girl, had given birth to a baby boy—a red little lump of flesh—whom she shamelessly coddled and fed at her breast! Her mother wept and screamed curses, her father beat her mercilessly, Pandit Dharam Das threatened her with the fires of Hell, and the elders of the village Panchayat coaxed and cajoled her to give out the name of the man who had fathered the child of sin. But Chanda would not speak. When she opened her mouth, it was only to say: "No, no, I will not betray him. I know I have sinned. You can give me any punishment for it. Kill me if you like. But I will not tell his name." And so, at the suggestion of Pandit Dharam Das, she was declared an outcaste and turned out of the village, along with her bastard child. Then the village folk came to know that she had found shelter in the Untouchables' quarter and, when he heard it, the Pandit said that it was as it should be, for in the eyes of God the sinner and the Untouchable were the same. . . .

Also, under that tree, was Mool Chand the moneylender. He belonged to the Rajapur but, as there was no moneylender in our own village, many of our people had dealings with him. Whenever anyone needed money for anything, for a marriage or a betrothal or for funeral ceremonies, he gave a loan, taking land or jewelry as security. It is true, no doubt, that he charged a high rate of interest and deducted the first year's interest in advance from the loan. But, as everyone said, that is the way moneylending business is done, and so no one ever blamed Mool Chand for it. On the other hand, all had a good word to say for the moneylender, for he was always generous in donating money for religious functions not only in Rajapur but also in our village. He was known as a truly God-fearing man. When he learnt that Mooloo Ram's daughter had been turned out of the village, he congratulated Pandit Dharam Das for thus punishing an evildoer and said: "But, Panditji, I still say you are too kindhearted and lenient. If we had found a girl like that in our Rajapur, I tell you we would have broken her legs and thrown her in a well." There was one other special thing about Mool Chand. He was always dressed in snow-white clothes—as if they had just come from the dhobi. [1] Also he always smelt of good strong attar of roses, though there were some who said he did that because his perspiration smelt so bad. Anyhow, he was fond of saying: "If the body is clean, the heart is clean; if the heart is clean, the body is clean."

The third man under the tree was Rehmat Khan, the village patwari,[2] who kept all the land records. Nowadays, son, these officials have lost much of their old glory. But in those days, for the village folk the patwari was King, Viceroy, Governor, and Collector, all rolled into one. All books and records of lands, their measurements, their transfers and sales were in his hands. The farmers could not read or write and they quietly put their thumb impressions where the patwari told them to, just as they put their thumb impressions where the moneylender asked them to. Rehmat Khan was always glad to make the different matters of land records easy for the villagers and, in return, they were glad to offer him a little money. You may call it bribe-taking if you like. But otherwise Rehmat Khan was known to be a man of God, with his long black-and-white henna-dyed beard,[3] praying five times a day in the village mosque. He had been on pilgrimage to holy Mecca once already and was planning to go there again. That was why those who had any dealings with him

[1] Washerman.

[2] Minor revenue official.

[3] Indication that the male Muslim has recently made pilgrimage to Mecca.

had to pay a little extra—to help him collect the steamship fare! He had two wives, the younger one being twenty or so, only a little older than his daughter from the first one. He was very particular about their purdah,[1] specially in the case of the younger wife. Being a Pathan,[2] he was a little hot-tempered. One day he hit Noor Bakhsh the weaver so hard that the poor man was down on his cot for three full days. Likewise, he once thrashed Chhidoo the cobbler, because he had dared to demand the usual price for a pair of shoes that the patwari had ordered from him. But one thing could be said about Rehmat Khan—that he used these rough methods only with the people of the lower castes. To the zamindar and his family, to the Pandit and the moneylender, he was most polite and respectful. And whenever an official from the district happened to visit our village in the course of his tour, Rehmat Khan moved heaven and earth to entertain him, so that everyone said that our patwari was not only hospitable but was also high up in the favor of the big officials. . . .

So these were the four who stood that day under the big neem tree, muttering prayers for the rain to stop. Every now and then there were flashes of lightning and peals of thunder like the beating of demon drums. It had grown quite dark. But once, when there was a lightning flash in the western sky, what should they see but the figures of Ruldoo the old cobbler and that wretched girl Chanda, the sinful daughter of the silversmith, coming straight towards them? Both of them were drenched to their bones and, as the downpour had just become even more intense, it was clear that they were coming to take shelter under the same tree.

Now, son, I forgot to tell you about Ruldoo, the kindly old cobbler whose wrinkled face looked like an old shoe of his own making. Though an Untouchable, he was called Ruldoo Kaka—Uncle Ruldoo—by all the village folk, most of whom had got their shoes made by him ever since their childhood. It was he who had given shelter to Chanda when she was driven out of the village. She was passing through the Untouchables' quarter, carrying her fatherless child in her arms, and crying piteously. Ruldoo, who was an old widower with one foot already in the grave, said to her: "Daughter, now that you have no caste, stay with your untouchable Uncle

---

[1] Seclusion of women; until recent times, practiced throughout India, but especially rigorously by Muslims.

[2] Muslim from northwest area bordering Afghanistan, reputed to be independent and quarrelsome.

Ruldoo. When the fire of your father's anger has burned itself out, I will go to him and ask him to take you back." A
blind man desires but two eyes, and one who is drowning
readily clutches at a straw, and so Chanda made her home in
Ruldoo's little broken-down hut. When her father heard of
this, he consoled himself by saying that instead of wandering
about in the streets, reduced to the fate of a beggar or even
worse, it was better that Chanda was staying with Ruldoo
who was known to everyone as a God-fearing old man, even
though he was an Untouchable! But there were high-caste
folk who said she should have thrown herself in the lake
rather than live in an Untouchable's house. Some hotheaded
young men even wanted to burn down Ruldoo's hut, but their
elders stopped them in time. Moreover, it was continuously
raining so hard that it was no easy job for one to light a fire
in one's own hearth, much less to set a fire to a hut.

Didn't I say, son, that strange are the ways of God? It was
rain caused its mud walls to fall. The cobbler was at his shop,
making shoes, and Chanda had gone to a neighbor's house to
beg for some herbs to give her child who had developed a
chill and was burning with high fever. The child was alone in
the hut when the east wall caved in and the roof came down.
Both Ruldoo and Chanda came rushing back, but the child
was already dead. Poor little soul, he had not even uttered a
single cry. Just died quietly, as quietly as he had been born!
When she saw her dead child, a deep and frightful silence
came over Chanda. Not a tear came out of her eyes, not a
sob or a sigh passed her lips. It was as if she had suddenly
turned into stone. People say she did not cry when her child
died and so the sorrow remained in her heart, and that made
her crazy. . . .

Oh, these eyes of mine! Son, will you do me a favor and,
when the rain stops, bring something for my sore eyes from
the Vaidji's [1] medicine shop? . . .

How my mind wanders from one thing to another! As I
was saying, those four were quite worried and taken aback
when they saw Ruldoo and Chanda coming towards that tree.

Pandit Dharam Das cried: "Ruldoo Kaka, don't you see
where you are going? Stop where you are."

Ruldoo stopped. After all he was an Untouchable, even
though they called him uncle, and was used to obeying orders
of the high-caste folk. With folded hands he said: "Take pity

---

[1] Vaidji, respectful form of address for Vaid, an Ayurvedic physi-
cian, or a doctor practicing the Indian system of medicine.

on us, Panditji, and let us also have shelter under the tree.
We will stand away from you in a corner."

Saying this, Ruldoo was about to take a step when he was
again stopped by a shout from Dharam Das: "Now, now, remain where you are. This is only a small tree, not a palace
that you two can stand in a corner." Then he turned to the
young Thakur and said: "Thakur Saheb, we should keep
them away or else we will all die with them. There is a terrible danger. . . ."

And patwari Rehmat Khan asked: "What danger, Panditji?"

The Pandit replied: "You don't know, Khan Saheb. Our
holy books say that lightning always strikes the unclean and
the sinful. One of them is an Untouchable and the other is a
daughter of sin. If they come under the same tree and the
lightning strikes, we will all be finished with them."

The patwari hurriedly mumbled a verse from the Holy
Quran to protect himself, and then said: "If that is so, Panditji, they must be kept away at all cost."

And the moneylender also agreed with them, saying: "Yes,
yes, after all we are not going to risk our lives for their
sake."

Chanda, who was staring fixedly at Thakur Harman Singh,
was now shivering with cold. Seeing her, Ruldoo once again
appealed, this time to the Thakur: "Sarkar,[1] this poor girl
will die of pneumonia if she remains in the rain any longer.
Her child is already dead—killed, when the roof of my hut
collapsed over him."

Chanda was still staring at the Thakur, but he turned his
face away, opening his gun and looking through its barrel, as
if all this talk was of no interest to him. And so it was, of
course. Wasn't he the lordly zamindar's son? What concern
had he with the lives and deaths of lowly folk like these?

When he heard about the death of Chanda's child, Dharam
Das said: "God be praised—the seed of sin is no more."

And Ruldoo once again pleaded: "Yes, Panditji, whatever
Bhagwan does is all to the good. What is done can't be undone. That is why I was taking Chanda to her father. Now
that the child is no more, she may be cleansed by a purifica-
tion ceremony and taken back in her home."

The moneylender, as always, tried to sound reasonable and
compromising: "That will all be seen later, Ruldoo, but now

---

[1] "My Lord," or "Your Highness."

you two go and find some other shelter. There is no place for you under this tree."

Ruldoo said: "Sahukarji, you know there is no other tree around here."

The moneylender now decided to explain matters to Ruldoo, and so he said: "Ruldoo Kaka, you are an old man so you must understand these things. We don't want any harm to come to you. But, after all, it is written in the holy books that lightning strikes people like you. You see it flashing all around. So why do you want to put our lives in danger? Leave us with our own Karma, and take your Karma away with you. . . ."

He was still speaking when they saw that wretched Chanda, shivering with cold, slowly walking towards them, slipping in the mud at every step—as if she was a woman possessed. Behind her, trying to stop her, was poor old Ruldoo. There was a flash of lightning just behind them so that, for a moment, they turned black against the light, like demon figures. Then came the sound of thunder, which shook the very earth.

The Pandit shouted as if death was staring him in the face: "Thakur Saheb, where is your gun? Don't let her come near us or we will all be killed. Look how the flashes of lightning are pursuing her."

The Thakur raised the gun to his shoulder but his hands were trembling. As she saw the gun aimed at her, Chanda became utterly mad and screamed: "You have already killed me, Thakur. Now if you want to shoot me also, what better destiny could I have? Shoot, shoot quickly, so that I can go and meet my son, my son that is also your son."

They all seemed to be convinced then that Chanda had gone completely raving mad. There was a rumble in the clouds, as if lightning was preparing to strike—the Sword of Shiva was being drawn out of its sheath. Chanda was now only four or five paces away from the tree. Still the Thakur did not fire. So the moneylender cried: "Shoot, Sarkar, or this mad girl will get us killed along with herself."

But, my son, who can kill those whom God protects? Before the Thakur could fire his gun, the Sword of Shiva struck with all its fury. There was a blinding flash as if the Sun-God had suddenly come through the clouds right down to the earth. Blinded by the light, Ruldoo and Chanda closed their eyes. Then there was a terrible crashing sound as if a hundred guns had been fired together. The earth shook and both Ruldoo and Chanda were violently thrown to the ground.

They were sure it was their end, that lightning had struck the unclean and the sinful. . . .

But when they opened their eyes they saw that the big neem tree had been struck by lightning and under it lay four dead men, their faces burned black, their lifeless eyes, still puzzled and full of wonder, looking up at the sky. As if, right up to the end, they had never understood! The gun was still in the Thakur's hand but its barrel was twisted out of shape as if it had been made of wax. . . .

That is why I ask: "Of what avail are the puny little guns and bombs of man against the Sword of Shiva?" Everything depends upon our Karma, my son. The deed is the seed, and we reap what we sow. The all-seeing eye of God sees everything, sees through sevenfold walls of stone and is not deceived by clean white clothes or princely turbans, or by the show of all the riches of the world. Believe me, son, God's eye sees right through into the hearts of men, sees the evil and untruth and rottenness that may be hidden inside there. And when the Sword of Shiva strikes, it cuts through the tallest and sturdiest tree, as if it was made of wax or even butter, and reaches the necks of the guilty ones. I know, my son, I know because I have seen. . . .

Perhaps you still think all this is the senseless talk of a mad old woman. But I swear to you that I tell the truth, my son. . . .

Look, the downpour slackens down. Now when you go out, don't forget to call at the Vaidji's medicine shop and tell him my eyes are sore again, and water flows out of them like rain out of heaven, and so let him send some medicine. Tell him you are sent by the crazy old Chanda. . . .

Why, you are gone already! Perhaps I bored you with my tale. You never heard anything I said? No one ever stops to hear my story. But you should have waited at least for the rain to stop, my son. . . .

KHUSHWANT SINGH

RIOT

The town lay etherized under the fresh spring twilight. The shops were closed and house doors barred from the inside. Streetlamps dimly lit the deserted roads. Only a few policemen walked about with steel helmets on their heads and rifles slung behind their backs. The sound of their hobnailed boots was all that broke the stillness of the town.

The twilight sank into darkness. A crescent moon lit the quiet streets. A soft breeze blew bits of newspaper from the pavements onto the road and back again. It was cooled and smelled of the freshness of spring. Some dogs emerged from a dark lane and gathered round a lamppost. A couple of policemen strolled past them smiling. One of them mumbled something vulgar. The other pretended to pick up a stone and hurl it at the dogs. The dogs ran down the street in the opposite direction and resumed their courtship at a safer distance.

Rani was a pariah bitch whose litter populated the lanes and by-lanes of the town. She was a thin, scraggy specimen, typical of the pariahs of the town. Her white coat was mangy, showing patches of raw flesh. Her dried-up udders hung loosely from her ribs. Her tail was always tucked between her hind legs and she slunk about in fear and abject servility.

Rani would have died of starvation with her first litter of eight had it not been for the generosity of the Hindu shopkeeper, Ram Jawaya, in the corner of whose courtyard she had unloaded her womb. The shopkeeper's family fed her and played with her pups till they were old enough to run about the streets and steal food for themselves. The shopkeeper's generosity had put Rani in the habit of sponging. Every year when spring came, she would find excuse to loiter around the stall of Ramzan, the Moslem greengrocer. Beneath the wooden platform on which groceries were displayed lived the big, burly Moti. Early autumn, Rani presented the shopkeeper's household with half a dozen or more of Moti's offspring.

Moti was a cross between a Newfoundland and a spaniel. His shaggy coat and sullen look were Ramzan's pride. Ramzan had lopped off Moti's tail and ears. He fed him till Moti grew big and strong and became the master of the town's canine population. Rani had many rivals. But year after year, with the advent of spring, Rani's fancy lightly turned to thoughts of Moti and she sauntered across to Ramzan's stall.

This time spring had come but the town was paralyzed with fear of communal riots and curfews. In the daytime people hung about the street corners in groups of tens and twenties, talking in whispers. No shops opened and long before curfew hour the streets were deserted, with only pariah dogs and policemen about.

Tonight even Moti was missing. In fact, ever since the curfew Ramzan had kept him indoors tied to a cot. He was far more useful guarding Ramzan's house than loitering about the streets. Rani came to Ramzan's stall and sniffed around. Moti could not have been there for some days. She was disappointed. But spring came only once a year—and hardly ever did it come at a time when one could have the city to oneself with no curious children looking on—and no scandalized parents hurling stones at her. So Rani gave up Moti and ambled down the road toward Ram Jawaya's house. A train of suitors followed her.

Rani faced her many suitors in front of Ram Jawaya's doorstep. They snarled and snapped and fought with each other. Rani stood impassively, waiting for the decision. In a few minutes a lanky black dog, one of Rani's own progeny, won the honors. The others slunk away.

In Ramzan's house, Moti sat pensively eyeing his master from underneath his charpoy.[1] For some days the spring air had made him restive. He heard the snarling in the street and smelled Rani in the air. But Ramzan would not let him go. He tugged at the rope—then gave it up and began to whine. Ramzan's heavy hand struck him. A little later he began to whine again. Ramzan had had several sleepless nights watching and was heavy with sleep. He began to snore. Moti whined louder and then sent up a pitiful howl to his unfaithful mistress. He tugged and strained at the leash and began to bark. Ramzan got up angrily from his charpoy to beat him. Moti made a dash toward the door dragging the lightened string cot behind him. He nosed open the door and rushed out. The charpoy stuck in the doorway and the rope tightened around his neck. He made a savage wrench, the rope gave way, and he leap't across the road. Ramzan ran back to his room, slipped a knife under his shirt, and went after Moti.

Outside Ram Jawaya's house, the illicit liaison of Rani and the black pariah was consummated. Suddenly the burly form of Moti came into view. With an angry growl Moti leapt at Rani's lover. Other dogs joined the melee, tearing and snapping wildly.

Ram Jawaya had also spent several sleepless nights keeping watch and yelling back war cries to the Moslems. At last

[1] Light wooden bedstead with interwoven rope "springs."

fatigue and sleep overcame his newly acquired martial spirit. He slept soundly with a heap of stones under his charpoy and an imposing array of soda-water bottles filled with acid close at hand. The noise outside woke him. The shopkeeper picked up a big stone and opened the door. With a loud oath he sent the missile flying at the dogs. Suddenly, a human being emerged from the corner and the stone caught him squarely in the solar plexis.

The stone did not cause much damage to Ramzan, but the suddenness of the assault took him aback. He yelled "Murder!" and produced his knife from under his shirt. The shopkeeper and the grocer eyed each other for a brief moment and then ran back to their houses shouting. The petrified town came to life. There was more shouting. The drum at the Sikh temple beat a loud tattoo—the air was rent with war cries.

Men emerged from their houses making hasty inquiries. A Moslem or a Hindu, it was said, has been attacked. Someone had been kidnapped and was being butchered. A party of goondas were going to attack, but the dogs had started barking. They had actually assaulted a woman and killed her children. There must be resistance. There was. Groups of fives joined others of ten. Tens joined twenties till a few hundred, armed with knives, spears, hatchets, and kerosene-oil cans proceeded to Ram Jawaya's house. They were met with a fusillade of stones, soda-water bottles, and acid. They hit back blindly. Tins of kerosene oil were emptied indiscriminately and lighted. Flames shot up in the sky enveloping Ram Jawaya's home and entire neighborhood, Hindu, Moslem, and Sikh alike.

The police rushed to the scene and opened fire. Fire engines clanged their way in and sent jets of water flying into the sky. But fires had been started in other parts of the town and there were not enough fire engines to go round.

All night and all the next day the fire burnt—and houses fell and people were killed. Ram Jawaya's home was burnt and he barely escaped with his life. For several days smoke rose from the ruins. What had once been a busy town was a heap of charred masonry.

Some months later when peace was restored, Ram Jawaya came to inspect the site of his old home. It was all in shambles with the bricks lying in a mountainous pile. In the corner of what had once been his courtyard there was a little clearing. There lay Rani with her litter nuzzling into her dried udders. Beside her stood Moti guarding his bastard brood.

Short Stories of
Southeast Asia

BURMA

Burma has offered one of the major trade routes between the subcontinent of India and the countries of Southeast Asia. More lasting than the material goods crossing her boundaries have been the cultural riches of the giant to her west. Considered to be among the most magnificent builders of Asia, the Burmese have monumentalized first the influences of Hinduism and next those of Buddhism. The latter are more obvious today in a nation that is officially Buddhist. At the impressive golden-domed Shwe Dagon pagoda in Rangoon, as in similar temples throughout the country, boys are regularly dedicated to the Buddha in impressive mass ceremonies followed by a noviate period of monastery service. Thereafter, periodic withdrawals into monastic seclusion are accepted as part of the normal male life, observed by Premier as well as peasant.

U Thein Han (1908–   ) broke ground for a new expression in Burmese literature with the publication in 1929 of his poem "Pitauk Pan." It was the first in a mode of writing called *Khitsan* (The Test of the Age).

Commenting on writers in this new school, U Thein Han has said: "We started writing in the old tradition. But there came a time when we started to rebel against unfruitful tradition, against pedantry, bookishness, conservativeness, and vanity." Writing under the pen name Zawgyi, U Thein Han turned from religious and classic themes to find rich sources of inspiration in the life of his day.

Now librarian at the University of Rangoon, Zawgyi finds time to write essays, fiction, and poetry. He has studied in Rangoon, Dublin, and London.

ZAWGYI (U THEIN HAN)

HIS SPOUSE

1

Ma Paw, the wife of Ko Hsin, worked in the market. Each morning she walked a mile to town with greens on a tray. If business was brisk, she returned early; otherwise, only when the sun had declined. Whenever she reached the bamboo bridge that crossed the stream beside the village on her return, thoughts of her husband and children arose in her mind.

She was tall with reddish hair and slightly protruding teeth, but it could not be said that she was ugly. Her husband, Ko Hsin, was a man of leisure who sat and ate at home. It was not wholly true that he did nothing. He had to cook the rice and look after the children.

Ko Hsin had been a novice in the Buddhist Monastic Order for nine years and had some learning. He was good-natured, fond of laughter, and was the prime mover at charities and weddings. He was not as tall as his wife, was small-chested, had a fine crop of hair and a thin strip of moustache. He was tattooed to his knees.

When they were married and after they had a son, Ma Paw kept shop and ministered to Ko Hsin's needs. When the second son was born, she could only keep shop. After the birth of their daughter, Ma Paw often became very tired. Once when she was hard hit by a business loss, her state was pitiable. But she did not complain.

She was heartened when one of her friends told her: "You should listen to your husband read the eulogy and blessing at a wedding in the village. Magnificent! He is a learned man." She was heartened when her fourteen-year-old son sometimes met her at the bamboo bridge and relieved her of her tray and basket. At these times her thoughts turned in gratitude to her husband.

Once when she and her children were talking on the raised platform of their house, a tipsy drinker of toddy appeared on the road and made insulting eyes at them. The children ran into the house in fear. Ko Hsin hurriedly appeared from within the house and stood with arms akimbo on the platform. The drunkard's eyes turned and whirled, leading away his tottering feet. Ma Paw was thankful. Were it not for my man, we would have suffered great indignities, she thought.

Ma Paw was now in her thirty-seventh year. Ko Hsin was six years older.

Ko Hsin, for all his years, had never really worked. When people said of him that he supported himself by clutching the hem of a skirt, he would reply jokingly, "I am able to live in leisure as I live now because of my past meritorious deeds. Don't be jealous." Though he said this, in his heart he was hurt. But the pain was almost forgotten in pride of his brilliant repartee. Because of his replies the others frowned on him or thrust their chins at him in derision. In time these acts of his neighbors spurred him to action. He borrowed money from a cousin and entered the bamboo business. He lost heavily. The next rains, he went down to the fields to plow. He returned home with blood dripping from his foot where he had run in the plowshare. It took fifteen days for the wound to heal.

2

He was forty-three on the day he got well. The wound of the flesh had healed but the wound of the heart had swollen.

Ma Paw had set off to market as usual, the elder son had gone on to the monastery school. The other two children were playing beneath the tamarind tree in front of the house. As Ko Hsin sat drinking a pot of green tea, he saw the carpenter father of six set out with his box of tools from a neighboring house. The man from next door crossed the stream to cut dani leaves on the other bank. Even the old man from the opposite house whittled a piece of wood to make a puddling stick.

At first Ko Hsin was filled with a sense of ease and pleasure as he drank cup after cup of tea and watched his children at play. But when his neighbors began to stir to work, his pleasure faded, and he remembered that he had yet to get the pot of rice on the fire. He suddenly recalled the taunts of his neighbors and the procession of his life passed before his eyes. His foppishness since leaving the monastery, his mar-

348   Modern Asian Literature

riage to Ma Paw, his business failure, his hurt foot. He became sad and ashamed. He desired to break out of this way
of life. He thought it would be good to become a monk.
Then he would not have to boil rice. He would be able to
turn his eyes toward the Supreme Good. His wife and children would gain merit by him. He felt certain that the time
for his release from the sorrows of rebirth was at hand. He
would endeavor to become a small god. Thus did he think.
But he remembered again that he must prepare the rice or he
would have nothing to eat and the children would cry. He
arose and entered the kitchen.

Meanwhile, in the market, Ma Paw was adding water to
her greens to make them heavier, whereby she might earn
more. With what more she earned, she intended to buy some
nice cheroots for her husband.

Ko Hsin was skilled at preparing boiled rice. He called the
children and gave them the rice with the remains of yesterday's curry. When the children had gone back to their play,
he sat with his feet dangling from the raised platform and
returned to his thoughts. When he became a monk, he would
come with his begging bowl to Ma Paw's house every morning and get a chance to meet Ma Paw and the children. But
Ma Paw was illiterate and ignorant of the religious Law.
When she died, she would pass to the lower worlds. For this
he pitied her. He wanted to open her eyes to the Law.

The quarrel of his children returned him to realities. The
sister had scratched the brother's face; in retaliation he had
pulled her hair. Now both were crying.

Ko Hsin called the children into the house and made them
sit in different corners. He then tried to return to his reverie
but could not pick up the chain of thought. He glanced at his
children and saw their little heads nodding into sleep. He felt
a yawn rise in him.

"Don't move," he commanded the children, and laid himself down for a nap.

The moment his eyes were closed the children opened
theirs. They threw speaking glances at each other and at their
father. They agreed to run down to play as soon as he fell

Ko Hsin awoke to Ma Paw's voice calling to her son in the

"Get down from there at once; you'll fall. Where is your

"At the streamside," the boy replied.

"Ko Hsin," Ma Paw cried, "do you leave your children un-attended like that? A good father you are!"

The daughter appeared with muddy hands and the boy climbed down from the tree.

Ko Hsin looked daggers at his children. They hid behind the mother.

"Here're cheroots for you," said Ma Paw, and thrusting them on him, she headed the children into the kitchen. Ko Hsin's eyes followed them. Ma Paw washed her daughter's hands and gave the children pea cakes to eat. Then, sitting down, Ma Paw spread her legs on the floor, untied her hair, bent forward, and let the hair hang above her legs.

"Massage my back with your elbows," she told her son. He did so while keeping his cake between his teeth. The shaking of the back under the pressure of the elbows and the swing of the spreading hair as her head swayed made Ma Paw appear as though possessed by the devil.

Ko Hsin looked and heaved a deep sigh of disgust. I must don the yellow robes, he thought.

However, he did not dare to tell his wife till the year had turned.

3

It was now three months, though Ko Hsin had said that he would wear the yellow robes for only a month. Ma Paw's aunt, who had come over to help look after the children, began to yearn for her own in her village.

"When will the Celibate return to lay life?" she had asked the monk one day.

The monk had not replied. Instead, he had quoted sacred verses extolling the life of a monk. The sacred verses did not enter the aunt's ears. Only anger rose in her because she felt that she was being kept here unfairly. When the monk had departed, she called Ma Paw to her.

"Ma Paw, I want to go back. Tell your monk to cast off the robes. I cannot stay on longer as a servant in your house," she threatened.

Ma Paw, too, wanted her husband to return home. She had alluded to the matter once or twice, only to have been turned back with sermons. Now the time was near when the monks would go into retreat for three months. Not knowing what to do, she conferred with a friend. After some talk they burst into laughter.

4

The morning was gold with sunlight. Doves cooed in the tamarind tree. Ma Paw did not go to market. Instead, she fried and cooked at home. Then she bathed and made herself fragrant with powder down to her toes. She smeared it lightly on her face. She gathered her straying strands and tied them in a knot to suit her features. The meager hair on her forehead was collected into a "dove's wing." She penciled her eyebrows in a wide sweep and made her lips red by chewing betel. She put on a jacket of fine white cloth and a new skirt of printed red flowers. The children, too, were dressed in clean clothes and the household things were packed. A bullock cart waited in readiness in the yard.

At ten o'clock the monk appeared, accompanied by his eldest son, who was in his monastery school. As he approached, he thought with apprehension, they will ask me again to forsake the life of a monk. He drew near the house and saw the cart. He entered the house and saw the packed household things. He sat on the mat the aunt had rolled out for him in the place of reverence in the house and searched in vain for Ma Paw.

After some time Ma Paw appeared with a tray of food. With sad eyes and movements, she offered the food. The monk took a quick glance at her. He noticed how dressed up she was. He took another glance. He was puzzled by her behavior, but his thoughts were occupied in steeling himself to refuse the request to return to lay life which he knew Ma Paw would surely make.

After the meal Ma Paw took away the tray and sat reverently at a distance. As the monk made to preach the sermon, Ma Paw spoke to her aunt.

"Aunt, hasn't the cartman arrived yet?"

The monk, unable to begin his sermon, looked toward the waiting cart.

"Ma Paw, what's going on here?" he asked.

"I will reveal all to the Celibate." Ma Paw addressed the monk without raising her head. "Aunt wants to return to her village. If she returns, I will be unable to keep shop and look after the children at the same time. That is why I beg permission of the Celibate to allow me and the two children to go live with Aunt in her village. The eldest son will be left in the Celibate's care."

She turned to her eldest son. "Son, stay behind with the

Celibate," she said, and wiped away a tear from her downcast face.

The monk remained silently thoughtful.

"The Celibate may continue to be a monk throughout his life if that is his wish. His humble lay woman will try to make a living somehow. The Celibate's world and hers are different worlds; there is a vast gap between them. Henceforth, there can only be the relationship of monk and lay devotee between them. Since she still has two children, if she can find someone to depend upon somewhere else, she desires to accept him. That is why she wishes to make things clear now so that complications may not arise later."

The monk uttered a cry of amazement. Ma Paw raised her eyes slightly. The monk's hands fluttered about his robes. He looked at Ma Paw.

Ma Paw continued: "This is said for the benefit of both. The Celibate will be able to follow the Law in freedom, and his humble devotee will be able, should she find someone—"

"There are too many toddy drunkards in your aunt's village," the monk said. "I will return to the lay life."

Ma Paw became Ko Hsin's wife again.

translated by U Win Pe

THAILAND

Prince Prem Purachatra, Thai professor of literature and magazine editor, asserts that Thai literature today flows in the direction of prose rather than poetry, the main literary stream of the past. And the numerous contemporary prose writers now publishing have been influenced to a great extent, he says, by the literature of the West. This is certainly true of the short-story type of writing.

And yet, could the Thai story in this volume have arisen from any culture other than that from which it came? "My

Thai Cat" is an imaginative story typical of North Thailand
and full of religious and cultural insights.

Pratoomratha Zeng (1918–   ), the author, is a native of
Ubol, the northern district of Thailand. He was educated in
Bangkok and New York. During World War II, he served as
a translator for the United States Army and, since that time,
has worked in the Thai government.

PRATOOMRATHA ZENG

My Thai Cat

Sii Sward was our Thai or Siamese cat in my hometown
Muang, a northern village in Thailand. She was a gift from
my father's friend to me when I was five years old. She had
piercing blue eyes and delicate dark brown fur which she
constantly cleaned with her tongue. I was completely devoted
to her. She was also very popular with my entire family, and
later was to be well known in the whole district.

During the drought in 1925, our Sii Sward was a heroine;
she had the great honor of being elected the Rain Queen.

We had been without rain for three months that summer.
It was hot and dry. Our public well was reduced to mud; the
river was at its lowest ebb. The grass and the trees were dry
as tinder. Many of the buffaloes and farm animals on our
farms died of heat, so we took the remainder to be fed far
away on the bank of the river Moon in the north. It seemed
as if farming that year would be impossible. We were on the
verge of chaos and famine. Already there were reports of forest fires in the other districts. Families from other villages
had migrated southwest seeking new places for farming.

Every day the villagers gathered in the village Buddhist
temple praying for the rain. All day long the Buddhist priests
chanted the sacred ritual for water from the sky. All the
farmers were worried and thought only of rain, rain, rain.

Then someone suggested that we perform the old Brahmo-
Buddhist rain ceremony called the Nang Maaw, the queen of
the cats. This ceremony has been performed by the peasants
since time immemorial.

No exact date can be given when the ceremony asking for
the rain started. In Brahmanism, Varuna, or the god of rain,
must be pleased. Varuna was the god or guardian spirit of the
sea, water, or rain. He was one of the oldest Vedic deities, a

personification of the all-investing sky, the maker and up-holder of heaven and earth. It is said that once Varuna, who was very militaristic, appeared in the form of a female cat to fight a demon. He won the battle and thus continued to give the world rain and prosperity.

Whether the Thai farmers knew the story of Varuna I do not know. All they thought during that time might be only to please Varuna, the god of rain.

One day, an old lady and her friends came to my father and begged him to help in the rain ceremony.

That day my father approached me and my cat seriously. He patted Sii Sward's head gently and said to me, "Ai Noo (my little mouse), the villagers have asked us to help in the ceremony asking for the rain. I promised them to use our cat—your Sii Sward."

I was stunned. How could they use my cat to get rain? I thought of those chickens that the Chinese killed and boiled during their annual Trut-Chine, the Chinese ritual days for sacrificing to and honoring the memory of their ancestors. To have my cat killed and boiled like a chicken! Oh, no.

I almost shouted to protest, "Oh, no, Father, I cannot let anyone kill my Sii Sward. Rain or no rain, I don't care."

In the Thai family, the father is the sole absolute authority of the house; to deny his wish is sinful and inexcusable. My father, however, was a very understanding man. He looked at me coldly and said calmly, "Son, no one is going to kill Sii Sward. Instead of doing that, and because our cat is the most beautiful and cleanest of all the cats in the village, she was elected by the people to be the Rain Queen of our district. This is a great honor to her and to our family."

I was reluctant to consent until Father said, "We can take Sii Sward back home as soon as the ceremony is over."

That evening there was an announcement from the temple ground by the old leader of the village that there would be a Nang Maaw ceremony starting in the afternoon of the following day.

Next morning everyone in the village went to the temple ground. The women were dressed in their bright blue skirts, Pha Sin, and white blouses, and the men in their white trousers and the Kui-Heng shirts. Children of all ages put on their new clean clothes; they walked along with their parents. Two artists built up a big bamboo cage and the people fastened flowers and leaves to it and dressed it up until it looked like a miniature castle.

At noontime, my cat Sii Sward had her usual lunch of dry

mudfish and rice, then my father gave me the great honor of carrying her to the temple ground. Some old ladies brushed and sprayed sweet native perfume upon her proud head. Sii Sward protested vehemently; she struggled to get away, and I had to put her into the adorned cage. However, once inside the cage, she became calm and serene as befitted her role and soon curled up in silent slumber. Buddhist priests came to sprinkle sacred water on her, but Sii Sward slept on.

In spite of the heat and the sun, that day people packed into the monastery to see Sii Sward, the Rain Queen, and to pray for rain. They carried the cage into the big Vihara, our best and most beautiful temple; and then the priests chanted a sacred prayer in front of the image of Lord Buddha, *Pra Kantharaj* (the image of Lord Bhudda asking for rain). Sacred water was sprinkled onto poor Sii Sward as a high priest lit a candle near the cage and chanted long moaning prayers in the sacred Pali tongue.

In mid-afternoon the sun was so hot that the villagers took refuge under the shade of the big mangoes and Po trees on the temple ground. A group of people began to chant the Nang Maaw song, softly at first, then louder and louder until everyone seemed to shout. Long native drums, Taphone, began to beat in chorus. People started to dance while chanting the song:

> Oh, mother cat, please give us rain from the sky
> So that we can make sacred water
> We need silver for the mother cat
> We need fish and we need honey
> If we do not get it, we will be ruined.
> Don't let the widow down to sell her children.
> Let them have all white rice
> To have pleasure, we need gold and silver
> We want to buy bananas
> We need provisions for the priests and the people
> Let us see the lightning and let us have rains
> Oh, let us have rain.

It was a most impressive ceremony and made me feel warm and confident of the queen's powers.

Sii Sward still slept peacefully in her adorned cage. Cool as a cucumber, she ignored the noise and the chanting until two men came to her miniature castle and lifted it to their shoulders, and then led the people out of the temple. A procession was formed; two drummers with Taphone drums led the crowd. They beat the drums incessantly as the people chanted and made a lot of noise. After the drummers there were a group of dancers dressed in the Thai theatrical style. They danced in front of the cage as if to perform the show for the Queen of Rain.

The procession moved toward the marketplace. There was a huge crowd following the procession; all of them chanted the Nang Maaw. On the narrow street people laid cakes and water which the pedestrians ate after Sii Sward passed. Some people gave the two men who carried the Rain Queen some rice wine. Both of them toasted the queen and drank the wine happily. These foods and drinks were to impress the Queen of Rain that ours was the land of plenty, and that the goddess of rain must give us water so that abundance of life would be preserved.

Sii Sward slept all the way; she was not impressed by the demonstration. Before we entered the open marketplace there was so much noise; someone fired many big firecrackers. A few women who were traders in powder and perfumes approached the cage and poured cups of sweet-smelling perfume and flowers onto the poor Rain Queen. At this moment, the noise of frantic shouting, of chanting, of firecrackers, and that perfumed water proved to be too much for the poor Sii Sward. More water and perfume were poured and splashed into the cage. Sii Sward stood up, her blue eyes staring at the culprits. Her brown and smooth hair was soaking wet. She began to cry and tried to find the way to escape in vain.

Seeing the whole condition going from bad to worse, I was almost crying asking Father to rescue the poor cat. However, Father said that everything would be all right. After a while, everyone seemed to be satisfied giving the Rain Queen perfumes; they stopped the noises completely as if to listen to the tormented noise of the Rain Queen. At that moment Sii Sward stopped crying, too. She was soaking wet and trembling with fear.

People chanted softly as they led the procession back to the monastery, even the drummers and the two men who ten minutes ago were chanting frantically now calmed down. Sii Sward continued crying on the way back to the temple as if her heart would break. I was helpless, but I followed the procession closely to the monastery.

When we reached the Vihara, the men placed the cage in front of the temple, and then all of them went into the Vihara to pray for the rain goddess again. At this moment, I saw the opportunity to help my poor Sii Sward. Having seen the last person enter the temple, I took Sii Sward out of the cage and ran home with her.

At nine o'clock that same night, it was pitch dark. Sii Sward now calmed herself down and seemed to forget the whole event in the daytime. She lay down under my bed and slept soundly. My parents were not yet returned from the temple ground; they joined the neighbors praying for rain in the monastery. I still wondered about the whole procession in the daytime, but I was too tired and did not know when I went fast asleep.

When my people came back from the temple ground at eleven o'clock, there was still no sign of rain. Someone came into my room to see Sii Sward, but seeing us asleep they went out quietly. It must have been about three o'clock in the morning when a sound like a train running and a big hurricane was heard. Later there was a strong sound of thunder over the mountains, and a few minutes later, a shower, a real tropical shower, came down. Everyone in the village got up from his bed. We were happy. The farmers started at once to their farms. It rained for three days, and three nights, and it seemed as if the showers would never stop until the water in the sky would be gone. Our crops were saved.

But Sii Sward ignored the whole rain. She slept happily the whole three days. Farmers and their families dropped down to see her afterward. They patted her delicate fur and left dry fish and meat for her, her favorite food. That year the farmers thought that Sii Sward saved their crops and their families. Sii Sward was a heroine.

PHILIPPINES

Philippine literature has been written and published in a variety of languages—Tagalog, Bisayan, Ilocano, and others. Today one of the most popular media, especially for the short story, is English. The use now of a "foreign language" for native literature should not make the product any more suspect than was Rizal's championship of the Filipino people, expressed in Spanish. Donald Keene, commenting on the volume *Modern Philippine Short Stories,* makes the point that, although Filipinos may speak one of the native tongues at home, their higher instruction has been largely in English and "their literary tastes were formed by English poetry and prose [and] many Filipinos feel that they cannot express themselves fully except in the language of their education."

It is true that, in earlier periods, tales and folk stories, indigenous in form as well as in theme, were naturally expressed in native dialect. However, the conscious literary genre of the modern short story, a Western form, is more naturally expressed in English, though content may remain as authentic to the local character and scene.

The two short stories from the Philippines included in this anthology were written in English and so reach us without, as Donald Keene puts it, "risking the terrible hazards of translation."

Amador Daguio (1912–) grew up in the mountain province of northern Luzon. He studied at the University of the Philippines, where he won several college and national magazine prizes for his fiction and poetry. In his early career as an educator, Daguio served several years in the southern islands. His first volume of poetry was completed while he was connected with the Zamboanga Normal School in the south. Shortly before the outbreak of World War II he went to Leyte Normal School.

During the war period, Daguio organized the Tacloban Theatre Guild, which produced two of his plays. These years also saw the publication of his second volume of poetry and a novel. In 1951 Daguio studied at the Stanford University Creative Writing Center, where his master's thesis was devoted to the translation of Kalinga tribal harvest songs, of the author's native province in the north.

On his return to the Philippines, Daguio settled in Manila, where he studied law and passed the bar in 1954. He has since held a variety of government positions, ranging from those with literary interest, such as chief of the editorial board of the Public Affairs Office, to those concerned with such mundane affairs as directing the Bureau of the Budget. He is also a regular university lecturer.

"Wedding Dance," which was first published in *Stanford Short Stories* in 1953, relates a heartwarming incident in the life of the non-Christian Kalinga tribes.

N. V. M. Gonzalez (1915–) was still a high-school boy when his writing was first accepted for publication—in *Graphic,* a Filipino magazine with which he was later to be editorially associated for six years. He was not yet twenty-one when a group of his poems was published in the American monthly *Poetry*.

A Rockefeller Foundation fellowship took him to the United States in 1949 where he studied under Wallace Stegner at Stanford University, as had Daguio before him. He also had opportunity for brief stays at the University of Denver and Kenyon College, and at writers' conferences at the University of Kansas and Middlebury College's noted Bread Loaf School in Vermont. In subsequent years, Gonzalez was to travel on Rockefeller lecture and writing grants throughout much of Asia. As a result, he is a favorite Filipino author and has been translated into Japanese, Thai, and other languages of the Orient and Southeast Asia.

Gonzalez has received a number of top Filipino literary prizes, including the Republic Award in 1954 for "advancement of Filipino culture in the field of English literature" and the first Cultural Heritage Award in 1960 for his novel *The Bamboo Dancers*.

"A Warm Hand" is a brief story packed with revealing insight into Filipino social customs and life in an archipelago setting.

AMADOR DAGUIO

WEDDING DANCE

Awiyao reached for the upper horizontal log which served as the edge of the head-high threshold. Clinging to the log, he lifted himself with one bound that carried him across to the narrow door. He slid back the cover, stepped inside, then pushed the cover back in place. After some moments during which he seemed to wait, he talked to the listening darkness.

"I'm sorry this had to be done. I am really sorry. But neither of us can help it."

The sound of the *gangsas* beat through the walls of the dark house, like muffled roars of falling waters. The woman who had moved with a start when the sliding door opened had been hearing the *gangsas* for she did not know how long. The sudden rush of the rich sounds when the door opened was like a sharp gush of fire in her. She gave no sign that she heard Awiyao, but continued to sit unmoving in the darkness.

But Awiyao knew that she had heard him and his heart pitied her. He crawled on all fours to the middle of the room; he knew exactly where the stove was. With bare fingers he stirred the covered smoldering embers, and blew into them. When the coals began to glow, Awiyao put pieces of pine on them, then full round logs as big as his arms. The room brightened.

"Why don't you go out," he said, "and join the dancing women?" He felt a pang inside him, because what he said was really not the right thing to say and because the woman did not stir. "You should join the dancers," he said, "as if— as if nothing has happened." He looked at the woman huddled in a corner of the room, leaning against the wall. The stove fire played with strange moving shadows and lights upon her face. She was partly sullen, but her sullenness was not because of anger or hate.

"Go out—go out and dance. If you really don't hate me for this separation, go out and dance. One of the men will see you dance well; he will like your dancing; he will marry you. Who knows but that, with him, you will be luckier than you were with me."

"I don't want any man," she said sharply. "I don't want any other man."

He felt relieved that at least she talked: "You know very well that I don't want any other woman, either. You know that, don't you? Lumnay, you know it, don't you?"

She did not answer him.

"You know it, Lumnay, don't you?" he repeated.

"Yes, I know," she said weakly.

"It is not my fault," he said, feeling relieved. "You cannot blame me; I have been a good husband to you."

"Neither can you blame me," she said. She seemed about to cry.

"No, you have been very good to me. You have been a good wife. I have nothing to say against you." He set some of the burning wood in place. "It's only that a man must have a child. Seven harvests is just too long to wait. Yes, we have waited too long. We should have another chance before it is too late for both of us."

This time the woman stirred, stretched her right leg out and bent her left leg in. She wound the blanket more snugly around herself.

"You know that I have done my best," she said. "I have prayed to Kabunyan much. I have sacrificed many chickens in my prayers."

"Yes, I know."

"You remember how angry you were once when you came home from your work in the terrace because I butchered one of our pigs without your permission? I did it to appease Kabunyan, because, like you, I wanted to have a child. But what could I do?"

"Kabunyan does not see fit for us to have a child," he said. He stirred the fire. The sparks rose through the crackles of the flames. The smoke and soot went up to the ceiling.

Lumnay looked down and unconsciously started to pull at the rattan that kept the split bamboo flooring in place. She tugged at the rattan flooring. Each time she did this the split bamboo went up and came down with a slight rattle. The gongs of the dancers clamorously called in her ears through the walls.

Awiyao went to the corner where Lumnay sat, paused before her, looked at her bronzed and sturdy face, then turned to where the jars of water stood piled one over the other. Awiyao took a coconut cup and dipped it in the top jar and drank. Lumnay had filled the jars from the mountain creek early that evening.

"I came home," he said, "because I did not find you among the dancers. Of course, I am not forcing you to come, if you don't want to join my wedding ceremony. I came to tell you that Madulimay, although I am marrying her, can never become as good as you are. She is not as strong in planting beans, nor as fast in cleaning water jars, not as good in keeping a house clean. You are one of the best wives in the whole village."

"That has not done me any good, has it?" she said. She looked at him lovingly. She almost seemed to smile.

He put the coconut cup aside on the floor and came closer to her. He held her face between his hands, and looked longingly at her beauty. But her eyes looked away. Never again would he hold her face. The next day she would not be his anymore. She would go back to her parents. He let go of her face, and she bent to the floor again and looked at her fingers as they tugged softly at the split bamboo floor.

"This house is yours," he said, "I built it for you. Make it your own, live in it as long as you wish. I will build another house for Madulimay."

"I have no need for a house," she said slowly. "I'll go to my own house. My parents are old. They will need help in the planting of the beans, in the pounding of the rice."

"I will give you the field that I dug out of the mountain

during the first year of our marriage," he said. "You know I did it for you. You helped me to make it for the two of us."

"I have no use for any field," she said.

He looked at her, then turned away, and became silent. They were silent for a time.

"Go back to the dance," she said finally. "It is not right for you to be here. They will wonder where you are, and Madulimay will not feel good. Go back to the dance."

"I would feel better if you would come, and dance—for the last time. The *gangsas* are playing."

"You know that I cannot."

"Lumnay," he said tenderly. "Lumnay, if I did this it is because of my need for a child. You know that life is not worth living without a child. The men have mocked me behind my back. You know that."

"I know it," she said. "I will pray that Kabunyan will bless you and Madulimay."

She bit her lips now, then shook her head wildly, and sobbed.

She thought of the seven harvests that had passed, the high hopes they had in the beginning of their new life, the day he took her away from her parents across the roaring river, on the other side of the mountain, the trip up the trail which they had to climb, the steep canyon which they had to cross —the waters boiled in her mind in foams of white and jade and roaring silver; the waters rolled and growled, resounded in thunderous echoes through the walls of the stiff cliffs; they were far away now but loud still and receding; the waters violently smashed down from somewhere on the tops of the other ranges, and they had looked carefully at the buttresses of rocks they had to step on—a slip would have meant death.

They both drank of the water, then rested on the other bank before they made the final climb to the other side of the mountain.

She looked at his face with the fire playing upon his features—hard and strong, and kind. He had a sense of lightness in his way of saying things, which often made her and the village people laugh. How proud she had been of his humor. The muscles were taut and firm, bronze and compact in their hold upon his skull—how frank his bright eyes were. She looked at his body that carved out of the mountains five fields for her; his wide and supple torso heaved as if a slab of shining lumber were heaving; his arms and legs flowed down in fluent muscles—he was strong and for that she had lost him.

She flung herself upon his knees and clung to them. "Awi-yao, Awiyao, my husband," she cried. "I did everything to have a child," she said passionately in a hoarse whisper. "Look at me," she cried. "Look at my body. Then it was full of promise. It could dance; it could work fast in the fields; it could climb the mountains fast. Even now it is firm, full. But, Awiyao, Kabunyan never blessed me. Awiyao, Kabunyan is cruel to me. Awiyao, I am useless. I must die."

"It will not be right to die," he said, gathering her in his arms. Her whole warm naked breast quivered against his own; she clung now to his neck, and her head lay upon his right shoulder; her hair flowed down in cascades of gleaming darkness.

"I don't care about the fields," she said. "I don't care about the house. I don't care for anything but you. I'll have no other man."

"Then you'll always be fruitless."

"I'll go back to my father. I'll die."

"Then you hate me," he said. "If you die it means you hate me. You do not want me to have a child. You do not want my name to live on in our tribe."

She was silent.

"If I do not try a second time," he explained, "it means I'll die. Nobody will get the fields I have carved out of the mountains; nobody will come after me."

"If you fail—if you fail this second time—" she said thoughtfully. Then her voice was a shudder. "No—no, I don't want you to fail."

"If I fail," he said, "I'll come back to you. Then both of us will die together. Both of us will vanish from the life of our tribe."

The gongs thundered through the walls of their house, sonorous and far away.

"I'll keep my beads," she said. "Awiyao, let me keep my beads," she half-whispered.

"You will keep the beads. They come from far-off times. My grandmother said they came from way up North, from the slant-eyed people across the sea. You keep them, Lum-nay. They are worth twenty fields."

"I'll keep them because they stand for the love you have for me," she said. "I love you. I love you and have nothing to give."

She took herself away from him, for a voice was calling out to him from outside. "Awiyao! Awiyao! O Awiyao! They are looking for you at the dance!"

"I am not in a hurry."

"The elders will scold you. You had better go."

"Not until you tell me that it is all right with you."

"It is all right with me."

He clasped her hands. "I do this for the sake of the tribe," he said.

"I know," she said.

He went to the door.

"Awiyao!"

He stopped as if suddenly hit by a spear. In pain he turned to her. Her face was agony. It pained him to leave. She had been wonderful to him. What was it that made a man wish for a child? What was it in life, in the work in the fields, in the planting and harvest, in the silence of the night, in the communings with husband and wife, in the whole life of the tribe itself that made man wish for the laughter and speech of a child? Suppose he changed his mind? Why did the unwritten law demand, anyway, that a man, to be a man, must have a child to come after him? And if he was fruitless—but he loved Lumnay. It was like taking away half of his life to leave her like this.

"Awiyao," she said, and her eyes seemed to smile in the light. "The beads!"

He turned back and walked to the farthest corner of their room, to the trunk where they kept their worldly possessions —his battle-ax and his spear points, her betel-nut box and her beads. He dug out from the darkness the beads which had been given to him by his grandmother to give to Lumnay on the day of his marriage. He went to her, lifted her head, put the beads on, and tied them in place. The white and jade and deep orange obsidians shone in the firelight. She suddenly clung to him, clung to his neck, as if she would never let him go.

"Awiyao! Awiyao, it is hard!" She gasped, and she closed her eyes and buried her face in his neck.

The call for him from the outside repeated; her grip loosened, and he hurried out into the night.

Lumnay sat for some time in the darkness. Then she went to the door and opened it. The moonlight struck her face; the moonlight spilled itself upon the whole village.

She could hear the throbbing of the *gangsas* coming to her through the caverns of the other houses. She knew that all the houses were empty; that the whole tribe was at the dance. Only she was absent. And yet was she not the best dancer of the village? Did she not have the most lightness and grace?

Could she not, alone among all the women, dance like a bird tripping for grains on the ground, beautifully timed to the beat of the *gangsas*? Did not the men praise her supple body, and the women envy the way she stretched her hands like the wings of the mountain eagle now and then as she danced? How long ago did she dance at her own wedding? Tonight, all the women who counted, who once danced in her honor, were dancing now in honor of another whose only claim was that perhaps she could give her husband a child.

"It is not right. It is not right!" she cried. "How does she know? How can anybody know? It is not right," she said.

Suddenly she found courage. She would go to the dance. She would go to the chief of the village, to the elders, to tell them it was not right. Awiyao was hers; nobody could take him away from her. Let her be the first woman to complain, to denounce the unwritten rule that a man may take another woman. She would break the dancing of the men and women. She would tell Awiyao to come back to her. He surely would relent. Was not their love as strong as the river?

She made for the other side of the village where the dancing was. There was a flaming glow over the whole place; a great bonfire was burning. The *gangsas* clamored more loudly now, and it seemed they were calling to her. She was near at last. She could see the dancers clearly now. The men leaped lightly with their *gangsas* as they circled the dancing women decked in feast garments and beads, tripping on the ground like graceful birds, following their men. Her heart warmed to the flaming call of the dance; strange heat in her blood welled up, and she started to run.

But the flaming brightness of the bonfire commanded her to stop. Did anybody see her approach? She stopped. What if somebody had seen her coming? The flames of the bonfire leaped in countless sparks which spread and rose like yellow points and died out in the night. The blaze reached out to her like a spreading radiance. She did not have the courage to break into the wedding feast.

Lumnay walked away from the dancing ground, away from the village. She thought of the new clearing of beans which Awiyao and she had started to make only four moons before. She followed the trail above the village.

When she came to the mountain stream she crossed it carefully. Nobody held her hands, and the stream water was very cold. The trail went up again, and she was in the moonlight shadows among the trees and shrubs. Slowly she climbed the mountain.

When Lumnay reached the clearing, she could see from where she stood the blazing bonfire at the edge of the village, where the dancing was. She could hear the far-off clamor of the gongs, still rich in their sonorousness, echoing from mountain to mountain. The sound did not mock her; they seemed to call far to her; speak to her in the language of un-speaking love. She felt the pull of their clamor, almost the feeling that they were telling to her their gratitude for her sacrifice. Her heartbeat began to sound to her like many *gangsas*.

Lumnay thought of Awiyao as the Awiyao she had known long ago—a strong, muscular boy carrying his heavy loads of fuel logs down the mountains to his home. She had met him one day as she was on her way to fill her clay jars with water. He had stopped at the spring to drink and rest; and she had made him drink the cool mountain water from her coconut shell. After that it did not take him long to decide to throw his spear on the stairs of her father's house in token of his desire to marry her.

The mountain clearing was cold in the freezing moonlight. The wind began to sough and stir the leaves of the bean plants. Lumnay looked for a big rock on which to sit down. The bean plants now surrounded her, and she was lost among them.

A few more weeks, a few more months, a few more har-vests—what did it matter? She would be holding the bean flowers, soft in the texture, silken almost, but moist where the dew got into them, silver to look at, silver on the light blue, blooming whiteness, when the morning comes. The stretching of the bean pods full length from the hearts of the wilting petals would go on.

Lumnay's fingers moved a long, long time among the growing bean pods.

N. V. M. GONZALEZ

A WARM HAND

Holding on to the rigging, Elay leaned over. The dinghy was being readied. The wind tore her hair into wiry strands that fell across her face, heightening her awareness of the dipping and rising of the deck. But for the bite of the *no-*

roeste, she would have begun to feel faint and empty in her belly. Now she clutched at the rigging with more courage.

At last the dinghy shoved away, with its first load of passengers—seven boys from Bongabon, Mindoro, on their way to Manila to study. The deck seemed less hostile than before, for the boys had made a boisterous group then; now that they were gone, her mistress Ana could leave the crowded deckhouse for once.

"Oh, Elay! My powder puff!"

It was Ana, indeed. Elay was familiar with that excitement which her mistress wore about her person like a silk kerchief —now on her head to keep her hair in place, now like a scarf round her neck. How eager Ana had been to go ashore when the old skipper of the *batel* said that the *Ligaya* was too small a boat to brave the coming storm. She must return to the deckhouse, Elay thought, if she must fetch her mistress's handbag.

With both hands upon the edge of the deckhouse roof, then holding on to the wooden water barrel to the left of the main mast, she staggered back to the deckhouse entrance. As she bent her head low lest with the lurching of the boat her brow should hit the door, she saw her mistress on all fours clambering out of the deckhouse. She let her have the right-of-way, entering only after Ana was safe upon the open deck.

Elay found the handbag—she was certain that the powder puff would be there—though not without difficulty, inside the canvas satchel that she meant to take ashore. She came dragging the heavy satchel, and in a flurry Ana dug into it for the bag. The deck continued to sway, yet presently Ana was powdering her face; and this done, she applied lipstick to that full round mouth of hers.

The wind began to press Elay's blouse against her breasts while she waited on her mistress patiently. She laced Ana's shoes and also bestirred herself to see that Ana's earrings were not askew. For Ana must appear every inch the dressmaker that she was. Let everyone know that she was traveling to Manila—not just to the provincial capital; and, of course, there was the old spinster aunt, too, for company—to set up a shop in the big city. It occurred to Elay that, judging from the care her mistress was taking to look well, it might well be that they were not on board a one-masted Tingloy *batel* with a cargo of lumber, copra, pigs, and chickens, but were still at home in the dress shop that they were leaving behind in the lumber town of Sumagui.

"How miserable I'd be without you, Elay," Ana giggled, as

though somewhere she was meeting a secret lover who for certain would hold her in his arms in one wild passionate caress.

And thinking so of her mistress made Elay more proud of her. She did not mind the dark world into which they were going. Five miles to the south was Pinamalayan town; its lights blinked faintly at her. Then along the rim of the Bay, dense groves of coconuts and underbrush stood, occasional fires marking where the few sharecroppers of the district lived. The *batel* had anchored at the northernmost end of the cove and apparently five hundred yards from the boat was a palm-leaf-covered hut the old skipper of the *Ligaya* had spoken about.

"Do you see it? That's Obregano's hut." And Obregano, the old skipper explained, was a fisherman. The men who sailed up and down the eastern coast of Mindoro knew him well. There was not a seaman who lived in these parts but had gone to Obregano for food or shelter and to this anchorage behind the northern tip of Pinamalayan Bay for the protection it offered sailing vessels against the unpredictable *noroeste*.

The old skipper had explained all this to Ana, and Elay had listened, little knowing that in a short while it would all be there before her. Now in the dark she saw the fisherman's hut readily. A broad shoulder of a hill rose beyond, and farther yet the black sky looked like a silent wall.

Other women joined them on the deck to see the view for themselves. A discussion started; some members of the party did not think it would be proper for them to spend the night in Obregano's hut. Besides the students, there were four middle-aged merchants on this voyage; since Bongabon they had plagued the women with their coarse talk and their yet coarser laughter. Although the deckhouse was the unchallenged domain of the women, the four middle-aged merchants had often slipped in, and once had exchanged lewd jokes among themselves to the embarrassment of their audience. Small wonder, Elay thought, that the prospect of spending the night in a small fisherman's hut and with these men for company did not appear attractive to the other women passengers. Her mistress Ana had made up her mind, however. She had a sense of independence that Elay admired.

Already the old aunt had joined them on deck; and Elay said to herself, "Of course, it's for this old auntie's sake, too. She has been terribly seasick."

In the dark she saw the dinghy and silently watched it

being sculled back to the *batel*. It drew nearer and nearer, a dark mass moving eagerly, the bow pointing in her direction. Elay heard Ana's little shrill cries of excitement. Soon two members of the crew were vying for the honor of helping her mistress safely into the dinghy.

Oh, that Ana should allow herself to be thus honored, with the seamen taking such pleasure from it all, and the old aunt watching, pouting her lips in disapproval! "What shall I do?" Elay asked herself, anticipating that soon she herself would be the object of this chivalrous byplay. And what could the old aunt be saying now to herself? "Ah, women these days are no longer decorous. In no time they will make a virtue of being unchaste."

Elay pouted, too. And then it was her turn. She must get into that dinghy, and it so pitched and rocked. If only she could manage to have no one help her at all. But she'd fall into the water. Santa Maria. I'm safe. . . .

They were off. The waves broke against the sides of the dinghy, threatening to capsize it, and continually the black depths glared at her. Her hands trembling, Elay clung tenaciously to the gunwale. Spray bathed her cheeks. A boy began to bail, for after clearing each wave the dinghy took in more water. So earnest was the boy at his chore that Elay thought the boat had sprung a leak and would sink any moment.

The sailors, one at the prow and the other busy with the oar at the stern, engaged themselves in senseless banter. Were they trying to make light of the danger? She said her prayers as the boat swung from side to side, to a rhythm set by the sailor with the oar.

Fortunately, panic did not seize her. It was the old aunt who cried *"Susmariosep!"* For with each crash of waves, the dinghy lurched precipitously. "God spare us all!" the old aunt prayed frantically.

And Ana was laughing. "Auntie! Why, Auntie, it's nothing! It's nothing at all!" For, really, they were safe. The dinghy had struck sand.

Elay's dread of the water suddenly vanished and she said to herself: "Ah, the old aunt is only making things more difficult for herself." Why, she wouldn't let the sailor with the oar lift her clear of the dinghy and carry her to the beach!

"Age before beauty," the sailor was saying to his companion. The other fellow, not to be outdone, had jumped waist-deep into the water, saying: "No, beauty above all!" Then there was Ana stepping straight, as it were, into the sailor's arms.

"Where are you?" the old aunt was calling from the shore. "Are you safe? Are you all right?"

Elay wanted to say that in so far as she was concerned she was safe, she was all right. But she couldn't speak for her mistress, of course! But the same seaman who had lifted the old aunt and carried her to the shore in his arms had returned. Now he stood before Elay and caught her two legs and let them rest on his forearm and then held her body up, with the other arm. Now she was clear of the dinghy, and she had to hold on to his neck. Then the sailor made three quick steps toward dry sand and then let her slide easily off his arms, and she said: "I am all right. Thank you."

Instead of saying something to her the sailor hurried away, joining the group of students that had gathered at the rise of sand. Ana's cheerful laughter rang in their midst. Then a youth's voice, clear in the wind: "Let's hurry to the fisherman's hut!"

A drizzle began to fall. Elay took a few tentative steps toward the palm-leaf hut, but her knees were unsteady. The world seemed to turn and turn, and the glowing light at the fisherman's door swung as from a boat's mast. Elay hurried as best as she could after Ana and her old aunt, both of whom had already reached the hut. It was only on hearing her name that that weak, unsteady feeling in her knees disappeared.

"Elay—" It was her mistress, of course. Ana was standing outside the door, waiting. "My lipstick, Elay!"

An old man stood at the door at the hut. "I am Obregano, at your service," he said in welcome. "This is my home."

He spoke in a singsong that rather matched his wizened face. Pointing at a little woman pottering about the stovebox at one end of the one-room hut, he said: "And she? Well, the guardian of my home—in other words, my wife!"

The woman got up and welcomed them, beaming a big smile. "Feel at home. Make yourselves comfortable—everyone."

She helped Elay with the canvas bag, choosing a special corner for it. "It will rain harder yet tonight, but here your bag will be safe," the woman said.

The storm had come. The thatched walls shook, producing a weird skittering sound at each gust of wind. The sough of the palms in back of the hut—which was hardly the size of the deckhouse of the *batel*, and had the bare sand for floor

—sounded like the moan of a lost child. A palm leaf that served to cover an entrance to the left of the stovebox began to dance a mad, rhythmless dance. The fire in the stove leaped intermittently, rising beyond the lid of the kettle that Obregano, the old fisherman, had placed there.

And yet the hut was homelike. It was warm and clean. There was a cheerful look all over the place. Elay caught the old fisherman's smile as his wife cleared the floor of blankets, nets, and coil after coil of hempen rope so that their guests could have more room. She sensed an affinity with her present surroundings, with the smell of the fishnets, with the dancing fire in the stovebox. It was as though she had lived in this hut before. She remembered what Obregano's wife had said to her. The old woman's words were by far the kindest she had heard in a long time.

The students from Bongabon had appropriated a corner for themselves and began to discuss supper. It appeared that a prankster had relieved one of the chicken coops of a fat pullet and a boy asked the fisherman for permission to prepare a stew.

"I've some ginger tea in the kettle," Obregano said. "Something worth drinking in a weather like this." He asked his wife for an old enameled tin cup for their guests to drink from.

As the cup was being passed around, Obregano's wife expressed profuse apologies for her not preparing supper. "We have no food," she said with uncommon frankness. "We have sons, you know; two of them, both working in town. But they come home only on weekends. It is only then that we have rice."

Elay understood that in lieu of wages the two Obregano boys received rice. Last weekend the boys had failed to return home, however. This fact brought a sad note to Elay's new world of warm fire and familiar smells. She got out some food which they had brought along from the boat—*adobo* and bread that the old aunt had put in a tin container and tucked into the canvas satchel—and offered her mistress these, going through the motions so absentmindedly that Ana chided her.

"Do offer the old man and his wife some of that, too."

Obregano shook his head. He explained that he would not think of partaking of the food—so hungry his guests must be. They needed all the food themselves, to say nothing about that which his house should offer but which in his naked poverty he could not provide. But at least they would be safe here for the night, Obregano assured them. "The wind is rising, and the rain, too . . . Listen. . . ." He pointed at the roof, which seemed to sag.

The drone of the rain set Elay's spirits aright. She began to imagine how sad and worried over her sons the old fisherman's wife must be, and how lonely—but oh, how lovely!—it would be to live in this godforsaken spot. She watched the students devour their supper, and she smiled thanks, sharing their thoughtfulness, when they offered most generously some chicken to Ana and, in sheer politeness, to the old spinster aunt also.

Yet more people from the *batel* arrived, and the four merchants burst into the hut discussing some problems in Bongabon municipal politics. It was as though the foul weather suited their purposes, and Elay listened with genuine interest, with compassion, even, for the small-town politicians who were being reviled and cursed.

It was Obregano who suggested that they all retire. There was hardly room for everyone, and in bringing out a rough-woven palm-leaf mat for Ana and her companions to use, Obregano picked his way in order not to step on a sprawling leg or an outstretched arm. The offer of the mat touched Elay's heart, so much so that pondering the goodness of the old fisherman and his wife took her mind away from the riddles which the students at this time were exchanging among themselves. They were funny riddles and there was much laughter. Once she caught them throwing glances in Ana's direction.

Even the sailors who were with them on the dinghy had returned to the hut to stay and were laughing heartily at their own stories. Elay watched Obregano produce a bottle of kerosene for the lantern, and then hang the lantern with a string from the center beam of the hut. She felt a new dreamlike joy. Watching the old fisherman's wife extinguish the fire in the stove made Elay's heart throb.

Would the wind and the rain worsen? The walls of the hut shook—like a man in the throes of malaria chills. The sea kept up a wild roar, and the waves, it seemed, continually clawed at the land with strong, greedy fingers.

She wondered whether Obregano and his wife would ever sleep. The couple would be thinking: "Are our guests comfortable enough as they are?" As for herself, Elay resolved, she would stay awake. From the corner where the students slept she could hear the whine of a chronic asthma sufferer. One of the merchants snorted periodically, like a horse being plagued by a fly. A young boy, apparently dreaming, called out in a strange, frightened voice: "No, no! I can't do that! I wouldn't do that!"

She saw Obregano get up and pick his way again among the sleeping bodies to where the lantern hung. The flame was sputtering. Elay watched him adjust the wick of the lantern and give the oil container a gentle shake. Then the figure of the old fisherman began to blur and she could hardly keep her eyes open. A soothing tiredness possessed her. As she yielded easily to sleep, with Ana to her left and the old spinster aunt at the far edge of the mat to her right, the floor seemed to sink and the walls of the hut to vanish, as though the world were one vast dark valley.

When later she awoke she was trembling with fright. She had only a faint notion that she had screamed. What blur there had been in her consciousness before falling asleep was as nothing compared with that which followed her waking, although she was aware of much to-do and the lantern light was gone.

"Who was it?" It was reassuring to hear Obregano's voice.

"The lantern, please!" That was Ana, her voice shrill and wiry.

Elay heard as if in reply the crash of the sea rising in a crescendo. The blur lifted a little: "Had I fallen asleep after all? Then it must be past midnight by now." Time and place became realities again; and she saw Obregano, with a lighted matchstick in his hand. He was standing in the middle of the hut.

"What happened?"

Elay thought that it was she whom Obregano was speaking to. She was on the point of answering, although she had no idea of what to say, when Ana, sitting up on the mat beside her, blurted out: "Someone was here. Please hold up the light."

"Someone was here," Elay repeated to herself and hid her face behind Ana's shoulder. She must not let the four merchants, nor the students either, stare at her so. Caught by the lantern light, the men hardly seven steps away had turned their gazes upon her in various attitudes of amazement.

Everyone seemed eager to say something all at once. One of the students spoke in a quavering voice, declaring that he had not moved where he lay. Another said he had been so sound asleep—"Didn't you hear me snoring?" he asked a companion, slapping him on the back—he had not even heard the shout. One of the merchants hemmed and suggested that perhaps cool minds should look into the case, carefully and without preconceived ideas. To begin with, one must know exactly what happened. He looked in Ana's direction and said: "Now please tell us."

Elay clutched her mistress's arm. Before Ana could speak, Obregano's wife said: "This thing ought not to have happened. If only our two sons were home, they'd avenge the honor of our house." She spoke with a rare eloquence for an angry woman. "No one would then dare think of so base an act. Now, our good guests," she added, addressing her husband bitterly, "why, they know you to be an aged, simple-hearted fisherman—nothing more. The good name of your home, of our family, is no concern of theirs."

"Evil was coming, I knew it!" said the old spinster aunt; and piping out like a bird: "Let us return to the boat! Don't be so bitter, old one," she told Obregano's wife. "We are going back to the boat."

"It was like this," Ana said, not minding her aunt. Elay lowered her head more, lest she should see those man-faces before her, loosely trapped now by the lantern's glow. Indeed, she closed her eyes, as though she were a little child afraid of the dark.

"It was like this," her mistress began again, "I was sleeping, and then my maid, Elay"—she put an arm around Elay's shoulder—"she uttered that wild scream. I am surprised you did not hear it."

In a matter-of-fact tone, one of the merchants countered: "Suppose it was a nightmare?"

But Ana did not listen to him. "Then my maid," she continued, "this girl here—she's hardly twenty, mind you, and an innocent and illiterate girl, if you must all know. . . . She turned round, trembling, and clung to me. . . ."

"Couldn't she possibly have shouted in her sleep," the merchant insisted.

Obregano had held his peace all this time, but now he spoke: "Let us hear what the girl says."

And so kind were those words! How fatherly of him to have spoken so, in such a gentle and understanding way! Elay's heart went to him. She felt she could almost run to him and, crying over his shoulders, tell him what no one, not even Ana herself, would ever know.

She turned her head a little to one side and saw that now they were all looking at her. She hugged her mistress tighter, in a childlike embrace, hiding her face as best she could.

"Tell them," Ana said, drawing herself away. "No, go on
—speak!"

But Elay would not leave her side. She clung to her, and
began to cry softly.

"Nonsense!" the old aunt chided her.

"Well, she must have had a nightmare, that's all," the merchant said, chuckling. "I'm sure of it!"

At this remark Elay cried even more. "I felt a warm hand
caressing my—my—my cheeks," she said, sobbing. "A warm
hand, I swear," she said again, remembering how it had
reached out for her in the dark, searchingly, burning with a
need to find some precious treasure which, she was certain of
it now, she alone possessed. But how could it be that they
should force her to tell them? "Someone"—the word was like
a lamp in her heart—"someone wanted me," she said to herself.

She felt Ana's hand stroking her back ungently and then
heard her saying, "I brought this on," then nervously fum-
bling about the mat. "This is all my fault. . . . My compact,
please. . . ."

But Elay was inconsolable. She was sorry she could be of
no help to her mistress now. She hung her head, unable to
stop her tears from cleansing those cheeks that a warm hand
had loved.

Short Stories of
China and Korea

CHINA

Fictional prose has never been very highly regarded in China. In fact, until very recent times it was so looked down upon that authors of imaginative prose preferred to remain anonymous. Novels have generally been mixtures of fantasy and religious precept, such as the sixteenth-century *Hsi Yu Chi (Monkey)*, or voluminous, picaresque, and often pornographic accounts of social life, such as the *Chin P'ing Mei (The Golden Lotus)* of the same period. Today, we regard these as early novels having considerable stature, yet the *Ssū Ku Chuen Shu (Encyclopedia of Chinese Literature)*, 1772, does not list them, nor—by order of Emperor Ch'ien Lung —does it include the novel as part of literature proper.

Relating stories chiefly for purposes of enjoyment has been foreign to Chinese literary traditions. Under communism it remains so today. Pearl Buck points out that through the centuries scholars have demanded that fiction must have social significance to be considered worthy. She gives the following as the conclusive syllogism:

> Literature is art.
> All art has social significance.
> This book has no social significance.
> Therefore it is not literature.

How neatly this precept, rooted in long-established culture

patterns, fits in with the preachments of Mao Tse-tung today!

Another strike against fictional prose was its use of *pei-hua*, the vernacular of the common people, rather than the classical *wen-li*, which, until Hu Shih's literary revolution, was the medium for verse.

That novels and short stories were written and published in the vernacular for the enjoyment of the masses despite such formidable obstacles is a tribute to the virility of the imaginative prose form.

Even though the modern short story is the product of an intermixture of Occidental and Oriental values and points of view, the Chinese story has tenaciously retained such aspects of its early expression as supernatural events and beings and Confucian and Buddhist preachment.

Chou Shu-jen (1881–1936) has been called "the father of the modern Chinese short story," because of his introduction of Western techniques into brief fictional pieces written in the vernacular *pei-hua*. Of a poor family, Chou managed to get to Japan to study medicine. While there he became deeply interested in the Western literature he read in Japanese translation. On his return to China in 1915 he abandoned medicine for teaching and writing, becoming his country's leading author of the 1920's. Writing under the pen name Lu Hsun, Chou produced only twenty-six short stories in all. However, these were to set a pattern that would be followed by other writers of the era. He was the first to choose themes of social concern, dwelling especially on the problems of the poor, women, and intellectuals. All three themes are interwoven in the "A Little Incident" that follows.

Because of his social criticism of the old order, Chou has been canonized by the People's Republic of China. A quotation from his writing which introduces Korean writer Yu-Wol Chong-Nyon's "The Nonrevolutionaries" (page 394) would not seem to qualify him for such honor, however.

Shen Yen-ping (1896–   ) writes under the pen name Mao Tun. He has had a varied and checkered literary career beginning with his emergence as an exponent of "revolutionary realism" early in the second decade of the present century. In 1920 he founded the Society for Literary Studies and in 1921 became editor of *Fiction*, a literary monthly. Five years later he moved on to the editorship of a Hankow daily paper devoted to the cause of the socialist revolution. When Chiang Kai-shek came to power in 1927, Shen left Hankow to return to Shanghai. It was then that he adopted the pseudonym he has used ever since.

For a period of some fifteen years Shen cooperated in the Kuomintang government. However, Chiang Kai-shek's political philosophy became too conservative for him and he withdrew from politics in order to devote himself entirely to his writing. Later he joined the Communist camp. During a period of political ascendancy, from 1949 to the present, Shen has held various cultural-political posts, such as Chairman of the Chinese Writers' Union, Minister of Culture in the Central People's Government, and (as of 1963) Minister of Culture. He is said to have become so involved in such governmental activity that he has produced no new creative work since about 1949.

Mao Tun is the author of a half-dozen novels, of which *Midnight* (1933) is considered to be his masterpiece. He has also published plays, articles, and essays, as well as many short stories.

"Spring Silkworms" depicts the uncertain life of village silkworm growers and is full of fascinating details concerning a way of life that is strange to most Westerners.

LU HSUN (CHOU SHU-JEN)

A LITTLE INCIDENT

Six years have gone by, as so many winks, since I came to the capital from the village. During all that time there have occurred many of those events known as "affairs of state," a great number of which I have seen or heard about. My heart does not seem to have been in the least affected by any of them, and recollection now only tends to increase my ill temper and cause me to like people less and less as the day wears on. But one little incident alone is deep with meaning to me, and I am unable to forget it even now.

It was a winter day in the Sixth Year of the Republic, and a strong northerly wind blew furiously. To make a living, I had to be up early, and on the way to my duties I encountered scarcely anyone. After much difficulty, I finally succeeded in hiring a rickshaw. I told the puller to take me to the South Gate.

After a while, the wind moderated its fury, and in its wake the streets were left clean of the loose dust. The puller ran quickly. Just as we approached the South Gate, somebody ran in front of us, got entangled in the rickshaw, and tumbled to the ground.

It was a woman, with streaks of white in her hair, and she wore ragged clothes. She had darted suddenly from the side of the street, and crossed directly in front of us. My puller had tried to swerve aside, but her tattered jacket, unbuttoned and fluttering in the wind, caught in the shafts. Fortunately, the puller had slowed his pace; otherwise she would have been thrown head over heels, and probably seriously injured. After we halted, the woman still knelt on all fours. I did not think she was hurt. No one else had seen the collision, and it irritated me that the puller had stopped and was apparently prepared to get himself involved in some foolish complication. It might delay and trouble my journey.

"It's nothing," I told him. "Move on!"

But either he did not hear me or did not care, for he put down the shafts and gently helped the old woman to her feet. He held her arms, supporting her, and asked:

"Are you all right?"

"I am hurt."

I thought, "I saw you fall, and it was not at all rough. How can you be hurt? You are pretending. The whole business is distasteful, and the rickshaw man is merely making difficulties for himself. Now, let him find his own way out of the mess."

But the puller did not hesitate for a moment after the old woman said she was injured. Still holding her arm, he walked carefully ahead with her. Then I was surprised as, looking ahead, I suddenly noticed a police station, and saw that he was taking her there. No one stood outside, so he guided her in through the gate.

As they passed in, I experienced a curious sensation. I do not know why, but at that moment it suddenly seemed to me that his dust-covered figure loomed enormous, and as he walked farther he continued to grow, until finally I had to lift my head to follow him. At the same time, I felt a bodily pressure all over me, which came from his direction. It seemed almost to push out from me all the littleness that hid under my fur-lined gown. I grew weak, as though my vitality had been spent, as though the blood had frozen in me. I sat motionless, stunned and thoughtless, until I saw an officer emerge from the station. Then I got down from the rickshaw as he approached me.

"Get another rickshaw," he advised. "This man can't pull you anymore."

Without thinking, I thrust my hand into my pocket and pulled forth a big fistful of coppers. "Give the fellow these," I said.

The wind had ceased entirely, but the street was still quiet. I mused as I walked, but I was almost afraid to think about myself. Leaving aside what had happened before, I sought an explanation for the fistful of coppers. Why had I given them? As a reward? And did I think myself, after my conduct, fit to pass judgment upon a rickshaw-puller? I could not answer my own conscience.

Till now that experience burns in my memory. I think of it, and introspect with pain and effort. The political and military drama of these years is to me like the classics I read in childhood: I cannot recite half a line of it. But always before my eyes, purging me with shame, impelling me to better myself, invigorating my hope and courage, this little incident is reenacted. I see it in every detail as distinctly as on the day it happened.

translated by Edgar Snow and Yao Hsin-nung

MAO TUN (SHEN YEN-PING)

SPRING SILKWORMS

Tung Pao sat on a rock along the bank of the canal with his back to the sun, his long-stemmed pipe leaning against his side. The sun was already strong, though the period of Clear Bright had just set in, and felt as warm as a brazier of fire. It made him hotter than ever to see the Shaohing trackers pulling hard at their lines, large drops of sweat falling from their brows in spite of their open cotton shirts. Tung Pao was still wearing his winter coat; he had not foreseen the sudden warm spell and had not thought of redeeming his lighter garment from the pawnshop.

"Even the weather is not what it used to be!" muttered Tung Pao, spitting into the canal.

There were not many passing boats, and the occasional ripples and eddies that broke the mirrorlike surface of the greenish water and blurred the placid reflections of the mud banks and neat rows of mulberry trees never lasted long. Presently one could make out the trees again, swaying from side to side at first like drunken men and then becoming motionless and clear and distinct as before, their fistlike buds already giving forth tiny, tender leaves. The fields were still cracked and dry, but the mulberry trees had already come into their own. There seemed to be no end to the rows along the banks and there was another extensive grove back of Tung Pao. They seemed to thrive on the sunlit warmth, their tender leaves growing visibly each second.

Not far from where Tung Pao sat there was a gray-white building, used by the cocoon buyers during the season but now quite deserted. There were rumors that the buyers would not come at all this year because the Shanghai factories had been made idle by the war, but Tung Pao would not believe this. He had lived sixty years and had yet to see the time when mulberry leaves would be allowed to wither on the trees or be used for fodder, unless of course if the eggs should not hatch, as has sometimes happened according to the unpredictable whims of Heaven.

"How warm it is for this time of the year!" Tung Pao thought again, hopefully, because it was just after a warm spring like this almost twoscore years ago that there occurred one of the best silk crops ever known. He remembered it well: it was also the year of his marriage. His family fortune was then on the upward swing. His father worked like a faithful old ox, knew and did everything; his grandfather, who had been a Taiping captive in his time, was still vigorous in spite of his great age. At that time too, the house of Chen had not yet begun its decline, for though the old squire had already died, the young squire had not yet taken to opium smoking. Tung Pao had a vague feeling that the fortunes of the Chens and that of his own family were somehow intertwined, though one was about the richest family in town while his was only well-to-do as peasants went.

Both his grandfather and the old squire had been captives of the Taiping rebels and had both escaped before the rebellion was suppressed. Local legend had it that the old squire had made off with a considerable amount of Taiping gold and that it was this gold which enabled him to go into the silk business and amass a huge fortune. During that time Tung Pao's family flourished too. Year after year the silk crops had been good and in ten years his family had been able to acquire twenty mou of rice land and more than ten mou of mulberry trees. They were the most prosperous family in the village, just as the Chens were the richest in town.

But gradually both families had declined. Tung Pao no

longer had any rice land left and was more than three hundred dollars in debt besides. As for the Chen family, it was
long ago "finished." It was said that the reason for their rapid
decline was that the ghosts of the Taiping rebels had sued in
the courts of the nether world and had been warranted by
King Yenlo to collect. Tung Pao was inclined to think that
there was something to this notion; otherwise why should the
young squire suddenly acquire the opium habit? He could
not, however, figure out why the fortunes of his own family
should have declined at the same time. He was certain that
his grandfather did not make away with any Taiping gold. It
was true that his grandfather had to kill a Taiping sentinel in
making his escape, but had not his family atoned for this by
holding services for the dead rebel as long as he could remember? He did not know much about his grandfather, but
he knew his father as an honest and hardworking man and
could not think of anything he himself had done that should
merit the misfortunes that had befallen him. His older son,
Ah Ssu, and his wife were both industrious and thrifty, and
his younger son, Ah Dou, was not a bad sort, though he was
flighty at times as all young people were inclined to be.

Tung Pao sadly lifted his brown, wrinkled face and sur-
veyed the scene before him. The canal, the boats, and the
mulberry groves on both sides of the canal—everything was
much the same as it was twoscore years ago. But the world
had changed: often they lived on nothing but pumpkins, and
he was more than three hundred dollars in debt.

Several blasts from a steam whistle suddenly came from
around a bend in the canal. Soon a tug swept majestically
into view with a string of three boats in tow. The smaller
crafts on the canal scurried out of the way of the puffing
monster, but soon they were engulfed in the wide wake of the
tug and its train and seesawed up and down as the air became filled with the sound of the engine and the odor of oil.
Tung Pao watched the tug with hatred in his eyes as it disappeared around the next bend. He had always entertained a
deep enmity against such foreign deviltry as steamboats and
the like. He had never seen a foreigner himself, but his father
told him that the old squire had seen some, that they had red
hair and green eyes and walked with straight knees. The old
squire had no use for foreigners either and used to say that it
was they that had made off with all the money and made everyone poor. Tung Pao had no doubt that the old squire was
right. He knew from his own experience that since foreign
yarn and cloth and kerosene appeared in town and the

steamer in the river, he got less and less for the things that he produced with his own labor and had to pay more and more for the things that he had to buy. It was thus that he became poorer and poorer until now he had none of his rice land that his father had left him and was in debt besides. He did not hate the foreigners without reason! Even among the villagers he was remarkable for the vehemence of his anti-foreign sentiments.

Five years back someone told him that there had been another change in government and that it was the aim of the new government to rescue the people from foreign oppression. Tung Pao did not believe it, for he had noticed on his trips to town that the youngsters who shouted "Down with the foreigners" all wore foreign clothes. He had a suspicion that these youths were secretly in league with the foreigners and only pretended to be their enemies in order to fool honest people like himself. He was even more convinced that he was right when the slogan "Down with the foreigners" was dropped and things became dearer and dearer and the taxes heavier and heavier. Tung Pao was sure that the foreigners had a hand in these things.

The last straw for Tung Pao was that cocoons hatched from foreign eggs should actually sell for ten dollars more a picul. He had always been on friendly terms with his daughter-in-law, but they quarreled on this score. She had wanted to use foreign eggs the year before. His younger son, Ah Dou, sided with her, and her husband was of the same mind though he did not say much about it. Unable to withstand their pressure, Tung Pao had to compromise at last and allow them to use one sheet of foreign eggs out of three that they decided to hatch this year.

"The world is becoming worse and worse," he said to himself. "After a few years even the mulberry leaves will have to be foreign! I am sick of it all!"

The weather continued warm and the finger-like tender leaves were now the size of small hands. The trees around the village itself seemed to be even better. As the trees grew so did the hope in the hearts of the peasants. The entire village was mobilized in preparation for the silkworms. The utensils used in the rearing were taken out from the fuel sheds to be washed and repaired, and the women and children engaged in these tasks lined the brook that passed through the village.

None of the women and children were very healthy looking. From the beginning of spring they had to cut down on their meager food, and their garments were all old and worn. They looked little better than beggars. They were not, however, dispirited; they were sustained by their great endurance and their great hope. In their simple minds they felt sure that so long as nothing happened to their silkworms everything would come out all right. When they thought how in a month's time the glossy green leaves would turn into snow-white cocoons and how the cocoons would turn into jingling silver dollars, their hearts were filled with laughter, though their stomachs gurgled with hunger.

Among the women was Tung Pao's daughter-in-law, Ssu-da-niang, with her twelve-year-old boy, Hsiao Pao. They had finished washing the feeding trays and the hatching baskets and were wiping their brows with the flap of their coats.

"Ssu-sao, are you using foreign eggs this year?" one of the women asked Ssu-da-niang.

"Don't ask me!" Ssu-da-niang answered with passion, as if ready for a quarrel. "Pa is the one that decides. Hsiao Pao's pa did what he could to persuade the old man, but in the end we are hatching only one sheet of foreign eggs. The doddering old fool hates everything foreign as if it were his sworn foe, yet he doesn't seem to mind at all when it comes to 'foreign money.'" [1]

The gibe provoked a gale of laughter.

A man walked across the husking field on the other side of the brook. As he stepped on the log bridge, Ssu-da-niang called to him:

"Brother Dou, come and help me take these things home. These trays are as heavy as dead dogs when they are wet."

Ah Dou lifted the pile of trays and carried them on his head and walked off swinging his hands like oars. He was a good-natured young man and was always willing to lend a hand to the women when they had anything heavy to be moved or to be rescued from the brook. The trays looked like an oversize bamboo hat on him. There was another gale of laughter when he wriggled his waist in the manner of city women.

"Ah Dou! Come back here and carry something home for me too," said Lotus, wife of Li Keng-sheng, Tung Pao's immediate neighbor, laughing with the rest.

"Call me something nicer if you want me to carry your things for you," answered Ah Dou without stopping.

[1] That is, the dollar coin. So called because the Chinese dollar is based on the Mexican peso, brought to China by European traders.

"Then let me call you godson!" Lotus said with a loud laugh. She was unlike the rest of the women because of her unusually white complexion, but her face was very flat and her eyes were mere slits. She had been a slave girl in some family in town and was already notorious for her habit of flirting with the men folk, though she had been married to the taciturn Li Keng-sheng only half a year.

"The shameless thing!" someone muttered on the other side of the brook. Thereupon Lotus's pig-like eyes popped open as she shouted:

"Whom are you speaking of? Come out and say it in the open if you dare!"

"It is none of your business! She who is without shame knows best whom I'm speaking of, for 'Even the man who lies dead knows who's kicked his coffin with his toes.' Why should you care?"

They splashed water at each other. Some of the women joined the exchange of words, while the children laughed and hooted. Ssu-da-niang, not wishing to be involved, picked up the remaining baskets and went home with Hsiao Pao. Ah Dou had set down the trays on the porch and was watching the fun.

Tung Pao came out of the room with the tray stands that he had to repair. His face darkened when he caught Ah Dou standing there idle, watching the women. He never approved of Ah Dou's exchanging banter with the women of the village, particularly with Lotus, whom he regarded as an evil thing that brought bad luck to anyone who had anything to do with her.

"Are you enjoying the scenery, Ah Dou?" he shouted at his son. "Ah Ssu is making cocoon trees in the back; go and help him!" He did not take his disapproving eyes off his son until the latter had gone. Then he set to work examining the worm holes on the stands and repaired them wherever necessary. He had done a great deal of carpentering in his time, but his fingers were now stiff with age. After a while he had to rest his aching fingers and as he did so he looked up at the three sheets of eggs hanging from a bamboo pole in the room.

Ssu-da-niang sat under the eaves pasting paper over the hatching baskets. To save a few coppers they had used old newspapers the year before. The silkworms had not been healthy, and Tung Pao had said that it was because it was sacrilegious to use paper with characters on it. In order to buy regular paper for the purpose this year they had all gone without a meal.

"Ssu-da-niang, the twenty loads of leaves we bought has used up all the thirty dollars that we borrowed through your father. What are we going to do after our rice is gone? What we have will last only two more days." Tung Pao raised his head from his work, breathing hard as he spoke to his daughter-in-law. The money was borrowed at 2½ percent monthly interest. This was considered low, and it was only because Ssu-da-niang's father was an old tenant of the creditor that they had been able to get such a favorable rate.

"It was not such a good idea to put all the money in leaves," complained Ssu-da-niang, setting out the baskets to dry. "We may not be able to use all of them as was the case last year."

"What are you talking about! You would bring ill luck on us before we even got started. Do you expect it to be like last year always? We can only gather a little over ten loads from our own trees. How can that be enough for three sheets of eggs?"

"Yes, yes, you are always right. All I know is that you can cook rice only when there is some to cook and when there isn't you have to go hungry!"

Ssu-da-niang answered with some passion, for she had not yet forgiven her father-in-law for their arguments over the relative merit of foreign and domestic eggs. Tung Pao's face darkened and he said no more.

As the hatching days approached, the entire village of about thirty families became tense with hope and anxiety, forgetting it seemed, even their gnawing hunger. They borrowed and sought credit wherever they could and ate whatever they could get, often nothing but pumpkins and potatoes. None of them had more than a handful of rice stored away. The harvest had been good the year before but what with the landlord, creditors, regular taxes, and special assessments, they had long ago exhausted their store. Their only hope now lay in the silkworms; all their loans were secured by the promise that they would be paid after the "harvest."

As the period of Germinating Rains drew near, the "cloth" in every family began to take on a green hue. This became the only topic of conversation wherever women met.

"Lotus says they will be warming the cloth tomorrow. I don't see how it can be so soon."

"Huang Tao-shih went to the fortune-teller. The character

he drew indicated that leaves will reach four dollars per picul this year!"

Ssu-da-niang was worried because she could not detect any green on their own three sheets of eggs. Ah Ssu could not find any either when he took the sheets to the light and examined them carefully. Fortunately their anxiety did not last long, for spots of green began to show the following day. Ssu-da-niang immediately put the precious things against her breast to warm, sitting quietly as if feeding an infant. At night she slept with them, hardly daring to stir, though the tiny eggs against her flesh made her itch. She was as happy, and as fearful, as before the birth of her first child!

The room for the silkworms had been made ready some days before. On the second day of "warming" Tung Pao smeared a head of garlic with mud and put it in a corner of the room. It was believed that the more leaves there were on the garlic on the day that silkworms were hatched, the better would be the harvest. The entire village was now engaged in this warming of the cloths. There were few signs of women along the brooks or on the husking grounds. An undeclared state of emergency seemed to exist: even the best of friends and the most intimate of neighbors refrained from visiting one another, for it was no joking matter to disturb the shy and sensitive goddess who protected the silkworms. They talked briefly in whispers when they met outside. It was a sacred season.

The atmosphere was even tenser when the "black ladies" began to emerge from the eggs. This generally happened perilously close to the day that ushered in the period of Germinating Rains and it was imperative to time the hatching so that it would not be necessary to gather them on that particular day. In Tung Pao's house, the first grubs appeared just before the tabooed day, but they were able to avoid disaster by transferring the cloths from the warm breast of Ssu-da-niang to the silkworms' room. Tung Pao stole a glance at the garlic and his heart almost stopped beating, for only one or two cloves had sprouted. He did not dare to take another look but only prayed for the best.

The day for harvesting the "black ladies" finally came. Ssu-da-niang was restless and excited, continually watching the rising steam from the pot, for the right moment to start operations was when the steam rose straight up in the air. Tung Pao lit the incense and candles and reverently set them before the kitchen god. Ah Ssu and Ah Dou went out to the fields to gather wild flowers, while Hsiao Pao cut up lampwick grass into fine shreds for the mixture used in gathering the newly hatched worms. Toward noon everything was ready for the big moment. When the pot began to boil vigorously and steam to rise straight up into the air, Ssu-da-niang jumped up, stuck in her hair a paper flower dedicated to the silkworms and a pair of goose feathers, and went into the room, accompanied by Tung Pao with a steelyard beam and her husband with the prepared mixture of wild flowers and lampwick grass. Ssu-da-niang separated the two layers of cloth and sprinkled the mixture on them. Then taking the beam from Tung Pao she laid the cloths across it, took a goose feather and began to brush the "black ladies" off gently into the papered baskets. The same procedure was followed with the second sheet, but the last, which contained the foreign eggs, was brushed off into separate baskets. When all was done, Ssu-da-niang took the paper flower and the feathers and stuck them on the edge of one of the baskets.

It was solemn ceremony, one that had been observed for hundreds and hundreds of years. It was as solemn an occasion as the sacrifice before a military campaign, for it was to inaugurate a month of relentless struggle against bad weather and ill luck during which there would be no rest day or night. The "black ladies" looked healthy as they crawled about in the small baskets; their color was as it should be. Tung Pao and Ssu-da-niang both breathed sighs of relief, though the former's face clouded whenever he stole a glance at the head of garlic, for the sprouts had not grown noticeably. Could it be that it was going to be like last year again?

Fortunately the prognostications of the garlic did not prove very accurate this time. Though it was rainy during the first and second molting and the weather colder than around Clear Bright, the "precious things" were all very healthy. It was the same with the "precious things" all over the village. An atmosphere of happiness prevailed; even the brook seemed to gurgle with laughter. The only exception was the household of Lotus, for their worms weighed only twenty pounds at the third "sleep," and just before the fourth Lotus's husband was seen in the act of emptying three baskets into the brook. This circumstance made the villagers redouble their vigilance against the contamination of the unfortunate woman. They would not even pass by her house and went out of their way to avoid her and her taciturn husband. They did not want to catch a single glance of her or exchange a single word with her for fear that they might catch her family's misfortune. Tung Pao warned Ah Dou not to be seen with Lotus. "I'll lay a charge against you before the magistrate if I catch you talking to that woman," he shouted at his son loud enough for Lotus to hear. Ah Dou said nothing; he alone did not take much stock in these superstitions. Besides, he was too busy to talk to anyone.

Tung Pao's silkworms weighed three hundred pounds after the "great sleep." For two days and two nights no one, not even Hsiao Pao, had a chance to close his eyes. The worms were in rare condition; in Tung Pao's memory only twice had he known anything equal to it—once when he was married and the other time when Ah Ssu was born. They consumed seven loads of leaves the first day, and it did not take much calculation to know how much more leaf would be needed before the worms were ready to "climb up the mountain."

"The squire has nothing to lend," Tung Pao said to Ah Ssu. "We'll have to ask your father-in-law to try his employers again."

"We still have about ten loads on our own trees, enough for another day," Ah Ssu said, hardly able to keep his eyes open.

"What nonsense," Tung Pao said impatiently. "They have started eating only two days ago. They'll be eating for another three days without counting tomorrow. We need another thirty loads, thirty loads."

The price of leaves had gone up to four dollars a load as predicted by the fortune-teller, which meant that it would cost one hundred and twenty dollars to buy enough leaves to see them through. There was nothing to do but borrow the required amount on the only remaining mulberry land that they had. Tung Pao took some comfort in the thought that he would harvest at least five hundred pounds of cocoons and that at fifty dollars a hundred pounds he would get more than enough to pay his debts.

When the first consignment of leaves arrived, the "precious things" had already been without food for more than half an hour and it was heartbreaking to see them raise their heads and swing them hither and yon in search of leaves. A crunching sound filled the room as soon as the leaves were spread on the beds, so loud that those in the room had difficulty in hearing one another. Almost in no time the leaves had disappeared and the beds were again white with the voracious worms. It took the whole family to keep the beds covered with leaves. But this was the last five minutes of the battle; in two more days the "precious things" would be ready to "climb up the mountain" and perform their appointed task.

One night Ah Dou was alone on watch in the room, so that Tung Pao and Ah Ssu could have a little rest. It was a moonlit night and there was a small fire in the room for the silkworms. Around the second watch he spread a new layer of leaves on the beds and then squatted by the fire to wait for the next round. His eyes grew heavy and he gradually dozed off. He was awakened by what he thought was a noise at the door, but he was too sleepy to investigate and dozed off again, though subconsciously he detected an unusual rustling sound amidst the familiar crunching of leaves. Suddenly he awoke with a jerk of his drooping head just in time to catch the swishing of the reed screen against the door and a glimpse of someone gliding away. Ah Dou jumped up and ran out. Through the open gate he could see the intruder walking rapidly toward the brook. Ah Dou flew after him and in another moment he had flung him to the ground.

"Ah Dou, kill me if you want to but don't tell anyone!"

It was Lotus's voice, and it made Ah Dou shudder. Her piggish eyes were fixed on his but he could not detect any trace of fear in them.

"What have you stolen?" Ah Dou asked.

"Your precious things!"

"Where have you put them?"

"I have thrown them into the brook!"

Ah Dou's face grew harsh as he realized her wicked intention.

"How wicked you are! What have we done to you?"

"What have you done? Plenty! It was not my fault that our precious things did not live. Since I did you no harm and your precious things have flourished, why should you look upon me like the star of evil and avoid me like the plague? You have all treated me as if I were not a human being at all!"

Lotus had got up as she spoke, her face distorted with hatred. Ah Dou looked at her for a moment and then said:

"I am not going to hurt you; you can go now!"

Ah Dou went back to the room, no longer sleepy in the least. Nothing untoward happened during the rest of the night. The "precious things" were as healthy and strong as ever and kept on devouring leaves as if possessed. At dawn Tung Pao and Ssu-da-niang came to relieve Ah Dou. They picked up the silkworms that had gradually turned from white to pink and held them against the light to see if they had become translucent. Their hearts overflowed with happiness. When Ssu-da-niang went to the brook to draw water, however, Liu Pao, one of their neighbors, approached her and said to her in a low voice:

"Last night between the Second and Third Watch I saw that woman come out of your house, followed by Ah Dou. They stood close together and talked a long time. Ssu-da-niang, how can you let such things go on in your house?"

Ssu-da-niang rushed home and told her husband and then Tung Pao what had happened. Ah Dou, when summoned, denied everything and said that Liu Pao must have been dreaming. Tung Pao took some consolation in the fact that so far there had been no sign of the curse on the silkworms themselves, but there was Liu Pao's unshakable evidence and she could not have made up the whole story. He only hoped that the unlucky woman did not actually step into the room but had only met Ah Dou outside.

Tung Pao became full of misgivings about the future. He knew well that it was possible for everything to go well all along the way only to have the worms die on the trees. But he did not dare to think of that possibility, for just to think of it was enough to bring ill luck.

The silkworms had at last mounted the trees but the anxieties of the growers were by no means over, for there was as yet no assurance that their labor and investment would be rewarded. They did not, however, let these doubts stop them from their work. Fires were placed under the "mountains" in order to force the silkworms to climb up. The whole family squatted around the trees and listened to the rustling of the straws as the silkworms crawled among them, each trying to find a corner to spin its chamber of silk. They would smile broadly or their hearts would sink according to whether they could hear the reassuring sound or not. If they happened to look up and catch a drop of water from above, they did not mind at all, for that meant that there was at least one silkworm ready to get to work at that moment.

Three days later the fires were withdrawn. No longer able to endure the suspense, Ssu-da-niang drew aside one corner of the surrounding reed screens and took a peep. Her heart leaped with joy, for the entire "mountain" was covered with a snowy mass of cocoons! She had never seen a crop like this in all her life! Joy and laughter filled the household. Their anxieties were over at last. The "precious things" were fair and had not devoured leaves at four dollars a load without doing something to show for it, and they themselves had not gone with practically no food or sleep for nothing; Heaven had rewarded them.

The same sound of joy and laughter rose everywhere in the village. The Goddess of Silkworms had been good to them. Every one of the twenty or thirty families would gather at least a 70 or 80 percent capacity crop. As for Tung Pao's family they expected a 120 or even a 130 percent crop.

Women and children were again seen on the husking fields and along the brook. They were thinner than a month ago, their eyes more sunken and their voices more hoarse, but they were in high spirits. They talked about their struggles and dreamed of piles of bright silver dollars; some of them looked forward to redeeming their summer garments from the pawnshop, while others watered at the mouth in anticipation of the head of fish that they might treat themselves to at the Dragon Boat Festival.

The actual harvesting of the cocoons followed the next day, attended by visits from friends and relatives bringing presents and their good wishes. Chang Tsai-fa, Ssu-da-niang's father, came to congratulate Tung Pao and brought with him cakes, fruits, and salted fish. Hsiao Pao was as happy as a pup frolicking in the snow.

"Tung Pao, are you going to sell your cocoons or reel them yourself?" Chang asked, as the two sat under a willow tree along the brook.

"I'll sell them, of course."

"But the factories are not buying this year," Chang said, standing up and pointing in the direction of the buildings used by the buyers.

Tung Pao would not believe him but when he went to see for himself he found that the buyers' buildings were indeed still closed. For the moment Tung Pao was panic-stricken, but when he went home and saw the basket upon basket of fine, firm cocoons that he had harvested he forgot his worries. He could not believe that such fine cocoons would find no market.

Gradually, however, the atmosphere of the village changed from one of joy and laughter to one of despair, as news began to arrive that none of the factories in the region were going to open for the season. Instead of the scouts for the cocoon buyers who in other years used to march up and down the village during this season, the village was now crowded with creditors and tax collectors. And none of them would accept cocoons in payment.

Curses and sighs of despair echoed through the entire village. It never occurred to the villagers even in their dreams that the extraordinarily fine crop of cocoons would increase their difficulties. But it did not help to complain and say that the world had changed. The cocoons would not keep and it was necessary to reel them at home if they could not sell them to the factories. Already some of the families had got out their long-neglected spinning wheels.

"We'll reel the silk ourselves," Tung Pao said to his daughter-in-law. "We had always done that anyway until the foreigners started this factory business."

"But we have over five hundred pounds of cocoons! How many spinning wheels do you plan to use?"

Ssu-da-niang was right. It was impossible for them to reel all the cocoons themselves and they could not afford to hire help. Ah Ssu agreed with his wife and bitterly reproached his father, saying:

"If you had only listened to us and hatched only one sheet of eggs, we would have had enough leaves from our own land."

Tung Pao had nothing to say to this.

Presently a ray of hope came to them. Huang Tao-shih, one of Tung Pao's cronies, learned from somewhere that the factories at Wusih were buying cocoons as usual. After a family conference it was decided that they would borrow a boat and undertake the journey of around three hundred li in order to dispose of their crop.

Five days later they returned with one basket of cocoons still unsold. The Wusih factory was unusually severe in their selection and paid only thirty dollars a hundred pounds of cocoons from foreign eggs and twelve dollars for the native variety. Though Tung Pao's cocoons were of the finest quality, they rejected almost a hundred pounds of the lot. Tung Pao got one hundred and eleven dollars in all and had only an even hundred left after expenses of the journey, not enough to pay off the debts they contracted in order to buy leaves. Tung Pao was so mortified that he fell sick on the way and had to be carried home.

Ssu-da-niang borrowed a spinning wheel from Liu Pao's house and set to work reeling the rejected cocoons. It took her six days to finish the work. As they were again without rice, she sent Ah Ssu to the town to sell the silk. There was no market for it at all and even the pawnshop would not loan anything against it. After a great deal of begging and wheedling, he was allowed to use it to redeem the picul of rice that they had pawned before Clear Bright.

And so it happened that everyone in Tung Pao's village got deeper into debt because of their spring silkworm crop. Because Tung Pao had hatched three sheets of eggs and reaped an exceptional harvest, he lost as a consequence a piece of land that produced fifteen loads of mulberry leaves and thirty dollars besides, to say nothing of a whole month of short rations and loss of sleep!

translated by Wang Chi-chen

KOREA

The development and role of fiction in Korea have been very much the same as in China. A similar respect for poetry (in early times, even following Chinese patterns and expressed in Chinese) tended to minimize the literary value of prose in the vernacular. However, Korea has an ancient and rich store of highly imaginative tales and fables. On the broad popular interest in such beginnings, the modern short story has been built.

Yu-Wol Chong-Nyon is the pseudonym for a young woman who is not a professional writer. The pen name is indicative of the author's generation since it means literally "Month of June Youth," referring to the post-civil-war generation. Members of the author's family now live in both North and South Korea. Her true name, therefore, cannot be revealed in connection with a story of the theme of "The Nonrevolutionaries."

A friend of the author's says of this story that it "was a burst of inspiration that came to her while she was describing the main scene in the story, at which she was actually present." She was then persuaded to put the incident into writing.

"The Nonrevolutionaries" has been selected because of its worth as a story and its insight into the hearts of those whose lives have been torn by a civil war which is now in abeyance but remains unresolved.

Choe Chong-Hi (1912–), a native of northeastern Korea, is one of the best-known writers in Korea today. Her first published work appeared in 1932. Since that time she has published novels, articles, and short stories. For a period she also wrote as a news reporter. Her collection of short stories, *The Village of Music,* is especially loved by the people.

As is indicated by "Chom-nye," Mrs. Choe is adept in her depiction of humble village life. Her empathic understanding of the simple, yet searing, problems of the poor and oppressed is evident here. The story is an interesting companion piece for "The Nonrevolutionaries" with its representation of the political dilemma of the common people.

YU-WOL CHONG-NYON

THE NONREVOLUTIONARIES

Revolution, counterrevolution, nonrevolution.
The revolutionaries are executed by the counterrevolutionaries and the counterrevolutionaries by the revolutionaries.
The nonrevolutionaries are sometimes taken for revolutionaries and executed by the counterrevolutionaries, sometimes taken for counterrevolutionaries and executed by the revolutionaries, and sometimes executed by either the revolutionaries or the counterrevolutionaries for no apparent reason at all.

—*Lu Hsun (1881–1936)*
translated from the Chinese by Wang Chi-chen

Cursed be the men of the East. Cursed be the men of the West. Cursed be those who have left my beloved homeland bleeding and torn.

They banged on the doors. They hammered at the walls. Out! *Out!* Everybody out! Everybody to the playfield.

With fear and with trembling we all got up, we got up out of our blankets into the chilly dawn. My father and my mother, my sisters and my brother. Out. *Out.* The shouting and the hammering continued. Out to the playfield.

"What about Ok-Sun?" my mother said to my father, pointing to me. "They don't know she's here. Maybe she should hide?"

"No, no," said my father. "They'll surely find her."

"But why? If we keep her hidden in the back, no one will see her."

"They will, they will. They're breaking in without warning. Only the night before, they broke into twelve houses in our district. In the middle of the night, at two and three in the morning. They banged at the doors and pushed their way in, stamped into the houses with their boots on and dragged the men away."

"With their boots on!" My mother was silent for a moment, shocked at this revelation of incredible boorishness. The poorest ragpicker, the most unlearned peasant, would never dream of entering another's home without removing his footwear.

But she returned to the argument. "I'm sure we can hide her safely——"

"No! No!" my father again protested. "Too dangerous. Better she go with all of us."

"But——"

But there was no time to argue. Out! *Out!* The shouting and the banging went on. They were still there, rounding up every man, woman, and child. Out I went, too, with my sisters and my brother, my father and my mother, out to the playfield.

I had returned home only a month ago. My year's scholarship had ended, and I was coming back to bring the wisdom of the West to my "underdeveloped" homeland. The boat had arrived at Seoul a day earlier than expected, but late at night. When I had reached home after midnight, none of the neighbors had seen me come. My father, glad as he and all the family were to see me, had said, "Enough. We'll go to bed and talk in the morning. She must be tired."

Tired I was, tired of the long, long voyage, still ill adjusted to the many-houred change in time, so tired that I developed a fever of exhaustion that night. It was as though I had been holding it in until I could get back to my own bed before letting it go. For weeks I lay there sick.

It was at the beginning of my illness that the armies suddenly and without warning swarmed down from the north, blasting their way through my homeland, leaving us overnight under a strange regime, ruled by men of our own nation, but men warped and twisted by their training in a foreign land, by the rule of an oppressive hand, of cruel and unfeeling heart and mind.

In a faraway country on the other side of the globe, the President of the United States, the Prime Minister of His Majesty's Government, and the chairman of the Supreme Soviet, accompanied by their Chiefs of Staff and other experts on human welfare, had met. The map had glistened brightly before them with its greens and reds and yellows and blues. The fate of the world was decided. Here a cut, there a snip, and here a line. "For purposes of military convenience," the history books say, my beloved homeland was cut in two. Our minds and hearts, our families and lives, were cut into shreds.

My beloved homeland! Will your rice and your wine ever taste the same again? Will your flutes and your harps ever sound the same again?

We were at the playfield once more. The playfield of so many mixed memories, now to be the site of the most sharply etched memory of them all. The playfield where with the girls of my class I had spent so many happy hours of childhood and adolescence. The playfield which had been built during the days of our Japanese lords, the days when here as everywhere in Korea we were taught to speak and to write and to think only in a foreign tongue, when a phrase spoken in our mother tongue in a public place brought a slap on the face from the lords or their Korean vassals. The playfield where my father with all the other fathers had had to go so often to prostrate himself before the Shinto shrines. The playfield where our masters revealed a change of heart to us, where they suddenly called us brothers, members of the same race, fruit of the same cultural heritage, and "invited" our young men to join their armies to fight for the glory of our "common primordial ancestors." Then we knew that the war was truly going badly for them, that their men were dying.

The playfield! We waited in the chilly dawn for our new lords to guide us. We were there by the thousand, fathers and mothers, children and elders. I saw many neighbors I hadn't seen for well over a year, but they were too preoccupied to be surprised at my sudden reappearance. We waited in the chilly dawn for our new lords to guide us.

They came. They came with their heavy boots and their heavy rifles. They came dragging twelve men behind them. Twelve men we all knew. Twelve men we had grown up with.

The men with the boots and the rifles distributed themselves among the crowd. A hundred men or more. A man here, a man there. Everyone felt the alien presence close to his skin, everyone felt the gnawing cancer digging into his soul.

Their leader climbed up on the platform and slowly turned his eyes over us, at the sea of faces all around him. A signal, and one of the twelve men was set up next to him, one of the twelve men we knew. He was a clerk in our municipal office, a man as inoffensive as he was inefficient, a man who did his insignificant work as well as his limited abilities permitted him, a man whose main interest in his job consisted in receiving his pay regularly and going home to his family at the end of each day.

I had noticed his wife and children in the crowd.

"Comrades!" bellowed the leader. "Behold a traitor to the people. As you all know, the man you see before you has for years held in his hands the lives and well being of all the people of this community. It is he who handles the rationing records, he who can decide how much rice you are to receive and when you are to get it. Comrades, an investigation of his records has revealed gross mismanagement of the rationing system of our community. When this treacherous criminal was directed to mend his ways, he offered nothing but resistance and reactionary proposals. For ten days now he has deliberately and malevolently sabotaged every effort on our part to establish the system of food distribution in this community on a rational and an honest basis. Comrades," he cried out again to the crowd, "what shall we do with this traitor?"

"Kill him!" The hundred men who had distributed themselves among the crowd had raised their fists and roared out this response with a single voice: *"Kill him!"*

The leader on the platform nodded in approval. "Thank you, comrades. That is indeed the only proper treatment for traitors."

He took his heavy pistol out of its holster, held it against the man's temple, and pulled the trigger. The clerk slumped to the boards of the platform. The crowd gasped.

"Death to traitors!" roared the hundred men. The man's blood trickled through the cracks between the boards and stained the soil of the playfield.

Another man was hoisted up onto the platform to take his place.

"Comrades," again cried the leader, "behold a traitor to the people. . . ."

An excited murmur went through the crowd as we recognized the man. I heard my brother whisper to my father, "Daddy! Isn't he the leader of the Communists?"

"Yes!"

"Then why?"

"Three kinds—Communists who've been in South Korea all the time; those trained in Russia and China; those trained in North Korea since the partition. They're fighting among themselves already."

The leader had finished his charges. Again he cried to the crowd; "Comrades, what shall we do with this traitor?"

"*Kill him!*" the hundred shouted as before.

But this time the leader looked displeased. "Comrades, I ask you what to do with a traitor and there is hardly any response! Comrades, think it over well. Take your time and reflect on the matter. I will ask once again a minute from now."

The hundred men glared at us, swung around in their places, and looked us each in the eye in turn. "I wonder if there could be any traitors here among us," they said for all to hear.

Then again the leader turned to the crowd. "Comrades," he bellowed once more, "what shall we do with this traitor to the people?"

"*Kill him!*" roared the hundred.

"*Kill him!*" we cried with our lips.

The leader looked pleased. He again unholstered his pistol, pressed it to the man's head, and his blood joined that of the other, dripping down to the soil of the playfield.

Ten more times did the leader harangue us. Ten more times did we shudder as we cried aloud with our lips, "*Kill him!*" Ten more times did the blood of a Korean stain the soil of Korea.

We watched and we trembled as the chilly dawn unfolded into the chilly day.

> *My beloved homeland!*
> *Will your rice and your wine*
>   *ever taste the same again?*
> *Will your flutes and your harps*
>   *ever sound the same again?*
>
> *Cursed be the men of the East.*
> *Cursed be the men of the West.*
> *Cursed be those*
>   *who have left my beloved homeland*
>   *bleeding and torn.*

translated by the author and D. L. Milton

CHOE CHONG-HI

CHOM-NYE

It is night. All the people of the village and of the upper village are gathered before a small house. There is no moon. The bushes, the pumpkin vines, and the corn stalks are gloomy. The ominous darkness is relieved only by the reflection of the stars in the flooded rice paddies, which stretch like an ocean before the door. But not one of them belongs to this house.

The house has only three parts: a half-size kitchen, a small porch, and one room. At this moment the front yard and the room are crowded. So many people have gathered that there is no space to move. Some of the men have wandered away, and some sit on the banks of the rice paddies, but the women press forward. Those with babies on their backs are screaming for the safety of their children, but they have no intention of leaving. The air is heavy with the smell of their clothes and dirty bodies.

There was not a single visitor—not even a dog—when the girl Chom-nye died last night, nor when her body was carried away late this morning by her father and her fiancé, Pogi. But tonight they have gathered to watch the practice of Shamanism for the clearance of her spirit. How callous they are! Because they thought that the death of Chom-nye was unnatural, they had gone to the blind soothsayer to get preventive pads for their protection. They have a superstition that, if a person is caught by the spirit of a dead girl, he is doomed to death. Then why have they come to witness this rite?

The rumor is that Chom-nye died because a chicken's spirit had caught her. Also, they have learned that her death has some connection with the family of Ho Sung-gu. The people are interested in these two facts. They did not care much for Chom-nye, but Ho Sung-gu is the richest man in this village. In fact, he is one of the richest men in the whole country, known even in Seoul. Poor people like these gathered about the house this evening, envy and honor a rich man; sometimes they even worship him as a god. If Chom-nye had died of an ordinary illness, people would not gather this way. Only her family, her fiancé, and a few of the neighbors would have come to her last ceremony.

When Chom-nye died, people whispered among themselves about a bride's or a virgin's death. But she had been neither a bride, nor a virgin; she had been too young for such terms. Her parents, because of their extreme poverty and in order to let one of their family be fed, had betrothed her to Pogi, who worked in an alekeeper's house at the marketplace. She was just fourteen years old; but since she was engaged, people called her a bride. Pogi had been chosen for her, not because he was rich, nor because he was good-looking, but because he had a job at the alehouse. If she married him, she could work with him in the kitchen. Then she could eat. To poverty-stricken people, eating is the most important thing.

After the engagement, they could not have the wedding ceremony, because the bride must have a suitable garment, but the bride's family could not afford one. The family had nine members, including the grandparents, the parents, and four other younger children. Eating was their biggest problem; they had no time to think of clothing. The fiancé was not much better off than her family. His monthly wage was only five hundred won in addition to his food. With the five hundred won he could not buy a rayon skirt and a blouse for his bride. So at last they decided to delay the ceremony for five months until he had accumulated enough money for that purpose.

At the end of five months Pogi went to his fiancée's house with his 2,500 won. Chom-nye's mother told Pogi to go to Seoul to buy material for the garments, and she herself hurried to the blind soothsayer to decide the date for her daughter's marriage. The twenty-eighth day of the fourth month in the lunar calendar was set for the wedding. Pogi went to Seoul and bought cloth of pink rayon and cotton, white cloth for a blouse, a box of powder, and a mirror, no better than a toy, for his bride; and for himself, he bought a pair of native shoes, made of worn-out tires, and a pair of socks. These purchases exhausted his money. When he brought them to the bride's home, her mother and grandmother complained about the mirror and said he should have bought cotton cloth to make native stockings for the bride. Pogi nodded and thought for a while. At last he spoke up and told them that his aunt had promised to give him two chicks for his wedding. He then went across the hill, got the chicks, and carried them to Chom-nye's home. When these were grown, the problem of the bride's stockings would be solved.

But there was another hitch in the wedding plan: a conflict of dates. The twenty-eighth of the fourth month in the lunar

calendar was June 16, which was the date set for the wedding
ceremony of Sun-haeng, the daughter of Ho Sung-gu. That
date had been chosen the preceding November, as everybody
knew; but Chom-nye's family did not realize that the two
dates were the same. Only ten days before June 16, when
Ho's household was busy with visiting relatives and the tenants of his lands, had Chom-nye's family realized the conflict.
For others, it would have had no meaning; but for Chom-
nye's family, who had been tenants of Ho's family for many
generations, it was a serious matter. They had not troubled to
notify Mr. Ho of their daughter's engagement to Pogi. Ho's
family would not have welcomed this news because Chom-
nye quite often worked for them. Another reason was that
the girl's parents were ashamed because she was too young to
marry. So Chom-nye's family lacked the courage to announce
the wedding of their daughter on exactly the same day as the
wedding of their landlord's daughter.

Helplessly, Chom-nye's mother again went to the blind
soothsayer to explain the matter and to ask for another favorable date, earlier if possible. But the blind man shook his
head and said that there was no good day before the fifteenth
of the seventh month. Any previous date would cause trouble
for the young people; one of them might even break a leg. So
finally they decided on the fifteenth of the seventh month.

Chom-nye was somewhat relieved to know that the ceremony had been postponed three months, not because she was
reluctant to be married, but because she knew that by then
the chicks would have grown so much larger that she could
buy, instead of the stockings, good material for a coat. She
remembered her friend Suni. After she had married, she had
appeared in a fine coat, her face white with cream. Chom-nye
wished to imitate her, but she had no foolish idea of aping
the rich and extravagant finery of Ho's daughter. She never
compared herself with the rich girl, nor complained of her
own poverty. She had no conception of human inequality and
accepted the fact that some were rich and some were poor.
Not only Chom-nye, but most of the people of this class accepted their lot. Such slavish submission had not been learned
in a day or two, not even in a decade or two, but in many
generations of serfdom.

The wedding ceremony of Ho's daughter was grand and
the entertainment lavish. Many people gathered to drink and
feast. Some said that there were over 10,000 people present;
others said over 100,000. Since Ho had only one daughter, he
had spared no expense for this occasion. Guests had come,

not only from the neighboring villages, but high officials from Seoul, and even a few American dignitaries.

Several days after the big ceremony and all its excitement, Ho's daughter, son-in-law, and the relatives departed for Seoul with all the bride's rich possessions and gifts. Three days later, one of Chom-nye's chickens went into the vegetable garden of Ho's home and was caught by Mr. Ho. Ho was usually not kind to tenants or to animals; now he became downright cruel with the chicken. Perhaps he was in low spirits after all the excitement of his daughter's wedding; perhaps he regretted having spent so much money; or perhaps he was sad that he had given his only daughter to another family. Whatever the cause, he was angry, and he tied the two wings of the chicken, fastened it to the tip of a long pole, and stood the pole in the hedge. At other times it had been his habit to kill stray chickens with stones or to break their legs. Because Ho's house was so big and the garden so broad that the small houses of the poor tenants surrounded his property, chickens often flew over the hedge into his garden to scratch for food; so Ho had ordered his neighbors to get rid of their chickens regardless of the custom throughout the country of allowing the birds to run free in the gardens and fields. The poor people obeyed the order without resistance. Some chickens were sold, some were eaten, and some were sent to Ho as gifts. There remained no chickens in this village except those of Chom-nye. Of course, Chom-nye and her family did not allow the chickens to run free. At first they tethered them with a long rope, and later they confined them to a narrow space in the fence; but on this day, when the door had been opened to give them fresh water, one of them had stolen out and had finally found its way into Ho's garden.

The chicken screamed in the sky and Ho talked angrily to himself: "Whose chick is this? Is it Chom-nye's father, Tae-chon's? He raises chickens and allows them to run free! The people are already changing for the worse. They talk about democracy. They are very impolite to me. They are now forgetting by whose grace they are living. From generation to generation they have lived on the bounty of my family. Now they are talking about equality. That Taechon must be one of the rude ones. He raises chickens and damages my vegetables." (He had just learned from a servant girl that the chicken belonged to Taechon.)

Chom-nye and her family knew that the chicken had been caught by Ho, but none of them dared to ask him to return it. They had a special reason to fear him. After the Liberation, a new order under the American military government had made a slight change in the tenant system: the tenant now returns a third of the crop to the landlord instead of a half. Designed to improve the lot of the tenants, this change has caused trouble in practice. The landlords immediately started to sell their unprofitable land. Ho was one of those who planned to dispose of undesirable and isolated plots. He wanted his tenants to buy them, but they did not have the necessary money; so he was willing to sell to any person who could pay. Chom-nye's family was among the victims. Her father tilled the part of Ho's land in front of his little house. He announced his willingness to sell the land, but Taechon was too poor to buy even a part of it. So Ho does not like him and plans to sell to someone else. The new landlord will lease the land to the favorite tenants, but Ho will not recommend Taechon. For this reason Taechon's family fears Ho.

There are many stories about this partially improved tenant system. After much thought as to how to save their families from starvation, some of the smarter tenants sold their houses, furniture, and cows for cash to buy the lands. When they found that they still had insufficient money, they went to private usurers to borrow more money by mortgaging the land to be bought. The interest on such loans was more than 10 percent per month, but the greedy usurers were more interested in the new type of mortgage than in mere interest. To satisfy that mortgage, the usurers claimed half of the year's crop from the land. The final result was much worse than the old fifty-fifty system. But the new system is established, and the poor tenants must find a way to eat and live; so they try every possible way. Even buying land in such a manner was not the privilege of any tenant who wished to do so; there were too few usurers with money enough to lend on such terms. So this system gives satisfaction to neither the landlord nor the tenant.

Chom-nye's family was the poorest among the poor who could not buy land. Meanwhile, Ho became irritable, not only because of his daughter's marriage, but because there were rumors to the effect that Communism would soon be established, a system which is much worse for the landowners than the Democracy of America. He asked his son, who was working in the military government, whether Communism or Democracy would win. The son's answer was that nobody could tell until the Korean interim government was established. Ho had little hope that the old system would be restored, and neither Communism nor Democracy was to his liking. For this reason Ho was uneasy. Chom-nye's chicken and Chom-nye herself became the cause of his anxiety.

The people of the village said that Chom-nye was dead because she had been obsessed by the spirit of a chicken. It is natural for ignorant people to hold such beliefs, but the facts of her death were quite different. For two days Chom-nye had been agonized by the sight of her chicken in the sky and by its screams. By the third night, she could endure her anguish no longer. When the moon shone through the white clouds, she crept out of the house and looked up at the chicken. The chicken screamed again. She stole into Ho's garden through the gate, went to the pole, untied the bindings, and brought down the chicken. As she started to run away through the same gate, she heard a rough voice inside the house. She was running fast and she fell. Then she was struck by a stone thrown by the cruel Mr. Ho; however, she rose again and fled in fear of him. When she reached her home, she fell senseless at the door. Her parents came out and found that her forehead was cut and bleeding profusely. Still she held the chicken in her arms, but it was almost dead. Her parents put some fermented soy-bean paste on the wound, which they thought was a simple scratch from the sticks of the hedge through which she had forced her way; but the bean paste caused serious infection instead of healing her wound. They also gave the chicken some rice, but it was unable to eat, and after a few hours it drew its last breath and died with a final scream. By this time Chom-nye was out of her head. In her delirium she continued to talk about her chicken, and in the middle of the next night she died. So it was that the people believed that Chom-nye was dead because she was obsessed by the spirit of a chicken.

Now, in the tiny room, under the flickering oil lamp, Chom-nye's parents, her four sisters, her grandparents, and her fiancé sit facing the witch. The spot on which the body of the girl had lain is spread with white rice, and at the corners of the room are branches of pine trees on which hang long pieces of white paper. The rest of the people are on the porch, in the yard, and on the banks of the rice paddies. The witch is going to call on the soul of Chom-nye to speak her wishes to the family. In preparation, she cleans the place by spreading ash water on the walls and ceiling of the room; then she sprinkles them with clean water. As a result, the people in the room and on the porch are covered with dirty water, but on this occasion everyone is obedient to the order or action of the witch. Then the witch shouts an order to the chicken spirit obsessing Chom-nye and to all other spirits, telling them to go away. She then scatches her wicker basket, and her assistant, who is her nephew, holds the witch stick. Chom-nye's soul is now supposed to arrive and to talk through the witch.

"Oh, my dear mother, father, grandfather, and grandmother, my sisters, and my dear husband, I am going, going to the unknown place, far, far away." Her voice is sad, and the gloom of the night adds to the sorrow of the family.

"How sad I am: I am leaving the world without having been in the arms of my husband." Her fiancé covers his face in embarrassment. Thus the nonsense of the witch continues in the name of Chom-nye.

"Oh accursed chicken! I fed you. I freed you from the terrible pole, and in return you capture my soul. Oh ungrateful chicken! Our master, Mr. Ho, is justly angered since you damaged his garden." (Thus the witch indirectly flatters the rich man.) "Dear mother and father, please get rid of the other chicken!"

At this moment, the assistant stands up and hurries out of the room to seek the chicken with his shaking stick. The frightened people stand aside to make room for him. Chom-nye's mother and father promise the witch—or Chom-nye's soul—to get rid of the chicken while her grandparents sit motionless as dummies. With the promise, the assistant, the executor, returns to the room and takes his seat. The soul again talks through the witch.

"Dear mother, please give away all the things we prepared for my use in the future. They are useless now." The assistant rises again with his shaking stick. By this time he himself is shaking under the influence of the spirit as he goes around in search of the clothes.

Chom-nye's mother sobs, "Oh, my daughter, do not worry. I will get rid of the chicken. Go your way in peace and without worry."

The assistant continues to seek Chom-nye's possessions until her mother finally takes a small carton from the shelf and gives it to him. He opens it with his shaking hand and stick, and removes its contents. There is nothing much: a pink skirt and a blouse. That is all. The witch is disappointed. She had expected a little more, although the family is very poor. Customarily the witch has the right to keep such things; that is really a witch's business. When she finds valuables and many possessions, she is excited and continues the séance; in this case she is disappointed and decides to wind up the performance in short order. So a concluding sentence comes forth.

"Good-bye mother, father, grandmother, grandfather. Good-bye, my sisters. And good-bye, my dear husband. Even though I was not fortunate enough to be in your arms, my heart was always with you. Good-bye! I am going to the unknown destination."

Chom-nye's mother goes out into the yard, catches the promised chicken, and brings it to the witch. The bridal clothes are again folded and placed before her, too. That morning when Chom-nye's body had been carried away by her fiancé, there was talk of dressing her in the new clothes to replace the ragged ones which she wore, but her family dared not do so because her new little garments were necessary for the witch's performance. They believed that this ritual was absolutely necessary following the burial of the body. Without it, they feared that woe would come to them, especially since this was the death of a bride.

Next, the witch looks down upon the rice spread on the spot where the body had rested and tells the family that Chom-nye has been transformed into a flower, saying that she sees the pattern of it in the rice. The assistant then collects the rice in a small sack. Now that the witch and her assistant possess everything of value, they take their leave. The crowd has already gone away. Only the members of the family sit motionless and without expression, as if they were petrified.

None of the crowd of neighbors knew the actual cause of Chom-nye's death. They did not try to discover it. They are content to think that the chicken's spirit possessed her and that she is dead because of it.

translated by Lee Chang-Hei

Short Stories of Japan

Storytelling in the old manner continues in present-day Japan, even in the face of the ubiquitous television. At village street corners the teller of tales sets up his little stall and soon collects about him a group of eager youngsters and a few amused adults to look at his "flick pix" and hear his accounts of heroic deeds. As in the puppet theater, the relator is a master of mimicry and empassioned declamation. His accounts live and move and have contemporary meaning.

When we combine this age-old love of storytelling with Japan's reputation as being one of the most literate nations in the world, we come up with a potent mixture that has produced some of the finest fiction in world literature. Everything—from early animistic superstition to today's news item—is grist to the author's mill. Ivan Morris has complained, however, that many of Japan's contemporary writers are unnecessarily verbose and do not observe as well as they might the emphasis on economy of expression and the focus on one image or issue that set the modern short story off from early tales. He finds this remarkable in a culture that has perfected and loved the *haiku*, the world's briefest poetry form.

Leading Western and Japanese critics agree in including Ogawa Mimei, Shiga Naoya, and Akutagawa Ryûnosuke among an elite of writers who are masters in the short-story form.

Ogawa Mimei (1882–1961) graduated in 1905 from the English Department of Waseda University, which was at that time the center of Japanese Naturalism. Ogawa is generally recognized, however, to favor by nature an idealistic romanticism, a literary mode that has not been popular in the modern period.

His first work, published in 1906, showed marks of naturalism; his subsequent writings turned more toward humanitarian socialism. In 1920—the year of "Kūchū no Geitō" ("The Handstand")—Ogawa joined the newly organized Socialist Union. After a period he became impatient with that movement and turned briefly to anarchism.

But Ogawa's sentimental nature could not long be happy with political violence, and his writing gradually returned to his earlier emphases. Ivan Morris speaks of him as being not so much a political revolutionary as "a poet with a violent loathing for the injustice that he saw about him." In his homeland today, Ogawa is most widely known for his poems and his children's tales.

"The Handstand" (or, as it has also been titled in English, "Wager in Mid-air") with mounting tension relates an incident that, through contrast, points up the drab boredom of a city worker's life.

Shiga Naoya (1883–) dropped out of Tokyo Imperial University to become a full-time writer. He came into prominence soon after the Russo-Japanese War (1904–5), while he was still little more than a youth. In 1910 he joined a coterie that became an important influence in modern literary developments. Taking its name, *Shirakabe* ("White Birch"), from its magazine, the group stressed idealistic humanism and the importance of the individual. Subsequently these writers were called the Neo-Idealists. Later Shiga became more of a realist, and his best works are marked by direct realistic themes and expression.

Shiga is preeminent as a master of the short story, in which he has excelled for over forty years. Richard N. McKinnon, professor of Japanese Language and Literature at the University of Washington, has written of Shiga: "He has . . . been one of the most influential, if not the most influential, in molding the character of Japanese prose literature, and especially the short story, during the last twenty or thirty years."

Ivan Morris remarks on Shiga's economy in style. It has resulted, he says, in "writing of exceptional beauty and deceptive simplicity which has become known as the 'Shiga style.' His language," he adds, "is clear, terse, delicate—and often unusually difficult to translate."

"The Patron Saint" (1920) is a semihumorous account of an unexpected benefaction to a city messenger boy.

Akutagawa Ryûnosuke (1892–1927), of all contemporary Japanese writers, is probably best known to the West because of his "Rashōmon," one of three stories used to provide the substance that was made into the prize-winning motion picture of the same name. Many of his compelling and strange stories have appeared in excellent translations at popular prices. Although he also wrote poems and essays, he excelled in short stories, of which 150 have been published in seven collections. They have been translated into French, German, and Spanish, as well as English.

Even though he never traveled farther from his native country than China and Korea, from youth Akutagawa read widely in Japanese, Chinese, and Western literature. He cited Anatole France, Edgar Allen Poe, Baudelaire, and Strindberg as among his favorite Occidental writers. Akutagawa developed his own meticulous and demanding style, yet we can note echoes of Strindberg in the cold objectivity of his treatment of character, and of Poe and Baudelaire in his preoccupation with gloomy and threatening themes, culminating in his suicide at the age of thirty-five. Critics find his short stories as finely worked, with as much care for nuance of expression, as are his *haiku* poems.

In reading Akutagawa one often witnesses a fascinating union of modern surrealism in style with ancient conventional themes. This is the blend in "Rashōmon," a traditional tale of medieval Japan, and in "The Spider's Thread," an exemplum on the theme of Buddhist morality. The dark and macabre quality of the former contrasts vividly with the delicate story of the Buddha's compassion told in "The Spider's Thread" in a style reminiscent of the early *Jatakas*.

OGAWA MIMEI

THE HANDSTAND

It was at a time when I had been reduced to painting street signs for a living. My days were spent entirely in drawing huge advertisements on billboards for toothpaste, circuses, bottled beer, and ladies' underwear. At first the novelty of my new life made it tolerable, but soon I came to loathe it and to long for some form of escape, even if only temporary.

Formerly when I had worked as a serious painter I had, of course, never taken the slightest interest in the pictures on billboards, let alone given any thought to the people who painted them. If anything, these pictures had struck me as an insult to my artistic sensibility. Yet now when I saw the little drawings printed on the covers of notebooks in the stationer's, or the designs glazed on the lids of paint boxes, or even the billboards outside theaters, I would stop and look, and sometimes I found myself actually being moved by them. I suppose it was because I had come to realize that among the people who produced these drawings there must be many who, like myself, had once aspired to be real artists but had been forced by circumstances into this drudgery.

What made me begin to hate my new occupation, however, was not just the feeling that I was prostituting such talents as I might have; it was the relentless monotony. I soon learned that almost all the workers with whom I had now come to spend my time suffered to a greater or lesser extent from this same sense of monotony. They were forever discussing possible ways of breaking the tedium of their lives.

We would gather in the evening by the benches near the suburban tenements where we lived. One by one we arrived from different directions, exhausted at the end of a long day's work in the heat. We sat down heavily on the benches or, if there was no longer any room, squatted beside them on the gravel, and indolently fanned ourselves as we chatted away, oblivious to the passing of time.

Along came a couple of young street-acrobats. One of them danced around with a lion's mask while the other accompanied him on a tambourine. A girl wearing a red sash came out of the ice-cream parlor opposite where we sat and gave the boy a copper. Later a young woman strolled past with a samisen, her hair fastened in a bun with a green comb, and carrying a baby on her back.

"Not bad looking, eh?"

"I bet she's an ex-geisha or something. What do you think?"

She walked up and down the street in front of us. Occasionally she stopped and strummed on her samisen. Later a huge, dirty-looking woman in an advanced state of pregnancy waddled past us. We looked at her in fascination. She was the most repulsive woman we had ever seen. So that day drew slowly to an end.

"A good job? Hell, there's no such thing as a good job! It's all a lot of sweat! If anyone thinks it's fun making a living, he's crazy."

"No, we'll never get anywhere this way. Just sweat away

till we croak, that's all! The only way to make money is gambling."

"Gambling, eh?" said a large, dark-skinned bricklayer who was squatting next to the bench in his undershirt. "I'll tell you about gambling. When I lived in Shitaya, there was a girl in the neighborhood about twenty-four years old. She was a pretty little piece, I can tell you! I used to watch her passing outside my window. She strutted past in her straw sandals with her head high in the air. She wore a big gold chain over her breast and always carried a shining patent-leather handbag. She had a gold chain on the bag also. She lived in a poor-looking sort of house and I got to wondering how she could afford to doll herself up like that. Then I heard she'd been gambling and made quite a pile. 'That's how to get rich,' I thought to myself. 'Even women can do it.' Then early one morning on my way to work I saw a girl hurrying out of a low-class brothel. I just saw her back but there was something familiar about the way she walked. I followed her for a while and then saw her face as she got on a tram. It was the girl with the gold chain, all right! So much for gambling!"

"That's right," said a serious-looking man on the bench. "You can't always hit it lucky. And even if you do, it doesn't always work out. Why, only last week I saw in the paper that a certain man won a gambling pool or something. He'd been hard up all his life and then all of a sudden about half a million yen fell in his lap. What did he do? He went stark raving mad and murdered his wife with a hatchet! No, it's no good when things change too much. . . . I'm not so sure it isn't best to jog along the way we do." The man sat looking straight ahead after he had spoken. He seemed quite moved by what he had said. After a while he got up and left. Then one by one the others began to leave, some to start their night shifts, some for the public baths, some for home. Soon they had all gone except myself, a tinsmith called Chō, and two others.

"Is it hard to learn the flute?" said Kichikō, an engineer's mate. "I'd like to play the flute."

"What an idea!" said Chō with a smile. "How's a clumsy ox like you going to play the flute? Anyhow it takes years before you can play an instrument."

"I suppose you're a great hand at the flute," said Kichikō.

"No, I can't play. I like listening, though," said Chō.

"Well, you're a fine one to tell me I can't play the flute. You're a clumsy brute yourself."

"I may not be able to play, but at least I know what it's all about. You haven't got the vaguest idea what art is. It's not something you can learn like playing tiddlywinks!"

"Oh, yes, I'd forgotten. You're a great artist, aren't you?" said Kichikō, laughing. "A great artist when it comes to singing songs in the beer parlor, I mean!"

"I'm good at standing on my hands," announced Chō, beaming all over but with a touch of genuine pride. Chō was a rather silent man. He had a large round face—almost bloated, in fact. There was something about his expression that made one feel he was smiling inwardly all the time in a warm, pleasant way.

"Standing on your hands? What a very original art!" I said without thinking. We all laughed, including Chō.

I did not know why, but for some reason Chō's handstanding excited my curiosity. In time I came to learn from Chō himself and from some of his friends how he had acquired this avocation. It appeared that he had once seen a girl doing a handstanding stunt in the circus. Standing upright on her hands, she had crossed a long narrow plank suspended between two platforms high over the arena. Chō had been greatly impressed. There seemed to be no catch in this as in so many other circus tricks; it was purely the result of long practice. Suddenly it occurred to him, as he sat there in the circus, that he could learn the trick himself.

From then on, he began practicing handstands whenever he had time—after meals, in the evenings, and in the brief rest periods between work. At least it broke the monotony.

Often he was discouraged and felt that he would never be any good. Yet he persevered. "It's that girl," he told me once, "that girl at the circus. I just can't get her out of my mind. She was a real beauty, you know. Fine white teeth, red lips, lovely breasts, big, dark, mysterious eyes—she's the prettiest girl I've seen."

He had never seen her again but by his handstanding he kept her memory alive. Apart from this there was, I guessed, a hidden motive that made him continue his exhausting pastime. By becoming an expert handstander himself, as great as this girl if not greater, was he not in some way derogating from the perfection which he had originally seen in her, thereby making her, in this respect at least, less wonderful? By surpassing her in the art of handstanding, by taking for himself the praise that had originally all been hers, was he not somehow punishing her for being so completely unattainable?

"The trouble was," said Chō, "I didn't have a high narrow plank to practice on. But I got round this in the end. I found a straw mat with a thin black border to do my handstands on. This black border becomes the plank and both edges become sheer drops hundreds of feet high. So when I practice walking along the edge of the mat on my hands, I'm as frightened of falling as I would be in the circus. Well, I've got now so I can do it every time without even swaying. And if I can do it on the mat, I don't see why I couldn't do it in the circus like she did. . . . But of course I'll never really know."

"That girl certainly did something to you," I said to Chō one day. Chō looked at me seriously. "It's the same as painting," he said. "When you see something beautiful, it gets you in some way, doesn't it, and that makes you want to paint it. You'll work away like mad trying to paint it, won't you? Well, it's the same with me. Only I can't paint so I've got to imitate what I've seen. Is that so strange?"

His explanation struck me as quite reasonable.

"Look, Chō," said Kichikō that evening when I first heard about the handstanding, "why don't you let us see you do it now?" He laughed and looked round. The last rays of the summer sun were fading; the sky had lost its brightness and become a light transparent blue. A slight wind had blown up and dull, vaguely colored clouds scudded past high above us.

"Would you really like to see?" said Chō cheerfully. He stood up, and leaned forward on one of the benches. As he put his weight on it, the bench shifted slightly on the gravel.

"I'd better do it here," he said. He planted his hands firmly on the ground next to the bench and raised himself a couple of times, falling back lightly in the same place. Then, keeping both legs closely together, he moved slowly up until he was standing vertically in the air. The soles of his straw sandals faced the surface of the limpid evening sky. His plump arms were slightly bent as they supported his heavy, squat body. As the blood ran to his head, his face became so dark that one could hardly distinguish it from the earth.

Kichikō whistled with admiration. "That's good," he said. "That's pretty damned good!" Quite a few people had gathered from the neighborhood to watch Chō's performance and they were all exclaiming their admiration as he held his feet immobile in the air. When he stood up again, a couple of the local errand boys and a few other enterprising young fellows began to try the trick. After I left, I turned back and saw them all in their light shirts standing upside down by the benches in the gathering dusk.

There was a large steelworks in the neighborhood. Most of the workers were regular employees, but there was also quite a number of casual laborers who drifted in from the other factories or from the mines and usually left again after a time. One evening as we were gathered by our benches, a small, intelligent-looking man joined us. "You're new around here, aren't you?" I said.

"That's right. I've just got myself a job as a lathe man in those ironworks over there. I've got lodgings near here, too."

He soon established himself as one of our group. We all found him interesting because he had spent his life moving from place to place and could describe all sorts of things that were unfamiliar to us. Although uneducated, he was a good talker and, as he told us of the hardships he had undergone, the strange places where he had worked, the odd customs he had observed in other parts of Japan, and the efforts of workers to improve their conditions, we felt that we were being lifted out of the prisons of our narrow lives.

His lively eyes shone as he described life underground in the Aso mines where he had formerly worked. "To get to the first pit, you go down a hundred and fifty feet in the cage. Then down you go another hundred and fifty feet to the next pit. There are twelve pits altogether. In the bottom pit the temperature was nearly a hundred degrees just from the heat of the earth. There was a whole lot of us working down there. The air was pumped down from the pit-head. But after you'd been down there awhile, it got so damned hard to breathe your lungs were fit to burst. I was in the war and I can tell you that to spend eight hours down there in that mine was worse than twenty-four hours under enemy fire.

"And don't let them tell you mining isn't dangerous! Down there you're at the mercy of machines and they're always going wrong. One of the fellows I knew was pulling a loaded trolley onto the elevator. At least he thought the elevator was there but something had gone wrong and instead he stepped backward into the empty shaft and went shooting down hundreds of feet with the loaded trolley on top of him. You could hear him screaming right down to the bottom.

"You see, the strain down there makes you careless in the end. Lots of the fellows get blown to smithereens by the dynamite they've planted themselves. Sometimes they even knock down the props when they're working and get buried alive.

"But I'll tell you something funny. While you're down there in the mine, you're so busy with your work, you're so damned glad you haven't had an accident yourself and trying so hard to watch out in the future, that you don't have time to worry about anything else. It's when you come out on the surface after a day's work that you start thinking. You see other people walking about up there who've never been down a mine in all their lives. And you get to asking yourself: 'What the hell! I'm no different from them. What do I spend all day down in that damned hole for?'

"That's the way lots of us began figuring. It wasn't hard to get the other fellows to see our point of view. What the hell, we were risking our lives down there every day to make profits for the company. We all got together and were going to make a set of minimum demands for our safety—not wages, mind you, just for our safety. But we had an informer among us. Our plan leaked out and the company put a stop to it all.

"Later on, a couple of smooth, well-dressed men came along and told us how we ought to organize ourselves. They'd never been farther down a mine than the pit-head but they pretended to know all about it. Well, we miners were a pretty uneducated bunch but we could tell fakes when we saw them. If these men really had our interests at heart, we'd have felt it and gone along with them all the way. But it didn't take us long to see they were the type who make their living out of our troubles—and a damned good living too. 'Better honor than life,' they used to teach us in the army. Well, these men wanted honor *and* life—and plenty of both—all at our expense. The dirty rats—what could they teach us? It's lucky for them they cleared out before I got my hands on them!

"No one who hasn't really been a worker knows what it's all about. You can't learn it out of a book. You've got to be a worker, you've got to live like a worker, day after day, year after year. That's the only way to get to understand the 'labor problem.'

"We weren't born to live like slaves or animals! We workers deserve the same share of the country's wealth as everyone else. That's what I'd like to tell society."

"A socialist," I thought to myself and wondered whether all the others realized it. They used to sit listening to him in silence and occasionally I noticed Chō sighing as if moved by something the man had said.

One day as I was strolling down the sunlit street, I stopped dead in my tracks. Some of the things the little man had said suddenly came back to me with extraordinary force. It was as if I had been walking along a narrow single-track railway bridge and had abruptly been struck by the thought "What shall I do if a train comes rushing toward me?" Perhaps the time would come when I'd have to make such a decision. The idea made my heart pound like a hammer.

The little man told us one day about a derelict mine. The ore had given out and the miners had all moved to other pits. The power was still connected, however, and one morning the lights were turned on for a party of visiting journalists. One of the men got separated from the rest of the group and, before he knew it, he was hopelessly lost in the maze of tunnels and passages which twisted about underground like the coils of some immense serpent. He must have rushed round, gradually becoming panic-stricken, in those weird, deserted corridors hundreds of feet below the ground. His shouts for help would have been deadened by the thick walls. And then he ran headlong into the open elevator-pit and fell hundreds of feet into pitch darkness.

This story made a great impression on me and it was long before I could rid my mind of the terrifying vision.

Gradually I came to think that, however monotonous and unrewarding my present work might be, I should at least be grateful that it was safe. "After all," I said one evening, "why do we work anyway? When all's said and done, surely it's so we can earn enough to keep alive. In that case, it's a complete contradiction to take a job where you're risking your life."

It seemed unbelievable to me that anyone should be so mad as to do work in which he might at any moment be killed. Later I was to learn that such logic does not always apply and that to break the unendurable monotony of their lives, some people will in fact do things which can only be classed as insane.

Chō and the little man became friends and I often saw them together. One evening as I was calling for Chō on my way back from work, I found him standing outside his shop talking to the little man. They both nodded to me. The man had a map in his hands. "Here it is," he said, pointing to a small corner of land sticking out into the blue northern sea, "here's Nikolaevsk. That's where I'll be heading now. A friend of mine's working up there and he's asked me to join him." He looked up at the deep blue sky. "When I decided to leave the mines," he continued, "I first thought I'd try my luck somewhere really far away—Sakhalin, Kamchatka, or somewhere. But then I thought if I came to Tokyo, I'd meet a lot of interesting people, people I could talk to, people who felt like I did about things. I've always been a great talker, you know, ever since I was a youngster. Well, I've got to like a lot of you fellows, but I'm not really your type. So now I'm pushing on. I won't be going straight to Nikolaevsk. I'll spend the winter working in Hokkaidō and try crossing over to the mainland next spring." He paused for a while. "I suppose the fact is I'm just a born wanderer," he added, laughing. We said good-bye, and Chō and I stood watching him walk away in the distance.

"He asked me if I wanted to go with him," said Chō. "And I would have, too, except for my old mother. She'd be lost without me."

We started walking along slowly. A few sprigs of wilted morning glory stood in a black, unglazed vase in a window opposite the shop. It was really amazing how blue the sky was. Under this deep, weird, silent blue, the black-tiled roofs of the houses seemed to roll sadly into the distance like dunes along a seashore.

None of us ever saw the little man again. We heard that he had found a job in a factory at Ōi. No doubt he made his way to Hokkaidō and perhaps he even reached Nikolaevsk. Wherever he may be, I am sure he is heatedly expounding his theories.

I thought about him often. I remembered the clear look in his eyes when he was not talking. In them were reflected the images of faraway mountains, of clouds floating across distant skies, of infinitely remote stars, and sometimes of the dark, raging ocean. Yes, he was a wanderer and I felt that like the wanderers of old he had within him a song that comforted him in his weariness and that constantly spurred him on to discover new places and new ideas. Compared to him the members of our group, rooted here in our dreary suburb, seemed to me men exhausted by the monotony of work, men in whom all spirit of adventure had atrophied. At least, that is what I thought until the following incident.

I had spent all day painting a huge advertisement for women's dresses on a tin billboard. In the evening when I had finished, I decided to pass by Chō's shop. It was a close, sultry evening and although the summer was almost over, the sun was extremely hot. There was not the slightest breeze.

When I arrived, Chō was standing in a shirt and a pair of khaki trousers working on a shiny tin bucket.

"Have you ever been to the girls' circus at Asakusa?" he said when he saw me.

"No, never. I've been to the opera once—that's all."

"I'd like to go to the amusement park at Asakusa," said Chō, wiping the perspiration off his face.

"Asakusa," I said. "That shouldn't be too difficult. It doesn't take all that long to get there."

"It's all right if you've got money. Then you can go to the mountains for the summer. But when am I going to have time to go to Asakusa? I suppose that's what they mean by no leisure for the poor." His face was wreathed in smiles; he looked as if he was imagining the gay, bustling pleasure grounds of Asakusa.

Presently Kichikō, the engineer's mate, joined us. He had on a short workman's coat.

"Well, hot enough for you?" he said in his gruff voice. "What's happening? Anything interesting?"

"No," said Chō. "By the way, Kichi, where were you last night?"

"Last night? Oh, yes, after work I went down to the river at Ryōgoku to cool off." He sat down on Chō's workbench and began fanning himself.

"Look, Chō," said Kichikō after a while. "What about you and me climbing that chimney over there by the spinning mill? We'd get quite a view."

"In this heat?" said Chō. "How high do you suppose it is?"

"Come on, don't be a coward," said Kichikō laughing. "It's two hundred and fifty feet."

"Heights don't bother me," said Chō. "I was always climbing trees when I was a kid."

"Well, then, let's go."

"What about you?" said Chō, looking in my direction.

I remember how I had once peered out of the window from the fourth floor of an office building. The pavement below had looked white and dry in the glaring sun, and the heat seemed to be flashing from the hard surface. Suddenly I had imagined how my blood would redden those burned, white stones if I fell out of the window.

I glanced at Chō but did not answer.

Just then Kichikō looked at me. "Come on," he said. "You can have a go at painting the top of the chimney. It'll be more fun than those billboards of yours!"

I was too much of a coward to admit that I was frightened

of heights. "All right, I'll come along," I said, even simulating a certain enthusiasm.

The three of us left Chō's shop. On our way we stopped at an ice-cream parlor and each had a glass of ice water. Then we set out for the spinning mill. It was on a huge dusty plain at the edge of the city. As we trudged along, the shriek of the crickets reverberated in my ears like the sound of a boiling kettle. The perspiration was streaming down my forehead. We were all looking ahead at the chimney which reared itself before us under the blue, cloud-speckled sky. It had only recently been completed and the scaffolding was still coiled around it all the way to the top like a monstrous snake. There was no smoke.

We reached the chimney in about fifteen minutes.

"Are you sure it's two hundred and fifty feet?" said Chō, looking up. "It doesn't seem that high from here."

"Come on and see," said Kichikō. "You'll get dizzy just standing down here staring at it." He bent his head back and looked up to the top. "Imagine working up there, though," he added. "They wouldn't get me to work on a chimney like that for anything."

We took off our coats and threw them on the ground next to the solid-looking brick foundation; then we removed our shoes and socks and wet the palms of our hands with spittle. I put one foot on the rickety scaffolding and glanced back at the city: under the deep blue sky the rooftops stretched out in solid black rows; they looked very safe.

Kichikō started climbing first; after him went the rotund Chō and finally myself. The steps were not built straight, but circled round the chimney in an endless-looking spiral. The narrow iron rungs dug sharply into the soft soles of my feet.

I had not realized what this climb would be like. As the other two moved steadily upward round the chimney, I gradually began to fall behind. When I had reached about the halfway mark, I suddenly felt I could not continue. But glancing down, I realized that it would be at least as hard to start going down. From now on, I forced every muscle in my body to continue climbing. My feet no longer hurt, but my legs were trembling uncontrollably, and although I planted myself firmly on each rung, I had the uncomfortable feeling that at any moment my body would float off into space of its own accord.

The wind was blowing quite hard up here and I could hear some of the looser boards of the scaffolding clatter noisily. If just one of these flimsy rungs should slip or break, I'd lose

my footing and go plunging headlong into space. At the
thought, a cold sweat ran over my whole body. My hands
were particularly clammy and I was certain that they would
slip as I grasped the rungs above. If only I could wipe them
or rub them with sand.

Looking up, I saw that Kichikō had reached the top of the
chimney. He was standing on the narrow bricklayers' platform that surrounded it and leaning with both his hands on a
low, perilous railing. He looked round at the scenery. Now
Chō reached the top and joined Kichikō in admiring the
view. From time to time they glanced down the side of the
chimney to see how I was getting on.

Finally I reached the top. It was broader than I had imagined while climbing—about six feet in diameter. My legs
were twitching with a sort of cramp and I realized that I
could not possibly stand on the platform with the other two.
Instead I squatted down carefully on the wooden boards and
held on to the bottom of the railing with both hands. My
teeth chattered and my whole body was trembling.

I no longer cared in the slightest what impression I was
making on my companions. My only object now was to elicit
their sympathy so that they might somehow help me to reach
the ground safely. Normally they would have laughed to see
me in this condition and probably they would have teased
me. But now they just glanced at me occasionally without
smiling or saying anything, as if it were quite normal that I
should be in such a state. In some way, this attitude of theirs
added still further to my anxiety. I should almost have welcomed some normal bantering. Instead I heard Chō saying:
"Take a look over there, Kichi. The sea's come right up
close, hasn't it? And look at those trams. They're just like little crawling bugs. . . . What's that tower over there?"

"That's the twelve-story pagoda of Asakusa," answered
Kichikō nonchalantly.

I just stared straight down at the wooden boards. My head
was blank and there was a haze in front of my eyes. Yet I
could not help noticing between the wide cracks of the
boards people down below like tiny black beans. At this sight
my throat became clogged and I could hardly breathe. I must
stay still, I told myself. If I try looking at the sea or the
twelve-story pagoda of Asakusa, I'm done for.

Gradually I noticed that the sun was sinking and that the
whole sky had turned crimson. Why in God's name had I
come up here? How would I ever get down? I was bound to
lose my footing on those endless steps. As my mind darted

back over my past life, which now seemed infinitely remote, I remembered with shame how I had cursed the monotony and never felt really grateful for its safety.

Only a few feet away gaped the huge, black, empty mouth of the chimney. I was aware of a distant rumbling sound coming from its depths, like the roar of some great monster. At the same time I suddenly realized that the entire chimney was swaying to and fro, even if only very slightly. I had forgotten that tall buildings and chimneys move in the wind.

A sense of despair came over me. Just then I heard an astounding remark from Kichikō.

"I don't suppose you could do that trick of yours up here?" he said.

I looked up at Chō, who was standing directly over me. His face at this moment seemed more enormous than ever. He smiled strangely and looked round.

"Of course I could," he said after a while. "I can stand on my hands anywhere. The trouble is, there's no proper place to rest my hands on up here. These damned boards bend every time you step on them. Besides, this platform's so narrow that the railing would get in the way when I raised my legs."

"Supposing we bet you? If you can do it up here, we'll each give you a yen," said Kichikō after a pause. "What about it?" he added, looking down at me. "You'd give him a yen, wouldn't you?"

The whole thing was a joke, he realized. Chō was a determined fellow, but he wasn't crazy. He obviously knew that this would be suicide. I nodded silently at Kichikō. I'd share in the joke, if that's what they wanted.

"You'd each give me a yen, eh?" said Chō. "That makes a whole day's wages."

"Only look here," said Kichikō laughing nervously, "if you make a mistake, it'll be the end of you. I'll have to go down and pick up the mess."

"You needn't tell me. I can figure that out for myself," said Chō. "The trouble is," he continued, as if speaking to himself, "where would I put my hands?" He looked all around the platform. Then his eyes came to rest on the thick iron mouth of the chimney. He bent over and looked into the great black opening.

"If I do it," he said, "I'll stand on this edge."

He felt the surface of the chimney top.

"The trouble is, it's damned slippery." Suddenly his expression changed, and with a sense of horror I knew that he was going to try the trick. I wanted to stop him and began to stutter out something, but the words wouldn't come. All I could do was to squat there gazing up at him intently with my sunken eyes. Surely, I thought, he could not be doing this for the two yen, however much he may have wanted to spend the day at Asakusa. Could it be that he was still trying in some strange way to get the better of that girl at the circus? Or was he emulating the little man and defying monotony in his own way? I never knew. The next moment I heard Chō say: "All right, I'll take the wager. I'll have a go." There was no longer the slightest trace of laughter in his voice.

"Wait a minute," said Kichikō, suddenly becoming dead serious. "You know what'll happen if you slip."

"If I slip, that's the end of me." There was a touch of defiance in Chō's voice as he threw out the words. He turned round in the direction of the city and stared at it for a few moments. The sun was rapidly disappearing now and strangely shaped tufts of cloud drifted past in the darkening sky. Yet the top of our chimney was brilliant red from the last rays of the sun, as if illuminated by giant flames.

Chō spat on his hands and rubbed his palms carefully with a handkerchief to remove any trace of greasiness. Then he hung the handkerchief on the railing and, bracing himself, planted both hands on the iron mouth of the chimney. For several moments he stood there peering down into the huge, black opening from whose depths emerged the continual roaring sound. I glanced at him. His eyes protruded from their sockets, his short fat back bulged, repeated tremors passed down his arms, and his close-cropped head was wet with perspiration. All this time the chimney swayed rhythmically to and fro in the wind.

Chō brought his legs together and drew them in as far as possible to avoid catching them on the railing. Once they were raised, it would be too late to make any adjustment. Should he then miscalculate and lose his balance, he would either fall headlong into the two-hundred-and-fifty-foot gullet of the chimney or backward over the railing and down to the hard ground below.

His legs had now left the platform and were already a few feet in the air. My head began going round and I had to look down. When I next glanced up, Chō was gradually straightening his legs. A moment later they were fully extended and now he stood there on his hands, his body a rigid line against the evening sky. A presentiment of relief ran through me.

Kichikō had not taken his eyes off Chō for a moment. He continued to gaze fixedly at him as he now slowly drew in his legs and began to retrace the line he had drawn in the air. Skillfully avoiding the railing, he gradually brought them back to the platform. For the first time since the performance had begun, I allowed myself to look straight at him. The strength of his entire body seemed to be concentrated in the bulging muscles of his arms. I noticed that a sort of spasm was passing from the nape of his neck to his shoulders. His hair was drenched.

The handstand was safely completed. For a while none of us spoke. Chō stood staring straight into space with unblinking, protruding eyes. His complexion was not even pale, but completely colorless like a dead man's. Round the corners of his mouth I detected a cool, dark, self-mocking smile.

In a flash I remembered seeing such a smile once before. A car had come hurtling along the street where I was walking and had almost run over a man working on the tramlines. By some miracle he had escaped, though the side of the car must have grazed his overalls. Afterward he had stood there rigid in the middle of the street still holding a large granite paving-stone. His eyes were wide open and there was a weird smile on his face. The car disappeared in the distance and the people who had stopped to look hurried on; but the man still stood there staring straight ahead into space.

Then I noticed a black bird skimming past directly over the chimney and silhouetted strangely against the dark sky.

Kichikō was the first to go down and I followed him. Glancing back, I saw Chō still standing there on the platform. His face was that of a dead man. He seemed sunk in thought.

translated by Ivan Morris

SHIGA NAOYA

The Patron Saint

Senkichi was an apprentice in a certain shop in Kanda where scales were sold.

It was a time when the soft, clear autumn sunlight was gently pouring into the store from beneath the faded navy blue shop curtain. Not a single customer was in the store.

The chief clerk looked bored as he sat smoking a cigarette behind the cashier's lattice. He began to speak to his junior clerk, who was reading a newspaper by the brazier.

"Say, Kô-san, isn't this about the season for your favorite tuna?"

"Yes, it is."

"How about tonight? Would you like to go out after we close up shop?"

"Fine idea."

"It'll take only fifteen minutes if we take the Sotobori line."

"That's right."

"Once you've eaten at that place, you couldn't possibly eat at any of the places around here. Don't you agree?"

"Absolutely."

Senkichi, the young apprentice, was seated at a respectful distance behind the young clerk. His hands were neatly folded under his apron. As he listened to the conversation he thought to himself, "Ah! they must be talking about the sushi house." [1] In the Kyobashi district there was another scale shop where he was often sent on errands. Senkichi, therefore, knew very well where that sushi house was. He longed for the day when he could attain the enviable position of a clerk, so that he too might talk like a connoisseur of sushi and patronize such an establishment whenever he wished.

"I hear Yohei's son has opened another place near Matsuya. Do you know anything about that, Kô-san?"

"No, I don't. Which Matsuya is that?"

"I'm not too sure, but it's probably the one at Imagawabashi."

"I see, and is the food supposed to be good there?"

"So I hear."

"Is it also called Yohei?"

"No, it's called something else. What was it now—I heard it, but I've forgotten it now."

Senkichi was thinking, "Goodness, there must be a lot of these high-class places," and his mouth watered as he continued to muse, "I wonder what they really mean when they say the food tastes good or bad?" He cautiously swallowed, taking care not to make a sound.

---

[1] An eating place that specializes in serving sushi, of which there are several varieties. The variety mentioned in this story is commonly called the Edo (Tokyo) style, and consists of bite-sized mounds of rice with small slices of fish on top.

2

It was near twilight several days later. Senkichi was sent on an errand to the scale shop at Kyobashi. The chief clerk gave him a round-trip fare.

When Senkichi got off the Sotobori streetcar at Kajibashi, he purposely walked past the sushi house. And as he gazed at the shop curtain of the sushi house, he visualized many clerks walking briskly through the curtain. Senkichi was at that time already quite hungry. In his mind's eye he saw sushi covered with fresh, juicy tuna. "How I wish I could eat just one," he thought. When Senkichi received his round-trip fare, he would very often buy only a one-way ticket, and walk back, instead. He did this again this time and as he walked along the four pennies which he had saved jangled in his inside pocket.

"With four pennies, I should be able to buy one; but, how can I go in there and say, 'One sushi, please'?" He gave up the idea and went on.

The business at the scale shop did not take long. He left the store after receiving a small but remarkably heavy paper carton containing several tiny brass weights.

As he retraced his steps Senkichi somehow felt that he was being drawn by some unseen force, and, without intending to do so, was about to turn the corner in the direction of the sushi house when he discovered a sushi stand on a side street beyond the intersection with identical markings on its shop curtain. Senkichi walked towards the stand.

3

A. was a young member of the House of Peers. His colleague, B., had often told him with a knowing look that one couldn't learn the true taste of sushi until he had sampled some at a sushi stand, where the sushi is eaten with one's fingers as soon as it is made. A. thought that someday he would have to try this himself. He therefore learned beforehand where he might find a good sushi stand.

One late afternoon, A. walked from the Ginza district across the Kyobashi bridge and stopped at the sushi stand which he had heard about earlier. Several people were already standing before the counter. He hesitated momentarily, but promptly summoned his courage and walked through the curtain. Still he could not bring himself to squeeze in between the people. So he stood behind them and waited a while.

Suddenly, a boy, thirteen or fourteen years old, entered the stand. The boy brushed past A. as if he were elbowing his way through, and pressed into a tiny space in front of him. He then hurriedly looked over five or six sushi placed on a thick wooden counter which was set at an angle.

"Do you have any rolled in seaweed?"

"Sorry, not today, son," replied the stocky proprietor, while he molded a sushi with his hands and eyed him narrowly.

With firm determination, the boy boldly reached out and picked up a sushi with tuna on top, as if to show that he had done this sort of thing before. Yet, for some reason, he hesitated. The hand, which reached out briskly for the sushi, faltered.

"Say, those are six pennies apiece, fellow," the proprietor warned.

The boy quickly put it back on the counter without a word.

"I wish you wouldn't touch things you aren't going to buy," the proprietor complained. Then, placing the sushi he had just made on the counter, he took the one that was touched, and set it down by him.

The young apprentice said nothing. He made a wry face and seemed unable to move. However, he quickly summoned his courage and walked out of the stand.

"Since the price of sushi has gone up, an apprentice simply can't afford to eat any," the proprietor muttered, looking a bit uncomfortable. And when he molded another sushi, he picked up the sushi the boy had touched and neatly tossed it into his mouth.

4

"I went to the sushi stand you told me about the other day."

"Well, how was it?"

"The food was quite good. By the way, I noticed that the people held their hand in this manner, and with the fish on the bottom, they simply tossed the whole piece into their mouth. Is that the way the connoisseur would eat?"

"That seems to be the usual way to eat sushi with tuna on top."

"I wonder why they turn it over that way, though?"

"That's simple. You see, in that way, if the tuna isn't fresh, your tongue would sense it right away."

"Oh, is that it. Well, I guess B. isn't much of a connoisseur of sushi, after all."

A. began to laugh. He then told the story of the young apprentice.

"Somehow, I felt sorry for that boy. I felt I wanted to do something for him."

"Why didn't you treat him? Think how happy you would have made him, if you had told him to eat as much as he wished."

"He undoubtedly would have been pleased, but I would have been very uncomfortable."

"Uncomfortable? In other words, you don't think you'd have the courage. Is that right?"

"I don't know if that's the word for it, but, at any rate, it isn't so easy to get up such courage. Now, if it's a question of taking that boy out somewhere else to eat, I might have been able to do that."

"Well, I guess you're right at that," B. agreed.

5

A. wanted to keep a record of the weight of his rapidly growing child, who was attending kindergarten. He decided to buy a small scale to be put in the bathroom. It so happened that one day he came upon the store in Kanda, where Senkichi was employed.

Senkichi didn't know A. A., however, recognized him.

Seven or eight baggage scales were arranged neatly in order of size along the side aisle of the store which led to the back room. A. chose the smallest one. He thought how happy his wife and child would be over such a cute miniature copy of scales commonly seen at the railroad station and the freight office.

"Where would you like to have this delivered, sir?" the chief clerk asked, holding an obsolete account book in his hand.

"Well," A. thought for a moment, while looking at Senkichi. "Can you spare this boy right now?"

"Yes, I guess so."

"Fine! I'm in a bit of a hurry, so can I have him come with me?"

"Very well, sir. I'll have this loaded on the wagon right away and have him follow you."

A. planned to treat the boy to a dinner that day, in order to make up for the other day.

When the money was paid, the chief clerk brought out a different book and asked, "May I have your name and address on this, sir?"

A. was a little distressed. He did not know that there were regulations which required the person who bought scales to register his name and address along with the serial number of the merchandise. To reveal his identity before treating the boy to a dinner was a little too embarrassing for him. Still, there was nothing else he could do. Turning this matter over in his mind, he wrote down a fictitious name and address and handed it back to the clerk.

The customer walked slowly, making allowance for Senkichi, who followed several yards behind with a handcart.

When they came to a certain rickshaw stand, the customer made Senkichi wait while he went inside. Presently, the scale was transferred to a rickshaw.

"Please see that this is delivered and collect the money at my house. I've written it down on my card." A. came out of the stand and then, with a smile, said to Senkichi, "Thank you for your trouble. I would like to treat you to something, so come along with me." Senkichi thought that this was too good to be true; yet, he felt vaguely apprehensive about it. Anyway he was delighted. He quickly bowed several times.

They walked by the noodle house, the sushi house, and even the store where meat is grilled on a skewer. "I wonder where he's planning to take me?" Senkichi began to feel uneasy. They passed under the viaduct by Kanda Station and came to the corner of Matsuya. Then they crossed the car tracks and stopped only after they had come upon a small sushi house around the corner.

"You wait here a minute." Senkichi set the cart handle down on the ground and stood waiting, while the customer went in alone.

Soon, he came out again, followed this time by a young graceful lady.

"Please come in," she said.

"I'll be going on home. But you stay and eat all you want," the customer said, and hurried out towards the main street as though he were fleeing from the scene.

Senkichi made short work of the three servings of sushi. Like a starved dog that had stumbled on to some food most unexpectedly, he gulped it down in no time at all.

Since there was no other customer and the lady had under-standingly closed the sliding door behind her, Senkichi did not have to bother about anything, least of all his table manners. He was able to eat in any way he pleased and to his heart's content. The lady returned with a pot of fresh tea and asked smilingly, "Can you eat some more?"

"No thank you—." Senkichi blushed and lowered his eyes. Then quickly he began to gather up his things.

"Well, in that case you must be sure to come again. You still have plenty of credit here."

Senkichi was silent.

"Have you known that gentleman for a long time?"

"No."

"Is that right? . . ." She exchanged glances with her husband who had just come in.

"He certainly must be a generous man. But, in any case, you must come again. We'll be in an awkward spot if you don't."

Senkichi merely bobbed his head, as he slipped his feet into his wooden clogs.

6

After he had left the boy, A. hurried out into the main street feeling as though he was being pursued. There he hailed a cab and headed straight to B.'s house.

A strange melancholy feeling overtook him. He thought to himself: I felt genuine sympathy for that boy who was caught in an awkward situation the other day. Today, just by chance, I succeeded in doing the very thing I have wanted to do for him ever since, and there is every reason why the boy, as well as I, myself, should be satisfied. To make people happy is not evil. I should rightfully feel a certain degree of satisfaction. Yet, how do I account for this sad and unpleasant feeling? Why is it, and where does it come from? Why, this is no different from the way a man might feel after he had secretly done something wrong. Could it be that there is within me a silly self-consciousness about having done a good deed, and that I am being criticized, betrayed, and mocked by the real me? I wonder if my feeling of melancholy is a reflection of this criticism, betrayal, and mockery. Maybe everything would be all right if I relaxed and stopped making such a big fuss about it. Unconsciously, though, I know that my mind is preoccupied with what I've done. But, at any rate, I haven't done anything to be ashamed of, and there is no reason why I should be left with this unpleasant feeling.

A. had promised to visit B. that day, so B. was expecting him. In the evening, the two left in B.'s car to attend a concert being given by Madam Y.

A. came home quite late. Having seen B. and having heard Madam Y.'s moving performance, A. was almost cured of his melancholy.

"Thank you so much for the scales."

Just as he had expected, his wife was very pleased with the size of the scales. The child was already asleep, but his wife told him how excited the child had been.

"By the way, do you remember my telling you about a young apprentice I saw at the sushi stand the other day? Well, I met him again."

"No! Where?"

"He works at the scale shop!"

"My, what a coincidence!"

A. told her about how he had treated the boy to some sushi and about the strange feeling which possessed him afterwards.

"I wonder why? It's funny that you should feel badly about it," his wife replied with concern. She seemed to be giving it some thought. Then suddenly she said, "Oh! I think I understand that feeling. Such things do happen. I can't think of it now, but, I think I've felt that way once myself."

"Do you think so?"

"Yes, things like that could very well happen. What did B. say?"

"I didn't mention it to him."

"Oh. Anyway, I'm sure you've made him very happy. Who wouldn't be, if he is treated to a meal like that so unexpectedly. I know I would. Couldn't you call them up and order some for me?"

7

Senkichi came back to the store with an empty cart. He was thoroughly stuffed. He had eaten his fill many times before, but he simply couldn't recall ever having stuffed himself with such delicious food.

Then, all of a sudden, he remembered the humiliating experience he had had at the sushi stand at Kyobashi. The memory of it returned to him at last. As he thought about it more, he realized for the first time that there must have been some connection between that experience and the meal he had today. Senkichi thought perhaps, yes, the man must have been there that day. I'm sure of it! But how did he know where to find me? There's something strange about the whole thing. Come to think of it, that was the very same sushi house that the clerks were talking about the other day. Now, how on earth did he know what they were saying!

The more he thought about it the more mysterious the whole thing became. It was inconceivable to Senkichi that A. and B. might talk about the sushi house in the same way that the clerks had done. He became convinced that the customer had heard the conversation that took place between the clerks, the very same conversation that he himself had overheard that day, and that this was the reason the customer had taken him there today. Otherwise, how was he to explain the fact that they had passed up any number of sushi houses on their way to that place.

Gradually he came to feel that the customer was no ordinary mortal. He knew about my humiliation; he knew what the clerks were saying, and above all, he even read my mind, and treated me to a splendid meal. This couldn't possibly be the act of a mortal. He might have been a god, or a wizard, perhaps. Maybe he was O-Inari, the god of harvest!

He thought of O-Inari, because he had an aunt who was a staunch believer in this god—so much so, in fact, that for a while she had almost gone out of her mind. She would go into a trance when O-Inari possessed her and make strange predictions and prophesy things that actually took place in distant places. Senkichi had once seen her in this state. He felt, however, that what had happened today was a bit too fashionable to be the work of O-Inari. Nevertheless, he became more and more convinced that it was an act of a supernatural being.

As the days passed, the strange feeling of melancholy gradually left A. until not a trace of it remained. All the same, he couldn't bring himself to walk by that scale shop in Kanda again. He couldn't help feeling a bit awkward about it. Moreover, he no longer had the urge to go to that sushi house.

"I think it worked out well for all of us. Now, all you have to do is to have some sushi delivered here so we could all enjoy it."

His wife laughed, but A. didn't.

"A timid person like myself has no business doing such a rash thing."

8

For Senkichi, "that customer" became more and more a part of his life. Whether he might have been a man or a supernatural being—this question mattered little to him now. All he felt was a deep sense of gratitude. The proprietor and the lady of the sushi house had repeatedly reminded him to return, but he didn't feel like going there again. He felt that to go again would be the height of impertinence, and this was too frightening to contemplate.

In moments of sorrow and distress, he always thought of "that customer." Just the thought of him was a comfort to him. He believed firmly that someday, somewhere, "that customer" would appear before him again and bestow upon him more undreamed-of favors.

This writer will lay down his pen at this point. He must confess that his original plans called for the young apprentice to go to the house of "that customer," for driven by his own desire to ascertain his true identity, he had learned the name and address of the customer from the chief clerk. The young apprentice, however, found no house at that address, only a small shrine of O-Inari. The young apprentice was astonished.—This is what this writer had in mind. However, he began to feel that this would be a bit cruel to the boy, and for this reason, he decided to end the story where he did.

translated by Michael Y. Matsudaira

AKUTAGAWA RYŪNOSUKE

THE SPIDER'S THREAD

1

One day the Buddha was strolling alone on the brink of the lotus pond of Paradise.

The lotus flowers in bloom in the pond were all as white as pearls, and the golden pistils and stamens in their centers ceaselessly filled all the air with ineffable fragrance.

It was morning in Paradise.

Presently the Buddha stood still on the brink of the pond,

and through an opening among the leaves which covered the face of the water, suddenly beheld the scene below.

As the floor of Hell lay directly beneath the lotus pond of Paradise, the River of the Threefold Path to eternal darkness and the piercing peaks of the Needle Mountain were distinctly visible through the crystal water, as through a stereopticon.

Then his eye fell on a man named Kandata, who was squirming with the other sinners in the bottom of Hell.

This Kandata was a great robber who had done many evil things, murdering and setting fire to houses, but he had to his credit one good action. Once while on his way through a deep forest, he had noticed a little spider creeping along beside the road.

So quickly lifting his foot, he was about to trample it to death, when he suddenly thought: "No, no, as small as this thing is, it too has a soul. It would be rather a shame to kill it inconsiderately," and he spared the spider's life.

As he looked down into Hell, the Buddha remembered how this Kandata had spared the spider's life. And in return for that good deed, he thought, if possible he would like to deliver him out of Hell. Fortunately, when he looked around, he saw a spider of Paradise spinning a beautiful silvery thread on the lotus leaves.

The Buddha quietly took up the spider's thread in his hand. And he let it straight down to the bottom of Hell far below through the opening among the pearly-white lotus flowers.

2

Here Kandata had been rising and sinking with the other sinners in the Pool of Blood on the floor of Hell.

It was pitch black everywhere, and when at times a glimpse was caught of something rising from that darkness, it turned out to be the gleam of the peaks of the dread Needle Mountain. The stillness of the grave reigned everywhere, and the only thing that could be heard now and then was the faint sighing of the sinners. This was because such sinners as had come down to this spot had already been worn out by the other manifold tortures of Hell and had lost even the strength to cry aloud.

So, great robber though he was, Kandata, choking with the blood, could do nothing but struggle in the pool like a dying frog.

But his time came. On this day, when Kandata lifted his

head by chance and looked up at the sky above the Pool of Blood, he saw a silver spider's thread slipping down toward him from the high, high heavens, glittering slightly in the silent darkness just as if it feared the eyes of man.

When he saw this, his hands clapped themselves for joy. If, clinging to this thread, he climbed as far as it went, he could surely escape from Hell. Nay, if all went well, he might even enter Paradise. Then he would never be driven on to the Needle Mountain or sunk in the Pool of Blood.

As soon as these thoughts came into his mind, he grasped the thread tightly in his two hands and began to climb up and up with all his might. Because he was a great robber, he had long been thoroughly familiar with such things.

But Hell is nobody knows how many myriads of miles removed from Paradise, and strive as he might, he could not easily get out. After climbing for a while, he was finally exhausted and could not ascend an inch higher.

Since he could do nothing else, he stopped to rest, and hanging to the thread, looked far, far down below him. Now, since he had climbed with all his might, the Pool of Blood where he had just been was already, much to his surprise, hidden deep down in the darkness. And the dread Needle Mountain glittered dimly under him. If he went up at this rate, he might get out of Hell more easily than he had thought.

With his hand twisted into the spider's thread, Kandata laughed and exulted in a voice such as he had not uttered during all the years since coming here: "Success! Success!"

But suddenly he noticed that below on the thread, countless sinners were climbing eagerly after him, up and up, like a procession of ants.

When he saw this, Kandata simply blinked his eyes for a moment, with his big mouth hanging foolishly open in surprise and terror.

How could that slender spider's thread, which seemed as if it must break even with him alone, ever support the weight of all those people?

If it should break in midair, even he himself, after all his effort in reaching this spot, would have to fall headlong back into Hell.

But meanwhile hundreds and thousands of sinners were squirming out of the dark Pool of Blood and climbing with all their might in a line up the slender, glittering thread. If he did not do something quickly, the thread was sure to break in two and fall. So Kandata cried out in a loud voice:

"Hey, you sinners! This spider's thread is mine. Who gave *you* permission to come up it? Get down! Get down!"

Just at that moment, the spider's thread, which had shown no sign of breaking up to that time, suddenly broke with a snap at the point where Kandata was hanging. Without even time to utter a cry, he shot down and fell headlong into the darkness, spinning swiftly around and around like a top.

Afterward, only the spider's thread of Paradise, glittering and slender, hung short in the moonless and starless sky.

3

Standing on the brink of the lotus pond of Paradise, the Buddha had watched closely all that had happened, and when Kandata sank like a stone to the bottom of the Pool of Blood, he began to walk again with a sad expression on his face.

Doubtless Kandata's cold heart that would have saved only himself, and his fall back into Hell, had appeared to the Buddha's eyes most pitiful. But the lotuses in the lotus pond of Paradise cared nothing at all about such things.

The pearly-white flowers were swaying about the Buddha's feet. As they swayed, from the golden pistils in their centers, their ineffable fragrance filled all the air.

It was near noon in Paradise.

translated by Glenn Shaw

BIBLIOGRAPHY

The following listings include books in English that give further background on the readings in this anthology or supplement its necessarily limited selections. Starred books are either referred to in the text or are those from which selections have been taken.

Since this is a volume of recent Asian literature, the bibliography is confined to works that have bearing on literature since the eighteenth century. It is merely representative and is not intended to be in any way definitive.

GENERAL

Anderson, G. L., ed., *The Genius of the Oriental Theater*. New York: The New American Library, 1966.

*———, *Masterpieces of the Orient*. New York: W. W. Norton & Company, 1961.

Bowers, Faubian, *Theatre in the East, A Survey of Asian Dance and Drama*. New York: Grove Press, 1956.

Cournos, John, and Norton, Sybil, eds., *Best World Short Stories: 1947*. New York: D. Appleton-Century, 1948.

Hanrahan, Gene Z., ed., *Fifty Great Oriental Stories*. New York: Bantam Books, 1965.

*Haydn, Hiram, and Cournos, John, eds., *A World of Great Stories*, 6th ed. New York: Crown Publishers, 1959.

Jose, F. Sionil, ed., *Asian PEN Anthology*. New York: Taplinger Publishing Company, 1967.

Kritzeck, James, ed., *Anthology of Islamic Literature from the Rise of Islam to Modern Times*. New York: Holt, Rinehart and Winston, 1963.

*Milton, Daniel, and Clifford, William, *A Treasury of Modern Asian Stories*. New York: The New American Library, 1961.

Nakamura, Hajime, *Ways of Thinking of Eastern Peoples: India, China, Tibet, Japan*, rev. English trans., Philip P. Wiener, ed. Honolulu: East-West Center Press, 1964.

Ross, Nancy Wilson, *Three Ways of Asian Wisdom: Hinduism, Buddhism, Zen, and Their Significance for the West*. New York: Simon and Schuster, 1966.

*Tietjens, Eunice, ed., *Poetry of the Orient: An Anthology of the Classic Secular Poetry of the Major Eastern Nations*. New York: Alfred A. Knopf, 1928.

Van Doren, Mark, ed., *An Anthology of World Poetry*, rev. ed. New York: Harcourt, Brace & World, 1936.

Yohannan, John D., ed., *A Treasury of Asian Literature*, 4th ed. New York: The New American Library, 1962.

CHINA

*Baur, Wolfgang, and Franke, Herbert, *The Golden Casket, Chinese Novellas of Two Millenia*, trans. from the German by Christopher Levenson. New York: Harcourt, Brace & World, 1964.

Birch, Cyril, ed., *Chinese Communist Literature*. New York: Frederick A. Praeger, Inc., 1963.

*Buck, Pearl S., *The Chinese Novel*. New York: The John Day Company, 1939.

Chai, Ch'u, and Chai, Winberg, eds., *A Treasury of Chinese Literature: A New Prose Anthology Including Fiction and Drama*. New York: Appleton-Century-Crofts, 1965.

Ch'ên, Jerome, *Mao and the Chinese Revolution: With Thirty-Seven Poems by Mao Tse-tung*. New York: Oxford University Press, 1965.

Ch'en, Shou-yi, *Chinese Literature: A Historical Introduction*. New York: The Ronald Press Company, 1961.

*Chou En-lai and others, *The People's New Literature: Reports at First-hand of All-China Conference of Writers and Artists*. Peking: The Cultural Press, 1950.

Davis, A. R., ed., *The Penguin Book of Chinese Verse*, 2d ed. Baltimore, Md.: Penguin Books, 1965.

*de Bary, William Theodore, and others, *Sources of Chinese Tradition*, 3d ed. New York: Columbia University Press, 1964.

*Fenollosa, Ernest Francisco, *The Chinese Written Character as a Medium for Poetry*, Ezra Pound, ed. San Francisco: City Lights Books, 1936.

Harrison, John A., *China Since 1800*. New York: Harcourt, Brace & World, 1967.

Hsia, C. T., *A History of Modern Chinese Fiction: 1917–1957*. New Haven, Conn., and London: Yale University Press, 1961.

Hsiung, S. I., *The Story of Lady Precious Stream, A Novel*. London: Hutchinson, 1950.

*Hsu, Kai-yu, trans. and ed., *Twentieth Century Chinese Poetry*. Garden City, N. Y.: Doubleday & Company, 1963.

*Hu Shih, *The Chinese Renaissance*. New York: Paragon Book Reprint Corp., 1963.

Lai Ming, *A History of Chinese Literature*. Preface by Lin Yutang. New York: The John Day Company, 1964.

*Lao Sheh, *Dragon Beard Ditch*. Peking: Foreign Language Press, 1956.

*———, *Rickshaw Boy*. New York: Reynal & Hitchcock, 1945.

Liu, James J. Y., *The Art of Chinese Poetry*. Chicago: University of Chicago Press, 1962.

Liu, Wu-chi, *An Introduction to Chinese Literature*. Bloomington, Ind.: Indiana University Press, 1966.

Mao Tse-tung on Art and Literature, 2d ed. Peking: Foreign Language Press, 1960.

*Mao Tun, *Midnight*. Peking: Foreign Language Press, 1957.

*———, *Spring Silkworms and Other Stories*. Peking: Foreign Language Press, 1956.

Payne, Robert, ed., *The White Pony: An Anthology of Chinese Poetry*. New York: The New American Library, 1960.

Scott, A. C., *Literature and the Arts in Twentieth Century China*. Garden City, N. Y.: Doubleday & Company, 1963.

Waley, Arthur, ed., *Chinese Poems*. London: George Allen & Unwin, 1961.

————, *Three Ways of Thought in Ancient China*. Garden City, N. Y.: Doubleday & Company, 1956 (first published, 1939).

Wang, Chi-chen, trans., *Contemporary Chinese Stories*. New York: Columbia University Press, 1944.

Yu, Kwang-chung, *New Chinese Poetry*. Taipei: Heritage Press, 1960.

INDIA, CEYLON, PAKISTAN, SOUTHEAST ASIA

*Abbas, Khwaja Ahmad, *Inquilab* (novel). Bombay: Jaico Publishing House, 1955.

Ali, Ahmed, *Twilight in Delhi* (novel). New York: Oxford University Press, 1966.

Anand, Mulk Raj, *Untouchable* (novel). Bombay: Jaico Publishing House, 1956.

Anantanarayanan, M., *The Silver Pilgrimage*. New York: Criterion Books, 1961.

Bhattacharya, Bhabani, *He Who Rides a Tiger: A Novel of Modern India*. Bombay: Jaico Publishing House, 1955.

Chatterjee, Bankim-Chandra, *Krishnakanta's Will* (novel). New York: New Directions, 1962.

Chatterjee, Debiprasad, ed., *Modern Bengali Poems*. Calcutta: The Signet Press, 1945.

Contemporary Indian Literature, A Symposium. New Delhi: Sahitya Akademi, 1959.

Coomaraswamy, Ananda K., *The Dance of Shiva: On Indian Art and Culture*, 2d ed. New York: The Noonday Press, 1959.

*de Bary, William Theodore, and others, *Sources of Indian Tradition*, 5th ed. New York: Columbia University Press, 1964.

Derrett, M. D., *The Modern Indian Novel in English: A Comparative Approach*. Bruxelles: Université, 1966.

*Dev, A. K., *History of Sanskrit Poetics*, 2d rev. ed. Calcutta: Ferina K. K. Mukhopadhyay, 1960.

Gargi, Balwant, *Folk Theater of India*. Seattle: University of Washington Press, 1966.

*————, *Theatre in India*. New York: Theater Arts Books, 1962.

*Kiernan, V. G., ed., *Poems from Iqbal*. London: John Murray, 1955.

Lubis, Mochtar, *Twilight in Djakarta* (novel). New York: Vanguard Press, 1963.

Malgonkar, Manohar, *A Bend in the Ganges: A Novel of Modern India*. New York: The Viking Press, 1965.

Markandaya, Kamala, *A Handful of Rice* (novel). New York: The John Day Company, 1966.

————, *Nectar in a Sieve* (novel). New York: The New American Library, 1956.

————, *Possession* (novel). New York: The John Day Company, 1963.

*Misra, Vidya Niwas, ed., *Modern Hindi Poetry: An Anthology*. Bloomington, Ind.: Indiana University Press, 1965.

Naim, C. M., ed., *Readings in Urdu: Prose and Poetry*. Honolulu: East-West Center Press, 1965.

Narayan, R. K., *The Bachelor of Arts* (novel). London: Eyre & Spottiswoode, 1951.

————, *The Financial Expert* (novel). New York: Farrar, Straus & Company, 1953.

————, *The Guide* (novel). New York: The Viking Press, 1958.

————, *The Man Eater of Malgudi* (novel). New York: The Viking Press, 1961.

Natwar-Singh, K., ed., *Tales from Modern India*. New York: The Macmillan Company, 1966.

*Premchand, *The Gift of a Cow* (novel). Bloomington, Ind.: Indiana University Press, 1968.

Premchand Reader, A, ed. by Norman Zide and others. Honolulu: East-West Center Press, 1965.

*Raffel, Burton, ed., *Anthology of Modern Indonesian Poetry*. Berkeley: University of California Press, 1964.

*Rama Rau, Santha, *Home to India*. New York and London: Harper & Brothers, 1945.

Rao, Raja, *Kanthapura* (novel). New York: New Directions, 1963.

*Singh, Khushwant, *Train to Pakistan* (novel). New York: Grove Press, 1961.

Tagore, Rabindranath, *Binodini: A Novel*. Honolulu: East-West Center Press, 1964.

*————, *The Collected Poems and Plays*. New York: The Macmillan Company, 1964.

*————, *Poems*, 3d ed. Calcutta: Visva-Bharati, 1946.

Tagore Reader, A, Amiya Chakravarty, ed. Boston: Beacon Press, 1966.

Vaid, Krishna Baldev, *Steps in Darkness* (novel). New York: The Orion Press, 1962.

*Vijayatunga, J., *Grass for My Feet*, 4th ed. London: Edward Arnold, 1953.

Yogananda, Paramahansa, *Autobiography of a Yogi*. Los Angeles: Self-Realization Fellowship, 1959.

JAPAN

Abe, Kobo, *The Face of Another* (novel). New York: Alfred A. Knopf, 1966.

————, *The Woman in the Dunes* (novel). New York: Alfred A. Knopf, 1964.

Agawa, Hiroyuki, *Devil's Heritage* (novel). Tokyo: The Hokuseido Press, 1957.

Akutagawa, Ryûnosuke, *Exotic Japanese Stories: The Beautiful and the Grotesque*. New York: Liveright Publishing Corporation, 1964.

————, *Japanese Short Stories*. New York: Liveright Publishing Corporation, 1961.

————, *Kappa*, rev. ed. Tokyo: The Hokuseido Press, 1949.

*————, *Rashōmon and Other Stories*, 2d ed. New York: Bantam Books, 1959.

Bowers, Faubian, *Japanese Theatre*. New York: Hermitage House, 1952.

*Bownas, Geoffrey, and Thwaite, Anthony, trans., *The Penguin Book of Japanese Verse*. Baltimore, Md.: Penguin Books, 1964.

Briggs, William A., ed., *Anthology of Zen*. New York: Grove Press, 1961.

Clark, W. L., ed., *Various Kinds of Bugs and Other Stories from Present-day Japan*. Tokyo: Kenkyu-sha, 1958.

Conze, Edward, *Buddhism: Its Essence and Development*. New York: Harper & Brothers, 1959.

Dazai, Osamu, *No Longer Human* (novel). New York: New Directions, 1966.

————, *The Setting Sun* (novel). New York: New Directions, 1956.

*de Bary, William Theodore, and others, *Sources of Japanese Tradition*, 4th ed. New York: Columbia University Press, 1960.

*Ernst, Earle, *Kabuki Theatre*. New York: Grove Press, 1956.

Gluck, Jay, ed., *Ukiyo: Studies of "The Floating World" of Postwar Japan*. New York: The Vanguard Press, 1965.

Hearn, Lafcadio, *Japan: An Attempt at Interpretation*. Rutland, Vt., and Tokyo: Charles E. Tuttle Company, 1963.

————, *A Japanese Miscellany: Strange Stories, Folklore Gleanings, Studies Here & There*. Rutland, Vt., and Tokyo: Charles E. Tuttle Company, 1967.

*————, *Tales and Essays from Old Japan*. Chicago: Henry Regnery Company, 1956.

————, *Tales Out of the East,* selected by J. I. Rodale. New York: A. S. Barnes & Company, 1960.

Henderson, Harold G., *Haiku in English*. New York: Japan Society, 1965.

*————, *An Introduction to Haiku*. Garden City, N. Y.: Doubleday & Company, 1958.

*Hino, Ashihei, *Wheat and Soldier*. London: G. P. Putnam, 1940.

Honda, H. H., trans., *The Poetry of Ishikawa Takuboku*. Tokyo: Hokuseido Press, 1959.

————, *The Poetry of Wakayama Bokusui*. Tokyo: Hokuseido Press, 1958.

————, *The Poetry of Yosano Akiko*. Tokyo: Hokuseido Press, 1957.

Introduction to Contemporary Japanese Literature, Part I (1902–1935), Part II (1936–1955). Tokyo: Kokusai Bunka Shinkokai (The Society for International Cultural Relations), 1939 and 1959.

Ishihara, Shintaro, *Season of Violence and Other Stories*. Rutland, Vt., and Tokyo: Charles E. Tuttle Company, 1965.

Iwasaki, Yozan T., and Hughes, Glenn, trans., *Three Modern Japanese Plays*. Cincinnati: Stewart Kidd Company, 1923.

Kawabata, Yasunari, *Snow Country* (novel). New York: Alfred A. Knopf, 1964.

*Keene, Donald, trans. and ed., *Anthology of Japanese Literature*. New York: Grove Press, 1960.

———, *Japanese Literature: An Introduction for Western Readers*. New York: Grove Press, 1953.

*———, *Modern Japanese Literature*. New York: Grove Press, 1956.

———, *Modern Japanese Novels and the West*. Charlottesville: University of Virginia Press, 1961.

———, *The Old Woman, The Wife, and The Archer: Three Modern Japanese Short Novels*. New York: The Viking Press, 1961.

Kondo, Ichiro, and Fukuda, R., eds., *An Anthology of Modern Japanese Poetry*, rev. ed. Tokyo: Japan Publications, 1962.

*McKinnon, Richard N., trans. and ed., *The Heart Is Alone: A Selection of 20th Century Japanese Short Stories*. Tokyo: Hokuseido Press, 1957.

Mishima, Yukio, *Confessions of a Mask* (novel). New York: New Directions, 1958.

———, *Death in Midsummer & Other Stories*. New York: New Directions, 1966.

———, *Five Modern Nō Plays*. New York: Alfred A. Knopf, 1957.

———, *Madame de Sade* (play). New York: Grove Press, 1967.

———, *The Sailor Who Fell from Grace with the Sea* (novel). New York: Alfred A. Knopf, 1965.

———, *The Sound of Waves* (novel). New York: Alfred A. Knopf, 1956.

*———, *The Temple of the Golden Pavilion*. New York: Alfred A. Knopf, 1959.

———, *Twilight Sunflower: A Play in Four Acts*. Tokyo: Hokuseido Press, 1958.

Miyake, Shūtarō, *Kabuki Drama*, 8th ed., Tokyo: Japan Travel Bureau, 1961.

Mori, Ogai, *The Wild Geese* (novel). Rutland, Vt., and Tokyo: Charles E. Tuttle Company, 1959.

*Morris, Ivan I., ed., *Modern Japanese Stories, An Anthology*. Rutland, Vt., and Tokyo: Charles E. Tuttle Company, 1962.

Morrison, John W., *Modern Japanese Fiction*. Salt Lake City: University of Utah Press, 1955.

*Ninomiya, Takamichi, and Enright, D. J., eds., *The Poetry of Living Japan: An Anthology.* London: John Murray, 1957.

Oe, Kenzaburo, *A Personal Matter* (novel). New York: Grove Press, 1968.

Ogawa, Mimei, *Rose and Witch & Other Stories.* San Francisco: Overland Publishing Company, 1925.

———, *The Tipsy Star & Other Tales.* Tokyo: Hokuseido Press, 1957.

Ooka, Shohei, *Fires on the Plain* (novel). New York: Alfred A. Knopf, 1957.

Osaragi, Jiro, *Homecoming* (novel), 2d ed., Rutland, Vt., and Tokyo: Charles E. Tuttle Company, 1956.

Reischauer, Edwin O., *Japan Past and Present.* New York: Alfred A. Knopf, 1947.

Scott, A. C., *The Kabuki Theatre of Japan.* New York: The Macmillan Company, 1966.

———, *The Puppet Theatre of Japan.* Rutland, Vt., and Tokyo: Charles E. Tuttle Company, 1963.

Seidensticker, E. G., and others, *Modern Japanese Short Stories.* Tokyo: Japan Publications Trading Company, 1961.

Soseki, Natsume, *Kokoro* (novel). Chicago: Henry Regnery Company, 1968.

———, *The Wayfarer* (novel). Detroit: Wayne State University Press, 1967.

Statler, Oliver, *Japanese Inn.* New York: Random House, 1961.

Stryk, Lucien, and Ikemoto, Takashi, trans. and eds., *Zen: Poems, Prayers, Sermons, Anecdotes, Interviews.* New York: Doubleday & Company, 1965.

Tanizaki, Junishiro, *Diary of a Mad Old Man* (novel). New York: Alfred A. Knopf, 1965.

———, *The Key,* (novel). New York: Alfred A. Knopf, 1961.

———, *The Makioka Sisters* (novel). New York: Alfred A. Knopf, 1957.

———, *Some Prefer Nettles* (novel), 2d ed. New York: Berkley Publishing Corp., 1965.

Tasaki, Hanama, *Long the Imperial Way* (novel). Boston: Houghton Mifflin Company, 1950.

Watts, Alan W., *The Way of Zen.* New York: Random House, 1965.

Webb, Herschel, *An Introduction to Japan.* New York: Columbia University Press, 1960.

KOREA

Buck, Pearl S., *The Living Reed: A Novel of Korea*. New York: The John Day Company, 1963.

Kang, Younghill, *The Grass Roof*. Chicago: Follett Publishing Company, 1966.

Kim, So-un, *The Story Bag: Collection of Korean Folktales*, 3d ed. Rutland, Vt., and Tokyo: Charles E. Tuttle Company, 1960.

*Korean Center of the International PEN Club, eds., *Collected Short Stories from Korea*. Seoul: Eomun-Gag Publishing Company, 1961.

*Lee, Peter H., ed., *Anthology of Korean Poetry: From the Earliest Era to the Present*. New York: The John Day Company, 1964.

——, *Korean Literature: Topics and Themes*. Tucson: University of Arizona Press, 1965.

McCune, Shannon, *Korea: Land of Broken Calm*. Princeton: D. Van Nostrand Company, 1966.

Zŏng, In-sŏb, ed., *A Pageant of Korean Poetry*. Seoul: Eomun-Gag Publishing Company, 1963.

PHILIPPINES

Arguilla, Manuel and Lyd, eds., *Philippine Tales and Fables*. Manila: Capitol Publishing House, 1957.

*Casper, Leonard, ed., *Modern Philippine Short Stories*. Albuquerque: University of New Mexico Press, 1962.

————, *New Writing from the Philippines: A Critique and Anthology.* Syracuse: Syracuse University Press, 1966.

Castillo y Tuazon, Teofilo del, and Medina, Buenaventura S., Jr., *Philippine Literature: From Ancient Times to the Present.* Quezon City: Del Castillo & Sons, 1964.

*David-Maramba, Asuncion, ed., *Philippine Contemporary Literature,* 2d ed. Rizal, Philippines: Bookmark, Inc., 1965.

Edades, Jean, *Short Plays of the Philippines.* Manila: Penipayo Press, 1950.

Fansler, Dean S., ed., *Filipino Popular Tales.* Hatboro, Pa.: Folklore Associates, Inc., 1965.

*Gonzales, N. V. M., *The Bamboo Dancers.* Denver: Alan Swallow, 1961 (copyright 1921).

————, *Selected Stories.* Denver: Alan Swallow, 1965.

Philippine Prose and Poetry, Vol. 4. Manila: Bureau of Printing, 1951.

*Rizal, José, *The Lost Eden (Noli me Tangere).* Bloomington, Ind.: University of Indiana Press, 1961.

————, *The Subversive (El Filibusterismo).* Bloomington, Ind.: University of Indiana Press, 1962.

☐ **CHINESE THOUGHT by H. C. Creel.** An incisive and penetrating history which traces three thousand years of Chinese philosophy and shows how traditional attitudes have shaped the politics of twentieth-century China. (#MQ888—95¢)

☐ **ASIA IN THE MODERN WORLD, Helen Matthew, editor.** Prominent authorities study the people, culture, and political history of Asia and provide the background needed to understand its decisive role in the shaping of world events today. Illustrated. (#MQ762—95¢)

☐ **THE NATURE OF THE NON-WESTERN WORLD by Vera Micheles Dean.** A timely, penetrating look into the ancient traditions and modern ideas by which half the world's people live. "Everything she writes in her lucid and persuasive style bears the stamp of a liberal and courageous mind."—**New York Herald Tribune.** (#MQ862—95¢)

☐ **THE NEW ASIA, Guy S. Metraux and Francois Crouzet, editors.** A provocative study of a world in ferment drawn from articles originally published in UNESCO's **Journal of World History.** (#MQ652—95¢)
